EMPTY VOWS

Also by Mary Monroe

The Wiggins Series
Mrs. Wiggins

The Neighbors Series
One House Over
Over the Fence
Across the Way

The Lonely Heart, Deadly Heart Series
Can You Keep a Secret?
Every Woman's Dream
Never Trust a Stranger
The Devil You Know

The God Series
God Don't Like Ugly
God Still Don't Like Ugly
God Don't Play
God Ain't Blind
God Ain't Through Yet
God Don't Make No Mistakes

The Mama Ruby Series
Mama Ruby
The Upper Room
Lost Daughters

Stand-Alone Titles
Gonna Lay Down My Burdens
Red Light Wives
In Sheep's Clothing
Deliver Me From Evil
She Had It Coming
The Company We Keep
Family of Lies
Bad Blood
Remembrance
Right Beside You
The Gift of Family
Once in a Lifetime

"Nightmare in Paradise" in *Borrow Trouble*

Published by Kensington Publishing Corp.

MARY MONROE
EMPTY VOWS

www.kensingtonbooks.com

DAFINA BOOKS are published by

Kensington Publishing Corp.
119 West 40th Street
New York, NY 10018

All Kensington titles, imprints, and distributed lines are available at special quantity discounts for bulk purchases for sales promotion, premiums, fund-raising, educational, or institutional use. Special book excerpts or customized printings can also be created to fit specific needs. For details, write or phone the office of the Kensington Special Sales Manager: Attn. Special Sales Department. Kensington Publishing Corp, 119 West 40th Street, New York, NY 10018. Phone: 1-800-221-2647.

The DAFINA logo is a trademark of Kensington Publishing Corp.

Library of Congress Card Catalogue Number: 2021949975

ISBN: 978-1-4967-3261-3
First Kensington Hardcover Edition: April 2022

ISBN: 978-1-4967-3263-7 (e-book)

10 9 8 7 6 5 4 3 2 1

Printed in the United States of America

This book is dedicated to the following queens: Priscilla Shipstad, Sheila Sims, Lauretta Pierce, Maria Sanchez, Deimentrius Clay, Meredith Riley, Tara Worthy, Rosemary Anderson, Pam Eisley, and Quiana Robinson. And to these two kings: James Seelen and Reggie Zellous.

Acknowledgments

It is such a blessing to be a member of the Kensington Books family.

My editor, Esi Sogah, is so awesome I don't know what I'd do without her. Thank you, Esi. Thanks to Steven Zacharius, Adam Zacharius, Vida Engstrand, Lauren Jernigan, Michelle Addo, Norma Perez-Hernandez, Robin E. Cook, Susie Russenberger, Darla Freeman, the folks in the sales department, and everyone else at Kensington for working so hard for me.

Things changed dramatically when the pandemic hit. I miss meeting in person with all you wonderful book club fans, bookstores, and libraries around the country. In the meantime, I love doing Zoom meetings and will continue to do them until things return to "normal."

To my awesome literary agent, Andrew Stuart, thank you for representing me. You're still the best!

Please continue to e-mail me at Authorauthor5409@aol.com and visit my website at www.Marymonroe.org. You can also communicate with me on Facebook at Facebook.com/MaryMonroe and Twitter@MaryMonroeBooks.

All the best,

Mary Monroe

Chapter 1
Hubert

Friday, November 17, 1939

I SAT STOCK-STILL AS THE DOCTOR AT THE COLORED CLINIC TOLD ME they had pronounced my twenty-one-year-old son Claude dead. Dr. Underwood looked young enough to be my son. I would have preferred somebody older with a lot more experience, but this "youngster" was the only doctor on duty that night. In a gentle tone, he told me, "I suspect it was either a heart attack or a stroke, or maybe something that can't be diagnosed here. I'm so sorry for your loss, Mr. Wiggins."

"You ain't as sorry as I am! You need to tell me more than that!" I blasted as I wiped tears off my cheeks.

"If I could, I would. I'm almost certain that it's a genetic issue," Dr. Underwood said, still speaking in a gentle tone, as if it was no big deal to him. I scolded myself for coming down so hard on him. With all the sick and dying folks he had to deal with, death was second nature to him. He couldn't let his emotions get in the way. Death was also second nature to me because I was a undertaker. I'd seen more dead bodies than this doctor had and I never let my emotions get in the way neither. But losing my son was almost more than I could stand.

"There ain't no genetic or any other health issues in my family," I protested.

Dr. Underwood furrowed his eyebrows and caressed his smooth chin as he gawked at me. "Didn't your daddy's brother die of a heart attack some years ago?"

My head was spinning like a tornado, and there was so much bile rising in my throat, I didn't know how I was able to keep talking. Somehow I managed to get a grip so I could answer. "Um, yeah, he did. But he was eighty pounds overweight and ate everything he shouldn't have."

"Maybe there is something defective on your wife's side," he suggested. "I heard that Maggie's daddy and mama died way before their time."

"My late father-in-law was a alcoholic and drunk hisself to death. His wife died when she caught that virus that was going around the world about twenty years ago. But Maggie has always been as strong as a bull. And so was Claude."

"Mr. Wiggins, I declare, even the most robust bulls die sooner or later."

My son had never been seriously sick a day in his life and neither had I. If what had happened to Claude was heredity, it had to have come from Maggie's side of the family, or his birth daddy's. Me and her was the only ones who knew I wasn't the boy's real daddy. We hadn't been able to create a child the normal way (I'll explain why later). Out of desperation, we'd set up a stranger and tricked him into getting Maggie pregnant. I never met the man and didn't know nothing about his background.

The staff at the clinic did the best they could for us colored folks, but they wasn't as sophisticated and knowledgeable as the doctors at the hospitals that only treated white folks. One of their doctors might have been able to offer a better explanation as to what killed Claude. Segregation laws varied from one county to another, so the coroner in our little country town couldn't perform autopsies on colored corpses. Sometimes we never found out exactly why one of us died.

When Maggie came home this evening after helping serve at a party given by one of the wealthy white women she knew, I was barely functioning. It took all of my strength for me to compose myself enough to tell her that our only child, Claude, had suddenly up and died a few hours ago. Maggie was devastated because she loved that boy more than she loved life. On top of that, he was the only blood relative she had left in the world. My nightmare continued.

Several hours after I'd told Maggie about Claude's passing, I found her unconscious on our living-room couch with puke all over the front of her nightgown. I refused to believe she was dead, even though it was obvious that she was. I drove her to the clinic anyway. The staff was just as shocked as I was that I had returned so soon with another body.

The doctor on the graveyard shift told me the same thing about Maggie that the evening shift doctor had said about Claude: She had died of a heart attack or a stroke. Words could not describe my pain. I went back home to grieve some more.

Less than a minute after I walked back into my living room, I blacked out.

I woke up the next morning in my old bedroom at my parents' house. Mama was hovering over me with her eyes so bloodshot and glazed over, she looked like she belonged in bed herself. "Was I dreaming, or is it true that Maggie is dead too?" I asked in a raspy tone.

Mama sniffed and nodded. "We done lost them both, son. Me and your daddy found you passed out on your couch last night, so we brought you over here. You must have fainted."

That was the last thing I remember before I fainted again. I didn't come to until the next morning. I was so weak and disoriented, Mama had to bathe and feed me. I don't know how I made it through the day without fainting again or losing my mind.

I wasn't doing much better the next day. Back at my house, me and Mama was sitting at my kitchen table. It was the middle of the afternoon, but I was still in my bathrobe. On top of the bags underneath my puffy eyes, I hadn't shaved in two days and my hair was so askew I looked like death warmed over. But I didn't care how bad I looked, it wasn't half as bad as how I felt.

"I can't believe God would allow all this misery to happen to me at the same time," I complained to Mama. I wondered if He had finally decided to punish me for loving men.

"Baby, don't question the Lord's actions. One thing you have to keep in mind is that He don't put no more of a burden on nobody than they can carry," she insisted.

"Hogwash! What kind of God thinks losing my whole family at the same time ain't more of a burden than I can carry?" I shot back.

"Don't put all the blame on God. Have you done anything that would deserve His wrath?"

Mama's last question threw me for a loop. "Who me?" was all I could say. If God was punishing me for loving men, how come He hadn't chastised me before now? I'd started having relationships with men when I was in my teens, more than twenty-five years ago. "Um . . . I can't think of nothing I done wrong," I mumbled.

I decided to change the subject. The last thing I wanted to hear was Mama implying that I was doing something that the devil had put me up to and that God was only trying to get my attention back. I blurted out the most appropriate thing I could think of: "I guess I shouldn't question God's mysterious ways, right?"

"Right. You and nobody else should be that brazen. Shoot. Jesus didn't and He was the Lord's son—and *perfect* in every way!" Mama screamed. She stopped talking and sucked in a deep breath. Her tone was much softer when she added, "Baby, try to remember that it was their time to go."

I had heard that phrase so many times, all it did now was irritate me. For one thing, it didn't make no sense. Whenever a person died, it was "their time to go." But I didn't like to argue with my mama because I usually lost anyway. I decided to be as cool and calm as I could. "I'm going to get through this and go on with my life as quick as possible," I declared.

"Me and your daddy will do all we can to help you do that," she said with a heavy sigh. "You ain't got no close friends to keep company with you, and you don't need to be by yourself too much right now. You want to move back home with us for a spell?"

I shook my head. "I want to be by myself tonight. The sooner I get used to being alone, the better off I'll be." I didn't give Mama enough time to respond before I went on. "Um . . . I'm going to get in touch with the Fuller Brother morticians. I want them to handle the funerals," I announced. I never thought I'd give business to my only competition.

Sixty-year-old Ned Fuller and his fifty-eight-year-old brother, Percy, had been thorns in my side ever since I'd inherited the business from my daddy's deceased older brother. They was so hifalutin and insensitive; their funeral home had a great big WELCOME sign tacked up on the wall by the side of their front door! Knowing how jealous they was of me because I got the most business, I knew they was going to charge me a pretty penny. But I didn't care. All I wanted was for this double funeral to be over and done with as soon as possible so I could move forward.

Mama scrunched up her face and threw up her hands. "The Fuller Brothers? I declare, I can't believe you want to give them snooty devils your business. Y'all been feuding for years. Besides, this involves our family. Don't you think Maggie and Claude deserve the best home-going possible? Folks will think you done lost your mind!"

"Mama, I don't care what folks think. It's bad enough that I ain't never going to see my wife and son alive again. After all I done already been through, the last thing I want to do is handle their funerals. And, as much as I don't want to admit it, the Fuller Brothers' work is almost as good as mine."

Chapter 2
Jessie

I DONE ATTENDED A LOT OF FUNERALS IN MY LIFE, BUT THIS WAS THE first one with two bodies. Looking at them caskets sitting end to end in the front of Reverend Wiggins's church chilled me to the bone. I was so numb, I couldn't even feel the hard pew I was sitting on.

I stopped crying so I could eavesdrop better on what the people sitting behind me was saying. "Mother and son. Don't they look peaceful? That rose-colored shroud Maggie got on suits her. S-she loved roses," sobbed a woman whose voice I didn't recognize.

"They both look as good in death as they did in life," remarked the man who lived next door to Hubert.

The person who spoke next had such a husky voice, I couldn't tell if it was a man or a woman. "I declare, Hubert must have spent a fortune on them bronze caskets and all of them flowers."

I tuned everybody out after the woman who used to help Maggie prune her and Hubert's pecan tree said, "I wonder what Hubert is going to do with all of them nice frocks and hats Maggie left behind. Me and her was the same size . . ."

I wanted to turn around and say something, but I was in so much grief, I didn't know what to say that I hadn't already said in the past few days.

When I couldn't stand to look toward the front of the church no more, I read the program over and over. By the fifth time, I had memorized every word, especially the ones that had been misspelled.

I started crying again.

"Sister Jessie, you look like you about to fall out. Can I get you a glass of water?" one of the ushers asked me as he leaned over.

"Thanks, but I'm fine." I sniffled and wiped my eyes and nose with my handkerchief. I had been crying off and on since Maggie and Claude died a few days ago. Ever since then, I'd had problems sleeping at night. When my husband, Orville, died last summer, I hadn't been able to sleep much them first few nights then neither. When I went without sleep for two whole days after his funeral, I knew I had to do something drastic. My money was tight, so I couldn't afford to buy nothing that would help me sleep. I was so desperate and exhausted, I didn't care what I had to do. I didn't have enough nerve to go in a store and steal something, so I "borrowed" some tranquilizers from the nursing home where I worked. Some of the nurses gave them to the unruly patients to keep them doped up so they wouldn't have to deal with them. I'd seen some of them old folks go to sleep at night and not wake up until after noon the next day. I had never took a whole pill because they was so strong. I would always crush one up and stir half of it into a glass of water when I got ready for bed. Within minutes after my head hit the pillow, I was out like a light and didn't wake up until the next morning. I'd relied on them pills several times in the last few months. That was the only way I was able to get a full night's sleep last night.

I didn't know how I was going to go on without Maggie. She had been my best friend for more than twenty years. It broke my heart to know that the last conversation I'd had with her before she died was about her son's death. "Jessie, that boy was my life. How in the world am I going to live without him?" she'd sobbed as she wallowed in my arms on her living-room couch.

"You going to go on because me and all the folks in this town who love you will help you get through this," I told her.

"If I hadn't gone to help out at that party tonight, I would have been home and he'd still be alive." Maggie's statement didn't make no sense to me. The boy had died of natural causes. I didn't want to make her feel no worse by asking her to explain what she meant. If I'd known it was going to be our last conversation, I would have asked.

I was going to miss Maggie's son as much as I was going to miss her. Claude was only a few years older than my son, Earl. They never got to be close friends because Earl was retarded. But Maggie had treated him as good as she treated Claude. She'd even babysat him for free when I went to work, and refused to take money, no matter how many times I offered to pay her. That was the kind of praiseworthy woman she was, even though she'd been raised by a used-to-be prostitute and the town drunk.

Maggie had always been there for me and Orville, no matter how mean and nasty my husband was to her. She'd even sung a solo at his funeral.

Now that Hubert needed to be consoled, I was going to do all I could to help him through this sad mess. I sighed and shook my head. After mopping my face with my handkerchief for the umpteenth time, I glanced around the room. Hubert's daddy's church was not that big, but it was the most ornate colored church in Lexington, Alabama. Pictures of the Lord, His disciples, Moses parting the Red Sea, and the Virgin Mary hugging Baby Jesus covered almost every wall. The floor was so clean you could lick it and not get a speck of dirt on your tongue.

I had been a member of this church all my life, but like a lot of folks who let other things get in the way, I didn't attend as often as I used to. And the last three times I'd come was to attend funerals, including my husband's.

The service hadn't started yet and people was still filing in. Hubert's parents was all over the place. His daddy was stomping up and down the aisle with the tail of his long black robe flapping like buzzard wings. He was trying to make sure everything was in order before he went up to the pulpit to get started. Hubert's plump mama was dressed in black from head to toe, including a wide-brimmed hat with a veil that completely covered her fleshy face and neck. Even though she was weeping and wailing up a storm, she was still able to make her way around the room so people could hug her.

I was so deep in thought, I didn't realize Hubert was talking to me until he poked my side with his elbow. I had almost forgot he was sitting right beside me on the front pew. "Oh? W-what did you say, Hubert?" I asked. I was so embarrassed my face got hot.

"I was just saying that I appreciate you dropping off that casserole and sweet potato pie yesterday, and helping me with my housekeeping chores these last few days," he told me in a low tone. "My icebox hadn't been cleaned out since Maggie . . ." Hubert stopped talking and dropped his head. He sniffled for a few seconds before he honked into a plaid handkerchief. He cleared his throat before he continued. "Maggie stayed on top of everything. It's going to be hard for me to carry on without her. When we got married, she took over doing everything for me that my mama had been doing all my life. She even washed my back, like Mama used to do." Hubert exhaled and gave me the most hopeless look I ever seen on his face. "Jessie, what am I going to do now?" He screwed up his mouth and started rubbing the back of his head. "My brain feels like it's fixing to explode. I been feeling so weak, I'm surprised I'm sitting here right now, still conscious."

I rubbed the side of his arm. "Hubert, you ain't going to be like this for long. You are the strongest man I know and the smartest. Besides, you got your mama and daddy, the church, *me*, and other people to look after you."

Sitting directly behind us on the next pew was twenty-eight-year-old Blondeen Walker. She was a pretty woman with big brown eyes, nut-brown skin, and a heart-shaped face. And she liked to draw attention to herself. Today she had on a low-cut black dress and enough rouge on her cheeks to coat a barn. She had been giving me side-eye glances ever since I entered the church.

When Blondeen suddenly tapped me on my shoulder, I turned

around. Even though I had a fake smile on my face, there was a scowl on hers. She was one of the many folks who had been bringing food to Hubert's house and consoling him since Maggie and Claude departed. "Jessie, in case you didn't know, the first pew is for the family," she snarled.

Before I could respond, Hubert whirled around and told her, "Jessie is like family. I'm the one who told her to sit here."

Blondeen's face got so tight, I could have bounced a dime off it.

We turned back around and she didn't say nothing else. But each time I looked in her direction, she gave me the evil eye. She wasn't the only one, though. I seen several other women glaring at me like they wanted to bite my head off. I didn't have to be a mind reader to know what they was all thinking: Hubert was up for grabs and they wanted dibs on him first.

Chapter 3
Jessie

I LOST TRACK OF ALL THE FOLKS WHO WENT UP TO THE PULPIT AND praised Maggie for being such a godly woman. One of the white ladies she used to work for showed up and spoke for ten minutes. She agreed with everybody that Maggie was one of God's favorite children because she had been so much like Him.

Several of Claude's friends and acquaintances spoke, including the mama of the first woman he'd been engaged to marry. His first fiancée's name was Daisy Compton, and she was the kind of woman that mothers warned their sons to stay away from. But Claude hadn't listened to Maggie. Not long after him and Daisy told everybody they was getting married, she suddenly packed a few clothes and took off with another man last June. Nobody had heard from her since. Some folks was even convinced that she was dead, because she hadn't even contacted her children, or anybody else in her family. Maggie had not cared much for that woman, but she'd always treated her with respect.

Toward the end of the service, I went up to the pulpit to say a few words. "Maggie was the most righteous, caring, and generous woman I ever met. God broke the mold when He created her. I'm sure she's up there in heaven helping Him and guiding the angels that might not be as saintly as she is, the same way she done with her friends down here on Earth." I wanted to say more, but I couldn't. I started crying again and Hubert had to run up and help me back to my seat.

After the long service, which included eight hymns sung by one of the ushers' godsons, and four more songs by the choir, things was finally coming to a close. More than two dozen women had fainted. Reverend Wiggins told the folks who wanted to eat to go to the dining area downstairs. I never knew anybody who went to a funeral who didn't stay long enough to eat.

Everybody stood around eating from plates overflowing with everything from macaroni and cheese to peach cobbler, reminiscing about all the good times they'd had with Claude and Maggie. "I'm sure going to miss poor sweet Maggie. I went to school with her," said a female who had bullied her almost every day from the first day of school to the last. This was the first time I'd ever heard this hypocrite say something nice about Maggie and it made me sick.

My mood went from grief to disgust when I overheard a woman ask another one the same thing that had been on my mind since Maggie died: "I wonder what lucky woman is going to land Hubert?"

If that wasn't bad enough, I overheard another one make a comment to Hubert when she didn't realize I was close enough to hear. "Folks wondering if you and Jessie are going to get together, now that both of y'all is single again," she said in a smug tone. Before Hubert could respond, the same woman added, "There is a heap of other women in this town who would suit you better."

"Jessie's been like a member of my family as far back as I can remember. She's a sweet, upstanding woman, but she ain't no more interested in me the way you mean than I am of her," Hubert replied.

I cleared my throat loud enough for him and that heifer to hear me. They whirled around at the same time to face me. "Hubert, excuse me for interrupting, but my son is getting fidgety, so I'd better take him home now," I said in a stiff tone. "I just wanted to come say bye and to thank you again for the ride over here."

"Oh, I'm sorry you and Earl have to leave. You want me to have somebody fix y'all a plate to eat later?" he said. "If you can wait a little longer, I can take y'all home."

"No, that's all right. I got leftovers from yesterday, and my sister and her husband can give us a ride home."

Hubert's eyes had dark circles around them and was slightly swollen from all the crying he'd done. Without all the makeup I had slathered on my face, my eyes would have looked as bad as his. "Okay, Jessie. You take care of yourself and your boy. I'll be seeing you directly," he told me as he gently massaged my shoulder.

"Thank you." I totally ignored the woman, but from the corner of my eye, I seen a grimace on her face as I walked off.

I couldn't wait to get out of that church. I didn't say nothing to Earl at first when I located him. I just took him by the hand and led him toward the door.

"Why do we have to go now, Mama?" he asked as he stumbled along.

"Um . . . I don't feel too good," I muttered.

He gulped some air. "You sick? You going to die too?"

"No, baby. I'm going to live for a real long time." I glared at some of the women who had been giving me the evil eye during the service. I didn't want to deal with them no more today. That was the reason I didn't plan on going to Hubert's house later, where a lot of the same folks who'd attended the funeral would end up so they could continue consoling him.

All I wanted to do was be alone and think about all the things I'd overheard. There was no telling what else them hussies had spewed about me behind my back. What amazed me was why some of them thought me and Hubert would get together in the first place. But since them busybodies had put the thought in my mind, I couldn't get rid of it. Especially since the notion of me and Hubert as a couple was so far-fetched. I was sure enough going to think more about it, though. And if I ever thought it would benefit me to be with him, I would definitely take action.

I wasn't too worried about growing old alone. There was other single men in Lexington. A few had asked me out, but I had turned them down. But if they had been anything like Hubert, I would have done everything I could to hold on to them. I was only forty-one, so I still had a lot of good years left. And I had a lot of love to give, so I didn't plan on being single for the rest of my life.

I wondered how Hubert felt about being single again now. He'd been with Maggie for so long, and had always seemed so happy as a married man, everybody was already predicting that he wouldn't be single for long.

Even though Maggie was gone, I was still determined to continue my friendship with Hubert. When he remarried—and there was no doubt in my mind that he would do so—I hoped that the new Mrs. Wiggins wouldn't be the jealous type. If she was, I'd let her know right off the bat that Hubert had always been like a brother to me, and as long as he wanted me in his life, I'd be in it.

Chapter 4
Hubert

*T*HE DAY AFTER THE FUNERAL, NOVEMBER 22, WHICH WAS ALSO the day before Thanksgiving, Mama, Daddy, and Jessie Tucker, Maggie's best friend, came to the house to help me pack Maggie's belongings. As much as I wanted to tackle this painful chore at a much later date, I couldn't put it off another day.

A hour after we got started, me and Jessie went in the bathroom to box up the more personal female items. "Jessie, Mama got dibs on the makeup and hair products, but you can have all of them smell-goods," I told her. "Maggie was so ahead of other women. She's the only colored woman I know who wore the same fragrances as the rich white ladies."

"Thank you. Bless your soul until the Rapture. She was always so generous about letting me splash some on whenever I wanted to," Jessie said. Her voice cracked when she added, "That woman was a saint in every way."

"You took the words right out of my mouth." My throat was so dry, it hurt every time I spoke.

Before I could say anything else, the door swung open and Daddy shuffled in. "Shake a leg, y'all. I want to get this over and done with as soon as possible. I'll let some of the church elders decide who to donate what to, and then they can oversee the distribution." He snorted and snatched a towel off the rack above the sink and used it to wipe sweat off his face. And then he covered his nose with the towel and honked into it. "All this stress is messing with my allergies," he griped. "This has been so tiresome. Let's finish up so I can return the truck I borrowed. And I need to get Mother home soon before she falls out. She's getting too overwhelmed looking at all the nice stuff Maggie left behind."

"I'm starting to feel like that myself, Reverend Wiggins," Jessie mumbled. I didn't make a remark, but I felt the same way too.

My beloved son's young wife, Maybelle, had took his death so hard, she had been too grief stricken to pack up his stuff. But she had packed hers and took off to Miami last night to live with relatives. I was glad she and Claude hadn't had a baby, because it would have been even harder for me to move on, with my grandchild living in another state.

By now, Daddy was as distressed as Mama. Nary one of them was able to go to Claude's house to help me and Jessie pack up his things. I was concerned about where everything was going to end up. If I would see a woman—especially a floozy—prancing around town in one of Maggie's sharp dresses or hats, or a young man decked out in one of Claude's dapper suits, I didn't know how I would react. I was so glad when we finally finished packing and delivered everything to the same folks who was to dispose of everything for us. I couldn't get back home fast enough.

With all of Maggie's things gone, the house felt so empty. I collected our wedding pictures and the ones we'd took on other occasions and put them under a stack of pillowcases in one of the drawers in my bedroom dresser. I had to. Because each time I gazed at Maggie's pretty face smiling from one of the framed pictures she'd hung on the living-room wall, I busted out crying. When I looked at her side of the bedroom closet, with nothing there except empty hangers, my stomach knotted up.

The two bottom dresser drawers was very special. Everything in them was going to stay there. It was where we had stored Claude's best school papers and drawings from the time he was in elementary school until he finished high school. I would keep them items until the day I died. I slept less than a hour that night.

* * *

When I dragged myself out of bed on Thanksgiving morning, the last thing I wanted to do was celebrate. It was such a gloomy day anyhow. Every cloud in the sky was black, so I knew a storm was in the making. But Mama had started planning for the holiday a month in advance and had invited a bunch of people to celebrate it with us. She offered to cancel everything, but I told her not to. Keeping busy was one way to help us get over our grief. But nobody was in a holiday mood. Half of the twelve folks she'd invited decided not to come. Daddy had even canceled the holiday evening program that him and Mama had spent weeks putting together.

After Daddy gave a ten-minute prayer of thanksgiving before we dug into the turkey and all the other scrumptious items on the table, a few people tried to lighten the mood by complimenting Mama on the great feast she had prepared. After that, almost everybody ate in silence and practically ran out the door as soon as they finished eating. "Y'all want to stay for some more prayer?" Mama asked the last couple when they started putting on their coats.

"No, thanks, Sister Wiggins," the husband said real quick with a woebegone expression on his face. "I just heard some thunder, so we need to get home to make sure we closed our windows before we left the house."

With a disappointed look on her face, Mama turned to me. I was still sitting at the table. "Son, you want to spend the night? I'd hate for you to be driving if the storm starts before you make it home."

I wiped my greasy lips with my napkin and made myself smile. "That's all right, Mama. I'd better get home to make sure I closed all my windows too. I ain't got but a few blocks to drive and I done drove in a lot of storms and ain't never had no problems." Before I could rise up out of my chair, Mama and Daddy started talking about so many different things, I couldn't get a word in edgewise. I didn't want to disrespect them by leaving when it was so important to them for me to stay longer. I felt like a hostage. It was another hour before I was able to leave without them saying to me, "One more thing I want to mention . . ."

* * *

The day after Thanksgiving, I had to pull myself together because I had to finalize the funeral arrangements for a woman who had been murdered in her own house three days ago. The woman's family was just as overwhelmed with grief as I still was. Losing loved ones to natural causes, like I had, was bad, but losing somebody to murder was unspeakable.

Everybody was on edge about the murder, and it was no wonder. Three other colored women had been murdered in the last six months and we was all convinced that the same maniac had killed them all. Each woman had lived alone. The oldest one had been seventy-eight and the youngest had just celebrated her twenty-first birthday. Since nobody I knew locked their doors, the killer hadn't had no problem getting into the houses of the first two. Because each woman he'd killed had been found naked, we assumed he'd raped them too.

The third woman had disappeared one night on her way to a juke joint—one of the numerous rowdy ramshackle houses we had in Lexington, where folks went to drink, dance, gamble, and behave like heathens. She had been beaten and shot. All four of the women's bodies had been dumped in the woods near Carson Lake, the same place where a lot of folks fished and had picnics. The fourth woman had been found with only half of her hair put in curlers and face cream on her face. The killer must have come at her while she was getting ready for bed. She'd also been shot before he dumped her.

Almost every man I knew liked to hunt, so they all owned at least one shotgun. Now, just as many women living alone owned guns too. The ones who couldn't afford a shotgun, or was too afraid to fool around with one, kept either a knife, a stick, or some other weapon nearby.

"I declare, if they don't catch that maniac soon, we ain't going to have no colored women left in this town," I complained to Daddy on Saturday a few minutes after he'd preached the latest murdered woman's funeral. Me and him was the only ones still inside the church. The pallbearers had carried the casket out to my hearse, which would be driven to the cemetery by one of the men who helped me with the funerals. I was going to follow in my trusty old Ford. I made it my business to be present at as many of the burials as possible. The families of the deceased always let me know how much they appreciated that.

"Son, I feel the same way. I'm glad you was able to get everything organized for this poor woman's family. Now, how are *you* doing?" My daddy was not that tall, but he was a big man. I wasn't no shrimp, but I was nowhere near as hefty as he was.

"I'm feeling better each day," I replied. "I'm going back to work at the turpentine mill on Monday because this is our busiest time of the year. And I like keeping busy, so I won't have too much time to dwell on everything that's been happening." I'd been supervising the colored workers at the mill since before me and Maggie got married. My bosses was so nice to me, I never had a problem taking off when I had business at the funeral home to attend to.

"You eating all right? I hope so, you need to keep up your strength."

"Yes, I am, Daddy. Some days I eat too good. I done already put on a few pounds, which I don't need. Several ladies from church and the neighborhood have brought me some mighty big plates. And Jessie, bless her sweet soul, she's a godsend. She calls me up every day to see how I'm doing, and she done brought me several plates in the last couple of days. Greens, pig ears, you name it. She even mopped my kitchen and did my laundry yesterday."

"Hmmm. That's good to hear. Jessie and Maggie was so much alike. I'm surprised some man ain't already snatched up Jessie. I hope your next wife will be as wonderful as Maggie and Jessie."

"I ain't going to settle for nothing less, Daddy."

I was glad he left a minute later, because I was beginning to feel uncomfortable.

My mama and Maggie was the only women I'd ever been close to. They'd catered to me so much, they'd spoiled me. I was so set in my ways now, I didn't even know how to go about finding another wife this late in life. But the loneliness I was experiencing now, when I was alone, was unbearable and scary. My house felt like a tomb and I felt like a man who'd died, but was still breathing. Tonight, just before midnight, while I was tossing and turning in bed, I heard loud footsteps on my back porch. I believed in ghosts, like everybody else I knew, so that was what I thought it was. I hoped it was the spirit of either Maggie or Claude, or both of them, coming to say one last good-bye to me. But I couldn't assume nothing. There was a whole lot of bad spirits that liked to torment living folks. That was why I'd grabbed my Bible before I left my bedroom and crept into the kitchen.

When I got to the kitchen window, I held my Bible close to my bosom before I took a deep breath and parted the curtains. There was a face pressed against the window gazing at me. But it wasn't Maggie or Claude, or a meddlesome demon. A deer had wandered into my backyard and moseyed up on the porch. As grief stricken as I was, I laughed.

Before I went back to bed, I dialed Jessie's number. She was the only person I knew who wouldn't be upset about me calling after midnight. Her phone rang six times, and I was about to hang up when she answered. "Jessie, I . . . I'm sorry," I stammered. "I hope I didn't wake you up."

"You didn't. I was already up using the bathroom. Is everything all right?"

"Um . . . I was just feeling a little lonesome. I thought if I talked to somebody, it would help me relax so I can get some sleep. I'm having a hard time getting used to being alone."

"Hubert, I know exactly how you feel. I felt the same when Orville died, and still do sometimes. I wish I would have had somebody to talk to when I was by myself during the first few nights. There was times when my misery was so bad, I was actually in pain. I had headaches, stomachaches, and my chest felt as tight as a drum. One night, I got out of bed and walked to the end of the street and back."

"I declare, Jessie. I didn't know all that. Did you talk to Maggie about how you was feeling? She was such a spiritual person, I'm sure she would have given you some good guidance."

"I didn't talk to nobody about it. The last thing I wanted to do was burden somebody with my problems. I didn't even want Maggie to think I couldn't cope on my own. Besides, I'd already dumped enough misery onto her plate."

"Jessie, I don't care how much misery is on my plate. You can always call or come see me when you start to feel low and need to talk to somebody. It's the least I can offer after all the happiness Maggie experienced by having a friend like you. You was just as much a friend to me as you was to her. I didn't show how much I appreciated having you in our lives, and I'm sorry I didn't."

Jessie took her time responding. "I can't tell you how often I used to wish when Orville was alive that he was more like you," she confessed. "Maggie hit the jackpot when she married you."

Her remarks surprised me. Nobody had ever gave me so much praise before. Not only did it make me blush, it also confused me and made me uncomfortable. I didn't know how to react, so I let go of the first thing that came to my mind. "I appreciate hearing you feel that way."

"I've always felt that way, Hubert."

"O . . . kay." Now I was feeling even more uncomfortable and confused. Was Jessie making a play for me? I wondered. I dismissed that idea right away. After all she'd been through with Orville, and the fact that she hadn't dated since he died, I didn't think she was interested in men at all these days.

Several seconds of silence passed before she spoke again. "I ain't sleepy, so I'm going to stay up for a while. You want to come over for a glass of cider or something?"

"No, I'm tired, so I better stay home." I was anxious to end this call now. "Bye, Jessie." I hung up before she could say something else that might have made me feel even more uncomfortable.

Despite the fact that Jessie had said some things that surprised me, our conversation had done me some good. It lifted my spirits.

Chapter 5
Jessie

WHEN ORVILLE PASSED, FOLKS DIDN'T WASTE NO TIME ADVISING me to get a boyfriend as soon as possible. One of my mama's friends, who'd been married six times, had the nerve to tell me during the funeral, "Don't waste no time, girl. It ain't natural to go too long without sex. Especially when you been getting it steady for over twenty years."

I didn't bother to let her know that the only thing I'd been getting steady for over twenty years from Orville was abuse. He used to beat me in advance for things he had convinced hisself I'd do in the future to tick him off. I'd rolled my eyes and gave the woman the most exasperated look I could. "I live by God's laws. I ain't about to wallow around in bed with a man I ain't married to!" I snapped.

"If you feel that way, that's all the more reason why you should find another husband right away," the busybody woman insisted, wagging her finger in my face. "I got engaged to my current husband while the one before him was still on his deathbed waiting to cross over."

One of the reasons I stopped going to church on a regular basis was because so many other people was saying some of the same kind of stuff to me.

The last couple of years of my marriage had been so bad, I used to fantasize about killing Orville. I didn't think I could get away with it, and prison was the last place I wanted to spend the rest of my days at. But the main reason I couldn't go through with it was because I didn't have the nerve to harm another person. And even if I got away with killing him, I wouldn't have been able to live with the guilt.

During one of the darkest days of my marriage last year, Maggie invited me to ride along with her to take Hubert's car to his mechanic to get the oil changed. On the ride to the garage, I actually told her what I'd been fantasizing about. Her response had been just what I'd expected from a woman as holy as she was. She gasped and gawked at me like I was crazy.

"I can't believe my ears! How could you even think about killing Orville! I know you know your Bible. Killing somebody is a sin against God."

I could still picture Maggie sitting behind that steering wheel, turning her head to glance at me every few seconds.

"I know that. But if you was in a bad situation, a *real* bad one, like I am, you couldn't kill nobody?"

"You know me. I can't even swat flies. I shoo them out the window. All life is precious."

"What if somebody was doing something mean and evil to you and making your life miserable? What if they threatened to kill you?"

Maggie shook her head. "I still couldn't do it. There ain't no excuse for taking somebody's life. That's only something God is authorized to do."

"Then what would you do to end the problem?"

"The same thing I'm advising you to do: pray about it. Ask God to intervene and make Orville stop beating and threatening you."

Maggie prayed with me before we got to the mechanic's place, and she prayed with me again on the way back home. God must have been listening, because I didn't have to put up with Orville much longer. A week later, the bad heart he'd been born with finally fizzled out.

Because of Hubert's expertise, Orville had one of the nicest funerals I ever went to. "He was in so much pain. He's much better off now," Maggie whispered to me during the service. "And so will you be," she added with a wink.

As close as me and Maggie had been, I never told her how much I'd rejoiced the day Orville died. But she was so wise and insightful, I had a feeling she knew anyway.

Hubert had had no idea how lucky he'd been to be married to Maggie. She'd made him so happy. It saddened me to know how miserable he was now. I was so glad he'd called me tonight. But I didn't know what to make of some of the stuff he'd said. Especially the part about me calling or coming to him whenever I needed to talk to somebody.

I was disappointed that Hubert hadn't took me up on my offer to come over and have some cider. My house seemed even more dreary and quieter than it normally did, so I was feeling even more lonesome than I'd felt before he called. I needed to talk to somebody. Most of the folks I knew didn't have no telephone. But it was too late to bother anybody anyway.

I was so antsy, I couldn't sit or stand still, and I wasn't ready to go back to bed. I still needed to talk to somebody, and I needed to do it before I went crazy. My only choice was Hubert. I wondered what he'd think if I called him up so soon after he'd told me I could. I took a deep breath and dialed his number before I lost my nerve. The phone rang ten times before he answered it.

"Hubert . . . uh . . . I'm sorry to be calling you so late. I know we just got off the phone a little while ago, but I forgot to mention something." I held my breath until he responded.

"You can call me at any time, day or night. And you can talk to me for as long as you need to. What do you need to discuss?"

"I forgot to tell you that I'm cooking some chicken feet tomorrow. Would you like for me to bring you a plate?"

He didn't answer right away. I figured he was wondering why I was calling him about something as trivial as a plate of chicken feet, when I could have called him tomorrow. "No, that's all right. But thank you for asking."

My heart dropped. "Oh. I know how much you like them. I

thought I'd ask so I could cook enough in case somebody comes to my house tomorrow and wants to stay for supper. I know I can't season them as good as Maggie did, though." I laughed and was pleased when he did too.

"That ain't the reason I don't want none of yours. The lady who lives in the yellow house at the end of the block is cooking some tomorrow too. She offered to bring me a plate. I just wish somebody in this neighborhood could whoop up a pot of gumbo as tasty as Maggie's."

"Tell me about it. I wish I had thought to ask her for her recipe."

"I wish I had too." Hubert sighed. "Oh, well. I enjoyed her world-beating gumbo as much as everybody else around here did. By the way, I been meaning to tell you that if you need something fixed around the house, or some weeds pulled, let me know and I'll make sure it gets done."

My heart skipped two beats. I had all kinds of things around my house that needed to be fixed, including me. "Thank you, Hubert. Now that you brought it up, I'm going to be needing a lot of handyman work done, now that Orville ain't around to do it no more. I'll need somebody to take over pruning my black walnut tree and trimming my backyard hedges in a few months. And I'll need to have that wobbly bannister on my back porch repaired. The man I hired a few months ago to help me around the house, moved to Nashville last weekend to live with his daughter."

His response stunned me. "All right. I'm trying to help one of the young ushers at Daddy's church find work to make a few dollars. He's saving up for college. I'll give him your phone number and he can deal with you directly."

This time, my heart felt like it had stopped beating. My tongue felt like it froze up and I sat there like a mute.

Chapter 6
Hubert

JESSIE HAD STOPPED TALKING SO ABRUPTLY, I DIDN'T KNOW WHAT TO think. "Jessie, you still there?"

"Yeah. I just had to lean over and swat a horsefly on my counter," she explained.

"You sound tired, so I'll let you go."

When I got back in the bed, all I could think about was what I was going to do with the rest of my life. I didn't have no close men friends who wasn't like me that I could do manly things with, such as fishing and hunting. Or to talk sports with. I occasionally played checkers and dominoes with a few of the regular men I knew, like my mechanic and the two cousins who helped me run my funeral home. But whenever I was with them, they would always get around to discussing all the women they'd been to bed with or wanted to go to bed with. When Maggie was alive, I had a good excuse to be closemouthed about my personal life, so I never discussed women I wanted to get involved with. The same men teased me about being such a "Goody Two-shoes," but that never bothered me. If they knew that I felt the same way about men that they felt about women, they wouldn't have even wanted to associate with me. And there was no telling how far they would go to chastise me for duping them.

It had been easy to keep my secret when I was a young boy because everybody thought me and Maggie was boyfriend and girlfriend. She had told me things she had never told anybody else, so I knew I could trust her. When I told her what I really was, she wanted to help me keep my secret hid. Shortly after my confession, I asked her to marry me so everybody would continue to think I was normal. I was twenty and she was seventeen when we exchanged vows.

We desperately wanted to become parents, so we'd appear to be a normal married couple. There was no way for us to get a baby the regular way because we had no desire or intention of ever having sex together. That was the reason we came up with a scheme to set up a stranger and trick him into getting her pregnant. After only a few visits to places where frisky men liked to drink and hang out, Maggie found a good prospect that looked similar to me. As soon as he got her pregnant, she dumped him and we focused on the baby she was carrying.

For more than twenty years, we'd had the perfect life raising our son, Claude. He was such a blessing, and he grew up to be as righteous and upstanding as me and Maggie.

"Hubert, I never thought I could be so happy. Even without sex, my life is complete," she told me on Claude's twenty-first birthday.

"I'm pleased to hear that," I replied with my face burning. I made it a point not to mention my sex life when I didn't have to. But that didn't bother Maggie at all. We conversated so much about everything else—from all the empty promises President Roosevelt was making on the radio to which movie we wanted to go see next—we didn't have time to talk about things that was too sensitive. And my sex life was the main one.

I had had several boyfriends before and during my marriage, but Daryl Hudson had been the love of my life for the past three years. A few weeks ago, we decided to leave our families so we could be together all the time. He told his wife and kids first, and I was planning to tell my folks the same day Maggie and Claude died. When I told her what I was planning to do, she took it real hard. Her main concern was how it was going to affect Claude, not to mention the pain it would cause everybody else we knew. She tried her best to talk me out of it, but when I explained that I was tired of living a lie, she gave up. She was hurt, but if anybody could bounce back from a trauma real quick, it was Maggie. Her strength was one of the many things I'd always admired about her. She'd been raised by a alcoholic and a former prostitute. On top of that, when she was a little girl, she'd been repeatedly molested by one of her daddy's friends. It took such a toll on her, she never developed any interest in ever having sex again with any other man. I was the only one she ever told, and if she hadn't told me, I never would have guessed that a woman with such a positive outlook on life had been through so much misery.

I was so sorry I had hurt her by telling her I was going to come clean and tell my parents what I'd been hiding from them all my life. But I was glad I'd had time to tell her that I wasn't going to go through with it before she died. That pleased her, and it pleased me to know that she'd died with some relief.

I hadn't communicated with Daryl since the day after we buried Maggie and Claude, and I hadn't been able to get in touch with him since. I'd left messages at the railroad station office, where he had been hired to work as a Pullman porter fifteen years ago, but he hadn't got back to me yet. We had never gone more than two or three days without seeing each other or talking on the phone, so I was beginning to worry.

Several more days went by and I still hadn't heard from him. If something bad had happened to him, I needed to know as soon as possible. The thought of losing my family and my boyfriend so close together was too much for me to deal with. I decided that if I hadn't heard from him in the next day or so, I'd drive to Mobile, where he lived, and try to find him.

He finally contacted me the week after Thanksgiving, the first Saturday in December. I had just got home from the funeral home fifteen minutes ago when he called. I was glad I was alone because Daryl told me the last thing I ever expected to hear from him.

"Hubert, I hate to tell you this over the phone, but I can't see you no more."

I couldn't believe my ears. I had never been so stupefied in my life. I held the telephone in front of my face and glared at it. I wanted to fling it across the room. I had to take a real deep breath before putting it back to my ear and to talk again. "W-what? Why?" Daryl was the man I had loved more than any of the others. He was the only one I'd been completely faithful to because I expected to spend the rest of my life with him.

"See, my wife forgave me and wants to work on saving our marriage. For her sake, as well as mine, but mostly for the kids."

"Do you mean to tell me she wants to stay married to you, knowing what you are?"

"Yup. After she thought about it for a while, she decided she would rather have a sissy husband than no husband. So long as nobody else knows about me, I think I can restore my relationship with her. My kids had a hard time forgiving me, but they did."

I sighed and rubbed the back of my neck. The muscles in it felt like they was about to snap. Other parts of my body felt like they wanted to shut down. I couldn't fall apart and end up in the crazy house. Then I wouldn't have nothing to live for. "So, where do we go from here?"

"*We* ain't going no place, no more. I done made up my mind. I ain't never going to see you again. I'm as sorry as I can be."

It felt like somebody had knocked the wind out of me. A split second later, my head started spinning and I had to lean against the wall to keep from collapsing. "Daryl, can we still be friends? For old times' sake, I hope we can still go out to supper from time to time and talk on the phone." I was so desperate to keep him in my life, I was willing to settle for just a friendship. I didn't even mind groveling. "Please, at least do that much for me."

It didn't take much to make Daryl cry. I listened to him bawl like a hungry baby for almost a whole minute before he replied, "Uh-uh. We can't have no contact at all. After I hang up this phone, I ain't never going to call you again. I don't want you to leave no more messages at my work." He hesitated and sucked on his teeth. After a loud snort, he continued. "I still care about you, but I can't give up my family for you. I thought I could, but now I realize I can't do it and be happy. How did your folks take it when you told them about me and you?"

"I didn't tell them. After I thought about it a little more, I changed my mind. But things was in such a uproar the last time you called, I didn't have a chance to let you know I'd changed my mind. I thought that after I buried my wife and son, you and me could go on like before."

"Well, we can't. With my wife and kids knowing about me now, I can't keep seeing you and come home and face them with more lies. I'm sorry."

It took me a few moments to respond. "I'll always love you, Daryl."

"I'll always love you too. Once my kids are on their own, my wife might decide she wants to be with somebody else. Or she just might be sick of me and want me out of her life. If so, me and you might have another chance to be together."

"For one thing, 'me and you' ain't kids. We don't have that kind of time left. I ain't going to wait around for you to be free and leave whoever I'm with then to resume a relationship with you."

There was a long moment of silence. "Then I guess this is it. Good-bye, Hubert."

Daryl hung up before I could say another word. I stumbled to my living room and literally fell down onto the couch. I was aching from my head all the way down to my feet. My chest was hurting the most. Even rubbing it didn't help. I wept like a old woman for the next several minutes. When I stopped, I sat bolt upright and asked, "Why me, God? Why me?"

Chapter 7
Hubert

*I*T WAS STARTING TO GET DARK OUTSIDE, BUT I DIDN'T TURN ON THE lights. I felt like I was in a trance. I couldn't believe I had lost so much, in so little time. I had been sitting on my living-room couch as stiff as a board ever since I got off the phone with Daryl two hours ago. I was too depressed to move. I was surprised I wasn't crying because I sure felt like doing it. For some reason, the tears wouldn't come.

My telephone had rang four times in the last half hour. I hadn't answered it because I was afraid Daryl was calling back to say something else hurtful. But when I thought about it a little more, if he was calling to do that, the sooner I heard what else he had to say, the better. When it rang again, it took all of my strength for me to get up and stagger to the kitchen to answer it. I was so relieved when I heard Jessie's voice.

"Hubert, I went to the meat market today. I bought more pig snouts than I got enough room for in my icebox. I don't want to let them sit on the counter and spoil. I wanted to know if I could bring some to you."

My throat was so dry and the lump in it was so big, it took me a few moments to respond. "I already got more than I need. I'm sure somebody else in the neighborhood would love to take them off your hands."

"I'll ask around then. Um, I didn't interrupt nothing, did I?"

"No, I wasn't doing nothing in particular. Just sitting here. I'm fixing to go read my Bible for a while."

"I ain't read mine in a few days, so I'm going to do the same thing. By the way, I talked to your mama this evening. She told me she called your house more than once today and you didn't answer. She's worried about you."

I blew out a short breath. "Did she ask you to check up on me?"

"Uh-uh. I thought I'd do that anyway. You don't sound too good."

"Jessie, I'm fine. I'm just a little tired, that's all. Thank you for your concern. When you talk to my mama the next time, tell her you talked to me and that I'm doing okay, so she can stop worrying."

"I'll tell her. I'll let you go now." Jessie hung up, and I returned to the couch.

One thing was for sure, I had to find myself a new man soon before I lost what was left of my sanity. And looking for somebody else was always risky. Not only was being a sissy against the law, everybody I knew thought that it was one of the worst sins anybody could commit. Daddy quoted words from Leviticus so often, I had memorized them: " *'You shall not lie with a male as with a woman; it is an abomination.'* " But the words that scared me the most was the punishment for the ones who violated this law: " *'They shall be put to death; their blood is upon them.'* "

Laws didn't mean nothing to people who couldn't help what they was. I had never had sex with a woman and didn't have no desire to do so. But I still needed one in my life so nobody would get suspicious about me and start asking questions and spreading rumors.

I couldn't decide which one was going to be the hardest to do: finding a new woman or a new man. From what I knew about women, the majority of them expected to be intimate when they was involved with a man. With that in mind, I figured I'd have relationships with several women at the same time so when one got antsy and broke it off with me because she wasn't getting no physical affection from me, I'd have others to fall back on. I wanted people to get used to seeing me socializing with women. I figured there had to be at least one out there who wasn't interested in having sex. If and when I found that woman, I'd drop all the others. Meanwhile, I could be hunting for a new boyfriend at the same time. With all that going on, I wouldn't have too much time to feel lonesome.

I couldn't consider men too close to home. Lexington was a small town and everybody I knew had big eyes and ears, and long tongues. It would be impossible to avoid getting caught eventually. Hartville was in the next county and I'd met a few good men there over the years. Since I'd been out of circulation for the last three years—wasting my time with Daryl—I didn't know what the dating scene was like these days. I only took a drink once or twice a year on special occasions, so I didn't have no reason to go to bars. But I'd found Daryl and a few other boyfriends in bars, so I figured I'd bite the bullet and start there.

I always knew I was a sissy, which was a word I had come to hate. I was manly in my looks, dress, and mannerism. The only thing I did that women did was love men. The only other word I'd ever heard folks use to describe men like me was "funny." There was nothing *funny* about it to me.

My first encounter with another male suddenly entered my mind. It had happened when I was sixteen. Just thinking about that experience made me smile. The other boy was the one who had initiated things. He was the seventeen-year-old son of one of my late uncle's friends and they lived in Mobile. His name was Xavier and he was as manly as they came. He was into sports, fishing, and everything else associated with men's behavior.

My uncle had run the funeral home until he died, and every time he had to go to Mobile to buy things he needed for the business that he couldn't find in Lexington, he took me with him. We always spent the night at his friend's house. There was four kids in the family, Xavier was the youngest boy. Like so many colored families, they didn't have much money, so they lived in a cramped tin-roofed house on a tree-lined dirt road. Xavier shared a rinky-dink bedroom and bed with his brother and two sisters. The girls slept at the top end of the bed; the boys slept at the foot. The first few times I stayed overnight, I slept on a pallet in the same room.

When Xavier's brother got married and moved out, I started sleeping in the same bed with him and the girls. One night after his sisters had gone to sleep, Xavier started rubbing me between my thighs. It felt so good, I had to hold my breath to keep from hollering. The next thing I knew, he kissed me smack-dab on my mouth. Things got a lot more serious and complicated after that. I didn't realize it until after it was over that we'd had sex. I left the next morning, and the next time I seen Xavier, we done the same things we'd done that night. It went on for around two years.

When Xavier told me he was going to get married, I was devastated. We made love one last time and he made me promise I'd never tell anybody about us. I never did and I never seen him again. Two years later, he joined the army and came home with no legs.

When I finished high school, I spent a lot of time in Hartville and other nearby towns looking for love. When I couldn't borrow a car, I took the bus. But I didn't have the nerve to initiate nothing with any of the men I ran into at the pool halls or any of the other places where colored men hung out, even if I suspected they was like me.

It was Mama, bless her heart, who had unknowingly steered me in the right direction. "Your daddy's brother stopped going to that bar in Toxey by the railroad tracks because he said a lot of sissies hang out there," she told me while I was helping her clean some chitlins in our kitchen sink a couple of months after my high-school graduation. "One had the nerve to get right fresh with your uncle one night and he beat that sissy's tail. He never went back because he was afraid he'd kill the next one that tried to get in his pants."

"Is that a fact? I declare, I didn't know Unc was the violent type," I'd said, trying to sound nonchalant.

"He ain't. But when something as unholy as another man trying to get him to do something vile with his body, he did what any other normal man would do. Wouldn't you have done the same thing if a sissy tried to move in on you?"

To this day, I could still feel how slimy them chitlins felt in my hands and how bad the stench was. It was a good enough reason for me to keep my face turned away from Mama. I didn't want her to see the anxious expression on my face. The place where my uncle had been approached sounded like a good prospect for me to do some hunting.

"I wouldn't be in a place like that in the first place. But if sissies ever come on to me, I ain't about to hit nobody, no matter what they do or say. I don't condone violence at all."

"Neither do I. You inherited that characteristic from my side of the family," Mama said proudly.

"The sissies in that place better be careful if they don't want to get run out of town or end up in prison. Exactly where is this wretched saloon?"

When Mama gasped, I turned to look at her. I ignored the curious expression on her face. "Why do you need to know that, Hubert?"

"I just wanted to know so I could tell all the boys and men I know who go to them kind of places to stay away from that one."

"That's a good idea, sugar. You must be the most thoughtful boy in this town." Mama told me more about the location of the bar. It was directly across the road from a deserted red barn on a dirt road right after the first bus stop off the highway in Toxey.

The very next day, while she and Daddy was about to leave to go to choir practice, I told them I was going to go to Mobile to visit a boy from my graduating class who'd recently moved over there. The bus I hopped on was the one that went to Toxey. It was a long walk from the bus stop to the saloon, but I made it. That night, I met somebody I liked right away. That relationship didn't last but a few weeks, but I went back every time I needed some affection.

The next few years, I had several relationships with men I'd met at that place, and a couple of others. I dreaded having to go back to square one. I didn't know what else to do if I wanted to love again.

It had been a hour since Jessie called. The telephone had rung two more times and I'd ignored it. I finally got off the couch, washed up, and put on some fresh clothes. I didn't even know if any of the haunts from my past was still in business. There was only one way to find out. Before I could leave the house, the phone rang again. This time, I answered. It was Jessie.

"Hubert, I just talked to your mama some more. She told me she's called your house several more times and you never answered. She sounded even more worried than before."

"After I talked to you, I got restless, so I went to visit one of my coworkers from the mill who just moved to this neighborhood. I just got back home."

"Oh? That's strange. I walked out to the curb fifteen minutes ago and seen your car in the driveway. Did he come pick you up?"

"No, he didn't. He lives close by, so I walked," I lied. "We played checkers for a little while. I just got back home a minute ago."

"Oh. If you still feeling restless, do you want me to come over and keep you company? I'll play checkers with you."

"That would be nice. But I promised my coworker that I'd come back tonight before it got too late to help him work on his car. I was fixing to leave when you called."

"Hmmm. How come you didn't stay while you was there and work on his car then?"

"His wife had drove it to go see her mama. He called just before you did and told me she just got back."

"Oh. I won't keep you then. By the way, I was going through my closet before I called you. I came across a blouse I had borrowed from Maggie. It made me so sad. It's the same one she had on the last time I ate supper with y'all." Jessie was whimpering like she was about to break down. I was glad she didn't, because I would have broke down too. "I can't tell you how much I miss coming to the house sitting for hours on end with you and her, listening to the radio, gossiping, eating and so on. Do you want me to bring the blouse so you can have them folks at the church donate it to somebody?"

"You can have it as a souvenir. Every time you look at it, you'll think about Maggie."

"Okay. Thank you. One more thing, and then I'll let you get going. If you ain't busy next week, would you like for me to come over and cook and do whatever chores you need done? Laundry, dusting, mopping. I'll do it every evening if you want me to. Afterward, we can spend a little time listening to the radio, playing checkers, or even going for a drive . . ."

"That's mighty generous and thoughtful of you. Ain't you got to go to work at the nursing home every night?"

"Not no more. Two people on the day shift recently retired, so they changed my shift to days. Starting this coming Monday, me and you will be working the same hours. I can take the bus to work, so I won't have to scramble around to find somebody to give me a ride, like Maggie did when my brother couldn't do it. His job is laying him off in two weeks, so this shift change came at the right time." Jessie paused and sucked in a loud breath. "I don't know about you, but I don't like being in a house all the time by myself."

"What about your son?"

"Earl? *Pffftt!* You know that boy don't talk much. Besides, since I'm going to be working days and ain't got nobody to look after him, he's going to Toxey tonight to stay a spell with my sister, Minnie. She came over a little while ago. Her daughter just moved back home with her three young kids and they love spending time with Earl. Besides, with Maggie not around no more to look after him while I'm at work, this is the best thing for me to do. My mama is sickly, and everybody else I know got to go to work, and I ain't been able to find another full-time person to look after my boy."

"That's a shame. I'll get back to you in the next day or so. I don't want to be taking up your time by having you cooking and cleaning for me when you could be doing something else."

"Hubert, since Orville and Maggie died, I ain't got nothing but time. I'd love to spend some of it with you."

I was so confused. Was Jessie hitting on me? I wondered once more. I immediately dismissed that notion. Jessie was not the type to do nothing that brazen. She was just as demure, virtuous, and godly as Maggie had been. She was also good-looking and faithful. Just the kind of woman any normal red-blooded man would love to get his hands on.

"You ain't got no boyfriend to keep company with?"

"Hubert, what's wrong with you? As fast as news travels around here, if I had a boyfriend, don't you think everybody in town would know about it by now?"

We laughed.

"Like I told you, I'll get back to you in a few days about your offer to help me out around the house."

"All right then, Hubert. I hope you'll enjoy the rest of your evening."

"I hope I will too."

Chapter 8
Jessie

I HUNG UP MY TELEPHONE AND SHOOK MY HEAD. EARL WAS IN HIS room gathering up some of the things he wanted to take with him to Minnie's house. She was sitting at my kitchen table guzzling her fourth cup of coffee. She had on a white cotton dress with such a plunging neckline, I wasn't even bold enough to wear one like it to bed.

People had been telling us all our lives how pretty me and her was. I never let it go to my head, but Minnie did. The way she strutted around in provocative clothes with rouge completely covering her cheeks, you would have thought she was a film star. We had the same copper-colored skin tone, oval-shaped faces, and thick black-and-gray hair that we always wore in the latest styles. At forty-eight, Minnie was the eldest one of my three siblings and had been married to the same man for thirty years. There was such a curious look on her face now, it made me nervous. "What was Hubert yakking about?" she asked.

"Gibberish. Nothing that would interest you. He's trying his best to act normal. But I know he's still in pain. I'm going to do all I can to make these next few months easy for him to get through. That's what Maggie would have wanted me to do." I plopped down in the chair across from Minnie. "I sure hope he finds another wife soon."

Minnie dabbed a few drops of coffee off her bottom lip and

patted her hair before she gazed at me with her eyes narrowed. "From what I keep hearing, you ain't going to have to wait long."

"What have you been hearing?"

"I heard that his mama and daddy is going to start match-making."

I knew that people had been talking about how much I gos-siped for years. It didn't bother me one bit because it was true. I enjoyed hearing news and reporting it. My sister was even more of a gossip than me, though. She lived in Toxey, which was in the next county, but she had so many friends in Lexington, she usu-ally heard stuff about people who lived in my neighborhood be-fore I heard it. She and her henpecked husband had raised their four kids, and she worked as a maid for a doctor only three hours a days, five days a week, so she had plenty of time to be a busybody.

Minnie swallowed hard and raked her fingers through her hair, which was in a French twist today. "I heard that Sister Wig-gins is planning to throw some supper parties soon. She's going to invite a few folks from church and at least one single woman, hoping she and Hubert will hit it off."

"So?"

"So I hope they invite you . . ."

Minnie knew how exasperating she was, so it didn't even faze her when I rolled my eyes. I calmly told her, "If they do invite me, it won't be because they want to match me up with Hubert. It wouldn't be fitting."

"Why not?"

I rolled my neck and looked at her with my mouth hanging open. "What's the matter with you? For one thing, Maggie was my best friend. How would it look for me to get involved with her husband?"

Minnie gave me such a disgusted look, I flinched. "You ain't that stupid. There ain't a colored woman in this town who would make a better wife for Hubert than you."

"*Wife!* W-what in the world—how did we get from me going to his mama's supper party to me marrying him? We ain't nothing but friends!"

"And that's all you and him will ever be if you don't get the spirit, baby sister." Minnie let out her breath and wagged her finger in my face. "Don't you let a golden-egg–laying goose like Hubert get away. Get the ball rolling before one of them other hussies get their hooks in him."

I gave Minnie a horrified look. "Stop talking crazy. If you think people are talking about me now, there ain't no telling what all they'll say if I got with my best friend's husband—less than two weeks after her funeral!"

"Your *dead* best friend. It would be different if you was still a young girl. When people of a certain age end up alone, like you and Hubert, they have to work fast at getting somebody else. And since when did you care about what the gossipmongers was saying about you? Shoot! If I wasn't married, I'd be on him like white on rice—and I'd be quick about it! That Blondeen and all the other women that's been taking him pies and casseroles and God knows what else since the funeral, you think they care about Maggie only being gone a couple of weeks?"

"They should. Going after a man who ain't finished grieving yet is unspeakable! What kind of women would do that?"

"Smart women." Minnie cleared her throat and folded her arms across her bosom. "You can sit around and wait for Hubert to finish grieving, if you want to. I heard that a couple of women started plotting to sink their teeth into him during Maggie's funeral! They ain't going to pussyfoot around and miss out on landing him."

"You make him sound like a piece of meat."

"He is! And a prime piece, at that."

"And another thing, I ain't even in love with Hubert."

"So what? This ain't about love. This is about being practical and looking out for your future. He's still a good-looking man with two jobs, a house that's paid for, a car, a telephone, and a flawless reputation. That's a mighty big jackpot up for grabs. Whoever marries him will eventually fall in love with him because he's got so much to offer. That's how it works. Do you think I was in love with that beady-eyed man of mine when I married him? Hell no. But he had everything I wanted, and I learned to love him." Minnie gave me one of the sternest looks she'd gave me since that time I got clumsy and spilled barbecue sauce on one of her favorite blouses. "Listen to me, baby sister. I want you to be happy and have somebody to grow old with. What you need to do is stay just friends with Hubert for now, but each day get a little bit closer. Offer to help him do things only a woman should be doing—laundry, cooking, house cleaning, you know the drill. Once you feel comfortable, and he gets to a point where he is dependent on you, go in for the kill. If you let him get away and he marries somebody else, you'll regret it until the day you die. Trust me."

I gave Minnie a thoughtful look. "You think I could be happy with Hubert?"

"If you can't, then there's definitely something wrong with you and the only man you need to be looking for is a psychiatrist. You know almost every unattached colored man in Lexington. Which one of them would be better for you than Hubert? And which one of them would want you, with you middle-aged self?"

I bit my bottom lip and gave some serious thought to her words. "When you put it like that . . ." I stopped talking and threw up my hands. "Oh, this is crazy! In the first place, it ain't easy to get a man who ain't never showed no interest in me that way. And you know I ain't the kind of woman to throw myself at nobody. If I was, I'd be with somebody new by now."

"All right, then. Don't say I didn't try to help you get back on track. You want to be lonesome the rest of your life, that's on you." Minnie shook her head just as Earl shuffled into the room.

"Mama, can I take my marbles with me?" he asked. I loved my poor slow-witted son, and I only wanted what was best for him. By living with Minnie, he'd have her three grandkids living in the same house to play with. They was all under the age of eight. His mental capacity was about the same as theirs, so he'd be happier, at least until there was another major change in my life.

"Sure, you can, sugar. And don't forget to pack up all your socks," I reminded. Earl's daddy had treated me and him both real bad. I told people I missed Orville. But I didn't miss that devil one bit and had been trying to put him completely out of mind since the day he died. That wasn't easy, though. Earl had his daddy's handsome features, peach-colored skin, and build, so it was impossible not to think about him every time I looked at Earl.

"Okay, Mama." Earl shifted his weight from one foot to the other and stared at me.

He would go for days at a time without talking. When he did say something, I tried to keep him conversating with me as long as I could. Some folks thought it was a curse to have a retarded child. I thought it was a blessing because he'd always need me. And being needed by somebody was important to me. "You can call me as often as you want."

"I don't like talking on no phone, Mama," he declared with a sour look on his face. "I don't like talking, period. After today, I ain't going to say nothing else for a real long time." Them was the last words to come out of his mouth before he went back to his room to do some more packing.

Minnie gazed at me and hunched her shoulders. "Don't worry. He'll be just fine. Now, you think about what I said about Hubert. And I advise you not to take too long to take my advice. You are forty-one years old. That's way too old to be taking your time in such a serious situation."

"I can still find somebody if I went out more. But most of the men around here are only interested in women who'll wallow around in bed with them. I ain't giving up my sugar too soon. I don't want men to think I'm easy."

Minnie rolled her eyes and waved her hand in the air. "Girl, you ain't got but a teaspoon of sugar left in your bowl. You ain't no Cinderella, so you don't have a fairy godmother with a magic wand to fall back on. And another thing, most men don't want a woman with feet bigger than theirs."

"Could you be a little more specific?" I shot her a hot look for a split second, and then I laughed. She never meant any harm with her wisecracks, but she believed in being brutally honest with everybody, especially me.

"Mama and the rest of the family don't want you to be alone too much longer. Now, that's all I got to say on this subject."

"Good!"

Minnie snickered and gave me a hopeless look before she went to help Earl finish packing. They left a few minutes later. I stood on my front porch and watched until her dusty old truck turned the corner. But her words was still ringing in my ears. The more I thought about what she'd said about me trying to land Hubert, the more I thought about doing just that. I had nothing to lose and a whole lot to gain.

Chapter 9
Hubert

I DIDN'T LIKE LYING TO JESSIE ABOUT WHERE I WAS GOING TONIGHT, but I didn't have no choice. I had a mission to accomplish.

I decided to start all over again at the first joint I'd ever visited in Toxey. I couldn't remember how to get there and I sure couldn't ask Mama again, but a man at a gas station pointed me in the right direction. I still took a wrong turn and got lost. I drove around for twenty minutes and passed some of the same places more than once. When I hit a possum, I almost ran into a ditch. I was distressed, to say the least, and was about to go back home, but then I finally found the place I'd been hunting for. The deserted red barn that used to face it had been tore down and the juke joint looked a lot more spruced up. It had been painted from a dull brown to a bright blue and it had a new roof.

Within minutes after I went in, I regretted it. Other than a blunt-featured, heavyset man in his fifties talking to a much older man sitting on a bench in front of a piano, I was the only man in the mix. There was almost a dozen women milling about and they couldn't pounce on me fast enough.

"What's your name, sugar?" the first one asked as she grabbed my arm. She was so skinny, I was surprised she could walk on her bony legs. And she wasn't much to look at neither. She had a long, horsey face and lips that stuck out like a carp.

"I just came in for a minute," I muttered.

Before I realized what was happening, another woman grabbed my other arm. She was a lot better-looking, but just as annoying. "I ain't seen you in here before," she slurred as she looked me up and down. "Baby, you look like you could really show a woman a good time! Let's go somewhere so we can talk in private."

"I just came in to ask for directions to get me back to the main highway," I lied. "I just left my lady friend's house and took a wrong turn." Both women let my arms go and spun around and walked away. I was glad when the heavyset man came up to me before another woman could approach.

"Good evening. I'm Ralph Cook. This is my place. I took it over nigh on twenty years ago when the man who'd owned it up and died," he announced in a loud, deep voice. "I ain't seen you in here before. What's your name?"

"Hubert Wiggins. I live in Lexington and I don't come out this way too often," I explained as I shook his huge, calloused hand. He had on bibbed overalls, a plaid flannel shirt, and a straw hat. He looked more like a field hand than a juke joint owner.

"Well, I hope you can stay a spell. Things been kind of slow lately, so everybody is welcome here." Ralph made a sweeping gesture with his hand. "I'm sure you'll have a good time."

"I'll come and stay awhile the next time I'm in this neck of the woods. But I really need to get on the road before it gets too late. It's done got too dangerous for a colored man with a nice car to be out at night on the highway by hisself. That's just the kind of thing that agitates the Ku Klux Klan."

He nodded and a hopeless look crossed his face. "Tell me about it. Them racist devils burned down my first place because it was too close to a white neighborhood. Peckerwoods, peckerwoods, peckerwoods!" He paused and perked back up real quick. "I can tell you which way you need to go, but don't you want a drink before you leave?"

"Oh no. Thank you for asking. I had a few before I left my lady friend's house."

As soon as he gave me directions, which I didn't need, I bolted.

I was so disappointed I didn't want to think about what I was going to do next to meet somebody. In the meantime, I planned to keep myself busy. Mama was going to host a supper next week, and Daddy had already put a bug in my ear about the single woman she had invited just for my benefit.

When I got back to Lexington and turned onto my street, I was surprised to see all the lights on in the little green house Jessie lived in, two blocks from mine on the opposite side of the same street. Without giving it much thought, I parked in front of it and stumbled up on her porch. I was so lonesome, all I wanted was some company. And I couldn't think of a better person to sit with for a little while than her.

Jessie opened the door right away when I knocked. She had on a shabby brown bathrobe and there was at least two dozen brown paper-bag hair rollers all over her head. She gasped and threw up her arms. "Hubert! I declare, I wasn't expecting nobody this time of night! I thought you was one of my neighbors coming to borrow something again. And I'm standing here looking like a fishwife."

"You look fine to me." I chuckled and glanced over her shoulder. "I hope I ain't interrupting nothing."

"Oh, I was just sitting on the couch listening to the radio. Come on in." She waved me into her neat little living room. "After Minnie and Earl left, I got kind of lonesome. I'm glad you came by. You want a glass of water or some cider? I got buttermilk too."

"That's all right. I don't need nothing to drink. I ain't going to stay long." We plopped down on her lumpy gray couch.

"You finish helping your friend?"

"What friend?" I asked dumbly. I had already forgot the lie I'd told her about where I was going tonight. "Oh! Um . . . yeah.

Everything is fine with his car now. A couple of things under his hood needed to be adjusted."

"I'm glad that's all it was." Jessie sniffed and scratched the side of her neck. "Um . . . have you thought about what I mentioned about me coming to cook and help you out around the house?"

"Yeah, I did give it some thought. It would be nice if you could do all that. But only when you have time. I don't want you to feel obligated to me in any way."

"I offered to do it, Hubert. How about me starting this coming Monday? I will get home from work between five thirty and six p.m., so I could be at your house shortly after that."

"Tuesday would be better. And I'll pay you five dollars a week."

I gasped. "You don't have to pay me. I offered to do this for you."

"I'd have to pay anybody else who did it. I'll still give you five dollars a week even if you don't cook every day."

"Okay, then. Why do you want me to start on Tuesday and not Monday?"

"Well, Mama will be hosting a few suppers in the next few weeks, and the first one is Monday evening. She's trying to team up with some of them single women who have been bringing me plates and consoling me, so they'll keep doing it. Mama's help ain't even necessary because them same women don't need no coaxing. Every time I look up, one is at my door with another casserole or a pan of corn bread. I enjoy their company, though, so I'm going to go along with the program." I laughed.

"Well, you know we will always be babies to our mothers. Every time I'm around my mama, she checks my ears to make sure I'm keeping them clean." We laughed. "Ain't it kind of soon for you to be looking for love?"

"Love? Ha! It ain't nothing like that. Mama and Daddy is worried about me being by myself and they know I ain't got no close friends. They think that if they can get some of them same women to spend more time with me, I'll get over my grief sooner. I let them have their way because I don't want to hurt their feelings. But I ain't too excited about the first single woman they invited to come."

"What's wrong with her?"

"Now, that's a loaded question. It's Zelma Hood."

A stupefied look crossed Jessie's face. "That no-neck, stout woman who takes care of the police chief's kids?"

"Yup."

She cleared her throat, snorted, and pressed her lips together. I could have swore she was trying her best not to laugh. "Zelma was a year behind me in school. She dropped out in seventh grade to get married."

"Well, she ain't married no more. She's the first one. And I ain't sure, but I think they planning to try and get me and Blondeen Walker together. I heard that from a couple of different people at church." I laughed.

"I hope them women don't get the wrong idea."

"Wrong idea about what?"

"Well, you might only be looking for somebody to keep you company, but they might be looking for something more. Especially Blondeen . . ."

"They can think what they want. But I ain't going to do nothing with them that I wouldn't do with somebody like you, or one of my female relatives. The minute I think they misunderstand my intentions, I'll cut them loose."

"Okay. I don't want to see you get in a situation that'll cause you even more grief. A scorned woman can be as deadly as a rattlesnake . . ."

"A 'scorned woman'?" I laughed long and loud. "That's funny. You have to be in a romance to scorn somebody, and that ain't about to happen with none of the women I know." I sighed. "Thanks for your concern, Jessie. I appreciate it. I'm mainly doing this for Mama. She loves to think that she's doing something that'll benefit me. But at the end of the day, she's more interested in doing things that benefit her and Daddy. Bless her soul."

"Well, if Zelma don't work out, I hope Blondeen will . . ."

"At least they are both in the church. Zelma don't belong to my daddy's church, but that don't matter. Church is church. But to be honest with you, I ain't too happy about getting more involved with neither one of them. Other than them bringing me meals, helping me out around the house, and keeping me company, I'll have to take them out from time to time. And when we don't go out, I'll have to sit around and conversate with them, for God knows how long, each time I see them. I might run into a few problems. Especially with Blondeen. She ain't but twenty-eight, so she might not be mature enough for a man my age. Zelma is forty and eats like a Clydesdale horse, so I'd have to spend a heap of money on food to keep her contented. On top of doing it to keep Mama and Daddy from worrying about me, I'm doing it to bide my time and keep myself busy, so I won't sit around for hours on end pining for somebody I ain't never going to see again. I thought about getting a dog or a cat, but cleaning up behind one of them critters don't appeal to me."

"What'll happen once you get over your grief? Will you find a woman you can have a serious relationship with?"

"I ain't thought that far ahead yet." I lowered my voice and leaned forward. "When I get to that point, maybe you can help me. You know almost all of the single women in this town and all their business. If you know a nice lady I might like, please let me know."

Jessie smiled. "I just want you to be happy again, Hubert. I'll do all I can to make that happen. I'll keep my eye out for somebody you might like enough to have a serious relationship with."

I sniffed and glanced around the room. It smelled so nice and fresh. Jessie didn't have attractive modern furniture like me. But every outdated, mismatched item she owned was neat, clean, and well-organized. "You sure keep a nice house, Jessie. And you can whip up some mean casseroles and other dishes."

She blushed and giggled. "I'm sure that if you decide to let me come cook and clean for you, you won't be disappointed."

"Jessie, I know you almost as well as I knew Maggie, so I know you would never disappoint me." And then it hit me like a ton of bricks: Jessie might be the perfect prop to help me keep my secret hid when I found a new boyfriend! But first I had to figure out a way to "woo" her into that position without her getting the wrong idea about my intentions. One way would be to take my time and see them other women until I felt comfortable enough to approach Jessie.

Chapter 10
Jessie

I WAS REALLY LOOKING FORWARD TO COOKING FOR HUBERT AT HIS house Tuesday evening, but the last thing I wanted to do was help him find a new lady friend! For one thing, I didn't know one single woman in Lexington who deserved a man like him.

I wasn't in love with him (yet), but my sister had convinced me that he had everything it took to make a woman happy. Just thinking about being the lady friend of the most eligible colored man in town was enough to get my juices flowing.

The only thing was, I had to do something to put some doubt in his parents' minds that would make them stop trying to get him interested in other women.

Two days after Hubert's late-night visit on Saturday, I called him up at half past eight p.m. He had just come home from his mama's supper party. All I wanted to know was if him and Zelma had hit it off. "How was Zelma?" I asked, trying to sound nonchalant.

"Fine, I guess. I didn't spend much time talking to her." He sucked on his teeth and mumbled some gibberish under his breath. "I declare, she was way more interested in Mama's pot roast and mashed potatoes than she was in getting to know me better. Judging from that huge bulge around her middle, she's been interested in a whole lot of other food since I seen her at that first murdered woman's funeral six months ago."

"Well, her appetite must not matter, because she's been married three times."

"And that's another thing, a woman with that many used-to-be husbands must have some serious issues with men. It would be different if they had all died, like yours."

Hubert's last comment got my attention. Now I couldn't wait to get my plan off the ground.

I went to his house Tuesday when I got off work and cooked him some pinto beans and fried chicken. While I was cooking, he took a long bath and spent about fifteen minutes on the telephone conversating with one of the men he supervised at the mill. As soon as he hung up, I told him, "I'll get to the laundry after supper." I assumed he expected me to eat supper with him, but that wasn't the case.

"I'll put everything in the icebox and eat later. You can do the laundry later in the week."

"Oh. Uh, do you want me to sweep the floors?"

"No, you can do that later in the week too. You can go home now. I'm going to the movies tonight and I don't want to leave you in the house alone."

I think what he meant was he was going to bring a woman home after the movies. If that wasn't mortifying enough, he'd probably serve her the supper I had cooked! "Oh. Well, I'd better get going so you can get ready." I got my coat off the rack by the door. "I hope you'll enjoy your movie." I was tempted to ask who he was going with, but I didn't want to be too nosy, too soon.

"Don't you want to take some of them beans and chicken home?" he asked.

"Oh no. I got some leftovers from last night."

"All right, Jessie. Thanks for cooking dinner. By the way, I'll be paying you every Friday evening. That suit you?"

"That'll be fine." He opened the door for me and closed it before I even got off the porch.

I was so confused and disappointed, I didn't know what to

think. If he was taking a woman to the movies tonight, there was no telling what else he had up his sleeve. Or what she had up hers, whoever she was. I knew now that I had to work even harder and faster.

Hubert's parents liked me a lot and it was time for me to get some mileage out of that relationship.

When I got off work on Wednesday, I paid his mama a visit.

Sister Wiggins pressed and curled women's hair in her kitchen and made good money, but I only had her do my hair when I had a few extra dollars. I had become so close to her over the years because of my relationship with Maggie and Hubert, I often dropped in on her just for a visit. I couldn't wait to see her today.

"Jessie, you are a sight for sore eyes!" she squealed when she opened the door to let me in. "It's so good to see you again. Hubert told us you working days now. Come on in and make yourself at home." She waved me into her large, well-organized living room.

"I know I should have called to make a appointment to get my hair done, but I decided at the last minute to come over today." I plopped down in one of the big chairs facing the couch. She stood in the middle of the floor with her arms folded.

"Oh? You ain't let me do your hair since before Orville died. How come you want me to start doing it again?"

"Now that Earl is living with my sister and she ain't charging me much for his food and whatever else he needs, I got a few dollars to spend on myself this week."

"Well, I can't help you out today." Sister Wiggins glanced at the clock on the wall above the couch. "I have to go over to the church in a little while to help organize this year's Christmas program. Otherwise, I'd be glad to fix you up." She sniffed and stared at my thick hair, which was all over my head because I had accidentally left my scarf at work and it was windy outside. "And you sure do need some help with that burning bush on top of your head."

"Tell me about it. That's why I'm here. Can I come back over here to get it done tomorrow?"

"I'm sorry, but I'm booked up for the rest of this week. I got a few minutes to sit and chat with you now, though." She flopped down on the couch. I was amazed at how Hubert was concerned about getting involved with a large woman like Zelma when he had a mama who was almost twice as big. "Me and the reverend are so pleased that you are helping Hubert out around the house. Other than that, what else have you been up to?"

"Nothing much. Just working." I cleared my throat and scratched the side of my head. "By the way, Hubert told me about the supper party you had on Monday. It's a shame him and Zelma didn't hit it off. I'm sure she would have enjoyed keeping him from feeling lonesome."

"We ain't gave up on her yet. Depending on how things go in the next few weeks, we might invite her to join us again soon." Sister Wiggins shook her head and gave me a sheepish look. "That boy is so pitiful right now, me and his daddy had to take some action. I loved Maggie to death, but her passing has left him heartbroken. I know she ain't been gone but a couple of weeks, and we had wanted him to wait at least six months or a year to get involved with another woman. But the way he's been moping around, we realized that he is way too fragile to wait that long. Now, don't get me wrong, we ain't trying to make him fall in love with nobody, we just want for him to have somebody to socialize with. We thought it would be a good idea to have him spend some time with some of the women who have been taking him casseroles and whatnot. He was so wrapped up in Maggie, he never took the time to make no close friends." A mysterious look crossed Sister Wiggins's face. "He ain't never had no men friends, to speak of, and me and his daddy could never figure out why. It's just as well. The men his age like to drink and get rowdy and that would be a bad influence on our baby. That's why we thought we'd try to match him up with a nice lady to be casual friends with until he finds romance again." Sister Wiggins blew out a sigh and lowered her voice. "I guess Zelma was a bad choice. They didn't interact much the other night. And she mean-mouthed all three of them men she used to be married to."

I cleared my throat. "Maybe it's just as well she and Hubert didn't hit it off. She might be a little too fast for a quiet, settled man like him. She got around quite a bit when she was married all them times," I tossed in. "If you know what I mean . . ."

Sister Wiggins blinked and gave me a concerned look. "She 'got around' how much?"

"More than a Fuller Brush man. I heard she has more fingerprints on her rump than the law got on file."

Chapter 11
Jessie

I WAS PLEASED TO SEE THAT I WAS MAKING SOME PROGRESS WITH Hubert's mama. Because of what I just said about Zelma, Sister Wiggins gasped so hard, her eyes crossed. "Good gracious alive! A woman like that would wreak havoc in any man's life. Even if she was just a friend."

"She'll give any man a run for his money, all right. My brother, Karl, took her out once. He told me she drank like a fish and flirted with other men right in front of him."

"I declare! I knew she liked to have a lot of fun, but I didn't know she was that frisky."

"I'm sure she's still a nice lady, though."

Sister Wiggins looked so disgusted, she yelled for Reverend Wiggins to come in the room. He stumbled in, already in his bathrobe, and stood by the side of the couch with a puzzled expression on his face. He looked like a older, much larger version of Hubert. "Hello, Jessie. I ain't seen you since Maggie's and Claude's funeral and I'm pleased to see you looking so well." He turned to Sister Wiggins with his hands on his hips. "What did you call me out here for?"

"Did you know that Zelma fooled around with a lot of men?" she asked him.

"Even while she was still married," I added.

Reverend Wiggins looked confused. "So?"

"Jessie tells me she likes to drink too. I don't think it's a good idea for her to get too close to Hubert. Her bad habits could rub off on him," Sister Wiggins said.

Reverend Wiggins took a huge gulp of air and looked directly at me. "Is that true, Jessie?"

I nodded. "I thought everybody knew that about Zelma by now," I answered in a smug tone.

"We try to avoid idle gossip as much as possible, which seems to be a popular sport with so many folks in this town. Maybe we should keep our eyes and ears open more so we can stay on top of who is doing what. The last thing this family needs is to get too close to somebody who'll tarnish our reputation!" Reverend Wiggins boomed.

"I know what you mean. I don't like gossip myself. But everywhere I go, somebody shares information with me. Oh, well. Whatever happens, I hope Zelma and Hubert can still have a nice relationship. Maybe he can tame her down some. And at least she'll keep him so busy, he won't have time to be lonesome."

Sister Wiggins was gazing at me with a distressed expression on her face. "Well . . . uh . . . we don't want our son to jump the gun. That's why we been considering other women besides Zelma," she said in a nervous tone. "Hubert tried to put up a fuss when we told him what we was up to, but that didn't stop us. He's still in somewhat of a dazed condition right now to do much for hisself. We invited Blondeen Walker to have supper with us next."

"Is that a fact? She's one of the best-looking women I know. And she's nice when you really get to know her." I added with a loud sigh, "With all the turmoil in her family's background, I'm surprised she ain't lost her mind. God must have His eye on her."

"Oh?" Reverend Wiggins's eyes got big and he started speaking in a gruff tone. "What turmoil?"

I gasped and threw up my hands. "Y'all ain't heard about them scandals a couple of her relatives got caught up in . . ."

"What scandals?" Sister Wiggins asked. She looked even more distressed now.

"Remember some years ago when that man got beat up and run out of town because he was going to bed with other men? That was Blondeen's uncle. And last year, one of her cousins was caught in bed with a man. His own wife found him, but he didn't stick around to get beat up. He took off the next day and ain't been heard from since."

"My Lord in heaven. That kind of behavior is a sin and a shame if ever there was one," Sister Wiggins said with a shudder.

"Sure enough. And then there was that mess Blondeen created at the nursing home I work at. We worked the same shift until they fired her for stealing some money from a patient. She got mad at me because I wouldn't stick up for her. I don't condone stealing. Especially when it involves helpless elderly people."

"I didn't know none of that," Reverend Wiggins responded. "Jessie, thank you for bringing all this to our attention." He snorted and turned to his wife. "Mother, I don't think it's such a good idea now, after all, to encourage Hubert to get involved with none of them women we picked out. Cancel that supper with Blondeen posthaste! Maybe we'll all be better off if we let Hubert decide who he wants to socialize with, and when."

"I guess we should let him choose his own friends, after all," Sister Wiggins said gently. "I just hope he don't get too antsy and pick the wrong friend when a better one might be just around the corner."

It looked like I had got my point across, but the last thing I wanted them to think was that I had unchristian motives. "I think it's wonderful that y'all want to help Hubert find a new lady friend. But I also think it's important for y'all to be aware of certain things. Hubert is like a brother to me, and I don't want his feelings to get hurt after all he's been through. Besides, people who have admired and respected him for years might lose respect for him if they knew he was friendly with certain types of women. That could have a negative impact on his business. Some folks can be real particular about who they let bury their loved ones." I paused long enough to come up with the next blow. "Look at it this way, the worst thing that could happen is that Hubert falls in love with Blondeen anyway and marries her and starts a new family. He'd probably have to find another line of work, but if he's happy, that's more important."

The reverend and his wife looked like they wanted to scream. Something told me I didn't have to say nothing else. My main concern was that they'd keep looking until they found a woman I didn't have no dirt on. I wasn't going to worry about that much, though. Now that I'd made up my mind to go after Hubert, I was going to go full steam ahead.

Hubert was on his way out when I arrived at his house after my visit with his parents.

"Hi, Jessie. I called your house a while ago to let you know I was going out again tonight," he panted as he darted out the door.

"I had to make a couple of stops on my way home. You don't want me to cook nothing?"

"Something came up at the last minute, so I'll be eating out tonight."

"I was going to do the laundry tonight."

"You can do that tomorrow." Hubert heaved out a loud sigh. "Now you have a blessed evening." He whirled around and galloped off the porch to the driveway and got in his car.

Hubert called me up before I left for work Thursday morning. "Jessie, I'm sorry I had to take off last night. I know you want to get a routine started and I promise we'll get one established soon."

"Well, on the nights you have to go out, I can cook something at my house for you and drop it off whenever you return."

"That ain't a bad idea. I'm glad you brought that up, because I'll be at my parents' house this evening doing a few chores for them. I don't know what time I'll be home."

"Well, just call me when you get home. I don't care what time it is."

Chapter 12
Hubert

I COULDN'T STOP THINKING ABOUT THE WAY I HAD TREATED JESSIE Tuesday night. I didn't enjoy giving her the brush-off. And I didn't enjoy taking one of my mill coworkers' girlfriends to the movies that night because he'd sprained his ankle. But he had promised to take his girl to see *The Adventures of Sherlock Holmes*. It had been released in September, and Tuesday was the last day it would be playing in Lexington. My coworker didn't want to deal with her wrath if she missed it.

I figured that by treating Jessie the way I had, on both Tuesday and then on Wednesday, it would make me look better when I started showing her more attention, and them other women less. That would make her feel special and more eager to get more involved with me.

I had just come home from visiting Mama and Daddy Thursday night when somebody opened my front door and walked in. It was Yolinda Crandall. She was a nice-looking, freckle-faced widow in her fifties who lived in the house across the street with a bunch of her relatives. She had lost her daddy last summer and I had handled his final arrangements. Shortly after his funeral, her mama moved in with one of her granddaughters several blocks away. She had decided that it would be too painful to stay in the same house where her husband had died.

Like Jessie and Maggie, Yolinda was a very caring, God-fearing woman. That's why I didn't mind her entering my house without even knocking—a habit that was common in our neighborhood anyway. She had also offered to cook and clean for me, but it was after I had told Jessie she could do it. I was so blessed to be surrounded by folks so determined to look out for me.

"Yolinda, I'm glad to see you looking so well," I told her as she pranced into my living room and sat down on my couch. She had on a floor-length dress with roses in various sizes all over it.

"I wish I could say the same about you, Hubert. I know you still in mourning, but you look so tired and underfed. Did you eat them gizzards I fried for you the other day?"

"Yes, I did. When you get a chance, bring me some more."

"I will. I know you missing Maggie and Claude something terrible, but it'll get better for you. There is a lot of women around here itching to help you get over your grief." Yolinda kicked off the men's house shoes she had on and crossed her legs.

I sat down in the chair facing her and rolled my eyes. "Tell me about it. But I'm particular, so it'll be hard to find one that suits me."

"I declare, I loved Maggie and I know she was the perfect wife. I hope that in the next few months, you find somebody new. Did I tell you my niece in Huntsville just left her husband? The one with the big brown eyes and shapely legs?"

"You told me about her the last time we talked. I'm going to take my daddy's choir director's cousin out to supper this week and I have a bunch of other things to take care of, so I'm going to be real busy for a while."

"That choir director's cousin is a little on the plain side, but I know some men don't care about things like that. Especially when the woman has a strong Christian background, like she got."

"And she's a very nice woman," I pointed out. "I've never heard anybody say anything unflattering about her."

"Well, if y'all don't hit it off, I'll call my niece."

Somebody else knocked before we could continue the conversation. I skittered to the door so fast, I almost tripped over my feet. It was Jessie. She was holding another casserole dish. "Oh,

Hubert, I didn't know you had company," she said as she strolled in, unbuttoning her dark brown wool coat. "Good evening, Yolinda. Hubert, I seen you drive past my house a little while ago. I wanted to drop off this macaroni and cheese I cooked for your supper this evening." She untied the white scarf she had on her head and stuffed it into her coat pocket.

"I had a few things to do this evening. I'm sorry I didn't let you know I would be getting home late. But I'm glad you went ahead and cooked. That was real nice of you. Is it that chilly outside now for you to be so wrapped up?"

"It is to me. I got low blood, so I figure that's why I catch colds more than everybody else."

"Maggie had that same problem. I'm sorry I bring up her name so much," I apologized, looking from Yolinda to Jessie. "But I can't help myself."

"You can talk about that sweet soul as much as you want to when you're around me," Yolinda said with a quick nod. "I do the same thing myself."

"Nobody could ever talk too much about Maggie in my presence," Jessie tossed in. "We should keep her memory alive as long as possible."

I swallowed the huge lump in my throat. "Let me take care of that casserole. Thank you for being so thoughtful again." I took the dish away from Jessie and she followed me to the kitchen.

Yolinda stuck her head in the doorway and snickered, "I'll leave you two alone! I better get back to the house before them crazy young'ns burn it down." She gave me a sly wink before she spun around and galloped to the door.

After she left, me and Jessie looked at each other and shrugged before we laughed. "I hope she didn't leave on account of me," she said.

"Oh, don't worry about Yolinda. I'm glad you showed up when you did." I put the dish in the icebox and motioned Jessie to a seat at the kitchen table. "She was trying to set me up with her niece."

Jessie shook her head. "I declare, I wish everybody would stop trying to make you fall in love with another woman. You ain't had time to get over Maggie yet."

"Jessie, I don't really mind all the attention I been getting. It's kind of nice. Anything is better than me moping around this house every day. I'm sure Maggie would want me to move on with my life as soon as I could."

"I'm sure she would too." Jessie sighed and glanced toward the doorway. "You want me to do any dusting or mopping before I leave?"

"No, that can wait."

"Then I guess I'll go on back home and let you get back to whatever you was doing. I like to read Scripture before I go to bed—"

I cut her off right away. I figured enough time had passed for me to give her more attention, and I'd show her a little more as the days went by. "Don't leave yet. If you ain't too tired, I wouldn't mind conversating for a little while. I need to read the Bible myself, so we could do it together. If you and Yolinda hadn't come over here, I would be sitting around twiddling my thumbs."

"Oh, okay. I'll stay awhile."

I sat down in the chair across from Jessie. She had such a anxious look on her face, I immediately told her that somebody had mentioned Zelma's loose ways and Blondeen being a thief to my folks. I couldn't believe how tight her face got. It got even tighter when I told her that Mama had called Blondeen up and told her not to come to next week's supper party she'd invited her to. And the reason she'd gave her was that she'd accidentally invited more folks than she could accommodate.

"Stealing ain't the only bad thing in Blondeen's background." Jessie told me about Blondeen's uncle and cousin getting caught with men. "Two members in the same family having them unspeakable desires is a bad omen any way you look at it. There ain't no telling how many more of their kinfolks have the same affliction."

I held my breath and tried to imagine what was going through her mind. The way she scrunched her face up, whatever it was had to be bad.

"Um, yeah. I heard bits and pieces about both of them scandals. Mama and Daddy hadn't heard nothing because they don't let folks spread too much gossip in their presence. Anyway, they finally heard about it recently. They didn't tell me who told them all that stuff, but it don't matter. I don't know anybody brazen enough to lie to a preacher and his wife, so I believe it's all true. As for Zelma, I wasn't too interested in her nohow. But even with so much going against Blondeen, I don't see nothing wrong with me spending time with her, so long as I don't let our relationship get serious—and my folks don't get the wrong idea. I don't like to judge people by something their kinfolks did and I believe everybody needs friends. She kept me laughing when I took her to supper at that chicken shack last week. When I'm around her, my burden don't feel so heavy."

Jessie let out a mild gasp and there was a sour look on her face. "I didn't know you was dating her."

"I don't know if I'd call it 'dating.' We are just two people at loose ends who happen to want to go out and enjoy ourselves. She done brought me a lot of pies, pig ears, chitlins, and other goodies since Maggie passed. Taking her out is one way for me to return her favors."

"I ain't surprised. Any red-blooded man would like to spend time with a pretty woman like Blondeen." The same sour look was still on Jessie's face. "I hope you can enjoy her company some more. I heard she can cook a mean pot of pig feet. If she's the jealous type, maybe I shouldn't keep coming over here so often, and maybe we should forget about me cooking and cleaning for you—"

I held up my hand to cut her off. "No, I don't want you to stop coming. I don't care how many other women I spend time with, everything between me and you will stay the same. For years you was the sister I always wanted and I'd like for us to become even closer. My time with Blondeen is about to run out because I could never have a real future with her. But I'm going to ease out of my relationship with her so her feelings won't be hurt." I laughed. "I almost had a fit when she told me she'd make me a good wife. She was joking, but I got a feeling she was also serious. Me marrying her is about as likely as me parting the Red Sea. Besides, Mama and Daddy are so convinced that bad habits are hereditary they would never accept her or forgive me. The possibility of me having a child with Blondeen who might become a thief is so unspeakable, they can't even discuss it without bile rising in their throats."

"I bet. But I could live with having a child being a thief. Stealing is almost at the bottom on the list of Ten Commandments. But that don't even hold a candle to that other thing. Having a son that loved boys or a daughter that loved girls would be way more than I could tolerate. I'd go crazy wondering when somebody was going to do harm to them. Not only that, but they could also end up in prison! I'd rather not have a child if they came in the world with unnatural desires."

Jessie's last statement made me so uncomfortable, I couldn't wait for her to leave now. The blood drained from my face and my heart was beating so hard, I could actually hear it thumping against the inside of my bosom. I couldn't look her in the eyes when I mumbled, "I know just what you mean. I feel the same way." I cleared my throat. "This subject is too unpleasant for me. Let's talk about something else. Anything."

"Well, I'd like to stay longer so we could discuss something that ain't so wicked. But I need to get home and wash out my work uniform." Jessie stood up.

"I'm glad you'll be cooking for me and I'm sorry we got off to a bad start. After this week, I should be home almost every evening in the week—unless something comes up. If you still want to come over every evening, or only when you feel like it, that's fine with me. I'll still pay you five dollars a week, no matter how many days you come."

Jessie's face lit up like a burning match. "You just made my day—which had been pretty dull since I got out the bed this morning. I just don't want to cause you no trouble with none of the other women you spend time with."

"Oh, you ain't got to worry about that. I'm just killing time with them. I'm going to ask my grave digger's sister to go out to supper with me one evening next week. It's her birthday. When her husband left her last year, she was so broke up, me and Maggie treated her to a birthday supper at the most expensive colored restaurant in Mobile. She ain't found a new man yet, so I thought it would be nice to take her again this year. She done called me up three times this week to make sure I ain't changed my mind. I just hope she don't get a notion that I'd be a replacement for her used-to-be husband." I laughed.

"Hubert, I am so glad to see you moving on with your life. I know Maggie would feel the same way."

"I'm sure she would. She always went out of her way to keep me happy." I had to catch my breath and blink back a tear. "I declare, I'm glad I spent the last twenty-plus years married. I don't think I would have lasted too long in the courting game." I tilted my head to the side and stared in Jessie's eyes for a few moments. "I'm so glad you ain't nothing like them other women I know. It's a shame Orville didn't appreciate you. If the Lord hadn't took him when He did, he probably would have killed you by now. And the world would have lost another wonderful woman. I hope we stay friends for a long time, Jessie."

"I'm sure we will," she said.

Chapter 13
Jessie

I COULDN'T DECIDE WHERE I FIT IN WITH HUBERT AS FAR AS HIM and women was concerned. Any way I looked at it, I had my work cut out for me and I wasn't too happy about that. I couldn't leave his house quick enough. I never walked so fast in my life to get back home.

When I made it to my living room, I flung my coat and scarf onto the couch and started pacing back and forth like a caged tiger. Getting Hubert interested in me as something other than a "friend" was turning out to be harder than I thought. But the fact that he was going to keep seeing other women was not going to stop me from going forward with my plan.

When I went to Hubert's house Friday evening, he met me at the door and told me I didn't have to cook. "You going out again?" I asked.

"Um, yeah. And tomorrow and Sunday, I'm having supper with Mama and Daddy. You don't have to cook again until Monday. And you can do the laundry and some light cleaning then too."

"Okay," I mumbled as he started to shut his door. "I'll see you then." I slunk back off his porch like a slug.

I was disappointed that it would be a few days before I'd see Hubert again. In the meantime, I still wanted to know what he was up to. I knew Yolinda loved to collect good gossip as much as I did, so I decided to pay her a visit around eight p.m. Hubert's car was gone.

Yolinda's front door was cracked open, so I just walked in. She was coming out of the kitchen wiping her hands on a bibbed apron. "I was at loose ends, so I thought I'd drop in on you for a little while," I told her.

She blew out a loud breath and gave me a sorrowful look. "I'm so glad you came, Jessie. I was at loose ends myself. I was getting so bored. Everybody in the house had plans for tonight, like they do almost every Friday. Even my nephew is on his way to a party—and his leg is in a cast! Lord, what I wouldn't do to be young again and not have to plan every move I make around my arthritis. I'd be ripping and running the streets myself instead of sitting alone in this big old house while everybody else is out having a good time." Yolinda blew out another loud breath. "I just baked some sugar cookies. You want some?" She motioned me to follow her into the kitchen, which always smelled like fresh baked cookies, even when she wasn't baking none.

"No, thanks. I just came over to talk for a spell."

We pulled out chairs and sat down at her kitchen table at the same time. "I hate spending so much time by myself. That piece of a boyfriend I been dragging along with for too long is at home dealing with *his* arthritis. I swear to God, he's the last geezer I'm getting involved with. Next time, I'll get me a young'n with fresh body parts." We laughed.

"Some of them got more problems than older men," I pointed out.

"I don't care. If I didn't have to do laundry and clean for the mayor's wife, I don't know what I'd do with myself every day. Or what I'd do with no money of my own coming in." Yolinda sighed and gave me a pensive look. "As evil as my daddy was, I miss having him around. Poor Mama. He treated her like a dog he didn't like, but she misses him too. She couldn't get used to him not being here. No wonder she was so anxious to move out of this house. At least he liked to talk. Even though it was usually to cuss us all out. That's why I kept moving in and out. Now that he's gone for good, I'm going to stay here until I get married again." Yolinda laughed some more. "But ain't too many men itching to marry a woman in her fifties."

"Being single ain't no picnic. As mean as Orville was to me, he kept me from being lonesome. I never thought living by myself would be so miserable."

"You ain't found nobody to rent your spare bedroom to yet?"

I shook my head. "I been trying, but so far, I ain't had no luck. A man who works for the railroad came by to take a look-see, but he decided that the room was too small for him. A woman who used to live next door to my mama came next. She told me up front that her man would be coming around all the time. And the reason she's leaving him is because he beats her." I shook my head. "It was bad enough when I was getting beat up in my own house by my own man. I ain't going to allow it to happen to another woman under my roof. The one nice newlywed couple that was really interested had to back out when the husband's job laid him off. They had to move in with his family."

"Well, you need to keep trying to find somebody to live with you. With that maniac that killed them colored women still on the loose, I worry about you living by yourself."

"I worry about that too. If I get more nervous and scared, I might move back in with my mama. But one of my sisters, her kids, and my brother is living there. Mama ain't got but three bedrooms, so them kids sleep on pallets. I'd have to sleep on one too. I don't want to live like that."

"I'm going to pray for you. You ain't exactly a hag yet, so there is some hope for you to get married again. A widow woman needs another husband to look out for her." Yolinda leaned forward and whispered, "And to play with in the bedroom."

I rolled my eyes. "It's been so long since I played like that with a man, I done almost forgot what it feels like."

"Then I'll pray even harder for you."

I had no interest in discussing my sex life, or lack of one, I should say. So I abruptly changed the subject. "Did I tell you I was going to be cooking for Hubert and helping him keep his house clean? He's going to pay me so that'll help me pay off them bills Orville left me with."

Yolinda looked surprised and amused. "Humph! You didn't tell me, but I'm glad to hear that. Most men can't fend for themselves. If they ain't got a mama, girlfriend, or a wife to take care of them, they are practically as helpless as babies. A strong man like Hubert needs a strong woman who also knows how to be demure and submissive, when she needs to be, so he'll always know he's the one in charge. Maggie was like that and so are you . . ."

My breath caught in my throat. "I don't know if you are complimenting me or putting me down."

"Why would I be putting you down?" A dreamy-eyed look crossed Yolinda's face. "I wish I could be more like you and Maggie."

Her last comment made me feel so much better. I smiled and puffed out my chest. "Thank you for that nice compliment. Anyway, I don't think Hubert is interested in me romantically. Besides, he's already seeing other women. On top of that, some folks might not like the fact that I got involved with my dead best friend's husband. Especially since she ain't been gone but a few weeks. There's no telling what they'll be thinking and saying." I was not about to let what people was saying stop me from going after Hubert. As far as I was concerned, being lonesome was worse than being gossiped about. Gossip eventually died down, but loneliness could do a lot of harm to a person's morale if it lasted too long.

"That's for sure. I ain't one to spread gossip, but a couple of them hussies is running around town talking about how much time you hang out at Hubert's house, before and after Maggie passed. One even suggested that you and him was getting physical before her death."

"That's a bald-faced lie!" I yelled. "Me and Hubert ain't never been nothing but friends. We ain't never done nothing more physical than hug, and I can count the number of times that happened on one foot. I'd like to get my hands on the neck of whoever came up with that."

Yolinda reared back in her seat, as if she was scared I was going to put my hands on her neck. "Don't get so upset. I already know the truth. Hubert ain't no more interested in you than he is a old crone like me." She laughed in such a sinister way it gave me goose bumps.

Her comment and that irritating laugh was a blow to my self-esteem. She made me sound like a dried-up hag. I was determined to prove her wrong, but I had to do it in a way that wouldn't make me look like a shameless hussy. "Having a man ain't that big of a deal to me. You know I ain't dated nobody since Orville died."

"I know you ain't. Before I captured my current boyfriend, I used to feel so lonesome and ugly, I'd actually get sick. Your innards must be as robust as a new tractor."

"They must be," I mumbled.

"By the way, I heard Sister Wiggins uninvited Blondeen to that supper she had planned, praise the Lord. She's the last woman I'd want to see Hubert in a serious relationship with. I seen her knocking on his door with another dish again last night." Yolinda narrowed her eyes and scrunched up her lips. "If he ends up marrying that floozy, I hope Maggie come back and haunt him until the day he dies."

Before I could say anything else, we heard a car door slam. Me and Yolinda didn't say nothing as we jumped up and ran to the front window and parted the curtains. Hubert got out of his car with a woman I used to babysit when she was a baby, and I was a teenager. He led her by the arm into his house. She was even younger and prettier than Blondeen. I could see my chances of hooking him dwindling.

"That's a new one. Last week, I seen that redbone schoolteacher with the good hair getting out the car with him when most folks is already in the bed. She stayed in his house two whole hours, so I know they got down to some serious busy, if you know what I mean. Oomph, oomph, oomph! How can that man keep up? He must be such a ball of fire in bed, it takes a harem to cool him off. Maggie must have been a world-beating lovemaker herself, because the whole time she was alive, I ain't heard nary bit of gossip about him fooling around with other women." Yolinda blinked and gave me a pitiful look. "I feel so sorry for you. You been out of practice for so long, you probably couldn't keep him happy in the bedroom nohow."

"I probably couldn't," I admitted.

Chapter 14
Hubert

JESSIE HAD BEEN COMING TO MY HOUSE TO COOK AND CLEAN FOR ALmost two weeks. This was much better than me waiting for neighbors, other women who knew me, and Mama to bring me home-cooked meals and me doing my own household chores.

I woke up with chills this morning. It was the one-month anniversary of Maggie's and Claude's deaths. It seemed like they had left me years ago. I was feeling better in some ways, but the loneliness I was still experiencing had become excruciating. I was willing to do just about anything to ease that pain. Taking out a few women to supper and the movies, and having Jessie at the house more often, took the edge off, but not enough.

Blondeen had started showing up on a more regular basis with casseroles and all kinds of other dishes. I was too numb with grief to turn her away. We'd eat, listen to the radio, discuss church and other things happening in our lives. After doing that for a few times, Blondeen told me how boring it was for us to sit around in my house. I never went to hers, since she didn't have no radio, and she didn't want me to bring my checkers or dominoes because she hated both. It didn't take long for her to let me know, she had other ideas. A couple Saturdays ago, she came to my house all dressed up and coaxed me into taking her to the movies.

The very next night, she showed up again. I took her to a ice-cream parlor owned by colored folks. We had fun, but I didn't like the fact that she liked to get demonstrative in public. As soon as we got out of my car, she grabbed my arm and wrapped it around her shoulder. Right after we got our ice cream and plopped down at a table, she hauled off and kissed me on my jaw. I balled up inside so tight, I could barely breathe. I hadn't been kissed by a woman since the day me and Maggie got married! A few folks I knew from church happened to be present and seen us. They didn't even try to hide the curious expressions on their faces. One woman's eyes got as big as the saucers our ice cream was in. I was embarrassed because them folks had known me all my life and had never seen Maggie get affectionate with me in public. Blondeen's boldness bothered me, but I let it slide for the time being.

I was horrified when she told me at the end of our last date, "Me and you got so much in common. I can't wait for us to get even closer. I been looking for a man like you all my life." That was when I realized I had to stop seeing her as soon as possible.

Besides that, when Mama and Daddy found out I had been taking her out behind their backs after they'd told me how they felt about her background, they was fit to be tied.

"Boy, why in the world are you spending time and money on a gal like Blondeen?" Mama hollered when I went to pick her up for church this morning. She was leaning up against the living-room wall checking the hem of the billowing blue dress she had finished making on her new Singer sewing machine last night. Daddy was going to church later because he wanted to stay home a little longer to rehearse the speech he'd prepared for the afternoon service.

"I know, I know," I whimpered. "Us going out was all her idea," I defended.

Daddy was standing in the middle of the living-room floor with his hands on his hips. His jaw dropped and he glared at me like I'd just sprouted a second nose. "What kind of man starts courting a woman because it was 'her idea'?" he yelled.

"She's just a friend. I ain't 'courting' her, or nobody else," I protested.

"If that's the case, you need to get that point across to Blondeen before she gets too carried away. A real man—especially one your age—knows how to keep women under control," Daddy grumbled.

Whenever somebody said something that sounded remotely like they was suggesting I was a sissy, my heart would skip a few beats and I'd start squirming like a worm on a hook. I was lucky nobody never noticed my demeanor during them uncomfortable moments. So far, using a woman as a prop to help me look like a real man had backfired.

"Y'all please calm down," I pleaded. "Another reason I took Blondeen out was because I just wanted some company. Maggie had been such a big part of my life, it's hard for me to be by myself now. But I realize now that Blondeen is too unpredictable, needy, and pushy for me. The next time she calls or comes to my house, I'm going to tell her I don't want to see her no more." That calmed my parents down for the time being.

I had been home from the evening church service for only a few minutes when Blondeen called me up. She started off talking in a real soft, cooing tone of voice. "Hubert, I thought I'd hear from you today. Why ain't you called me?" Before I could answer, her voice got cold and hard. "What's the matter? You mad at me?"

"No, I ain't mad at you. But I been real busy. I was at church most of today. Several folks got saved and so Daddy had to preach longer."

"Oh. What about all the days before today?"

"I was busy then too."

"Too busy for me, I guess," she snarled. Then her voice got soft again. "When will I see you again?"

I took a deep breath before I answered. "Now you look here, Blondeen, I like you, but I don't think me and you have enough in common to keep spending so much time together," I clarified as gently as I could.

"Oh? When did you figure that out? How come you didn't tell me that to my face the last time I seen you?"

"It don't matter. Besides, I'm getting serious about another lady. I like her a whole lot."

Blondeen gasped so loud, it sounded like she was in the same room with me. "It's that buffalo-butt Zelma Hood hussy, ain't it?"

I knew Blondeen was a little on the crude side, but I was surprised to hear her say something so unflattering about another woman. "No, it ain't her. She decided to remarry her last used-to-be husband anyway." I had to clear my throat so I could speak more clearly. But I stammered anyway. "I . . . uh . . . I been spending a lot of time with Jessie and we get along so well, I want to see more of her."

"Jessie Tucker?" She huffed out Jessie's full name like they was cusswords. "W-why . . . I can't believe my ears. Your mama let it slip while she was doing my godmother's hair yesterday that Jessie told her a bunch of mess. Now I know why! She wants to claim you for herself!"

"A bunch of mess about who?"

"Don't play dumb. I figured out the reason Sister Wiggins changed her mind about me having supper with y'all. It's all because Jessie put a big nasty bug in her ear about me and my family! And I ain't going to forget it!"

"I don't care what anybody told my mama. I just don't think me and you would have lasted too much longer anyway. Besides, I ain't never gave you no reason to think that we was going to have something serious and permanent. I ain't never even kissed you."

"Tell me about it! Them other women you been taking out like to run their mouths. I heard you ain't kissed nary one of them, or done nothing else like a real man would! I ain't never in my life met a man that was as restrained as you! What's your problem—"

I couldn't let her finish her sentence. To me, it sounded like she was hinting that I was funny and I had to squash that right away. "Hold up, Blondeen. I got some issues going on that's affecting all my decisions. I'm still trying to get used to the idea of not having a wife to have intimate relations with no more. Maggie was the only woman I was with since me and her got married. To me, sex is a holy experience."

"Humph! That's all the more reason why you should be having 'intimate relations' with somebody by now."

I was more than a little mad. I wanted to make sure Blondeen got the message loud and clear. So I told her, "Well, when I do have relations with somebody, it won't be you."

I was surprised at how defeated Blondeen sounded when she spoke again. "All right, then. That's fine with me. You and Jessie have a nice life. But you better tell her to keep my name out of her mouth!"

I was glad she hung up on me. I stared at the phone for a long time before I dialed Jessie's number. She answered right away. "Hello, Hubert. I was just thinking about you."

"That's nice. I was just thinking about you too. I was wondering if you ain't going to be too busy tomorrow if you'd like to go out for supper? I could pick you up around seven."

She didn't waste no time replying. "I would love to go out. I'll be ready. How should I dress?"

"You can wear whatever you want." Even though I had a bad taste in my mouth that Blondeen had caused, I managed to chuckle. "Uh, somebody is at the door. I'll see you tomorrow."

When I peeped out the front window and seen it was one of them pesky Fuller Brush salesman, I cracked open the door and shook my head before he could even go into his sales pitch.

I thought about calling Jessie back, but I decided not to. I'd said what I had to say to her for the time being. Besides, I'd be seeing her soon enough and I was looking forward to it. I had to work fast and hard to get in good enough with her so folks would think we had something going on. I'd hug her when the occasion called for it and I'd kiss her now and then—on her jaw—but I'd never do more than that. All I had to do was come up with a good enough excuse to satisfy her *when* and *if* she acted like she wanted more.

I patted myself on the back for finally making a practical decision about my social life with women. Of all the ones I knew, Jessie would be the best cover for me when I found a new boyfriend. I couldn't understand why it had took me so long to figure that out. She didn't look as good as Maggie, but she had a cute little shape and a pretty copper-colored face with the biggest and brightest brown eyes I ever seen. If my manly desires was on the right track, I would be all over her like the measles.

Chapter 15
Jessie

I HAD PLANNED TO DO SEVERAL THINGS TOMORROW EVENING WHEN I got home from work. My mama wanted me to come over and help her kill and pluck a couple of chickens and I'd promised I would. After that, I was supposed to help Sister Wiggins finish a quilt we was making to donate to the colored kids' orphan asylum. And my sister Minnie wanted to come to the house to get some more of Earl's things.

I called them all up right away and told them something had come up and I'd see them later in the week. I wasn't about to pass up supper at a nice restaurant with Hubert. Mama and Sister Wiggins didn't get upset about me canceling on them and didn't even ask what had come up. But Minnie did.

"What came up?" she asked in a harsh tone.

My sister could be rude when somebody disappointed her, but I never let her get under my skin. "It ain't none of your business, but if you really want to know, Hubert wants to take me out to supper," I said sharply.

"Well!"

"Why do you sound so surprised?"

"I'm surprised it took him so long. I was wondering when he was going to see that his next best woman was already in plain sight. A little birdie just told me that he definitely won't be seeing Blondeen no more."

"I didn't know that. You way over in the next county, how did you hear it before me?"

"Girl, you know as well as I do that some of them gossips in your neck of the woods got long tongues. I shudder when I think about how much news can be spread by the ones who make enough money to afford telephones. Blondeen told a bunch of folks today and she ain't so happy about being dumped by another man. I bet she done lost count by now. I heard she gave Hubert a big piece of her mind."

"I'm sure she did. I'm glad he woke up and seen the light before he got too involved with her. A wonderful man like him deserves a woman who will make him happy, not sass him, or upset him in any way. But I don't know nary woman who can follow a tough act like Maggie. Not even me."

Minnie sucked on her teeth. "Hubert likes you enough to ask you out, so don't sell yourself short, girl. I'm glad he ain't letting the grass grow under his feet like some widowers. Most of the men who lose their wives don't even look at another woman for months, let alone take them out to supper."

"Hubert ain't like most men. Maggie was the only woman he was romantically involved with."

Minnie guffawed like a hyena. "You believe that? How do you know he didn't see other women before he married Maggie? Most men have been involved with a heap of women by the time they get married. And how do you know he didn't see other women *after* him and Maggie got married? After all, he is a normal man."

"You, of all people, should know that if there was any other women in Hubert's life other than Maggie, the gossips would have reported it," I snapped.

"He could have been with women who didn't live in Lexington," she shot back.

"It don't matter, so I don't even know why we are discussing it. At the end of the day, the poor man is still out of sorts and needs all the support he can get right now." I sighed. "I wish there was more I could do to cheer him up. But I still don't think Hubert wants nothing from me but my cleaning and cooking services, and a companion to go out with."

"Humph! I'm telling you now, you better start cooking up more than his food. He's a mighty big fish, so it ain't going to be easy for a gal with as little man-catching experience as you to hook him and reel him in. And to do it in a underhanded way so he ain't none the wiser."

"You telling me to trick Hubert into getting involved with me?" I chuckled.

"If you don't tighten the screws, all you'll get from him is a few suppers and trips to the movies. I advise you to use every trick in the book, and some that ain't in the book. Once you get him in the bag, sew it up with double stitches."

"Maybe I will be a little more aggressive with him." I sounded so meek and uncertain, even I wasn't convinced that I could pull off such a outrageous scheme. I didn't know what to do to get him interested in me the way my sister meant. I was already doing the same things them other woman had been doing: fixing meals for him, keeping him company, and such. I was afraid that if I went overboard and tried to kiss him or seduce him, he'd get offended. And I wasn't willing to risk losing his friendship. Or give up them few dollars he was paying me to cook and clean. I thought the smartest thing for me to do was wait and let him make the first move. Once he did, then I'd figure out ways to "sew" him up.

I was still thinking about Hubert making a move on me when we got back to his house after eating supper at a rib joint tonight. "Make yourself comfortable, Jessie. I'll go make you some tea."

I held up both hands and eased down on the couch. "That's all right. I drunk enough with my supper. Let's just sit here and talk for a little while." I smiled and patted the spot next to me.

Hubert gave me a puzzled look before he hunched his shoulders and sat down—at the other end of the couch. A Christmas tree that he'd asked my brother, Karl, to chop down for him in the woods by Carson Lake three days ago was laying on the floor by the wall.

"When are you going to put up your tree?" I asked.

"Not until I get some new ornaments. I had almost decided not to bother with one this year," he replied in a raspy tone. "I ain't got much holiday spirit."

"If you want me to, I can come over and decorate it for you. You can use my ornaments. With Earl out of the house, I ain't putting up a tree this year."

"Thank you. If I don't put it up in the next day or so, I'll take you up on your offer." He sniffed and crossed his legs. I enjoyed seeing such a serene expression on his face now. "I declare, Jessie. I am so blessed to have a friend like you."

There was a lot more things I planned to say and do to help increase my chances of becoming more than "a friend." But in due time. For now, I needed to be more subtle, so I just smiled and mumbled, "Thank you. I feel the same way about you." I couldn't think of nothing more neutral to say. I was still going to leave it up to him to get our "romance" up on its feet. If I still needed to do something devious to help him along, I would. I just didn't know what or when yet.

We spent the next ten minutes talking about some mundane things related to the church and work. He suddenly scooted a little closer in my direction. "You look so nice in that pink dress. It reminds me of all the cotton candy I used to eat at the fair when I was growing up."

It wasn't the kind of compliment I expected or wanted to hear, but I assumed it was his way of telling me I looked like something he liked. "Thank you," I said shyly. "It's been a long time since a man told me I looked nice."

"That's a shame. A lovely lady like you ought to get complimented every day. I don't know what's wrong with the men in this town. I can't believe you ain't remarried yet."

I took a deep breath before I asked what I'd been wanting to ask him since Maggie died. "Do you think you'll ever fall in love with somebody else?"

His lips quivered, but he didn't say nothing at first. He just dropped his head and stared at the floor for a few seconds before he looked back up at me. My breath caught in my throat when I seen tears in his eyes. "I'm sorry for asking you that. It ain't my business, so you don't have to answer me."

He waved his hand. "I don't mind telling you. Yes, I would love to fall in love again. I'd even like to get married again. But . . ." He stopped talking and put his head in his hands.

"Uh, I can tell that whatever it is, it ain't something pleasant, so you ain't got to tell me. I don't want to make you uncomfortable, so I'm going to go home now. You ain't got to drive me, I can walk." I stood up.

"Please don't go yet, Jessie." He motioned me back to the couch; this time, I sat so close to him, our knees touched. "Losing Maggie was the most god-awful thing that ever happened to me. It affected me in the worst-possible way."

"Like how?" Before I realized what I was doing, I started rubbing his back. He didn't say nothing, but when I felt his body get stiff, I stopped.

With even more tears in his eyes, he looked at me and grabbed my hand and squeezed it. "I . . . I can't function no more."

I was confused, to say the least. "What do you mean? Other than you grieving, you seem to be going about everything like you always did."

He wrung his hands and shook his head. "I done lost my nature. I can't function as a man and I don't know how long this affliction is going to last. Or if I'll ever be able to perform again."

If a bolt of lightning had struck me, I couldn't have been more stupefied. I never thought I'd hear such a unthinkable confession coming from a strapping man like Hubert. Maggie had told me more than once that he was the best lover she ever had. I had to take several deep breaths before I could speak again. "Lord, have mercy." The way I was wheezing, you would have thought I'd lost my nature too.

I reached over to rub his back again, but when I recalled how he'd flinched the first time, I kept my hand to myself. "My brother-in-law had the same problem after he had that mild stroke six years ago. He eventually got over it. Him and Minnie even went on a second honeymoon and she claimed that the only time they got out the motel bed was to use the bathroom and to get something to eat." I forced myself to laugh, hoping it would get a chuckle out of Hubert too. I was wrong. There was a puppy-dog expression on his face. I cleared my throat and went on, making sure I sounded serious. "I know you'll be the way you was sooner than you think."

Hubert shook his head. "I don't know about that. I done spent time with several women since Maggie died, and it ain't done no good. Blondeen didn't like the fact that I'd never kissed her and it bothered her. That's one of the reasons I had to cut her loose. I would never tell her or any other woman what I just told you. I don't want nobody to think of me as a freak, the way they do that philandering sugarcane field hand whose jealous wife stabbed him in the crotch with a pitchfork."

"You ain't nearly as bad off as that man is. The only thing he can do with his pecker now is empty his bladder."

"And that's all I can do."

The wind felt like it had been knocked out of me. I couldn't believe what came out of my mouth next. "Sex ain't everything. I ain't been with a man since Orville died and I ain't had no desire to do so. Me and you riding in the same boat, so I understand what you are going through."

"I figured you would understand. I'm sorry I hadn't told you before now. I would really like to let all of them other women go and only spend time with you. Going out with so many and dealing with all of them different personalities was getting to be too much trouble. I realized that they was looking for something I can't give them."

I almost laughed out loud. I was looking for something he couldn't give me, but I still thought I'd be better off with him, no matter how long I had to wait for his problem to heal. If I could go without sex since Orville died last summer, I could go longer. "I'd love to spend more time with you." I bit my bottom lip before I spoke again. "Uh . . . by the way, my sister's husband's problem went away on its own in a few months. But before it did, he was too embarrassed to go to a doctor to see if they could help him. Have you thought about seeing a doctor?"

Hubert nodded. "I done been to see a doctor at the colored clinic in Lexington, and one at the clinic in Mobile. Ain't nothing they can do. They say this is the kind of problem that has to sort itself out. I don't think they know enough about it yet to figure out what to do to help."

"Hubert, I don't care about your problem."

His jaw dropped and his eyes got big. "You don't?"

"I'm sorry. I didn't mean that the way it sounded. I do care. But if you think I wouldn't want to spend time with you because of that, you ain't got nothing to worry about. And don't worry about me telling nobody what you told me. All I care about is you being happy again. I'm going to go out of my way to help you be the fun-loving, outgoing man you used to be."

He seemed as stunned by what I'd just said as I was for saying it. "Jessie, Maggie used to tell me all the time that you was a special lady. Now I see what she meant. No wonder you was able to stay with that devilish Orville all of them years. You got the patience of Job, bless your soul."

Hubert was full of surprises. The next thing I knew, he slid closer to me with his lips puckered! My heart started racing because I thought he was going to kiss me. He did, but it was on my jaw.

Chapter 16
Hubert

I WAS GOING TO ENJOY SPENDING MY TIME WITH ONLY ONE WOMAN and I was glad it was Jessie.

I wished I had told her sooner about my inability to perform in the bedroom. Maybe if I had, I could have avoided the aggravation of trying to juggle more than one woman at a time and seen only Jessie. On Wednesday, two days after my confession to her, I got a visit from Mama and Daddy shortly after eight p.m. I never locked my doors, but they didn't bother to knock when they visited me nohow.

I wasn't surprised to see them sitting on my living-room couch when I came out of the bathroom after taking a nice hot bath. It had been a very long day. I'd spent the first few hours at the turpentine mill and had to leave before noon to collect the body of a woman who had passed last night. I'd spent the rest of the day at my funeral home.

I flopped down in the chair facing them. "I wish y'all had let me know y'all was coming over."

"Since when do we have to make a appointment to see our only son?" Daddy snapped. Him and Mama spent so much time at the church, they dressed like that's where they was going even if they was just going to the market. Today, he wore a dark blue suit, white shirt, and his favorite red tie. Mama lived in loud-colored floor-length dresses that looked more like bedspreads. Today, she had on a green one with big orange dots.

I laughed. "If I'd known y'all was coming, I could have put on some tea and brought out some of them pickled pig feet that Jessie cooked the other day," I said as I rubbed the back of my head. Even though I was going to turn forty-three next year, sometimes I still felt like a young boy. "Um . . . I decided to stop taking Blondeen out. She got real agitated with me the last time I talked to her and she said some disturbing things. So I ain't even going to allow her to come to the house no more."

"Good! I'm so glad you came to your senses before things got too serious. Thank God Jessie opened our eyes about that gal. I declare, we dodged a mighty big bullet!" Mama blasted. "Blondeen still owes me money for the last time I pressed and curled her hair, and something tells me I ain't going to get a plugged nickel from her. I'll never do her hair on credit again. That heifer." Mama paused to catch her breath and fan her face with her hand. She gave me a apologetic look before she went on. "And another thing, me and your daddy ain't going to stick our noses in your business no more. We never should have tried to set you up with a woman nohow, especially so soon after Maggie's passing. But you'd been looking so miserable since the funeral, the thought of you taking months or even years to find somebody else, the way most people do, didn't seem like such a good idea. It's a shame you never had many men friends to hang out with. Not even when you was a young man."

I had to reply to that as quick as I could. "That was because of Maggie. She wanted me to focus on our marriage and my work back then. Besides, all the men my age was running around cheating on their wives, drinking, gambling, and fighting."

"And that's still true today," Daddy piped in. He was nodding his head so hard, his fleshy jowls shook like jelly. "But it wouldn't hurt for you to make at least a couple of men friends to keep your mind off women."

I had to cover my mouth to keep from laughing at Daddy's last comment.

"I'm going to be seeing a lot more of Jessie," I announced. "She's a nice settled-down woman. And the icing on the cake is that we know one another real well. I ain't got to worry about her sassing me, the way Blondeen did."

Mama and Daddy looked at each other, then at me, with puzzled expressions on their faces. "You going to see more of Jessie? How much more of her is there for you to see?" Mama asked with her eyebrows raised. "She comes over and cooks and cleans for you all the time."

"Well, I'm going to be taking her out every chance I get. She reminds me so much of Maggie, I just couldn't help myself. She is such a practical and godly woman. I wonder how in the world she ended up married to a hound from hell like Orville. I'd like to get to know her better."

"'Better'? You been knowing her over twenty years. Before Maggie died, she spent half of her time in this house." Daddy paused and made a sweeping gesture with his hand. "More time than she spent at her own. You should know her as well as you knew Maggie."

I cleared my throat and rubbed my hands together. "I was hoping y'all would like hearing I'm going to court Jessie."

Mama and Daddy looked at each other again, then back at me. This time, they looked more puzzled than before. And then Mama smiled. "I love Jessie almost as much as I loved Maggie. I hope she'll make you happy."

"I do too," Daddy said with a firm nod. "She's a fine specimen of a good Christian woman. She's honest, clean, knows her Bible, and, most important of all, she ain't no fornicator. Other women who done lost their husbands started hopping in and out of bed with other men before their husbands even got put in the ground. Why don't you invite that sweet woman to spend Christmas with us?"

"I'm glad y'all feel the way you do. I had already decided to invite her."

Right after my folks left, I trotted to the telephone and dialed Jessie's number. Like me and most of the folks I knew who could afford a phone, hers was in the kitchen. She must have spent a heap of time in her kitchen because it seemed like every time I called, she answered by the end of the first or second ring. This time, she picked up halfway through the first ring.

"Hello, Jessie. How are you feeling this evening?"

"Blessed, and I hope you feel the same way," she chirped.

"I won't keep you long. I just called to see if you had plans for Christmas. If you don't have none, me and my folks would love for you to eat supper with us."

"I'd love to," she squealed. "I'm so glad you asked. I didn't want to spend my first Christmas alone, or with that mob at my mama's house."

"You know how Mama and Daddy like to entertain, so there'll be a 'mob' at their house too."

"I know. But they won't be drinking and getting rowdy like they will at Mama's house. Thank you for inviting me, Hubert."

Chapter 17
Jessie

I WAS DUMBFOUNDED WHEN HUBERT INVITED ME TO GO WITH HIM to his parents' house for Christmas. The minute I got off the telephone with him last night, I immediately called up Minnie. "I think he's coming around," I blurted out without even saying hello first.

"Who's 'coming around'?" she asked dryly.

"Girl, what's wrong with you? You going senile already? Who do you think I'm talking about?"

"If I knew that, I wouldn't be asking," Minnie snarled.

"Hubert." I loved the way his name rolled off my tongue.

"Oh. What makes you think he's 'coming around'? You done let him play with your kitty cat?"

"Can't you keep your mind out of the gutter? I wish you wouldn't think about sex so much. For your information, Hubert ain't that kind of man. He ain't never *hinted* that he got a itching to go to bed with me."

"If he ain't even done that, what did he do for you to say he's 'coming around'?"

"He's taking me to his folks' house for Christmas."

"Is that all? You racking up charges for a long-distance call to tell me that?"

"Don't you see what's happening? First he stopped seeing all of them other women. I'm the only one he wants to take out now. I'm the only one he tells his secrets to."

"What secrets?"

I rolled my eyes. "If I told you, then they wouldn't be secrets. The bottom line is, I done made a lot of progress in the last few days."

"I'm glad to hear that. And I hope you don't do nothing to run him off."

"I won't."

I was sorry I'd called Minnie up. I was glad she had to abruptly hang up to go shoo a stray dog off her porch.

I had a good time spending Christmas with Hubert, his parents, and some of their friends. We ate a huge feast that Sister Wiggins had cooked, had a gift exchange, and sung a few hymns.

Me and Hubert was the only unmarried folks in the mix, so I wasn't surprised when the same few folks asked us both when we was going to find another mate. I told each one the same thing: "I'm still looking for the right man."

Hubert made light of that question by just shrugging his shoulders and grinning. But the last time he was asked, he replied, "I know a lot of good women, but I don't want to settle for any particular one too soon."

That was not the response I wanted to hear. Hadn't he told me in so many words that he wanted to "court" me? What was I supposed to think now? But the bottom line was, he still hadn't gave me a reason, so far, to think that I'd ever be anything more to him than a servant/friend who could accompany him when he didn't want to go out alone.

On the way home, he kept praising me about how much he'd enjoyed my company and how impressed he'd been with the way I had handled myself around his parents' nosy friends. I was tempted to bite the bullet and ask him if he had any romantic feelings for me. The ones I had developed for him was getting stronger by the day. I was glad I didn't bring that subject up, though. I had made too much progress with him to say something that might scare him off. And I wasn't about to let that happen. Now I had to make myself so indispensable, he wouldn't be able to function without me. When it got to that point, he wouldn't have no choice but to marry me.

When we got to my house, he parked and gently patted the top of my head, the same way you'd pat a dog. "Thank you again for spending the day with me, Jessie. I love that new necktie you gave me. Do you like them pot holders and that apron I gave you?"

"Oh yes. I ain't never had some as nice as them."

"Good! I thought you'd appreciate useful gifts like that. You was born to be a domesticated woman. I would have also bought you a new eggbeater and washboard, but the notions store had sold the last ones the day before I got there. I'll get them for your birthday." Hubert gently tapped the steering wheel and turned his head just long enough for me to see the self-satisfied expression on his face. "I had been dreading the holiday, but you really helped me get through it with flying colors. I hope you had a good time."

"I sure did," I said in as cheerful a tone as I could manage under the circumstances.

"I have to go to Hartville this weekend. I'll head over there Friday night or Saturday morning. The folks in Mobile that I usually buy embalming fluid from decided to close up for the rest of the year and my workers told me this morning that our supply is real low. I declare, I just bought some last month. The place in Hartville is cheaper, so I think I'll be doing business only with them from now on. Unless I find a even cheaper place."

"Why don't you buy a big supply so you won't have to go get more for a while?"

"I buy quite a bit every time. But folks have been dying like flies these past few months. I don't mind going to Hartville or Mobile. I like having a reason to get on the road. It kills a lot of time, and I enjoy the drive."

"Oh. Well, if you want me to ride along with you, let me know."

"I will. But I plan on spending the night over there and I might stay longer. There's a barber I like to go to, and a few white-owned stores that don't make colored folks come and go out the back door. And they treat us nice. If I get back home on Saturday and it ain't too late, maybe we'll go to a restaurant for supper again."

"Okay. If you don't mind, I would rather you let me cook supper and we spend the evening in my house. I got a possum my brother gave me from his last hunting trip. I'd like to cook it before it gets stale. Besides, with the New Year coming up soon, most restaurants will jack up their prices and you already spend enough money feeding me. We could play checkers and you could even spend the night at my house, if you want to . . ."

Hubert started fidgeting in his seat like a baby in a wet diaper. "Spend the night with you? Me? Good gracious alive." I had never seen a man—a single one, at that—react like this over something I thought was so innocent. "A home-cooked meal would be nice, but we can't do nothing that would go against our Christian beliefs. Other than my mama and my wife, I ain't never spent the night alone with a woman under the same roof."

I sighed. "Hubert, I want to say something else, but only if you promise me, you won't get mad."

He stopped fidgeting, but now his eyes looked as big as saucers. "What could you say that I'd get mad about?"

"I won't know until I say it."

"Go on and say it. I ain't going to get mad."

I took a deep breath before I continued. "Maggie ain't coming back. I know you'll always love her, and I know that no other woman can take her place, not even me." He reminded me of a hoot owl the way his eyes stared at me without blinking as I went on. "I'm sorry for what I just said about you spending the night with me. I had no idea it would make you so uncomfortable. I'm ashamed of myself and I hope you'll forget I was brazen enough to suggest such a thing." I paused long enough to blow out some hot air. "I guess I should remind myself that I'm just a friend to you."

"Jessie, you are more than 'just a friend' in my book. Inviting a man that ain't your husband, or your fiancé, to spend the night with you took a lot of guts. One thing I appreciate is a gutsy woman." This time, he patted my shoulder before he added, "We'll see how things go in the next few months."

Months? There was no way I was going to just go out to eat, sit at opposite ends of his couch, listen to the radio, play checkers, and yak about one mundane thing after another for the *next few months!* Him marrying me was a long shot, but I was determined to be intimate with a man again before my body outlived its usefulness.

Chapter 18
Hubert

THINGS WAS REALLY LOOKING UP FOR ME. WITH JESSIE IN A stronger position in my life, I was feeling less and less lonesome. I was surprised she was willing to settle for a platonic relationship, especially her being as attractive and independent as she was. But I would never let myself forget that Jessie was still a regular woman in a lot of other ways. I didn't care how much she claimed she'd settle for the little bit I had to offer; it was a woman's nature to be fickle.

In the meantime, I planned to get as much mileage out of our flimsy relationship as I could. So long as I didn't hurt her in some way, I didn't see nothing wrong with how I was using her. Shoot. In a way, she was "using" me too. She was benefiting more than I was by me treating her to meals in nice restaurants and paying her cash money to help out with household chores that didn't require much time and effort at all.

I took Jessie to the Seafood House for supper on Friday. It was a cute little place near downtown, and the only one in the vicinity that was owned by colored folks. It was the same restaurant I took Blondeen to the first time we went out together. A lot of folks had went out of town for the holidays, so the place wasn't as crowded as it usually was.

Me and Jessie each ordered a three-way combination: deep-fried oysters, jumbo shrimp, and catfish, with sides of potato salad and hush puppies. "I love eating out. Even when I cook the same things I order in restaurants, it don't never taste as good. There ain't nothing I miss more than that scrumptious gumbo Maggie used to cook," Jessie stated with a wistful look on her face.

"That was the last meal Claude ate," I mumbled. "Maggie ate some too. She had puked when she had that spell before she died. Gumbo was splashed all over the front of her nightgown when I found her." Just speaking Maggie's and Claude's names made my chest tighten. I was glad Jessie changed the subject.

"My mama is going to cook a big pot of black-eyed peas to serve on New Year's Day for good luck. She wouldn't mind if I brought you to her New Year's Eve party."

I shook my head. "Thank you for inviting me. But I might stay in Hartville until after the holiday."

We discussed a few mundane things until our orders arrived. The way we dove into our food, you would have thought we hadn't ate in days. I was really enjoying myself, but not for long. A few minutes later, who I seen strutting through the door made me want to crawl up under the table: Blondeen.

It never dawned on me that she would show up at the same restaurant, at the same time, as me when I was with another woman. I was surprised to see her with two other women instead of a man. And they was two of the most annoying busybodies in town: Sukey Kirksey and Wilma McGinnis. They was both still in their twenties, but they looked almost as old as me. Everybody was convinced that Blondeen had picked them to be her side-kicks because they was homely and dull. They made her look even better so she got all the attention from men when they went out together. Wilma had six kids and she helped her husband serve drinks at the juke joint he operated, so she didn't get out much. Sukey's widowed mama lived next door to Jessie, so when she visited her mama, which was at least two or three times a week, she dropped in on Jessie without notice and pestered her.

The women approached our table and stopped right next to me. "My Lord, speak of the devil. Happy New Year!" Blondeen hollered. Then she scrunched up her nose and started fanning her face. "It sure smells funky up in here. If I didn't know no better, I'd swear they done put chitlins on the menu." She looked straight at Jessie and added, "Unless somebody in here didn't wash up." Her remarks offended me, but I didn't show it. Jessie's face suddenly got as tight as a drum.

Blondeen had on a tapered wig-hat with reddish-brown hair that she shared with her two older sisters. Each one wore it two or three days at a time. Wig-hats was expensive. But a generous white lady Blondeen did laundry for gave her one that she didn't want no more.

Blondeen had already been married twice and lost both husbands to other women. Each marriage had lasted less than a year. Nobody could figure out what a good-looking woman like her was doing to turn men off so fast. Each time she got a new one, she went out of her way to keep him happy, but so far she hadn't done enough. Her last live-in boyfriend had threw in the towel after living with her for only two weeks. It had been a rumor for years that she'd even resorted to hoodoo to improve her love life, but even that hadn't done her no good. And it was more than a rumor that she was jealous of women who had better luck with men, especially ones like Jessie, who'd had the same husband for over twenty years.

"I declare, Hubert. I can't get over how good you look for a man your age! You'd look even better without all of them wrinkles on your face," Blondeen blurted out loud enough for everybody in the place to hear. She looked at Jessie with pity and shook her head. "The same goes for you, sister woman." She and her friends snickered and so did the young couple at the table next to us.

Jessie looked straight ahead and didn't say nothing. The tight expression was still on her face.

If Blondeen wanted to resume her relationship with me, her crack about my appearance—and Jessie's—wasn't helping none. I was so glad I had removed her from my life. If I hadn't dumped her when I did, there was no telling how much damage she might have done to my morale. I cleared my throat and reared back in my chair. "Happy New Year, ladies. Y'all looking mighty spiffy this evening," I said in a casual tone.

Blondeen wore a tight red silk blouse and a black corduroy skirt up under a brown corduroy coat. Her makeup was flawless. The other two women had on cute bright-colored dresses and makeup, but none of that made them look half as glamorous as Blondeen.

"Thank you, Hubert. You should have seen us last night. Especially me," Blondeen cooed as her eyes roamed over my face. She glanced at Jessie again, then back at me. "Well, we'd better leave you two old folks alone so y'all can finish eating and go home and get as much rest as possible. Otherwise, them wrinkles is going to double up real soon."

Me and Jessie didn't laugh at her comments, but Blondeen, her two cohorts, and the young couple at the other table snickered again. I was glad when them heifers spun around and pranced toward a table in the back of the room.

Jessie exhaled and shook her head. "I guess she thinks it's cute to low-rate people to their faces."

Another reason I had chose Jessie over Blondeen was because she was a real lady. Most of the other women I was acquainted with probably would have cussed Blondeen out for saying something so inappropriate to them in public.

"She can low-rate me all she wants. It don't faze me one bit," I said in a stiff tone.

"Hubert, you ain't even got that many wrinkles."

I squinted, leaned closer to Jessie, and gazed at her for a few moments. "I didn't even notice you had any until she brought it up. But they are so faint, I can barely see them."

Jessie laughed and pinched my hand. "I think we need to change the subject." She heaved out a sigh and glanced around the room. "I love this place. I ain't been here since Maggie treated me to supper on my birthday last year."

"Any day you don't feel like cooking for me, or just want to get out the house for the evening, just let me know and we can

come here, or go to any other place you want to go. Do you want
to do something in memory of Maggie's and Claude's birthdays
coming up next month?"

Maggie's birthday was two days before Claude's. We'd always
celebrated them on the same day each year. Our wedding anniversary was two weeks after Maggie's birthday. I was dreading
next month because I knew it was going to be a hard time for
me to get through.

"No, I don't want to do nothing special. It'd be too painful.
All I plan to do is go put some fresh flowers on their graves,"
Jessie said.

"That's nice. I was planning to take a mess of flowers over
there myself."

If Blondeen hadn't been on the premises, giving us the evil
eye every minute or so, I would have stayed longer and ordered
some dessert. We left right after I paid the check.

We cruised along in silence for a few minutes before Jessie
slapped the dashboard so hard, it rattled. It startled me so
much, I almost lost control of my car. I had never seen her show
any anger. "What's the matter?" I yelled.

"Oh, I can't stop thinking about how mean Blondeen was to
us tonight."

I whirled around so fast to face Jessie, I almost pulled a muscle in my neck. "Don't let something that petty get to you."

"I can't help it. We got feelings just like everybody else. I
would never say anything mean to another woman, the way she
does to me."

"It ain't just you that she's mean to. I've heard her say nasty
things to Sukey and Wilma and they are her best friends."

"That don't make me feel no better. I guess she'll be taunting
me in some way from now on," Jessie grumbled. "All because
I'm the one going out with you now and not her."

"I thought the beef she had with you was because you wouldn't
lie for her at the nursing home when they accused her of stealing."

"Well, that's part of it. But I think she's madder about me and you being together. And I don't know if she knows it yet, but I'm sure she'll eventually hear that I'm the one who told your mama and daddy about her stealing at the nursing home."

"She probably knows that already."

"And I told them about Blondeen's uncle and cousin being sissies. But I heard that even with his unnatural affliction, her uncle was still a nice man and would give anybody the shirt off his back. And everybody that knew the cousin said the same thing about him. To tell you the truth, I don't understand what's so bad about folks being that way."

I was so confused. I wondered how Jessie could call something a "unnatural affliction" and at the same time think that there was nothing bad about people being like Blondeen's uncle and cousin. "You don't think being like that is bad?"

"Not really. That's probably because everybody in my family is normal, so I don't have no firsthand experience in that area. But the way folks carry on about what them people do to each other in bed, you'd think they'd been born with hooves." Jessie paused and let out a loud breath. "I think there is worse things a person can be born with than hooves for feet. But the bottom line is, the Bible condemns people like Blondeen's two kinfolks. I'm glad me and you don't know any."

I didn't know what to say after her last comment and she must not have neither; we didn't talk no more until I dropped her off at her house a few minutes past eight p.m.

"Hubert, if I don't see you until after the New Year, have a happy one."

"The same to you." I gave her a one-armed hug.

I would have kissed her on the jaw, but I didn't want her to get slaphappy and say something mushy or insist on me coming into her house for a nightcap. I rushed off before she could say anything else.

Chapter 19
Jessie

TEN MINUTES AFTER HUBERT DROPPED ME OFF AT MY HOUSE, I went to close the curtains at the front window in my living room. If I'd waited five seconds longer, I wouldn't have seen his car cruising past my house. I assumed he had decided to go to Hartville tonight instead of tomorrow. I couldn't imagine him going anywhere else this time of night. It saddened me to know that I wouldn't see him again until after the New Year.

I had no idea what I was thinking when I decided to sneak into his house that night to do some snooping. I wasn't going to look for nothing in particular. It's just that I was so nosy, I couldn't help myself.

I changed out of my dress and put on a pair of pants and more comfortable shoes. I had just put my coat back on and was about to leave when my telephone rang. I cussed under my breath and ran into the kitchen to answer it. It was Sukey Kirksey.

"Hey, Jessie. I'm at my mama's house and I was wondering if I could come over and borrow some flour from you? She wants to make biscuits, to go with the black-eyed peas she's going to cook for New Year's."

"I'm sorry, Sukey. I ain't got no flour."

She sucked on her teeth and said in a gruff tone, "I was standing smack-dab behind you in the checkout line at the grocery store last week when you bought some. And it was a big bag! You mean to tell me you done used it all up that quick?"

"Um, I didn't shut the bag up all the way when I made biscuits on Monday. Weevils got in it, so I had to throw it away." I didn't mind lying to a pest like Sukey. I did it all the time.

"Okay. Then I'll pay a visit to Yolinda to see if she got some. I'll let you get back to whatever you was doing."

We hung up and I was about to walk out the door when the telephone rang again. I was annoyed when I heard Sukey's voice this time too. "I forgot to ask you if I could borrow a few dollars. I need to get my hair done so I can look good at Blondeen's New Year's Eve party."

"I ain't got but a few dollars until I get paid next week, so I can't help you this time."

"Okay."

I knew Sukey well enough to know that she wasn't just calling about no flour and a few dollars. She often called me up or came to my house when she wanted to grill me for information that she could pass on to her friends. But she shared a lot of juicy stuff with me—mostly some of the nasty things Blondeen said about me—so I put up with her. I thought it was important to know what Blondeen was saying about me so I wouldn't get too lax and let my guard down.

"I was fixing to walk out the door, so can we talk some other time?"

"Where you going?"

"Nowhere in particular. I just wanted to get out the house for a little while."

"Who goes 'nowhere in particular' in this chilly weather, this time of night?"

"I was just missing my husband. I thought a short walk to the end of the block and back would do me some good."

"I don't see how. You'd probably be better off spending time with a close friend." Sukey sniffed and sharpened her tone. "You and Hubert looked mighty kissy-poo in that restaurant tonight. I would think y'all would still be together. How come he ain't with you now?"

"He had to go over to Hartville for a few days. He wanted me to go with him, but I couldn't go. My mama's having a big New Year's Eve celebration and she wants me to be there."

Sukey suddenly switched gears. "I guess you know Blondeen still wants to get her hooks in Hubert."

"What else is new?" I rolled my eyes.

"I just thought I'd mention it. She's real possessive when it comes to her men friends. Remember when she punched the girl who works at the meat market for flirting with the man she was seeing at the time?"

"I heard about it, but that don't faze me. Besides, I'm not seeing her man. I'm seeing Hubert."

"Well, she ain't nobody to mess with if you can help it. I declare, if I seen her fighting with a alligator, I'd help the alligator."

"I ain't worried about Blondeen. The way she keeps behaving, she ought to be the one worried about me. And you can tell her I said so."

"Oh, I done already told her that. She knows you ain't no pushover. But she'll push you as long as she can—until you stop her."

"When and if I have to, I will. But Hubert is my friend and I do a few things around his house for him. You can let Blondeen know that so long as Hubert wants me to spend time with him, I will. I hate to cut this conversation short, but I have to hang up."

"Wait a minute!" Sukey yelled. "Me and you been friends for a long time, so I thought I should let you know that Blondeen is talking more trash about you than ever before these past few days. She done told a bunch of folks she wasn't going to lay off you until she ruined your reputation so bad, you wouldn't have no choice but to leave town. She even had a notion that you and Hubert was fooling around before Maggie died."

"That's a damn lie!" I boomed.

"Oh, I don't believe y'all was that bold, and I doubt if anybody else believes it. Blondeen couldn't even back that up with no evidence." Sukey cleared her throat and continued. "One more thing she told me—which I never thought she'd be mean enough to say, even about you—was that she hopes the next funeral she goes to is yours."

A chill crawled up my spine. "Thanks for letting me know all this. Tell her I said I'd probably be attending her funeral before she attends mine."

I didn't care how many more vicious things Blondeen had said about me. I'd heard enough for tonight, so I wasn't going to listen to nothing else Sukey wanted to tell me. I wondered if she was telling me all this mess to get me riled up enough to confront Blondeen so she'd finally see us fight. That wasn't going to happen. I had never got into a physical conflict with a woman over a man and I wasn't about to start now.

"I'll talk to you again soon, Sukey." I didn't give her time to say nothing else. I hung up and rushed out the door.

Since that man started killing colored women, most of the folks I knew had started locking their doors for the first time. Even in the nice quiet neighborhood me and Hubert lived in. He still didn't, so I didn't have no trouble getting into his house.

Even though it was pitch dark, I knew the layout of his house so well that I didn't have no trouble making it to one of the living-room end tables to turn on the lamp. I glanced around for a few moments before I went into his bedroom and turned on one of the bedside lamps. I dropped my coat on top of the dresser and flopped down on his bed and closed my eyes.

I drew in a deep breath and tried to imagine what it would be like to actually lay in this bed with him on top of me. The way Maggie used to brag about his performance, I knew I had a real treat in store for me. I got so hot, I had to fan my crotch. I wallowed around under the covers for fifteen minutes, hugging a pillow, wishing it was Hubert in my arms.

I was getting too comfortable, so I got up and remade the bed. I didn't know what to do next, so I moseyed over to the other side of the room to his dresser and opened the top drawer. I was surprised to see how orderly everything still was, since I'd done his laundry last week. I fished out a few of his under shorts and smelled them before I put them back. As careful as I was, I couldn't stack them as neat as they was or put them back in the order they was in when I opened the drawer. It was such a little detail; I knew he wouldn't notice, so I didn't fret over it. I didn't bother to look in the other drawers because I knew that every other thing I'd washed and put away would still be just as orderly.

Hubert was such a well-organized man; I couldn't understand why he'd offered to pay me to help him out around the house. Just being with him was enough compensation.

I rifled through a bunch of papers in one of the nightstand drawers, but I didn't see nothing interesting at first. Just bills and insurance papers from the families of some of the people he'd buried. When I seen a copy of the program they'd passed out at Maggie and Claude's funeral, I gasped and slammed the drawer shut. It was such a shock to see that ominous piece of paper again, I had to sit down on the bed and rub my bosom. I composed myself as quick as I could and sprinted to the kitchen.

I didn't see nothing in his icebox that I wanted to nibble on, but I found a piece of hard candy on the kitchen counter, so I ate it.

If things went the way I hoped they would, I'd be the new Mrs. Wiggins as soon as Hubert realized I was the *only* woman who could take over where Maggie left off.

Chapter 20

Hubert

WHEN I GOT HOME AFTER DROPPING JESSIE OFF, I DECIDED TO GO to Hartville tonight instead of Saturday. I packed a few changing clothes, some underwear, and shaving items because I was pretty sure I'd stay until the New Year rolled in. I didn't think I could stand to be alone in the same house where me and Maggie had celebrated our last New Year together. I didn't feel like celebrating this one with anybody I knew in Lexington because I didn't want to be bombarded with more questions about my personal life. And I knew that no matter where I went out, I'd run into some of them women I was avoiding now.

As much as I liked Jessie's company, I didn't want to ring in this New Year with her because me and Maggie had made plans for it. We had spent the last four years celebrating the holiday with church family friends, and it was one of the few times me and her drunk alcohol. Last year, me and Daryl celebrated the holiday two days before because his wife had planned a big party and he had to be there.

There was only a couple of motels in Hartville that rented to colored folks. They was both real gloomy, but spending the night in one of them was better than sleeping in a car or on the ground, like some colored folks chose to do when they had to stay out of town overnight. I was real familiar with the one on State Street. It was where me and Daryl used to hole up at when we couldn't get a place in Mobile, where he lived, which was one town over from Hartville. When we didn't have enough time or money to pay for a room, we got cozy in the backseat of my car or his.

After I checked into my room and unpacked, I rinsed my mouth out with warm water from the bathroom sink. And then I got antsy. I wanted some affection so bad; I didn't know what to do with myself. I even considered going back to that juke joint in Toxey, hoping to run into somebody there that I could connect with. But just thinking about the way them frisky women had pestered me the last time I was there, I dismissed that notion right away.

I missed Daryl so much, I wanted to cry. He was the most interesting and affectionate man I'd ever met. And he was a hardworking one too. He had been a Pullman porter most of his adult life. The route the train he worked on went through all the little country towns in our part of the state, so he knew a heap of nice places along the way that served colored folks. One of the restaurants we used to visit in Hartville was called the Half Moon Diner. It had been closed for remodeling since last March and had recently reopened. It was a popular little hole in the wall on a dead-end street, not too far from the motel I was in now. I'd ate so much a few hours ago, I knew I wouldn't eat nothing else until the morning, but I had a itching to go to the restaurant anyway. Despite my full stomach, I could still guzzle a few glasses of tea or lemonade.

The Half Moon Diner was one of the few places in town where men like me hung out. Several years ago, I'd had several encounters with one of the waiters. I met other short-term boyfriends through him before he moved to Kentucky four years ago. The owner didn't have a problem with us, so long as we spent a lot of money and wasn't too obvious.

Not only was it hard to find partners, but it was also dangerous. Before I met Daryl, I was at another restaurant in Hartville one night that somebody had since burned down. Anyway, as I was sitting there gnawing on some frog legs, I could have swore that another male customer who was also eating by hisself was giving me the eye. When I left, I waited in my car until he came out. I sidled up to him with a wall-to-wall grin on my face. I didn't even get a chance to make a play for him. He reared back on his legs and cussed me out for even thinking he was interested in a man. Before I could get away, he clobbered me upside my head with his fist.

When I returned to that restaurant a month later, it was so crowded that I had to share a table with a stranger, who turned out to be Daryl. It didn't take long for him to show some interest in me. We checked into a room that night.

During the drive to the Half Moon Diner tonight, the thought crossed my mind that I might run into Daryl there. It was one of his favorite hangouts. But I wasn't about to let that stop me. If I ran into him, I figured he'd probably ignore me anyway.

When I reached my destination, I didn't see nobody in the place that I liked, so I didn't plan on staying long. Just as I was finishing up my second glass of lemonade, a moonfaced, middle-aged man, who looked familiar, pulled a chair out and plopped down at my table.

"I hope you don't mind me sitting here until my order is ready for me to pick up," he said.

"Excuse me?" I glared at him with my jaw twitching.

He gave me a dismissive wave and snickered. "Don't you remember me?" He reached out his hand to shake mine.

"Should I?" I raised my eyebrows, but I shook his hand anyway.

"You came into my place in Toxey recently. You didn't stay long because you'd only stopped to get directions."

I squinted and looked at his face until I realized why he looked familiar. "Oh yeah! Your name's Ralph, right?"

"Ralph Cook. I noticed you as soon as I walked in the door. My sister lives over here. After I paid her a visit, I decided to swing by here to pick up some hush puppies and other snacks for my guests. And the drinks are pretty good here. Sometimes I need a change from that moonshine I sell. This place will be jumping like a Mexican jumping bean on New Year's Eve. But I'm staying close to home that night. You welcome to come by, if you want to. I just bought a brand-new phonograph and I got all the latest records."

"I would love to, but I'm meeting a lady friend later. We'll hole up at her place until I go back to Lexington on Monday," I lied. "She's running late, so I decided to come in here for a spell. They serve a mean glass of lemonade."

"Lemonade?" Ralph chuckled. "I'm surprised that a brawny man like you wets his whistle with something that tame."

I chuckled too. "Well, I don't like to drink nothing too strong when I have to drive. And I like to be nice and sober when I'm with my lady friend."

Ralph winked. "I don't blame you. It's a waste of time to be with a woman who is ready, willing, and able and not get the full impact of her talents. Is she the same one you was visiting the last time I seen you?"

"Uh-huh. She's a lovely woman."

"I bet she is. You are the kind of man lovely women go far." Ralph lowered his voice and leaned across the table. "And some men . . ." He snorted and gave me a serious look. "Some of the folks that come to my house like to gossip. I hear all kinds of stuff about men getting together with other men. Sissies ain't got that many places to go and socialize with each other, so a few come here from time to time. The owner told me he don't mind them coming so long as they spend money and don't act so sissi-fied they'll give his business a bad name. I done heard that some will get real drunk and approach regular men at a few of them other places they hang out at. Do you know where not to go in this town so you won't get pestered?"

"Not really. But other than seeing my lady friend, the only thing I'm going to do in Hartville is pick up some embalming fluid for my job."

Ralph reacted the same way most people did when they found out what I did for a living. His face froze. The only thing moving on it was his blinking eyes. "Embalming fluid? Good God. You work for a undertaker?"

"I am a undertaker."

He screwed up his lips and flinched. "Well, somebody got to do that spooky job. It don't give you the heebie-jeebies?"

I laughed. "No, it's just a job to me. Deaths done almost doubled since last year, so I been using a lot of embalming fluid. Nobody in Lexington sells it, so I have to come over here or go someplace else to buy some. I'm also going to visit that barber on Noble Street to get my hair cut."

Ralph drew in a sharp breath and narrowed his eyes. "You talking about Leroy Everette?"

"Yeah. Do you know him?"

"Uh-huh." He looked around before he told me in a low tone, "I advise you to start going to a different barbershop."

"Why? I been going to him for years and I ain't never had a bad experience. Did his place go out of business?"

"Nothing like that. Um, y'all ain't got no barbers in Lexington?"

I laughed. "Yeah, we do. But Lexington is smaller than Hartville and a lot more country. We got a lot of dirt roads, and there is so many woods in all directions, it ain't nothing for me to get up in the morning and find a possum playing possum on my back porch. No matter what part of town you in, if you walk long enough, you'll run into blackberry patches, fishing holes, cotton and sugarcane fields."

"That is country," Ralph agreed with a frown.

"Anyway, we got a couple of barbers. One is elderly and only works part-time. The other one got folks lined up, back-to-back, every day. He closed up yesterday and won't reopen until after the holiday. So it ain't so easy for a colored man to get his hair cut in Lexington, unless he cuts it hisself or let some random person with a pair of scissors do it. I decided to get a haircut during one of my visits over here, about four years ago, because I had some time to kill. I asked a man on the street where I could find a colored barber and he sent me to Leroy. I've been back to him several times since. He's a nice guy and I enjoy talking to him. I know he has a lot of business and I usually show up without making a appointment, but I don't mind waiting. Now, tell me why you think I should find another barber?"

"Because Leroy ain't what you think he is." Ralph looked toward the entrance, around the room, and then back at me. He told me in a much lower tone, "He is as funny as a drunk clown—and I don't mean funny 'ha-ha.' I mean the other kind . . ."

I gulped a mouthful of air. "For real? He don't look like it, and he sure don't act it. At least he didn't none of the times I was with him."

"That's the problem with most sissies these days. Some look as normal as me and you. You rarely see the kind that struts around like bandy roosters in loud-colored glad rags and such, and speak in high-pitched voices like they are trying to sound as womanish as possible. They get their tails kicked left and right. I know one that got bold enough to show his true colors to the wrong people. After a couple whupped him good, they set the white folks on him and now he's sitting in the state prison." Ralph paused and took a deep breath. There was a solemn expression on his face as he went on.

"I been knowing Leroy for years. Him and his boyfriends used to come to my place. They spent a lot of money and I didn't mind their presence, so long as they didn't get too affectionate with each other in front of normal folks," Ralph said. "But every now and then, a few of them quacks got too outrageous. They'd be dancing cheek to cheek, sitting in each other's laps, hugging and kissing, and whatnot. And some of my other guests got offended and stopped coming."

"Is that fact? What did you do?"

"I didn't want to lose money, so I made them pay double for their drinks—and I didn't allow them to get too friendly with each other. They eventually found other places to go drink at. But a few still slide in every now and then. And I still make them pay double." Ralph gave me a grievous look and shook his head. "It's such a waste when handsome, strapping men like Leroy swing that way."

"He sure had me fooled. I thought he was a happily married man. I've seen pictures of his wife and two sons," I commented.

"*Pffftt!*" Ralph did a neck roll and waved his hand. "He probably was a happily married man at some point. That don't mean nothing, though. A lot of his kind get married and raise children. Sometimes a wife and kids ain't enough, even for normal men like me. The Lord blessed me with the best wife in the world and wonderful children, but I still have to see other women on the side to feel completely contented." Ralph turned his head to the side and looked at me with his eyes narrowed. "You married?"

"I was. We had a wonderful life for more than twenty years. She passed the week before Thanksgiving."

"I'm sorry to hear that. Well, did you ever cheat on her with other women?"

"Not one single time," I said proudly. "The whole time I was married, I never even looked at another woman."

Ralph looked at me in awe. "Bless your heart. I wish I could say that. I been trying to behave myself, but the women that come to my place won't let me alone."

I shifted in my chair and caressed my chin. "Well, just be careful. I'd hate for you to lose your woman over one of them juke joint jezebels. Anyway, I still like Leroy and the way he cuts my hair. I hope he don't close up before I can get over there tomorrow."

"All right, then. But if he decides to get fresh with you someday, don't say nobody warned you." Ralph glanced toward the kitchen. "I'm going to go see if my order is ready, so I can skedaddle. You have a blessed night. Happy New Year, and be careful."

"The same to you." I shook his hand again and he left. I left a few minutes later. I couldn't wait to get to Leroy's barbershop tomorrow.

Chapter 21
Hubert

AFTER I PICKED UP THE EMBALMING FLUID SATURDAY MORNING, I went directly to Leroy's barbershop. A customer was on his way out, so he held the door open for me. Leroy's shiny black eyes lit up when he seen me. "Hubert! It's good to see you again!" he greeted as we shook hands.

"I try to drop in every time I come to Hartville," I said as I eased down in a chair along the wall. Everything Ralph had told me about Leroy was still ringing in my ears. I liked Leroy's looks and his personality, so I was more than interested in getting to know him better. But what Ralph had told me still wasn't enough for me to make the first move. I prayed that Leroy would give me the slightest hint that he was interested in me.

"You are always welcome. I hope you had a nice Christmas. I'm glad you got here when you did. I was thinking about closing early today." Leroy had told me during a previous conversation that he'd graduated from high school the same year as me. I figured we was the same age, but he looked younger. There wasn't a wrinkle in sight on his square-jawed, butterscotch-colored face. His hair was thicker than mine and there wasn't a gray strand in sight. His body was still lean and firm. I was a little on the pudgy side and my eyes didn't sparkle the way his did, but the way women behaved around me, I knew I still had something going for myself. I just hoped that Leroy thought the same thing.

"I had a wonderful Christmas, Leroy. But a lot has happened since the last time I was here." I told him about losing Maggie and Claude.

"I'm sorry to hear that. How are you getting along?"

I climbed into the barber's chair and got comfortable as he draped a white towel around my shoulders. "I was feeling real low the first couple of weeks. But things done started to turn around for me. I'm moving on with my life as fast as I can. I've already started socializing again."

"That's good to hear. Ain't nothing like being alone." Leroy's voice trembled as he spoke. "My wife took off with my kids back in September on Labor Day morning. I can't tell you what a miserable, lonesome holiday it was for me. I spent the whole day by myself, so depressed I couldn't even barbecue the two slabs of ribs I had bought. When I did cook them later that evening, I brought them to work the next day for my customers to enjoy."

"That's a shame. Is she coming back?"

"I doubt it. She decided that there was another man who suited her better than me. She done already got a job working at the same hotel where he works."

"My Lord." I didn't want to sound nosy, but I didn't see nothing wrong in what I asked next. "You dating again yet?"

"Every now and then," he muttered. I was glad my back was to him. He sounded so woebegone; I didn't want to see what kind of look was on his face. "You want the same pomade as the last time?"

"Huh? Oh yeah. But not too much. I don't want to smell too sweet."

Leroy was surprised when I told him that I was going to spend New Year's Eve alone in my drab motel. "Lord, have mercy. That's where I spent my honeymoon and a few wedding anniversaries. I know how dreary that place is."

"Tell me about it. They didn't have but one room left and it's the one at the very end," I complained.

Another customer shuffled in and sat down in one of the seats along the wall facing us. He was a regular, so him and Leroy had a lot to talk about. I stayed quiet until he finished with me. "I hope to see you again soon, Hubert," he told me as I was leaving.

"Oh, I'm sure I'll be coming back again in a few weeks," I said on my way out the door. I picked up some ribs and Nehi soda pop on the way back to the motel.

I couldn't stop thinking about what Ralph had told me about Leroy. I found it hard to believe that such a good-looking, strapping man liked men. After all the conversating we'd done since he'd been cutting my hair, I thought I knew everything there was to know about him. He'd lost his first barbershop eight years ago when his bank went under and spent the next year unemployed. His wife cooked for a wealthy white family and she was the one who'd kept the family afloat during that time. That had caused a lot of tension between them and drove her into the arms of several other men. He'd stayed with her because of his boys. He'd slowly got back up on his feet by taking over the barbershop, which he owned now, when the previous owner passed away. He'd been doing well ever since.

He sounded like the kind of man I was looking for. I was glad he had never gave me a hint that he was interested in men. If he had, I wouldn't have acted on it. At the time, I was hopelessly in love with Daryl and I would have never cheated on him.

I went to bed a few minutes before nine p.m. and tossed and turned so much, I couldn't go to sleep. I was feeling so humdrum, I was tempted to get back up and go back home and sleep in my own bed. But that long drive in the dark by myself didn't appeal to me.

When I got up Sunday morning, I decided to visit a church I was familiar with. Their preacher was often a guest speaker at Daddy's church. After that, I drove to Mobile for supper at a restaurant me and Maggie and Claude used to eat at. I got hungry again a couple of hours before the New Year arrived, so I got up and drove back to the Half Moon Diner. There was a lot of cars parked out front and on the side, so I had to park a block away.

I wasn't inside no more than ten minutes before I seen Leroy. He didn't see me, and I didn't want to bother him because he was busy talking to a young man in a red suit. I did a little mingling, but only to kill time. All of the women was with men, so I didn't spend much time talking to any of them. I wasn't keeping track of the time and didn't know we was so close to the New Year until folks started the ten-second count.

The next thing I knew, men and women was hugging and kissing like it was going out of style. I even allowed a woman to kiss me but it took my breath away. When I seen another one staggering in my direction with her lips puckered, I moved to the other side of the room before she got to me. I caught my breath and looked around the room. Some folks was still hugging and kissing. The same man I'd seen Leroy talking to, when I came in, took his hand and led him to a corner in back of the room and kissed him on the mouth. They did it so fast, I was probably the only one that seen them. I wondered how they could behave in such a way out in the open. They had to know that what they was doing was illegal and dangerous. I didn't see none of the other men getting too close to one another, but I had feeling some of them did when they was in private. Before I could get my bearings, Leroy moved away from the man he'd kissed and came up to me.

"Hey! Happy New Year! I didn't expect to see you here!" he yelled. "I guess that motel room got too lonesome, huh?"

"It sure did," I agreed. "It seems like everybody here is with somebody, so I'm going to head on back to that room. I feel like a third leg."

We laughed. And then Leroy lifted his chin and stared at me with his eyes narrowed.

"Well, it was good to see you again, Hubert. I hope to see you again soon," he told me. And then he added, "Real soon."

"I hope so." Our eyes locked and he winked. I winked back and nodded. Leroy took off because the man in the red suit suddenly motioned him to join him in another part of the room. The sight of him kissing another man and winking at me was all the proof I needed to believe that Leroy was one of my kind. The only problem was, he didn't seem to have no interest in me. If he had any, how come he didn't give me a kiss to ring in the New Year? I wondered. Me winking and nodding at him, and being in the same place with at least one other sissy tonight, should have told him that me and him was on the same team.

Then it suddenly dawned on me. The man in the red suit was in his twenties or early thirties, like most of the other customers. Who was I trying to kid? I asked myself. As hard as it was for men to connect with each other, who was going to take a chance on me with my old self? Some men in their forties, and even older, preferred younger men. I left before I could get depressed.

It looked like I was going to be without a man for a long time, if at all again. One good thing was I still had Jessie. She didn't come close to being in the same league as a man was for me, but at least I'd have somebody to kill time with. The only thing I had to worry about was keeping up the hoax that I couldn't perform in bed. Would she still go along with it a year from now or longer? Could I come up with another medical lie that would make my condition permanent? Wondering about them things was making my head spin, so I put them aside for the time being.

Ten minutes after I got back to my room, somebody knocked on my door. I assumed it was a drunk guest knocking on the wrong door, because nobody knew where I was at. Except Leroy. I snatched the door open. He was standing there holding a bottle of champagne.

"W-what are you doing here?" I stammered as I waved him in.

"Well, you didn't want to stay at the party, so I decided to bring the party to you."

He set the bottle on the scarred dresser and plonked down on the side of the bed. I eased down next to him.

"This place is so tacky, they don't even put glasses in the rooms," I complained.

"I already knew that. If you ain't got no problem drinking out the same bottle, I ain't neither."

He took the first sip before he handed the bottle to me and I took a long pull. I got a slight buzz right away. Before I knew what was happening, he leaned over and took my hand in his.

"You know about me?" he whispered.

I nodded. "When I seen you and that young buck kissing earlier tonight, I had a feeling me and you was cut from the same cloth." I didn't see no reason to mention what Ralph had told me about him yet, if at all. I suddenly felt so free and light, I probably could have rose up and floated around the room.

"Hubert, I swear to God, I had no idea about you."

I gave him a big smile. "Well, now you know. What's the story about the red suit?"

"What red suit?"

I reared back and gave him a surprised look. "The one I seen you kissing on."

"Him? *Pffftt!* He ain't nobody to me. His name is Oscar Porter and he's that friendly with everybody. He must have kissed half the people at the place tonight."

"You was the only one I seen him kiss."

"Well, the old man he lives with was also there. But he knows how frisky Oscar is. Everybody knows. He ain't nobody for you to worry about. Besides, he ain't my type."

I chuckled. "What is your type?"

Leroy looked me in the eyes and mouthed, "You."

Chapter 22
Hubert

*I*ALREADY FELT SO COMFORTABLE WITH LEROY, I TOLD HIM ABOUT my first encounter with Xavier when I was a teenager. I also told him about how hopeless I'd felt at several low points in my life, like when I realized what I was and couldn't do nothing to change it.

He was quick to share his story with me. "I always knew I was different. I was attracted to boys when I was a teenager, but I only dated girls. I was way too shy and afraid to do anything out of the ordinary." He paused and a wistful look crossed his face. "Things changed for me when I joined the army. It all happened in France. Me and some of the other guys used to hang out at the bars. Them prostitutes in Paris was all over every colored American soldier they seen. I went at it with a couple, but one night I went home with one I hadn't seen before. Come to find out, she was he."

I gasped. "You couldn't tell it was a man?"

"No! He looked and acted exactly like a woman. Anyway, I had the best time I ever had in my life in that dingy little room with that French boy. I found out later that almost everybody who hung out at that bar knew what he was. Some of the same men in my company had been with him—and out in the open, at that! After him, I spent time with two others, but they didn't walk around dressed and acting like a woman. I seen so many men over there showing affection to each other in public. If it hadn't been for my mama and daddy needing me to help out at home, I would have gone back to France when I got discharged and stayed there."

"I declare! France sounds like a wonderful place. Now I'm sorry I didn't join the army or get drafted. I could never get away with loving a man—colored or white—in this country."

"That's for sure. It's amazing how the white folks in this country, whose folks originally came from Europe, can be so close-minded about them things. When I got back to the States, I returned to my old routine. The girl I had been seeing before I enlisted pressured me so much to marry her, I finally did. Not because I loved her, but because I wanted to live the kind of life everybody expected. By the time I reached my middle twenties, I was convinced that I'd never feel the touch of another man. I was driving for a nice old white man who owned a lot of property at the time. He was in his fifties and had grandkids, but his wife was dead. One night after he'd been drinking, he offered me money to . . . you know."

"Did you do it?"

"Yes, I did. He paid me more in one night for showing him some affection—that's what he called it—than he paid me for driving in a whole week. He was into dark meat, so he let me in on these parties he'd throw at least once a week. There would be me and at least three or four other young colored men present so he could take his pick. Half of the men he partied with was normal, but they was the kind that would do anything for money. And some of them suckers had the nerve to look down on men like me! Even after I left that job, I stayed in touch with one and it was through him that I met my next few boyfriends. I don't look for new people these days. I let them look for me. You are the first one I've approached in years."

"I'm glad to hear that," I said with a sheepish grin. "By the way, my daddy's first name is also Leroy. He's got his own church, but he's been our used-to-be mayor's brother's butler for over forty years. Part-time now, though. I call him Daddy, and everybody else—including my mama—have been calling him Reverend Wiggins for so long, I bet most of them done forgot what his real name is."

"That's a nice coincidence. It's a name that'll be easy for you to remember."

I nodded. "Are you seeing somebody now?"

Leroy gave me a dry look and hunched his shoulders. "Something like that."

"Either you are seeing somebody, or you ain't. Which one is it?"

"Well, I have somebody I go see for maintenance purposes only. I ain't seen him in over a month." Leroy pursed his lips, tapped mine with the tip of his finger, and said, "I probably won't see him no more after tonight."

"Oh." I smiled.

"My last long-term relationship ended two years ago. I was depressed every day for a whole month."

"Oh? Did he find somebody else?"

"No, he died in a car wreck. He had a wife and he had convinced her, and everybody else, that we was just fishing buddies. It took me a while to get over losing him, and I tried to do everything I could to get back on track. I closed my shop for a month and went to Miami to grieve. And at the same time, I tried to ease my pain by jumping in and out of bed with strangers I picked up on the beach. When I got back to Hartville, I slid back into a relationship with one of my used-to-be lovers. But he had changed so much, he didn't even seem like the same man I'd once been in love with. He had never asked me for nothing, but now he was asking for free haircuts and money, sometimes twice in the same day. When I found out he was spending my money on other men, I was fit to be tied. I ain't one to be fattening frogs for snakes."

Leroy looked so sad, I leaned over and kissed him. When I pulled away, I kept my arm around his shoulder. "I had somebody up until last month." I told him everything there was to tell about Daryl.

He gave me a sympathetic look. "I feel for you. Losing your

wife, your son, and your man so close together must have been awful! How do you stand being so alone now? You don't have a new boyfriend yet?"

"Not yet. But I had a heap of lady friends coming in and out of my house for a while. That got to be too much of a hassle, so I whittled it down to just one in particular. I'm content with her for now."

"Well, in desperate times, tail is tail."

I shook my head and gave Leroy a sheepish grin. "Not exactly. I ain't been with no woman that way."

"Oh? You mean not since your wife passed?" he asked with his eyebrows raised.

"Me and her never done it. Having sex with a woman was one thing I couldn't bring myself to do. It seemed unnatural. Maggie didn't have no problem with that. She'd been molested for years when she was a child, and because of that, she didn't want nothing more to do with sex, period."

"Hmmm. Then it was your play son that died? Y'all got him from a relative or that orphan asylum?"

"No, Claude was *our* boy," I boomed. "Well, at least he was Maggie's." Leroy's mouth dropped open when I told him about the devious way me and Maggie had become parents.

"My God. I never would have guessed you was holding something that deep inside you."

"Nobody else would neither. It ain't easy. It feels like I been stuck in a tornado since I lost my family and my boyfriend, and the wind is blowing me every which way."

Leroy gave me the most pitiful look I'd seen in a long time. "Brother Hubert, I do believe you been in the storm too long." The next thing I knew, he gently pushed me down on the bed with one hand and he unzipped my pants with his other.

After we finished pleasuring each other, I felt like a new man. What had just happened took a lot of the edge off me. It also took my mind off Maggie's and Claude's upcoming birthdays and my wedding anniversary.

We cuddled and discussed a bunch of things. He liked playing sports and going fishing with his two teenage sons, who lived in Branson, the next town over. They took the train or the bus to Hartville so they could spend at least a couple of weekends each month with him. I never gave sports much thought and I'd only been fishing a few times in my life, but I made it clear to him that I'd like to get more involved in both.

"Do you think I can go fishing with you and your boys one day?"

"Um . . . I don't think that's such a good idea. One rule I made for myself when I got married was that I'd never take my kids around nary one of my boyfriends."

"Is it because you think they'd get suspicious and start asking questions about me?"

A woeful look crossed his face. "No, it ain't that. I wouldn't do or say nothing that would make them suspicious. I feel bad enough about deceiving the people I love. Me bringing my boyfriends around them would be like rubbing it in their faces."

"I understand. I never took any of my boyfriends around my wife and son, or anybody else I knew. That's the main reason I never get involved with men who live in Lexington. And I always made it clear to them that they could never come near my house."

"What about the funeral home you run? Has that always been off-limits too?"

"Well, because of the nature of the business, most folks don't want to be nowhere near such a ominous place—unless they have to be. Of all the men I've been with, not a single one wanted to come over there."

"I can understand that. A funeral home is the last place I want to be. And it will be the last place I visit before they cart me off to the church for my funeral." Leroy laughed. Then he paused and gave me a serious look. "I want to say something, and I hope it don't sound too forward."

"You can say whatever you want to me," I told him as I squeezed his hand. "We are two mature men enjoying each other's company."

"I'm looking for somebody who is looking for the same things

I want. The next time we get together, I'll pay for the room. Better yet, you can come to my place. I live in a small apartment above my barbershop. It's got a back entrance, so my next-door neighbors can't be peeping out their front windows seeing who comes and goes to my place."

"Oh? So, are you telling me you'd like to see me again?"

"Sure enough. And . . . and I hope you feel the same way. I been cutting your hair for a long time and done got to know you really well. I believe we can make each other real happy."

"I believe we can too. We can figure out a plan to get together that'll work for both of us. I live in a neighborhood with a lot of busybodies and I just started a relationship, if you want to call it that, with the woman I mentioned a few minutes ago. Like my wife was, she's the perfect cover to help me keep my secret hid. Her name is Jessie. She was my wife's best friend."

"Uh-oh. I'm sure that's raising a lot of eyebrows."

"That's for sure. I know folks are saying all kinds of things about me behind my back. But I don't care. If they don't have nothing to gossip about, they'll make up something. So I'm damned if I do, and damned if I don't," I shared.

"I feel the same way about my own situation. But I have several female friends, mostly from church that I spend time with. I've even been to bed with one, but it didn't do nothing for me, so I don't do that no more. It was a real challenge for me to have a physical relationship with my own wife, and most of the time she had to hound me to do it. Otherwise, a woman couldn't turn me on with a monkey wrench." We laughed.

"I won't have that problem with the woman I'm seeing. I got Jessie believing that I lost my manly functions because my wife's passing traumatized me. She lost her husband to some kind of heart problem a few months ago, but he was mean as hell to her. Because of him, she ain't had no desire to get in bed with another man yet. Or so she claims."

"Jessie sounds like a good woman to use if you think you still need a prop. I keep to myself, so most of the folks don't know much about my personal life. But some men like to gossip as much as women, especially when they come to a barbershop. When they ask me about my love life, I always tell them my lady friend is married to a ferocious ex-con/ex-bootlegger and we have to be discreet. So I can't give out her name or too much information about her. That always shuts them up. You ever thought about telling folks you seeing a married woman if they ask?"

"*Pffftt.* My daddy is the most respected and beloved colored preacher in town, and every woman looks up to my mama. I been on the straight and narrow all my life. If I suddenly started telling folks I was seeing another man's wife, my name would be mud. I couldn't bring that kind of shame on my family."

"That's a good point. You need to keep Jessie on the hook as long as you can. I just hope she don't start pestering you to be more than friends."

"If things get out of hand with her, I'll turn her loose and find another woman. It would be a dream come true if I could find one who was only interested in women, but needed a man as a front to make folks think she was normal. Me and her could cover for each other." We laughed again.

"I am so glad we *finally* got each other's number," Leroy told me as he stroked my arm.

"I wish it could have been sooner," I cooed.

Chapter 23
Jessie

Monday, January 1, 1940

RIGHT AFTER NOON ON SUNDAY, I DEVELOPED A HEADACHE THAT wouldn't go away, no matter what I did, so I didn't feel up to going to Mama's New Year's Eve party. I went to bed two hours before New Year rolled in.

I woke up at daybreak the next morning with the cramps. My monthly had started during the night and I was bleeding like a stuck pig. After I took a bath, I stretched out on my living-room couch to read yesterday's newspaper, something I didn't do every day. It was too depressing. There was always some article about how them folks over in Europe was fighting and fighting. Everybody I knew was predicting that America would get caught up in that mess eventually.

I put the newspaper aside a few minutes before ten a.m. After I took a long hot bath and got dressed, I decided to sneak into Hubert's house again.

This time I made myself some tea and drunk it as I laid in his bed. I had planned to stay longer, but when somebody knocked on the front door, I got spooked. They was gone by the time I got to the window to peep out. When the telephone rang three times in ten minutes, I thought it would be best for me to haul ass.

When I left, I took one of Hubert's shirts with me in case I ran into Yolinda or some other nosy busybody. I'd claim that I'd forgot to take the shirt before Hubert left and had come back to get it because I'd promised him I'd sew on some new buttons. I'd even snatched off the first two and put them in my brassiere to be more convincing. I'd return to his house before he did and put the shirt back in the closet and do some more snooping and lounging. I felt so at home in his house now, it was hard for me to stay away.

Afterward, I decided to go to my mama's house to see if there was any black-eyed peas left so I could take a plate home. She lived within walking distance in the same crooked little house me and all my siblings grew up in.

"How come you and Hubert didn't come to the party last night?" Mama asked, looking over my shoulder as I shuffled in the front door. My mama didn't look like a woman in her seventies. Some folks found it hard to believe she had four grown children and eight grandchildren. She was petite like me and had similar features. "I thought he was courting you?"

"I was too tired to come over here last night. And Hubert had to go to Hartville on Friday night for business and probably won't be home until this evening. I'll see him when I go to his house to cook his supper tomorrow evening after I get home from work."

"Well, he's a keeper in my book, so I hope you don't let him escape," Mama advised, wagging her finger in my face.

"How come it's so quiet up in here?" I asked as I followed Mama into the kitchen. Dirty glasses and dishes, noisemakers, and party hats was all over the place.

"This place was a madhouse last night. I'm so glad it's quiet now! I didn't get to bed until two in the morning. Ten minutes after New Year got here, your sister Annie Ruth got drunk as a skunk and was so slaphappy, she took off with that new joker she latched onto last month. Your brother left a hour ago to go hunting. I don't know where everybody else is at. They all scattered like roaches when I mentioned cleaning up." Mama rolled her eyes, but she wasn't complaining. She hated being alone as much as I did. After my daddy died, my sister Annie Ruth left the man she'd been married to for ten years and moved back home with her three teenagers.

As soon as I sat down at the kitchen table, Mama took a damp dishcloth and wiped a smudge off my chin. She spent the next ten minutes grilling me about who was doing what on my street.

I was glad when I got back to my street, even gladder when I seen Hubert's car in his driveway. I rushed inside and dialed his number. He picked up right away.

"Happy New Year, Hubert," I sang.

"The same to you, Jessie. Did you go anywhere?"

"No, I was feeling under the weather so I decided to stay home so I wouldn't get sicker. I'm fine now. Did you get all of your business taken care of in Hartville?"

"Yup. And I ran into a old school friend on Sunday. He invited me to his house where him and his wife was having a New Year's Eve party. They ain't got no phone, or I would have called you."

"I hope you enjoyed yourself."

He cleared his throat before he answered, "I did."

"I just came from Mama's house. I brought a bowl of black-eyed peas home, if you want me to bring you some."

"Thanks, but that's all right. My mama just called me up and told me she had set aside a heaping bowl of some for me."

"Okay. You sound tired, so I won't keep you. I'll come over to cook tomorrow evening around six. I'm going to marinate some fish heads overnight so I can make you a pot of stew."

"Thank you. I can't wait to dive into it. By the way, I been meaning to ask, how you like working the day shift so far?"

"I love it. But I'm even busier than before. At least when I was on the graveyard shift, a lot of the patients was asleep most of the time and I didn't have to deal with them too much. I miss how quiet the place was then. Now there's crabby old folks getting violent with the workers and screaming bloody murder throughout the day. And now I have to change bed linen for the same ones three or four times a day."

"Are they that messy?"

"Hubert, diarrhea and puke visits that place more than the patients' loved ones," I said with a shudder. "And when somebody dies, we usually don't find out until the next morning. By the time I have to go in the rooms, they been dead for hours. I swear, sometimes it feels like I'm working in a haunted house."

"Well, at least you got a steady job. Just think about all the folks scrambling from one week to the next for work so they can keep food on the table."

"Tell me about it. I got too many blessings, so I ain't complaining."

"Let's look at the bright side of our work. As bad as the economy still is, me and you got job security. So long as white folks dump their elders in the nursing home and colored people die, our services will always be in demand." He laughed, but it was brief and hollow. "I'm sorry. I shouldn't have said that. I hope that didn't sound uncaring. I was just making conversation."

"Hubert, I feel the same way you do," I chuckled.

"Good night, Jessie. I'll see you tomorrow. It was a long weekend, so I need some rest."

"What else did you do in Hartville other than pick up that embalming fluid and visit your friend?"

"Huh? Uh . . . on Saturday, I went to buy some new shirts and socks. And doing all that footwork from one store to the next wasn't no cakewalk, with the bunions and corns I got. But I needed a few new items. Maggie loved to shop, so she used to buy whatever I needed."

"I wouldn't mind adding shopping for you to my duties. I used to do it for Orville, and I enjoy shopping as much as Maggie did."

"I'll let you know the next time I need to buy something. Thanks for offering. I . . . I guess I'll get used to being a widower sooner or later."

"Yes, you will. I'm going to help you get used to it as much as I can," I assured him.

Poor Hubert. I felt so sorry for him. He had depended on

Maggie so much, now he was practically helpless. That was bad enough. But it must have been hell for a man like him not to be able to perform no more. I didn't care what he thought, I believed he would come out of this mess even more passionate than before. And I hoped to God that I was the one on the receiving end.

Chapter 24
Jessie

*T*HE ONLY REASON I SLEPT LIKE A BABY LAST NIGHT WAS BECAUSE I'd talked to Hubert before I went to bed. I couldn't wait to see him again. Even though I'd originally wanted to be with him because he'd be a good catch, now I was beginning to have real feelings for him. I got teary-eyed when I imagined what it would be like the first time he made love to me.

I was anxious to get my day going, so I got to work about fifteen minutes earlier than I was supposed to. It was always nice to get in early and gear up for whatever was in store. Especially since the people who supervised the place was so unpredictable. We colored workers didn't have no lockers to put our personal items in, like our white coworkers, so we had to store our things in the same closet where we kept the bedpans, spittoons, linen, and cleaning supplies. As hard as it was to believe, everybody used the same restroom at the end of the hall. That was only because the outhouse they'd had in the backyard for colored staff to use had been blown away in the last tornado we had, and the Westville Nursing Home hadn't got a new one.

There was one other nursing home in Lexington. I had applied for a job there the same time I'd applied at Westville almost eighteen years ago. Westville, which was a well-tended facility located on the outskirts of town, called me the next day. I never heard from the other place. I was glad they hadn't called me, because I'd heard that they was real mean to their colored workers. They couldn't enter the break room area if a white person was present, and they couldn't use the bathroom. They didn't have no outhouse. The colored workers had to relieve themselves in the woods behind the facility and wipe off with old newspapers, or corncobs they brought from home. I'd had some miserable jobs in my life, so I was glad to finally have one where I got treated more like a human being.

I'd been part of the Westville staff ever since and didn't have no desire to return to them other jobs I'd dealt with: dishwashing in dingy restaurants, cooking, cleaning, tending to unruly white kids, and doing their laundry.

We had twenty-eight patients, and every time one died, it didn't take no time for another one to take their place.

Three hours after I got to work, two patients died minutes apart. We already had two new ones scheduled to check in before the end of the day.

"White folks sure don't want to be bothered taking care of their elderly relatives," my coworker Quinette Pickett said to me. "If they ain't putting them away like old clothes, they got us coming to their houses to tend to them." She sniffed and raked her fingers through her bone-straight brown hair and then rubbed her thin nose. Quinette was a year older than me; she was so light-skinned, she could almost pass for white. She was one of the only two other colored women on the day shift.

We was sitting on the back steps of the building, which was where we took our breaks. The only time colored folks was allowed to be in the break room was to clean it. And, boy, did we do a lot of cleaning each day. My hands would be so dry when I got home, I had to coat them with calamine lotion. And when I ran out of that, I coated them with bacon grease.

"If the nursing homes allowed us to shut away our elderly loved one, I'm sure we all would," I said, giving Quinette a hopeless look.

"That's for sure. I love my mama to death, but moving her in with me and my husband and kids last year when my daddy died, it done took a toll on me. Thank God my sister helps sometimes. But she and her husband just took in both of his sickly parents, so she got enough on her plate. Girl, I wish I had it easy like you."

I laughed. "'Easy'? My life ain't *easy*. I'm struggling to pay bills and I don't like living by myself. Every time I hear a little noise at night, I almost jump out of my skin. I'm concerned about my safety these days, with that maniac still running around killing colored women."

"I know just how you feel," Quinette responded in a shaky tone. "You should get a big dog or a gun."

"Dogs make me sneeze and I'm scared of guns."

"Then you better find another husband, and quick."

"I will," I said with confidence.

The only other colored woman who worked on our shift was a widow in her late forties. Glennola Mays was so sweet, everybody loved her to death. She was so pretty, all the men patients fawned over her. So did the tall, muscle-bound man who did the maintenance work on the day shift. His name was Conway Dawson, and he was one of the best looking colored men I ever seen. He had a strong jawline, juicy-looking lips, and bright hazel eyes. His skin was so smooth and flawless, it looked like he'd been dipped in a vat of honey. He was only twenty-nine, but that didn't stop him from flirting with all three of us older women every chance he got.

"Hello, ladies," Conway greeted as he approached us from around the side of the building with a whisk broom in his hand. He looked at us like we was something to be served on a platter. "Y'all mind if I join you?"

"Suit yourself. I have to get back to Mrs. Garra," Quinette said, wobbling up off the steps. "If you want a ride home today, Jessie, let me know before three."

"Okay," I muttered. I cleared my throat as Conway plopped down next to me. He laid the whisk broom in his lap and then wiggled it from side to side for a few seconds, as if he wanted to draw attention to his crotch. I forced my eyes not to look below his chin. It seemed like every day, he looked a little more handsome than the day before.

Hubert was still a good-looking, honey-colored man, and had once had a real nice body. He still had a full head of hair, but half of it was gray now. Father Time and too many plates of pig ears and his other favorite dishes had caught up with him.

"Jessie, you can get a ride with me anytime. I love being in the company of pretty women," Conway said with a wink.

"I don't mind taking the bus," I told him. I stood up and held my breath. There was something about this man that made me nervous. He was too handsome for his own good and he knew it. But he wasn't the kind of man I could have a real relationship with. I couldn't put up with all the attention he gave other women. At least when I was with Hubert, he only had eyes for me.

"Well, what about going out for a drink one evening after work?"

I shook my head. "I don't think my boyfriend would like that." I couldn't believe I'd let them words slip out of my mouth. Me and Hubert was going out together, but him being my boyfriend was a whole different story. I would never tell anybody that all he'd done so far was kiss me on my jaw.

Chapter 25
Jessie

HUBERT DIDN'T MENTION MAGGIE'S BIRTHDAY OR CLAUDE'S when they came up in the first part of January. And I made sure I didn't mention them either. It was the same thing when his wedding anniversary rolled around a week after Maggie's birthday.

I couldn't wait for January to be over, it was such a painful time for Hubert. I don't know what he would have done if I hadn't been available to help him keep his mind off his wife and son. Being with him helped keep me from thinking about them myself, so it was a winning situation for us both.

We liked to eat out, but there was only a few nice places in Lexington where colored folks could go that was owned by colored folks.

We'd been back twice to that seafood place where we'd run into Blondeen that Friday before New Year's. I was glad we hadn't seen her since then, but living in a small country town, a person was bound on a regular basis to run into folks they didn't want to see.

The last Thursday in January, I stopped at the fish market on my way home from work to pick up some catfish to cook for Hubert's supper. While I was still talking to the man behind the counter, I seen Blondeen from the corner of my eye. I had already paid for my order so I bolted, but not quick enough. As soon as she spotted me scurrying toward the door, she headed in my direction. I was surprised she didn't say nothing. But the expression on her face spoke for her. She glared at me like she wanted to bite my nose off. I practically ran all the way back to my street.

I didn't even stop at my house; I went straight to Hubert's. He was standing on his front porch talking to Yolinda.

"Girl, why you huffing and puffing so hard?" she asked as soon as I headed up the porch steps. "You running from somebody?"

"Something like that. You know that big black dog that lives in the house by the bus stop? He was outside in the yard. When he started growling and inching toward me, I took off running," I explained.

It was easier to lie than tell the truth. They knew that Blondeen didn't care for me, so I didn't need to remind them.

I smiled at Hubert. "I thought I'd go by the fish market and pick up some catfish to cook for supper this evening," I told him as I held up the bag that contained two hefty catfish that still had their heads and tails. Cleaning them suckers was a nasty chore, but I didn't mind doing it for Hubert.

"I better get back home before them young'ns burn down the house," Yolinda piped in as she gave me a knowing look. She excused herself and darted back across the street to her house, and me and Hubert went inside.

"Jessie, did I tell you I have to go to Hartville again tomorrow evening? I won't be back home until sometime Sunday."

My heart sunk as I followed Hubert into the kitchen. "Oh? Why do you have to go over there again so soon? Don't tell me you need to go get more embalming fluid already?" I asked as I dumped the fish into the sink.

Hubert was standing next to me. Even with the fishy stench in front of us, I could still smell the lavender-scented hair pomade he used. It always turned me on. I was glad I wasn't the kind of pushy woman who would try to seduce Hubert. If I had been, I would not have been responsible for my actions, and there was no telling what I would have done, or tried to do, to him by now.

"Ain't but four people died since the last time you went to go buy some. You done ran out already?"

"Oh no. I got enough to last for a while. Um . . . you remember that elderly midget woman who used to play the piano at Daddy's church?"

I wiped my hands on a towel and sat down at the table. Hubert dropped down into the seat facing me. "Yeah, I remember her. She had the fluffiest white hair and the prettiest gray eyes. I thought she was dead."

"Almost. She been sickly ever since she moved to Hartville to be closer to her kids. She told me years ago that she wanted me to handle her funeral and that she'd sit down with me to sort out all the details before she got too feeble to do it."

"What about her family? Didn't one of her sons move in with her when he got discharged from the army?"

"*Pffftt!*" Hubert rolled his eyes and waved his hand. "Yeah. But that sucker's been drunk for the past five years. She got a bunch of kids and grandkids and ain't nary one got a lick of sense. They done already started fussing over who is going to get what out of her house. If it was left up to them, they'd have her put away in a cardboard box. She wants to be laid to rest in style, so she plans to spend every dime she saved up from scrubbing floors and commodes for sixty years."

"It's a shame that lady can't count on her family to do right by her. Is it going to take the whole weekend for you and her to make her final arrangements?"

"Well, she wants me to come Friday evening so I can take her out to supper at her favorite restaurant one more time. She's real slow, so I suspect it'll take most of Saturday for her to decide on everything she wants me to do for her home-going. I even have to help her pick out her burial dress."

Hubert was such a considerate man. That was one of the many things Maggie used to brag about. "I declare, that's a lot for a woman to be asking a undertaker to do. Why don't I go with you? I can help pick out her dress."

He shook his head. "If you don't mind, I'd like for you to stay here at my house. A man is coming on Saturday to take a look-see at the commode to try and figure out why it backs up so often. He couldn't tell me what time he's coming, so somebody needs to be here all day. I would have asked Mama to come over, but she got a habit of rummaging through my things when I ain't here. I suspect she's coming more often now and doing more snooping. Some of the things in my drawers wasn't the way I left them. And one time, I could tell she'd laid down in my bed."

"That's because she loves you and wants to make sure everything is all right on your end."

"She ain't got to sneak into my house for that."

"Well, so long as she don't break nothing, you shouldn't worry about it." I cleared my throat. "Okay, I'll come and stay until the man comes to fix the commode. If the bus is running late when I get off work on Friday, I might not get here until six or later."

"I was planning to head to Hartville around four p.m." Hubert caressed his chin and gave me a thoughtful look. "I don't never lock my doors, so you can let yourself in whenever you do get here and just make yourself at home."

"O . . . kay," I muttered. I wondered what he'd think if he knew I was already doing exactly that.

Chapter 26
Hubert

*T*HE MIDGET LADY WAS TOO TIRED TO GO OUT TO SUPPER WHEN I got to her house Friday evening. She led me to her parlor and described some of her health issues in great detail. I could have kissed the neighbor who dropped in halfway into the second hour.

"Thank you for listening, Hubert," she wheezed. "I'll tell you the rest tomorrow. Be sure you get here around noon so I'll have enough time."

I excused myself and bolted.

Leroy's used-to-be wife had called him up earlier in the week to let him know that the boys had colds and wouldn't be coming to visit him this weekend. So I made a beeline for his place.

He had closed up his shop early and was in his apartment, freshly bathed and spruced up, waiting for me. As soon as I got inside, he closed and locked the door. Even though his place was on the second floor, he never opened his curtains. But he did always lock his door when I was there. Southern folks had a habit of entering somebody's house without knocking if the door was unlocked. We couldn't take a chance on somebody he knew walking in and catching us in the act.

"I thawed out some pig tails in case you wanted to nibble on something later this evening," he told me after we'd kissed passionately for a full minute.

"I'd rather nibble on you for now." I grinned as we moved to the couch. He swooned when I took his hands in mine and kissed the tips of his fingers.

Each time I seen Leroy, my feelings for him got stronger. I had almost forgot how much pain I'd been in since losing my family.

"Hubert, I'm so pleased to see you ain't half as tense as you was our first night together. I know you still miss your wife and son, and you will for the rest of your life. But I want you to know that anytime I can make you feel better, I will."

"I appreciate hearing that. I don't like to bog you down with my misery, so I won't bring them up unless I have to."

"You can bring them up all you want. I don't care," Leroy assured me. "I know I can't take Maggie's place, or that sucker Daryl that dumped you when you needed him the most!"

Leroy was serious, but his face was scrunched up in a way that looked funny, so I laughed. I was glad he did too.

It was a wonderful visit. My spirits was about as high as they could go. You would have never believed that I'd experienced so much tragedy a little over two months ago. But every time I thought about Maggie and Claude too long, I felt sad. I thanked God that them moments didn't happen as often now and last as long as they used to. Surrounding myself with other folks who cared about me helped more than I'd thought it would.

I was feeling so good when I got home Sunday evening. I chuckled when I went in the kitchen. It looked like Mama had struck again. I'd left a cup on the table and it was in the sink now. There was a fresh dishrag on the table. A candy bar I had left on the counter was gone and the wrapper was in the trash can. I wondered if she'd been rifling through my bedroom drawers again like she'd done a few other times. Then it dawned on me that Jessie could have ate the candy bar and done some light housekeeping while she was waiting for the man to come fix the toilet. It didn't matter which one had done what. I didn't have nothing to hide. But then, something hit me that I had forgot about.

I still had some love letters Daryl had sent me. I trotted to the bedroom and squatted down on the floor and pulled a shoebox from under my bed, where I'd hid them letters. Daryl had sent me a bunch, but I'd only kept three. He didn't mean nothing to me no more, so I didn't see no reason to keep his letters. After the cold way he had dumped me, they didn't even have sentimental value neither. If Mama ever seen some of the mushy stuff he'd wrote, all hell would break loose and my life wouldn't be worth a plugged nickel. I tore the letters up and went out to my backyard and burned them. I didn't go back in the house until I scattered the ashes.

I was getting so attached to Leroy, sometimes he had a better effect on me than a tonic. Being away from him for a day was hard. I had just been with him a week ago, but it felt like a year. Thursday when I got home from work, I had a itching to give him a call. I wanted to know if I could visit him again for a couple of hours after I ate my supper. Otherwise, I couldn't see him again until next week because he'd have his kids with him this weekend.

He sounded real excited. "I'd love to see you tonight, Hubert. I just feel guilty about you being the one to spend money on gas to come see me. I wouldn't mind driving over to Lexington now and then. So long as we don't slip up and get too affectionate in public, I don't see why we need to be worried about your neighbors or somebody else getting the wrong idea about us."

My breath caught in my throat. "No, I don't want you to come over here, period. There is way too much traffic in and out of my house and I don't want none of them to even know about you. The same way you don't want your kids to know about me."

"I understand. Well, the least I can do is help you cover the gas."

"That would be okay, but you don't have to."

"Look, like I told you, a lot of them young bucks I used to mess around with took advantage of me by asking for money and free haircuts. The last thing I want to do is let somebody else foot bills for me."

"I don't see it that way and we don't need to even be talking about this. Besides, the last three or four times I came over, I ate food you'd paid for."

Leroy laughed. "We ain't got to be so petty. Let's drop it. What time can you be here?"

I glanced at the clock on my living-room wall. "It's twenty minutes after six. If I leave in the next fifteen minutes and traffic ain't too heavy, I should be there before seven thirty. Um . . . I think I should take a bath first, though, so it'll be a little later."

"Don't worry about taking no bath. You can do that here. I enjoy scrubbing your back, as well as every other part of you."

"Okay." I was getting so hot and heavy, I needed to get off the phone before I started sweating.

Jessie usually showed up around this time. I had to try and catch her to let her know I didn't have no appetite, so she didn't have to cook for me this evening. I immediately dialed her number.

I was glad she answered right away in a cheerful tone. She didn't sound so cheerful when I told her what I was calling for.

"You don't want me to cook today? Aw, shoot! I was looking forward to fixing you a casserole using a recipe I got from one of the ladies at work. All right. I'll come anyway so I can get the laundry done in case we go out to supper this weekend—"

I cut her off right away. "Don't worry about the washing. That can wait a few more days. I forgot to bring home some insurance papers from the funeral home the other day that I need to process. I'm going to go over there to take care of that. I'm sure Tyrone and Floyd misfiled them again, so there ain't no telling how long it'll take me to find them. I'll fill them out while I'm there."

"Ooh wee. You ain't scared to be there by yourself?"

I laughed. "Jessie, it's a little late for me to be getting scared to do my job. Did you want to come with me and keep me company? You can sit in the calling hours' room and read a magazine or dust off the caskets."

"Good God, no!" she yelled.

Jessie couldn't get off the telephone fast enough.

I made it to Leroy's place in almost half the time it usually took and enjoyed one of the most passionate nights I ever experienced. If he dumped me tomorrow, I would not hold a grudge against him. Instead, I would be forever grateful to him for enhancing my life. I planned to spend the rest of my days with Leroy—if he let me.

Chapter 27

Jessie

I PLANNED TO SPEND THE REST OF MY DAYS WITH HUBERT—IF HE LET me. Even if we never got married, I'd be there for him, no matter what. I knew several couples who had been together for thirty or forty years and never got married. I wasn't going to worry about no legal issues, like what I'd get if he up and dropped dead or something. I refused to let my mind go in that direction. I didn't think that was something I had to worry about anyway. A righteous man like Hubert would never leave a woman high and dry.

I got a thrill out of going into his house when he was gone. Stretching out in his bed was like wallowing on a cloud, it was just that comfortable. And I enjoyed eating the snacks he left laying around, like that piece of hard candy I'd found on his kitchen counter during one of my visits.

I smiled to myself every time I thought about the wonderful life I was going to have with Hubert. What amazed me was how I had started out just being very fond of him, the same way I felt about my brother and other male relatives. Before Orville turned from a lovable oaf into a teeth-gnashing beast, and started treating me like he'd bought me by the pound, I'd loved him. At the time, he was the only man I'd ever loved with so much passion. That was the way I felt about Hubert now. He was such a luscious and sanctified man, I couldn't see myself giving my love to nobody else. Fate had been laying the groundwork for years for us to end up together when the time was right. Having him would make up for the raw deal I'd got with Orville.

A few other men had tried to get close to me since Orville died, but I made it clear to them right off the bat that I was not interested. That didn't make no difference with Conway at work. Every day, he either winked at me or said something he didn't have no business saying—especially after Glennola told me he had moved in with his girlfriend.

"Ain't one woman enough for you?" I teased when he made another pass at me on Friday. I was sitting on the ground under one of the trees behind the home, knitting a cap for one of Minnie's grandsons.

Conway squatted down next to me. "She would be if she was a real woman like you," he replied with a hungry look in his eyes as they roamed all over my body.

My dull gray uniform was so plain and loose-fitting, I could have been nine months pregnant and nobody would have noticed it. I didn't wear much makeup to work or do nothing fancy with my hair, so I couldn't understand why he found me so appealing.

"If she is so bad, how come you stay with her?"

For the first time, I seen a sad look on Conway's face. "I ain't got nowhere else to go, and I don't make enough here to eat good and pay rent on a place by myself. I *need* her."

I was not surprised to hear that he was the kind of man who used women. "Don't you think that's unfair to her? I'm sure she thinks you care about her."

"I can't help the way I feel. She is the one who wouldn't stop coming at me until I broke down and got with her. Besides, I give her all the attention she deserves from me. But . . . well . . . at the end of the day, she ain't the one for me."

I gave Conway a disgusted look. "I would hate to find out a man was staying with me just so he could get a scot-free ride. You ought to be ashamed of yourself," I scolded.

Conway snickered. And then he let loose with a long-winded

rant that made my head spin. "Where you been, girl? People do what I'm doing all the time! And I ain't getting no scot-free ride. She makes me help with the bills and all. But she's one of the meanest, most controlling women I ever met. Even my mama didn't make me do as much dusting, sweeping, and mopping as this fishwife makes me do. Shoot! Slavery ended a long time ago, but she don't care. Every time I look up, she is accusing me of cheating on her. She even goes through my pockets and opens my mail. Sometimes she follows me when I leave the house without her. I done seen her peeping at me from behind trees, ducking down between parked cars, and all kinds of other crazy shit! No matter what I do or say, I can't please her.

"Everybody keeps telling me to leave that battle-ax because she's as mean as a rattlesnake. But ain't none of them offering me a place to stay. I'm trying to save money so I can get my car in shape enough to drive up to New York, where my folks is at. They done all flew the coop and I'm the only Dawson still living in Lexington," he finished.

I shook my head and gave Conway a sympathetic look. "I'll pray for you. But the main thing you need to concentrate on is getting away from that woman before she hurts you."

"Oh, she threatens me all the time."

"I'll pray for her too. I'm sure she ain't as bad as you make her sound. Even the meanest people got some good in them."

"If you knew her like I do, you wouldn't say that." Conway snorted. "I declare, this man of yours must be right special to you if you won't even give me a chance."

"He is. It's just a matter of time before we get married." I couldn't believe I'd said something that was still such a long shot.

Conway snickered again and then he leaned back and gave me a thoughtful look. "Shoot. It's just a matter of time before I get married myself."

My eyes widened and my mouth dropped open. "You ain't making no sense at all. I thought your girlfriend was so mean," I teased. "Why would you marry somebody you ain't happy with?"

"I ain't said nothing about marrying *her*. Shoot. With her

mean streak—which is getting worser by the day—she wouldn't make a good wife for nobody, especially me. But until I find the right woman, I'll keep me a spare like you no matter who I'm with. I do it all the time."

"Humph. I don't do it all the time. What's the point of being in love with a man, or a woman, if you going to mess around with somebody else at the same time?"

"I can't argue with you about that." Conway sighed and gave me another thoughtful look. "Your man is lucky. He'd be a god-damn fool if he lets you get away."

Them comments made me smile for the rest of the day.

Chapter 28

Hubert

I WAS GOING TO TURN FORTY-THREE ON FEBRUARY 17, WHICH WAS about two weeks away. I had never cared much about celebrating birthdays, at least not for myself.

Maggie and Claude had made a big deal out of theirs every year, so it had always been a big event in our family. The only thing I was glad about was that their birthdays was only a few days apart, so we always celebrated both on the same day. We had done that every year until they died. My mama would bake a cake, folks from church would show up with all kinds of snacks, and at least two or three neighbors brought some champagne. Mama and Daddy rarely touched alcohol, but me and Maggie would always have at least one glass. When Claude turned twenty-one last year, we allowed him to have a glass too.

I didn't want to do nothing for my birthday this year. I told everybody not to even give me no presents. But Jessie insisted on baking a cake and inviting Mama and Daddy to eat supper with us at my house.

The next two weeks zoomed by.

I didn't feel a year older when I woke up this morning before dawn. I was anxious to get the day over with so I could move on to other things, especially after what I'd been through last night. A teenage girl had fell in Carson Lake and drowned yesterday.

Immediately after, I got the call from her hysterical mama a hour after they'd pulled her out of the water. I notified one of my assistants, Tyrone McElroy, to bring the hearse so we could go collect the body.

I always did most of the embalming and paperwork myself. But I usually had Tyrone spruce up the folks with a thorough scrubbing and makeup so it wouldn't be so hard for the family and other mourners to look at them. Mama always did the women's hair. I'd also put Tyrone in charge of the burials. And if the deceased was somebody I had been close to, I took it upon myself to help place the heavy caskets over the graves on straps and slings and ease them down into their final resting place.

When I'd inherited the business from my uncle shortly after me and Maggie got married, Tyrone came with it and had been with me ever since. When another guy who'd also worked for me for years recently quit and moved up north last month, I immediately hired Tyrone's cousin Floyd McElroy. We'd all attended high school together. He was as dependable as Tyrone and they had families to support, so I was glad I could help them out. I had promised them that when and if I decided to give up undertaking, I'd sell the business to them real cheap.

I made sure at least one of my workers was at my funeral home every day, except Sunday, from nine in the morning until six p.m. I wanted to have somebody on the premises to answer the phone in case a family member of a deceased person couldn't reach me at home. On top of that, there was always a lot of paperwork to be processed for payments, insurance issues, and whatnot. Tyrone and Floyd helped with that too.

I kept the hearse parked by the side of the funeral home, so Tyrone and Floyd always had access to it. When I wasn't available, which was very rare, I sent them to collect the bodies. And after each funeral, I had them transport the dearly departed to the colored cemetery. They was also the only two colored grave diggers in Lexington, so when they wasn't digging graves for me, they did that chore for the Fuller Brothers.

After I'd shaved and put on a pot of coffee this morning, my telephone rang. It was Jessie. "Happy birthday, Hubert," she chirped.

I was so glad she didn't sing "Happy Birthday" to me the way she used to before Jessie passed. That and "Jingle Bells" was the two most irritating and overused songs I could think of.

"Thank you," I mumbled. I was hoping she didn't notice how humdrum I sounded. This day meant more to her than it did me and I didn't want to spoil her glee.

"You sure don't sound like a man should sound on his birthday."

"I just feel so bad about that young girl drowning," I said, my voice cracking.

"I can understand that. She was a sweet child. Her whole family belongs to your daddy's church. I went to school with her mama, so I'd better get over to her house right away so I can hug her."

"Don't do that today. The family is so upset, I don't think they want no company right now."

"When is the funeral?"

"The girl's whole family is so distraught, they don't want to have one. All they want is a graveside deal with only the immediate family present and Daddy to officiate. This is so hard on that poor family. They don't want no mourners to come over and sit with them, or bring food after the funeral."

"Them poor folks. That girl was their only child. They tried for eight years before they had her. Every time I think about that, I feel like crying."

"I do too. But Daddy tells his congregation all the time, we all got to go sometime. I'm so thankful the Lord has allowed me to live as long as I have."

"I feel the same way, Hubert."

Jessie drew in a loud breath before she continued. "You sure you don't want to change your mind about inviting some more folks to the party this evening?"

She gasped when I abruptly said, "I ain't going to change my mind. I told you, I don't like nobody making a fuss over me."

"I just thought you'd like to have Tyrone and Floyd and their wives join us. And I know Yolinda would love to come."

"If we invite Yolinda, everybody in her house will want to come. The same goes for Tyrone and Floyd."

"Okay, then. Your mama and daddy will be picking me up around seven, and I'll bring over the cake I'm going to bake and some champagne. I'll see you then."

Right after I got off the phone with Jessie, I called up Leroy.

"'Happy birthday to you, happy birthday to you,'" he sang in a low tone.

I didn't mind him singing that annoying song. I held my breath until he finished.

"Leroy, I wish you could be here tonight."

"I wish I could too. If my boys wasn't here, I'd ask you to come over later so we could celebrate in style," he whispered.

"I'll come over at least one night next week and then on the weekend," I assured him.

"Is there anything special you want to do next week?"

"Just being with you is special."

After I hung up, I stared at the telephone for a few moments with some serious thoughts going through my head. They was all about Leroy. I never thought I'd find a man who'd make me stop wishing I'd been born normal. When I was a confused little boy, and couldn't figure out why I felt the way I did about other boys, I prayed for God to either change me or make me appreciate what I was and find some way to be happy with my condition.

After all these years, I knew I was never going to be changed. But I was no longer confused, and I was happy with the way I was. Happier than I'd ever been in my life. If Maggie hadn't helped me carry out my hoax as long as she did, there was no telling what my life would be like now. If somebody hadn't killed me, I'd probably be rotting away in prison.

Chapter 29
Hubert

GETTING OLDER DIDN'T BOTHER ME. OTHER THAN HIGH BLOOD pressure and some mild arthritis, my body was in good shape. I didn't have no more wrinkles or gray hair than I'd had the year before, so as far as I was concerned, I still looked the same. I hoped I would for as many more years as possible.

Jessie kept my house so clean, you could eat off the floors, so there wasn't anything for me to do to get it ready for tonight. Since I had time on my hands, I decided to pay my mechanic a visit. I had him change the oil in my car and then I swung by my parents' house, but they wasn't home.

Even though their minds was still sharp, and they didn't have no disabilities, I didn't want to get too lax as far as their well-being was concerned. I knew that someday they wouldn't be able to function, and I'd have to assist them. I also knew that if me and Jessie was still close then, she'd be more than happy to help me take care of them. That's the kind of woman she was.

I decided to swing by the funeral home to make sure everything was under control. When I shuffled into the room where we had laid out the young girl's body, Tyrone was standing there, gazing at her. When I coughed to get his attention, he whirled around and did a double take.

"W-what you doing here? I didn't expect to see you today," he grunted.

"Oh, I was at loose ends," I explained as I glanced at the corpse. I could barely stand to look at somebody so young and pretty and lifeless without tearing up. Especially since I knew firsthand the kind of pain the family was going through.

"I declare, this is the last place you should want to be on your *birthday*," Tyrone said with a grimace. "You know me and Floyd can take care of business on our own when you ain't here." Tyrone was a year younger than me. But every hair on his head was gray and he had so many wrinkles on his mulish face, I couldn't tell where one ended and another one started. "Floyd must be at loose ends too. He just called and told me he's on his way over here. But as you can see, I got everything under control. We dug the grave at the crack of dawn this morning. She'll be right next to her grandmamma." Tyrone waved his hand toward the corpse.

"That's good. I'm going to go through the paperwork to make sure everything is in order."

After I made sure we had all the necessary information, I went outside to check on the hearse. As usual, it was shining like new money, thanks to Tyrone and Floyd. The only thing they slacked up on was keeping the gas tank full. I got in and drove to the first filling station I seen and gassed up. I didn't like driving it down the street unless we had a funeral procession going on, because folks got spooked when they seen a hearse go by. I returned it to the funeral home and got back in my car.

On my way back home, I paid a brief visit to a member of Daddy's church who was on his deathbed. He liked to chew tobacco, so I took him a few plugs. I liked to stay in good with potential customers. So, when it was their time to go, they usually chose me over them greedy Fuller Brothers.

When I got back home, I took a long, hot bath and rearranged a few things in the kitchen before I stretched out on the couch to take a nap. I didn't wake up until Jessie and my parents arrived at half past seven p.m.

"Hubert, you look like you done lost weight," Mama commented as she set the big cake, which Jessie had baked, on the kitchen table. Then she turned to Jessie. "Maggie kept him plumped up. Every time she cooked a pot of gumbo, he ate two or three bowls. That was the last meal she cooked before . . . well . . . We don't need to go there." Mama paused to catch her breath before she continued. "I just want you to make sure my baby starts eating more when you come over here to cook."

"Hush up, woman," Daddy scolded as he put down the snacks they had brought and then helped Mama remove her coat. "If you don't think your 'baby' is a man by now, he never will be. Happy birthday, son. I hope you'll have forty-three more before the Lord calls you home." He patted me on the back and gave me a one-armed hug.

"I hope he lives even longer," Jessie said.

It was pretty chilly outside, so everybody had on a coat. Before I could collect them all and go lay them on my bed, Jessie beat me to it. When she got out of earshot, Mama leaned close to me and whispered, "You don't know how lucky you are to have Jessie looking out for you."

"Sure enough," Daddy added.

Before I could say anything on that subject, Jessie strolled back into the kitchen, clapping her hands and grinning from ear to ear. "All right, let's get this party started."

After a fifteen-minute prayer session, we munched on the deviled eggs, hush puppies, and ham sandwiches that Mama had prepared, and then cut the cake. And, for the first time since Daddy's niece in Birmingham got married last year, him and Mama each drunk a glass of champagne. I had one too. Jessie was on her second, but that didn't bother me. But when she let out a mighty belch, Mama and Daddy gave her sideways glances, but they didn't say nothing.

My parents usually went to bed every night almost right after it got dark. This night was no different. Mama wrapped up some of what was left of the cake and the snacks and they took off, huffing and puffing and complaining about how much they had eaten.

"You don't have to give me a ride home, Hubert. I can walk," Jessie said as we sat down at the kitchen table. "I told Yolinda I'd bring her a slice of cake on my way home. You know how long-winded she is, so God knows how long she'll hold me hostage."

Jessie laughed. "If she don't get a dose of gossip every day, she'll be as cranky as a teething baby."

"After all you did to make this day special, I don't mind taking you home. That way, you won't have to put up with Yolinda tonight. Why don't you wrap up a slice of cake and I'll take it to her now? When I get back, I'll drive you home. It's too late for a woman to be out walking by herself at night, with that killer still on the loose."

"Okay," Jessie said, already reaching for the cake knife.

When I got back from delivering the cake, Jessie was sitting on the couch, drinking her third glass of the champagne. It had been quite a while since I'd seen her guzzle up more than two glasses in the same day, which was at me and Maggie's last anniversary party. I gasped and reared my head back.

"Ain't you had enough?" I was shocked to see that she had poured more into another glass and set it on the coffee table.

"Oh, it'll help me sleep better when I get home. Um . . . you didn't have but one glass, so why don't you help me finish the bottle. I already poured one for you." She giggled and tapped the side of the other glass.

I drew in a sharp breath and gazed at her like she was speaking Gaelic. "You kidding?"

"No, I ain't kidding. Hubert, you need to loosen up more. Come on. Don't make me drink alone. If we don't finish what's left, it'll get so flat, it'll be weaker than tap water."

I laughed, but I glared at the bottle like it was a time bomb. "There is more left in that bottle than I'd drink in a whole year."

"Aw, come on. Do it this one time for me. Just one more glass. I don't want to pour it back into the bottle, and I can't drink no more after I finish the one I got now."

"Oh, all right." I flopped down onto the couch and picked up the glass. I figured the sooner I finished it, the better. I took a long pull until my glass was empty.

That was the last thing I remembered until I woke up in bed Sunday morning with Jessie in my arms.

"WHAT THE HELL IS THIS?!" I roared.

Chapter 30

Jessie

I HAD ALREADY BEEN AWAKE FOR HOURS BEFORE I HEARD HUBERT'S loud voice on Sunday morning. But I rubbed my eyes and tried to look as groggy as possible. I thought he was going to have a heart attack when he lifted the covers and seen that we was both naked. He looked like he'd seen a ghost—his own. His eyes was as big as walnuts and his lips was quivering so hard, his teeth was click-clacking against each other.

"W-what's the matter?" I asked with a hiccup. There was such a nasty taste in my mouth and I had a slight hangover.

"Jessie, we got a mess on our hands!"

"W-what's going on?" I touched my bosom and whimpered. I had to act as alarmed as I could. And from the horrified expression on Hubert's face, my acting skills was pretty good. "Hubert, w-what did you do to me?"

"I don't know!"

The poor thing. He was so frantic he slid off the bed and hit the floor so hard, the lamp on his nightstand rattled. He was back on his feet before I could say another word. He snatched a pillow off the bed and covered his private parts, and that didn't make no sense. I'd already seen the nice package Maggie used to brag about.

"I guess we had way too much to drink," I mumbled as I swung my legs to the side of the bed. Hubert still had his socks on, but I was completely naked.

He looked around the room and moved a few steps away from the bed, where his clothes and shoes laid in a pile on the floor. Mine was on the floor next to the side I was on. After he'd passed out on the couch last night, it had took me about five minutes to drag him by his feet to the bedroom. It took another ten to hoist him up onto the bed and take his clothes off. He was out pretty good, because the whole time, he didn't make a sound or move a muscle.

"H-how did you end up in my bed, Jessie?" He leaned down and snatched up his clothes and started putting them on.

"Me? I ain't sure. All I can remember is that after we finished our drinks, you put your arm around me and hauled off and kissed me. Not on the jaw like you did that other time, but on the lips. Then you pulled me up into your lap and started rubbing up and down my rump. That's the last thing I can recall."

"I . . . you . . . Did something else happen?"

"If you mean sex, it must have. I'm a little sore down there." I winced as I gently massaged my crotch.

"My Lord in heaven!" he boomed. He zipped up his pants and paced back and forth for a few seconds before he stopped and looked at me with such a extremely scared expression on his face, I got scared. "Do you mean to tell me, I got so drunk I took advantage of you? I r-raped you?"

"Well, I was just as drunk as you was, maybe even more so. I don't know if you can call it rape. Unless you did it while I was too out of it to realize what you was up to and couldn't stop you . . ."

"Look-a-here, Jessie. If I did something to your body without your knowledge or permission, rape is what it was!"

"Hmmm. Now that's debatable, so stop beating yourself up." I sat up straighter and pulled the sheet up to my neck. "If I'd had my wits about me, our first time wouldn't have happened this way."

"Our *first* time? Lord, have mercy on my soul!"

Hubert dropped down onto the bed with a groan. Then he put his arm around my shoulder, but he snatched it away so fast, you would have thought I'd scorched him.

"Listen . . ." He paused and looked around the room again. His hands was trembling, and the muscles on one side of his face was twitching. "I'm a God-fearing man. I ain't never broke the law."

"I ain't never broke the law neither. And I'm just as God-fearing as you. But we both know that even women in the Bible enticed men. For all we know, I could have been so drunk, I could have led you on." I was trying to sound as cool and calm as possible. The last thing I wanted to do was behave like a hysterical victim. Especially when the real "victim" was Hubert.

"But you don't have to keep trying to convince me that you didn't mean to do what you done." I sucked in a deep breath and touched Hubert's arm. It and the rest of his body was shivering like he'd just climbed out of a icebox. "It's a shame we had to find out this way that you done finally got over your problem."

Hubert's face froze with a confused expression on it. "What problem?"

I gazed at him and blinked. "Hubert, you ain't been able to perform since Maggie died, remember? I always knew you'd get over it sooner or later."

He snorted, mumbled some gibberish, and rubbed his head. "Um, I . . . I promise you, this ain't *never* going to happen again."

"Hubert, it ain't the end of the world, and I hope it ain't the end of our relationship."

He narrowed his eyes and gave me such a cold stare, I almost started shivering myself. "Huh? What do you mean by that?"

"I'm just as guilty as you, because if I hadn't goaded you to drink that second glass of champagne, nothing like this would have happened. I'm so ashamed of myself, I could ball up and die! I'll get in my clothes and get up out of here. I'm as sorry as I can be," I choked out as I eased out of bed. I figured it was time for me to show more emotion, so I started crying.

Hubert reached out his hands toward me, but he didn't get off the bed. "Aw, come on now, Jessie, stop that crying. There ain't no reason for you to feel that bad. You didn't do nothing wrong. I'm the culprit and I take full responsibility. I . . . we . . . Let's keep this between us. If the wrong person ever finds out what happened last night and blabs, I could go to prison."

I stopped crying, but now tears was flooding his eyes. "You ain't got to worry about me telling nobody about this. And you ain't got to worry about me coming around no more, so this will never happen again," I whimpered. I sniffled and cleared my throat. "I really appreciate you letting me cook and clean for you, but I'm sure you won't have no trouble finding somebody else to take over. Sukey and Wilma, Blondeen's best friends, told me they was looking for work. I'll tell them to give you a call." I blinked to hold back more tears that was threatening to flow, but a couple oozed out anyway.

"I told you to stop crying! I'm the one that ought to be breaking down." He tumbled off the bed, rushed over to me, and wrapped his arms around my waist. "And I don't want nothing to do with Sukey or Wilma, or nobody else close to Blondeen. Do you hear me?"

"Uh-huh." Things was going just the way I'd hoped they would.

"We made a mistake and we learned from it. I still want you to come to the house and cook and clean for me, and we can still play checkers and go out together." Hubert shook his head and suddenly there was a hangdog expression on his face. "I . . . I am so sorry, Jessie. This is the last thing I ever expected to happen. Me raping a woman? I don't know how I was even able to perform, but I *know* nature ain't cured me. I feel as limp down there now as I been feeling since Maggie died. What happened last night was nothing more than a fluke of nature. And a onetime fluke, at that."

My heart dropped. Them was the last words I wanted to hear. But I still wasn't going to give up on getting some of that good loving Maggie got.

Chapter 31
Jessie

I GOT DRESSED AS FAST AS I COULD. I GRABBED MY COAT OFF THE dresser, where I had tossed it last night, and put it on. I had to lean against the dresser to keep from falling as I slid my feet into the shoes I'd bought especially for Hubert's birthday celebration.

"You got your shoes on the wrong feet," Hubert told me in a raspy tone. He was sitting on the side of the bed, looking like a condemned man. He had been acting so distressed since he woke up, I was surprised he wasn't running around the room, weeping and wailing.

"That's all right. I can run faster with them on that way," I muttered as I buttoned my coat.

"Run? Jessie, you ain't got to be running from nothing, especially me. You can even stay longer if you want to, in case you want to discuss what happened some more."

I shook my head. "I don't know what else to say about it. Something happened last night that shouldn't have happened. As soon as I get home, I going to read my Bible."

"You can stay here and read mine. I'll read along with you. We are in this mess together."

"That's all right. I need to get home anyway," I insisted.

He stood up and came back up to me, but he didn't get too close. "You are in such a frantic state, I'm scared you might go out there and walk in front of a bus. I'll drive you home."

"Thank you, but I'll walk," I insisted. "I need to be alone now." I didn't turn around to look at his face, but I could picture how far his jaw had dropped as I rushed out of the room.

When I got to the living room, I peeped out the front window. I didn't see none of our neighbors out and about, so I eased out the door and stumbled down the porch steps. Just as I made it to the sidewalk, Yolinda flew out of her front door like a burglar, sprinted across the street, and stopped in front of me. She was still in her housecoat and slippers and had a stocking cap on her head.

"Jessie, what you doing at Hubert's house this early in the morning?" she asked with her hands on her hips. She glanced toward his door, then back at me, with her eyes squinted. "I thought you just came over in the evenings."

"Yeah, that's when I usually come. But I came over last night to celebrate his birthday with him and his mama and daddy. It was pretty late when we got through. His mama and daddy had left, and Hubert didn't feel like driving me home, so he made a pallet for me on his living-room floor and I stayed all night."

"'A pallet'?" she tee-heed. "Why would a able-bodied, single woman spend the night with a able-bodied, single man and sleep on a pallet . . . in his *living room*? How come you didn't sleep in the bed in Claude's old room?"

"Well, Hubert don't let nobody go in that room out of respect for Claude's memory."

"I can understand that. But I don't see the logic in you sleeping on a pallet while Hubert is by hisself in a bed big enough for two people."

"He offered me the couch, but that's where Claude and Maggie both took their last breath. I can sit on the same couch, but I know I couldn't sleep on it."

"I'm skittish, so I know I couldn't neither." Yolinda shook her head real slow and gave me a grievous look. "So you and him didn't have no fun?"

"We had fun, but not the kind you mean. We ate snacks and cake, sung 'Happy Birthday' and a few hymns, and drunk some champagne. Hubert is too much of a gentleman to expect something like what you thinking from a woman he ain't married to."

"Girl, please! Every 'gentleman' is still a man, especially when alcohol is involved. And we both know what a man likes to do with a woman—unless he's crazy, disabled, or sissified."

I didn't want to make Yolinda mad, so the mean look I gave her was pretty tame. "Well, Hubert ain't nary one of them," I defended. "Like I said, we still had fun."

I guess to a normal person, what I was saying not only sounded funny, but downright ridiculous. She let out a sharp laugh. "You better get on your job before Blondeen or one of them other hussies get his attention back. You practically got Hubert in the palm of your hand and ain't doing nothing about it."

"What are you talking about?" I was getting annoyed and wanted to end this conversation and be on my way. But I knew Yolinda would follow me home, so I decided to stay and finish hearing her out.

"Ain't he courting you?"

"Well, he takes me out to supper and stuff. We go on drives and whatnot. And I do cooking and cleaning for him."

"Humph! And you the only woman beside his mama that he let help celebrate his birthday this year? If that ain't courting, I don't know what is."

"What are you trying to say, Yolinda?"

"I ain't 'trying' to say nothing, I'm saying it. If you don't take care of that man's natural needs, some other woman will. You might not think of yourself as his girlfriend, but I guarantee you, everybody else around here thinks it. Don't look a gift horse in the mouth, girl. Luscious men like Hubert are hot natured. He may be contented for now because of his religion and out of respect for Maggie, but that can only restrain him for so long. He'll eventually run out of patience. When that happens, all hell will break loose and he won't settle for you being just a *glorified housekeeper*."

Yolinda was talking so crazy, I was horrified. "In the first place, there is no reason for Hubert to run out of patience for something that ain't even on his mind. He wasn't raised like other men we know. Maggie told me they didn't do nothing until their wedding night. As far as I know, Hubert ain't been to bed with a woman like you mean since she died. His daddy and mama would have a fit if he started acting that worldly."

"'Worldly'?" Yolinda threw her head back and cackled long and loud. "Jessie, you get around almost as much as me, so you know who is doing what. Since when did religion ever stop healthy people from going at it in the bedroom? Maybe Reverend Wiggins and some of them geezers in his church ain't never fell from grace, but a handsome man like Hubert? Something must be wrong with him if he ain't—"

I held up my hand as fast as I could to cut Yolinda off. "Shame on you! There ain't nothing wrong with that man except he's still mourning the loss of his beloved wife!"

Yolinda dropped her head and got such a woeful expression on her face, I was sorry I'd hollered at her.

"You got a point there. I ought to be ashamed of myself for saying something so unholy. If there was something wrong with Hubert, you'd be the first to know. And I know that with your loose lips, you wouldn't be able to keep it to yourself."

"I'm glad you finally see things my way. Let's give Hubert a break and let him come around in his own time. Maggie's only been gone three months. He needs more time to finish grieving."

Yolinda puffed out her chest and suddenly shifted gears back to her badgering mode. "In the first place, if how long Maggie's been dead was a issue, how come he's been seen out on the town with you and other women before you? All that started when Maggie had only been gone less than one month."

"I know all that. But nobody knows what all is going on inside Hubert's head. Let's give him the benefit of the doubt. He ain't disrespecting Maggie by seeing me or any other woman so soon. He's just trying to get through life the best way he can. Everybody grieves in their own way."

Yolinda sighed and gently touched my shoulder. "All right. I need to keep that in mind." She glanced toward Hubert's front door again and drew in a loud breath. "Good God! Don't turn around. He's peeping out the window at us. I hope he don't think we saying nothing unflattering about him." Yolinda wrung her hands and gave me a sheepish grin. "Please don't tell him nothing I just said. I wouldn't want him to think I been gossiping."

"I won't say nothing about our conversation, and I don't think he'll ask what we was talking about anyway. You have a blessed day." I gave Yolinda a quick hug before I whirled around and started walking toward my house.

My feet couldn't move fast enough. I had to get home so I could compose myself and decide the best time to move on to the next phase of my plan.

I was glad that Yolinda already had a notion that Hubert was interested in me as a woman. Now she wouldn't be surprised when she heard he was going to marry me.

Chapter 32
Jessie

THERE WAS NO TELLING WHAT I WAS THINKING WHEN I CRUSHED up two of them tranquilizers I took from work and stirred them into Hubert's drink last night when he went to take that cake to Yolinda. If half a pill made me sleep like a log when I needed help getting to sleep, I should have known that one would have done the trick on him.

A scary thought suddenly popped into my mind: What if two of them pills had killed Hubert? There was even a label on the bottle warning folks not to take more than one without a doctor's approval. My goose would not have been just cooked, it would have been burned to a crisp. I pushed that thought out of my mind and promised myself that when and if I ever had to drug him again, I'd never use more than one pill. But I didn't see no reason in the future when I'd have to do it again. I'd accomplished my mission. Hubert thought he'd made love to me.

When I got to my house, I took a bath, made a pot of coffee, and stretched out on my couch. Before I could get comfortable, my telephone rang. I leaped up and sprinted to the kitchen and grabbed it on the third ring. The minute I heard Hubert's voice, my heart started beating like a drum.

"I was just calling to make sure you are all right," he said with his voice trembling.

I had to remind myself to speak in a meek tone. At least for the next few times I talked to Hubert. "Well, I'm still a little bit shaky, and other than being a little sore *down there*, I'm doing okay. Thank you for c-checking," I stammered. I coughed and let out a low moan for good measure.

"You sure? You don't sound too good."

"Honest to God, I'm fine. Nothing like this has ever happened to me before. Not even with Orville when he was on one of his lustful rampages." I paused to let my words sink in. I was pleased to hear him gasp. "How about you?"

"I just finished praying. I'm sure I'll be redeemed, so I feel much better now." He paused, and just as I was about to speak again, he blurted out, "That suspicious Yolinda just left my house. She claimed she wanted to borrow some butter, but I knew she was fishing. I was looking out the window when you left here and seen you talking to her. Did you tell her anything that could be misconstrued?"

"No, I didn't. I just told her about the celebration."

"Was she surprised you spent the night?"

"Not really. But she was surprised when I told her I'd slept on a pallet in your living room. I explained to her why I didn't sleep in Claude's old bed, or on the couch. Or with you."

"*With me?* Why would she think you'd sleep in the same bed with me?"

"I don't know. Now listen, when she comes back, don't let her badger you into letting nothing slip out about what you did to me last night . . ."

He gasped again and there was a long moment of silence before he said anything else. "You ain't got to come over and cook supper for me this evening. I'll eat some of that baloney in the icebox."

"All right, then. What about tomorrow and the rest of the week?"

"You can skip tomorrow too. I need to finish up things with that little girl that drowned so I can have everything ready for her burial next week. So I'll have to spend the next couple of days at the funeral home and with her family to sort out the details. I'll let you know when I want you to cook again."

"Okay, Hubert." He got silent again, so I didn't know what to think. I wondered what was really on his mind. If it was something I didn't want to hear, the sooner I heard it, the better. "What's on your mind, Hubert?"

"I been thinking. Maybe we shouldn't spend so much time together no more. Instead of you coming here every day, you can come only when I call for you. I'll let you know a day in advance each time. I'll still pay you every week, so you ain't going to be out nothing."

I wanted to howl. I was happy to hear that I'd still get paid, but hearing him say he wanted me to cut back on my visits made me bristle. I was not about to let him know that, though. If he thought for one second that I was mad at him, he'd eventually probably cut off my visits and even end our relationship! If it came to that, I didn't know how I'd be able to contain myself until enough time had passed so I could tell him I was pregnant with his baby.

A thought I hadn't even considered suddenly entered my mind. What if his "crime" eventually shamed him so bad that he moved to another town where he had relatives before I could tell him about the alleged baby? I'd be up a creek without a paddle. My head was swimming and my heart felt like it had dropped down to my stomach. Shoot!

I made sure my voice sounded as whiny as possible. "I ain't got nothing else to do with my time but go to work and visit folks and work for you."

"That's enough to have on your plate. I know how hectic it is taking care of them old folks at the home, and I know how vexing some of the folks you associate with can be. Now that includes me . . ."

"I could do my job in my sleep and I'm used to dealing with all the annoying folks I know, so them two things ain't no big deal. But I don't think of you as being vexing, Hubert. So please be up front and say what you really mean.

"If you don't want to see me no more, you ain't got to beat around the bush. I done almost forgot about what happened last night, so it ain't no issue with me and it shouldn't be one with you. I mean, after all, it was a mistake. If anybody should be blamed, it's Satan. It was that low-down, funky black devil who encouraged me to encourage you to drink more." I cut the comment short because I was beginning to sound ridiculous.

"It don't matter. I'll get over my shame." Hubert sounded so beat-down, I felt sorry for him. But it was too late for me to turn back now. I had to ride this horse until the race was over. "Like I just said, I'll let you know a day in advance when I want you to come cook or clean. We'll do it this way for a while and see how it goes. Another thing is, you can just cook something for me at your house and bring it over. That way, you won't be away from your home so much. I'll buy the food I want you to cook and drop it off at your house."

"What about your laundry and housecleaning?"

"I'll let you know when it needs to be took care of." Hubert exhaled and then he started talking in a low, controlled tone. It almost sounded like he was reading a speech he had wrote. "Bless my soul, I need to go to church today. I could use all the spiritual nourishment I can get after what I done to you. I feel like hell mentally, and even worse physically."

"I got some pain pills if you want some."

"No, I don't like taking no kind of pills. But I can tell you one thing is for sure, I will never get that carried away again with no alcohol. My head ain't never felt this bad, and I'm so tired, I can barely keep my eyes open. As soon as I get back from church, I'm going to drink a pot of coffee and get back in the bed. If I don't call you later today, I'll call you tomorrow or later in the week."

"Okay, Hubert. God bless you."

When I hung up, I was smiling from ear to ear as I pranced over to the calendar on the wall above the counter. I needed to check the dates so I could determine the best time to tell him he was fixing to become a daddy. My birthday was April 1. Telling him on that day would be a birthday present to myself. And it being April Fools' Day was so fitting.

I was so hyped up when I went to bed, I was still awake at midnight. I didn't want to look like a hag at work tomorrow, so I got back up and broke another one of them tranquilizers in two so I could get some sleep.

Chapter 33
Hubert

*I*T WAS BAD ENOUGH THAT I WAS ONE OF THE LOWEST FORMS OF humanity, according to the Bible. "Maggie, you must be rolling over in your grave," I said out loud as I gazed in the bathroom mirror this morning. Now there was a sissy and a rapist looking back at me.

When Jessie left my house this morning, I gathered my underwear and the rest of the clothes I'd wore the night before and dumped everything in my garbage can. The pants was one of my favorite pair, and I'd only wore the shirt and tie once, but I would never wear them glad rags no more. They was part of my crime so I knew I'd never feel comfortable in them again.

The next thing I had to do was wash off as much of my shame as I could. I took a bath in water as hot as I could stand without scalding myself. I scrubbed between my thighs long and hard, so by the time I stopped, my private parts was numb.

I had planned to get my vile tail back to church today, but I changed my mind at the last minute. I felt too soiled, unworthy, and corrupted to be in a hallowed setting so soon after my crime.

I didn't want to mope around the house all day neither. I called Leroy a few minutes before ten a.m. and a young boy answered his phone. I hung up without saying nothing. I tried again at four p.m. and nobody answered. Just as I was about to get ready for bed, Leroy called me.

"Did you call here earlier today?" he asked.

I had promised Leroy from the get-go that I would never lie to him and I wasn't about to start now. "Yes, I called. I got spooked when I heard your boy's voice, so I hung up. I forgot you'd told me that your kids usually spend most of Sunday with you when they come for their weekend visits."

"I just put them back on the bus a little while ago."

"Oh. Well, I had just wanted to hear your voice this morning."

"How was your birthday?"

"It was okay. But . . ." I couldn't finish my sentence.

"But what? Did something happen? If it did, you know you can talk to me about it."

"I know that. But some things is hard to talk about," I mumbled. "I don't want to upset you."

"You upsetting me by dragging this out. Hubert, you should know by now that I don't judge you or criticize any decisions you make. And I don't interfere in your business unless you bring me into it. Something is bothering you and that's bothering me. Please tell me what it is."

I took a long, deep breath and told him everything about what had happened while I was drunk. He sucked on his teeth, but he didn't say nothing until I finished telling him.

"Hubert, under similar circumstances, what happened to you could happen to any man. Even me. You made a mistake."

I almost choked on the huge lump in my throat. I had to cough hard to dislodge it. "Yeah, but I ain't never made a whopping mistake like this one!" I pointed out. "Poor Jessie. The last thing I want to lose is her respect. I'm so ashamed of myself, I can't even think straight."

"Well, judging by what you just told me she said, she'll get over this mishap in no time and she won't hold it against you." Leroy's voice was so gentle, and he sounded so sympathetic, I felt bad that I'd hesitated to tell him.

"I hope she meant it. She is the only woman I feel comfortable with these days and I don't want our friendship to end because of something I did. If I was available again, them other women I used to spend time with would be on me like white on rice. And at this point, I don't want to start looking for another woman as tolerable as Jessie and start from scratch molding her to be a good front for me."

"I can understand that. So, where do you and Jessie go from here?"

"We decided that we would never drink together again and go on like this never happened."

"That sounds like a good plan. I'm sure the relationship will continue to be strong and productive. In the meantime, I wouldn't mind having some company tonight . . . if you feel like driving."

Them words was music to my ears. "I'll be out the door and on my way in ten minutes."

It was a fast and enjoyable drive to Hartville.

Before I could knock on Leroy's door, he opened it. He hadn't shaved and was already in his bathrobe. "You must have flew to get here this fast," he laughed. "I didn't have time to get gussied up." He draped his arm around my shoulder and led me to the couch.

"If I could have flew, I would have. And you don't have to gussy up for me."

We smooched for a few minutes and then listened to a comedy on the radio. After the program ended, we moved to the kitchen table and discussed a few miscellaneous issues. I was glad he didn't mention what I'd done to Jessie, but I knew it would come up again.

"I'm glad to see you looking more relaxed now," he commented as he poured two glasses of iced tea.

"Every time I'm with you, I feel like I been reborn and I'm starting all over again," I said with a grin.

I was paying him a compliment, but evidently he didn't see it that way. Instead of him grinning, he looked as grim as a pallbearer. I panicked right away. At the rate I was going, if I kept panicking so much, I was bound to have problems with my health down the road. Each time I had a panic attack, my heart raced, my blood pressure shot up, and my head throbbed.

"Did I say something wrong?"

He shifted in his chair and there was a hangdog expression on his face. "If you feel like you starting over every time you are with me, maybe I ain't doing my job."

"Huh? What do you mean?"

"I thought that by now our relationship was complete. If you have to keep reinventing yourself, something is wrong . . ."

I couldn't believe my ears. I got up and ran around the table and put my arms around Leroy's shoulders. "I am more complete than I ever was. All I meant was that I'm so happy, I feel like a brand-new man each time I see you. There ain't nothing else you can do to make me no happier."

"You ain't just saying that?"

"No, I ain't. If I was feeling something was lacking, don't you think I would have said something to you about it by now?"

"I guess," he mumbled. I caressed the side of his face and kissed his forehead. "Now let's finish the tea before I leave."

Me and Leroy didn't have sex every time we got together, and I liked that. Today, all we did was kiss and cuddle. I was pleased that our attraction to each other wasn't just physical. I couldn't say that about nary one of my previous relationships. He was the perfect man for me.

Chapter 34

Hubert

*L*IFE WAS GETTING BETTER AND BETTER—BETWEEN ME AND LEROY, and between me and Jessie. Neither one of them brought up what I'd done to Jessie after the last time we'd discussed it, and I sure didn't. I wasn't sure Leroy would ever bring it up again, but something told me Jessie would. Well, so long as I knew she wasn't going to hold a grudge against me, I was fine.

To sweeten the pot, I planned to do things that would convince her that I was treating her like the queen she was. I was already doing something like that, but I could do more. Helping with her finances was one way. She never complained about her living expenses. But it was no secret around the neighborhood that she'd been robbing Peter to pay Paul ever since Orville died and left her with a bunch of bills. To ease that burden, I'd add another dollar to the five I gave her every week. I'd take her out to eat more often and that would save her a few dollars on food.

But I still had to keep everything else in perspective. I had to continue working on strengthening my relationship with Leroy.

Him and Jessie had pulled me back up out of a bottomless pit and I was going to bend over backward to keep them both happy.

The first weekend in March, Leroy's used-to-be wife called

him up and asked if she could borrow fifty dollars to take the boys to visit some of her relatives in Georgia next weekend. I was sitting close beside him on the couch and heard his end of the conversation. He told her he couldn't spare that much money at such short notice. I reached into my pocket in a flash and pulled out two twenties and a ten and handed it all to him. Leroy's eyes got so big, I thought they would pop out the sockets. He hesitated, but he told the boys' mama that he'd send the money right away.

When he got off the phone, he looked at me with his mouth hanging open. "Hubert, you didn't have to do that. I don't want you to start lending me money."

"Let's look at it this way. So long as we're together, what's mine is yours. So, technically, it ain't a loan."

"It is a loan to me and I'll pay you back next month. In the future, don't offer me nothing I don't ask for. I've never been dependent on no man in my life and I ain't about to start now."

"I'm dependent on you," I said shyly.

Leroy gawked at me with a confused expression on his face. "What's that supposed to mean?"

It gave me a lot of pleasure to tell him. "I have a good life again and a lot of the credit belongs to you. I know that whenever I call you up or see you, it'll brighten my day. I can depend on you to keep me happy."

"Oh. Well, when you put it that way, I guess I depend on you too." We laughed. "I don't know how I got along without you for so many years."

Nobody had ever said something so endearing to me in my life. I had to force myself not to overact and get too giddy. It felt good to know how much I was appreciated by Leroy and Jessie. I knew that so long as I balanced my two lives enough so that neither one of them got too little attention from me, all three of us would benefit.

The second Saturday in March, Jessie accompanied me to a wedding that Daddy was going to officiate at. The bride had once lived next door to me and Maggie and had babysat Claude from time to time when he was growing up, so it was important for me to attend. Unfortunately, the bride was also friends with Blondeen, so, naturally, she was one of the guests.

I tried to avoid looking at Blondeen, but that was easier said than done. She had on about a pound of rouge and face powder, a low-cut orange dress with a huge fake white rose pinned on it close to her bosom, and her wig-hat had a white bow clamped on the side. Compared to Jessie and some of the other female guests, she looked like she was dressed for Mardi Gras. I seen Mama, Daddy, and just about everybody else giving her the side eye.

Her sidekicks, Wilma and Sukey, looked as dowdy as usual. They had on the same drab frocks they wore to the last wedding I seen them at. This time, Sukey had a safety pin holding one of her sleeves in place.

"I don't know who looks worst, Blondeen or her two minions," Jessie whispered in my ear. We occupied a pew behind the bride's family.

"They couldn't look more outlandish if they tried," I said under my breath.

I was glad it was a short wedding. Immediately after the bride and groom kissed, Jessie tugged my sleeve and gave me a pleading look. "We can leave now if you want to," she told me.

I gave her a stern look. "Jessie, I can't leave now. Mama and Daddy expect me to stay until everything is over with, like always," I protested. "But, if you feel uncomfortable, you can leave. You can drive my car home and I'll get a ride home with somebody."

Jessie poked out her lip and heaved out a sigh. "I'll stay. But if Blondeen says something mean to me, I won't be responsible for my actions. She's been needing a good butt-whupping for a long time!"

My mouth dropped open. As far as I knew, Jessie didn't have a violent bone in her body. That was another thing she and Maggie had in common.

"Jessie, I'm surprised at you. Would you show out like that in church?"

A puppy-dog expression crossed her face, and she bit her bottom lip. "You know I didn't mean that," she muttered. "You ain't got to worry, I'll behave myself."

Blondeen was seated on a pew on the other side of the church and hadn't acknowledged me and Jessie until everybody gathered for the reception in the dining area.

"Hello, Hubert," she said as she strutted up to me. She acted like Jessie wasn't even present. "I hope you enjoyed your birthday last month. If I hadn't been so busy, I would have brought you a cake or a gift or something. Did you have a party?"

"Yes, but only for immediate family. It was a very nice affair."

"That's nice," Blondeen hissed with a smirk on her face. "I hope your 'immediate family' enjoyed themselves."

I nodded toward Jessie. "Jessie was kind enough to bake me a cake and bring a bottle of champagne."

Blondeen's face froze so fast, it looked like she had put on a mask, one with a scowl so extreme, it made me shudder. I was glad to see that her presence wasn't fazing Jessie no more than it already had. The whole time, Jessie gazed straight ahead.

Blondeen's eyebrows rose up so high they almost touched the hairline of her wig-hat. "I declare, I thought you only drunk on special occasions."

"It was a special occasion," I said.

"I hope you have a lot more 'special occasions.' Well, I better start stepping if I want to get home before dark. I ain't going to make it easy for that killer to pick his next victim. I'll see you around, okay?"

I didn't like the fact that her last sentence was a question, not a statement.

"I'm sure you will. This is a small town," I said with a laugh.

The second that Blondeen was out of earshot, Jessie heaved out a huge sigh of relief. "She's the rudest woman I know. You would have thought I was invisible. Ain't you glad you decided not to get too close to her?"

"Sure enough. I can't put my finger on it, but there is something about that woman that scares me," I admitted. "I don't think there is nothing she could do that would surprise me."

"I feel the same way," Jessie said with her face scrunched up. "My chest tightens every time I see her. I won't be satisfied until the day she leaves me and you alone for good."

"I got a feeling we'll have to put up with her until she gets tired or finds somebody else to pester."

"I got that same feeling," Jessie said with a deep sigh.

Chapter 35
Jessie

I HAD REHEARSED SEVERAL DIFFERENT WAYS I WAS GOING TO TELL Hubert on my birthday that I was pregnant with his baby, but I wasn't sure which one I was going to go with. I had to decide soon. April 1 was coming up in a few days.

The Friday evening before my birthday, Hubert told me he had to go to Hartville *again* to pick up more embalming fluid. This time, he also wanted to price some new caskets. We was at his kitchen table eating the hog jowls and turnip greens I had cooked for supper. I was disappointed that he didn't ask me to go with him. I believed that because of what he'd done to me, he didn't think it was a good idea for us to be going out of town together overnight.

I had told everybody weeks ago that I didn't want to do nothing special to celebrate my birthday. Getting old was bad enough, I didn't need to highlight it with a cake and a bunch of rowdy folks in my house acting like kids. Hubert had insisted on us having a celebration at his house. I agreed but only if his parents was the only guests.

I was glad he hadn't brought up the "rape" no more. I wasn't going to, unless it was necessary. Whenever it seemed like I was losing ground with him, I'd ease it into a conversation.

"When will you get back from Hartville?" I asked as I finished off the last jowl on my plate.

Hubert picked up his napkin and wiped pot liquor off his lips before he answered. "I think I'll get a room, like I usually do, and spend the night. If I get back home early enough tomorrow, we'll get together and go see a movie. I got a few acquaintances over there that I ain't seen in a while—a undertaker and his crew, and a sharecropper that used to live over here. I buried the sharecropper's mama, daddy, and his grandparents on both sides. I might look them up and stay until Sunday."

I stared at him for a few seconds with a curious expression on my face. There was a minor issue on my mind that had been there for quite some time now and it felt like it was about to burn a hole in my brain. I decided to finally bring it up so I could stop thinking about it.

"How come you socialize with so many out-of-town folks, when you know so many in Lexington that you could hang out with?"

"What are you talking about?" Hubert asked so fast, spit flew out the sides of his mouth. "I play checkers and dominoes with a few here." He wiped his lips some more.

"That's only every now and then."

"Well, all that time I spent with them women before you only caused me a lot of confusion and complications. And I don't have much in common with the men I know in this town. Some don't like the fact that I'm doing so well and that everybody looks up to me and my family."

"It's probably because they are jealous!" I threw in, waving my hand in the air. "Your out-of-town friends must be as well-off as you, so they ain't got no reason to be jealous, huh?"

"Sure enough. They all got great jobs, and a few is doing even better than me."

"I guess the hard times ain't hard on everybody. It's nice to hear that other colored folks are having some successes with the economy still being so bad. President Roosevelt ain't doing much to help Americans—colored or white. I got a itching to go with you one of these days so I can meet some of your prosperous out-of-town friends. I'm sure they'd like to meet me too."

"Um . . . I know they would. I talk about you to them all the time. I'll let you know in advance when it's a good time for you to go with me."

"Why don't you invite a few over here? You shouldn't always be the one buying gas to go see them."

"Jessie, I go out of town because of my business. I don't see no reason not to call on friends in a town when I'm already there. They would do the same thing if they was the ones coming over here. But they got kids, so it ain't so easy for them to up and travel out of town as easy as it is for me."

"That makes sense, I guess. But I'm still anxious to meet at least one or two. I hope there ain't no females in the mix that I need to be worried about."

"*Pffftt.* All the friends I spend time with, in Hartville, and every other place, are men. The wives and girlfriends always got something else going on when I'm there."

"I'm glad to hear that. At least when I do meet them, I ain't got to worry about them treating me like Blondeen's been doing since me and you got closer." I gave Hubert a thoughtful look. "Thanks for offering to take me to a movie when you get back. I'll pass on it, though. The last time we went, I couldn't hear nothing from them back-row balcony seats where we had to sit," I griped.

"We can't do nothing about the rules in this state. Whatever the white folks say, we got to go along with it," Hubert reminded.

When we finished our supper, I told him to go on to Hartville and I would stay and clean up the kitchen. He was fine with that.

I waited until he'd been gone for fifteen minutes before I did some more snooping. Hubert was so meticulous; it was a waste of time to go through his drawers. Every time I did, it looked like nothing had changed. But I did stretch out in his bed again for a few minutes, hugging one of the pillows, pretending it was him.

I didn't want to go home. But I didn't want to get too comfortable, so I left right after I smoothed over the covers on his bed.

I always left a light on at my house at night, whether I was home or not. They'd found the fifth murdered colored woman's body in the woods last week, so everybody was even more on edge now. This victim had been a member of Reverend Wiggins's congregation all her life and was one of the Wigginses' closest friends. Naturally, the woman's family wanted Hubert to handle the funeral arrangements. Just like with the other four victims.

We felt so helpless because there was nothing we could do to stop the killings, except be more careful and keep weapons handy. People had stopped talking about us getting together and storming the police station and demanding that they do more to try and find the killer.

The last time a group of colored folks confronted the police about them needing to look out for our needs, they all ended up behind bars for "agitating" and "disturbing the peace." It was up to us to protect ourselves.

I still hadn't been able to find somebody to rent the spare room in my house, but I wasn't trying so hard no more. If my plan worked with Hubert, I wouldn't be living by myself much longer.

I was as pleased as I could be when Hubert called me up Saturday evening at five thirty. "I wanted to let you know I was back. If you ain't too busy, do you mind coming over to cook some more of them hog jowls?"

"Oh, I ain't busy at all," I lied as I set aside the sewing I'd been doing. I was late finishing up a quilt I'd promised one of my neighbors, but I'd work twice as fast on it when I got back home. I immediately slid into my shoes and trotted all the way to Hubert's house. He was standing on his front porch, waiting for me.

I had changed the way I was going to tell him I was pregnant. I wasn't going to wait until my birthday. Life was so unpredictable, I realized something could happen before Monday that would cancel out my birthday supper, like him having to collect another dead body, which usually put him in a gloomy mood.

When I thought about telling him while we was celebrating my birthday in the nice restaurant he wanted to take me to, that idea didn't seem so smart, after all. Doing it after we got back home from the restaurant didn't sound smart either. He would probably get upset because I had put off telling him something that he should have been told as soon as I found out.

I had to tell him *now*. It would probably mean he wouldn't want me to cook them jowls this evening and he might not be in the mood to take me out for my birthday. I didn't care, because I wanted to get this over with before I lost my nerve.

At first, Hubert was smiling and looking like he was glad to see me, and I believed he was.

"Good news, Jessie! I picked up that eggbeater and the washboard for your birthday and I hope—" He stopped talking just as I reached his porch steps. He narrowed his eyes and his jaw dropped. The way he was gazing at me now, you would have thought he was seeing me naked again. "Why is your face so puffy and your eyes so red? What's the matter?"

"I . . . I'm glad you asked me to come over," I mumbled as he ushered me into his living room. "I need to talk to you about something that's very important."

I stumbled to the couch and flopped down. He sat down next to me.

"What's wrong, sugar? Did you have a run-in with Blondeen? I ain't never seen you looking so out of sorts."

I was having a hard time getting the words out. "Oh, Hubert. I don't know what I'm going to do!"

"Whatever it is, you need to tell me now so I can help you."

"I been waiting all day for you to come home so I could tell you." I sniffled and wrung my hands. The more I hesitated, the more distressed he looked. I held my breath and blurted the words out as fast as I could. "I just found out last night that I'm fixing to have your baby."

Hubert's eyes rolled up in his head and the blood instantly drained from his face. A split second later, he fainted and fell sideways across my lap.

Chapter 36

Hubert

WHEN I CAME TO, I THOUGHT I WAS WAKING UP FROM A BAD dream. What Jessie had just told me was the last thing I ever expected to hear from her—next to her telling me I'd raped her. I didn't know how I was going to go on living as a Christian with this sword dangling above my head. What made it even worse was the fact that I couldn't remember a single thing about the rape!

I was laying on the couch and Jessie was hovering over me wiping my forehead with a damp rag, so I knew I wasn't dreaming. I felt so weak, it was a struggle for me to sit up.

"Hubert, lay still. You don't want to go into shock."

"I . . . I'm already in shock," I managed to say. "I got you *pregnant?* I . . . I don't know what to say." I gazed at her for a few seconds. "You sure? You been to the doctor?"

"Do you think I'd be telling you this if I didn't know for sure? I don't need no doctor to tell me nothing. I been pregnant before, so I know what I'm talking about."

I suddenly felt much stronger, so I swung my legs to the floor and scooted back on the couch. Jessie sat down on the other end. I was surprised she didn't look more upset than she did. If somebody had raped me and got me pregnant, I would be screaming bloody murder all over the place.

"B-but there was just that one time on my birthday!"

"All it takes to make a baby is one time, Hubert." She dropped her head and gazed at her feet for about half a minute. I sat stiff as a board, with all kinds of thoughts whirling around in my head.

"This could cause a scandal of biblical proportions. I ain't never ever had to deal with nothing like this!" I slammed my fist into the palm of my other hand. "Why did you let me drink that second glass of champagne? You know I ain't much of a drinker."

"Hubert, I didn't force you to have that second drink. You didn't even protest that much before you guzzled it down."

"I declare, I wish I hadn't. This is disgusting!"

Jessie gave me a hopeless look. "I'm sorry you think I'm disgusting," she whined.

"Don't put words in my mouth. That ain't what I said."

"That's what you meant, though. I know I ain't nowhere near as cute and young as some of the women you know, and my body done seen better days. But I'd like to think that under normal circumstances, some men still find me attractive and not—"

I held up my hand. "Jessie, slow down. You going way off the rails. I ain't said nothing about you not being attractive and your body looks as healthy as all the other women I know. You taking everything out of context."

"I don't know what to say or think anymore. I'm responsible for you getting drunk that night, I don't deny that. I'm sorry. But what's done is done and we have to deal with it."

"I know, I know, and we will. But at the end of the day, I can't bring this kind of shame on my mama and daddy! Daddy done spent most of his career as a preacher warning his congregation about fornication and the consequences. He'll look like a fool when they find out his own son done—"

Jessie cut me off. "Hush up!" I was glad she did before I said something I'd regret. "He ain't got to know!"

I winced and shook my head, which felt like it was the size and weight of a great big pumpkin. "How can we hide something like a baby?"

She coughed to clear her throat and stared at her feet again. "I don't want to ruin your reputation, so I'll make it easy for you. Ain't nobody in Lexington got to know about this baby."

I blew out a mouthful of air. "If you thinking about getting rid of my child, I ain't going to let you do nothing like that! No matter how this baby was conceived, it's still a gift from God."

"I ain't talking about getting rid of it. I would never do something like that. I got some cousins in Detroit. I could go up there until I have it and let them raise it."

I glared at Jessie like she had lost her mind. "You call my baby a 'it' and want to give him or her away to folks I don't even know?"

"Well, at least nobody would ever have to know what you done to me. I'll even stay on in Detroit and get a job, so you won't never have to see me again. Maybe I'll meet a nice man who will marry me and raise the baby like it's his . . ."

I held up both hands and shook my head. "Uh-uh. I done lost one child, I ain't going to lose another one if I can help it." I stopped talking and stood up, facing Jessie. She looked so pitiful and I felt so bad. I couldn't believe the fix I was in. But I was going to face my responsibility like the man my folks raised me to be. If I had a child, I'd want him or her to know me. It had been bad enough that Claude hadn't known his birth daddy. Jessie hadn't been with no man except me since her husband died, so there was so doubt in my mind that the baby she was carrying was mine. "I ain't going to let another man raise my child."

"Then what do you think we should do?"

"There ain't but one thing fitting for us to do: get married."

Chapter 37
Jessie

I WAS FIXING TO BECOME THE NEW MRS. WIGGINS! IT WAS TOO good to be true. I couldn't believe how much God was blessing me. If somebody had gave me a million dollars, I couldn't have felt no better than I did now.

I couldn't imagine the look on Blondeen's face when she heard the news. I'd probably never see it, because I went out of my way to avoid her. We shopped at the same meat market and a few other places, so now I only went just before each one closed for the day. Most of the folks I knew liked to do their shopping earlier in the day.

But three days ago when I got home from work, I seen that heifer heading into the house next door where Sukey's mama lived. She saw me long enough to give me a dirty look, but she didn't say nothing. When I left to go to Hubert's house, she was leaving at the same time. She didn't say nothing to me, but she said something to Sukey I couldn't hear and then she busted out laughing. I didn't care how she treated me no more. I was fixing to get married and that was enough to cancel out all the other negative stuff going on in my life.

My plan was working out better than I thought it would. I knew Hubert would step up to the plate when I told him about the "baby," but I never expected him to come through so fast. I was rising up on cloud nine and it seemed like the sky was the limit. One of the next things I hoped to do was quit my job. Hubert could afford to support me. Folks was dying left and right lately, so he was making more money burying folks than ever before. If he allowed me to stop working, I could move my son back to Lexington and look after him myself. I was grinning so hard, my cheeks ached.

"Are you sure you want to marry me?" I whimpered. I stood up and went up to him. I got so close, I could feel his breath on my face.

He hunched his shoulders and mumbled, "Yeah, I guess. What else can we do to keep everybody happy and dodge a scandal? Besides, I need to atone for my crime."

"What crime?"

Hubert's jaw dropped again, even lower this time. "I raped you. As far as I know, that's still a crime."

"Oh," I said in a flat tone. "I had pushed that to the back of my mind."

"I had done the same thing. But now that we got a baby to deal with, it's going to be in the front of my mind until the day I die."

"When do you want to get married? The baby will be here in less than eight months. Somebody is bound to count the months when I give birth. They'll come to the conclusion that we had been fooling around before we got married, and we'll have to face a scandal anyway."

"Then we ain't got no choice."

"What do you mean?"

"I'll have to marry you right away. We'll say the baby was born premature. That happens all the time. I came two months early myself."

I was so excited and happy, I wrapped my arms around Hubert and squeezed him so hard, he started squirming. I turned him loose and just stared at him in awe. "God broke the mold when He made you, because there ain't a more upstanding and wonderful man in this world than you."

Hubert looked embarrassed and happy at the same time. He

snorted and gave me a weak smile. "I'm glad you feel that way about me, Jessie. You deserve some praise too. For you to be so forgiving about the rape, your heart must have been shaped in a bowl. I hope I can live up to your expectations."

"You already have, and I promise I'll live up to yours. And another thing, I swear to God, I won't never touch another drop of alcohol."

"You ain't got to worry about doing much cooking and cleaning for a while. I don't want you to do nothing that might wear you out. A woman your age can't breeze through a pregnancy like a younger woman. Babies born to women your age are more likely to come with afflictions."

His last sentence made my heart drop. "I was in my twenties when I had Earl. I took care of myself, ate right, got enough rest, and he still came out retarded. I don't think a woman's age got much to do with something like that. Afflicted children is even more special in God's eyes."

I wasn't trying to make Hubert feel guilty about what he'd just said. But from the hangdog look on his face, that was exactly what I'd done.

"I'm sorry I said that. I know better." He narrowed his eyes and stared at me so hard, I flinched. "Jessie, I don't care if that baby comes here with scales and a forked tail. I'll love it as much as I loved Claude. And as much as I love your boy. I want you to bring him back to Lexington eventually so he can be closer to us. Once we get married, he'll be my son too."

I had so much on my mind now, I didn't know which thought to process next. One of the main things I had to look forward to was the fact that I'd be moving into Hubert's house. Not only would I no longer be alone and in danger of that killer still on the loose, but I'd also have a lovely new house to fiddle around with. The first thing I'd do was make new curtains for every window. I was glancing around the living room, wondering what else I could do to liven up this place even more, when Hubert interrupted my thoughts.

"Jessie, you listening?"

"Huh? Yeah, I'm listening?"

"I just asked if we could get married next Saturday? I'm sure Daddy will be able to officiate. But"—Hubert stopped talking and sucked in a deep breath—"like with my birthday, I don't want no big splashy shindig. Just family and a few friends from church. So long as we keep things simple, we won't have to deal with a lot of questions. And one thing is for sure, there won't be no champagne served!"

"That's fine with me." I had to hold my breath to keep from dancing a jig. I couldn't wait to get back to my house so I could go over everything in my head that Hubert had told me.

"Let's cancel going out to supper for your birthday on Monday. We'll eat here. I'll give you your eggbeater and washboard then. I even had the lady gift wrap them for you."

"That's wonderful, Hubert. They'll sure make my work easier, so I can't wait to get them."

He hugged me. I cut it short because being that close to him excited me, so I left a minute later.

Chapter 38
Hubert

TEN MINUTES AFTER JESSIE LEFT, I CALLED MAMA. "I NEED TO COME over and share some news with you and Daddy," I blurted out.

"Oh?" Poor Mama. She sounded worried already. There was no telling how she'd react when she heard my news. "I was just about to roll up my hair and soak my feet. Can't you tell me over the phone?"

"No, this is too important," I protested.

"Is that so?" Mama sounded even more worried, so I had to squash that right away.

"It ain't nothing bad, Mama. I ain't sick and I ain't lost my job at the mill and my funeral home ain't burned down."

"I didn't think it was nothing that bad. But whatever it is, you need to get over here posthaste so we won't be in suspense."

"I'm on my way."

I was so distressed. My head was throbbing and my ears was ringing. I couldn't believe that I'd stepped into a new phase of my life in just a matter of weeks.

The short drive to my parents' house, which was less than five minutes away by car, seemed much longer. Everything me and Jessie had discussed was playing in my head, over and over, like a broken record. I had a hard time concentrating on the road. There was a car in front of me that was moving so slow, I swerved around it and almost ran up on the sidewalk. I had to get a hold of myself before I caused a accident or something worse.

Mama and Daddy was standing on the front porch with puzzled expressions on their faces when I drove up.

"What's going on, son?" Mama asked as I followed them into the living room. They sat down on the couch and I started pacing back and forth in front of them.

"Say something, boy. And you better be quick about it," Daddy ordered.

I stopped pacing and let the words slide out of my mouth. "I'm fixing to get married again." Mama's eyes got big; Daddy reared back and raised his hands in the air so fast, he looked like somebody had pulled a gun on him. "To Jessie."

"Married? Maggie ain't even been gone five months!" Mama boomed. She placed her hand over her heart and started rubbing. "I thought you was just keeping company with her so you wouldn't feel lonesome. We had no idea you was contemplating *marriage* this soon. And certainly not to *your dead wife's best friend.*"

"Well, I'm going to do it and I don't see no reason to put it off. I'm sure Maggie would approve," I defended.

"When did you decide this?" Daddy asked.

"Um, I been thinking about it for weeks. I just decided to bite the bullet and propose to Jessie tonight," I answered in a meek tone.

Daddy groaned and mopped sweat off his face with his hand. I couldn't tell if he was confused, in pain, or what. He snorted and went on. "I declare, I didn't know you was that serious about her. We thought y'all was more like brother and sister. You know how this is going to look to folks?"

Mama slowly shook her head and fanned her face at the same time and wheezed. "What I want to know is *when* you realized you felt this way about Jessie?"

I rolled my eyes. "If y'all thinking I had feelings for Jessie while Maggie was still alive, that ain't the case. I've always cared about her, but now in a different way. And of all the women I know, she'd be the best one to take Maggie's place."

"Bite your tongue, boy! There ain't a woman alive who could take Maggie's place. She was the salt of the earth," Mama boomed.

"Ain't it the truth!" Daddy added. Then he lowered his voice and let out a long, loud sigh. "But you ain't getting no younger, so I can see why you don't want to put off marriage too much longer."

"We love Jessie and will treat her as well as we did Maggie. The thing is, folks will say that you marrying your late wife's best friend ain't fitting. And it ain't. With God's help, we won't fret none over that, though. But I'm a little worried that some of them busybodies might make life miserable for y'all until somebody else gives them something to talk about." Mama heaved out a loud sigh. "Son, if you really love Jessie, don't let society's opinion stop you from marrying her. When was y'all planning to do the deed?"

"This coming Saturday," I mumbled.

Mama gasped so hard, she had to catch her breath. "That soon? Can't y'all put it off a few more months, or until November when Maggie will be gone a year? You know how the folks around here like to talk. There ain't no telling what all they'll be saying if y'all get married so soon after Maggie's death."

"Even if I waited ten years, folks will talk about me marrying Maggie's best friend. My mind is made up. I done already proposed to Jessie and she said yes. Besides, we want to get started on trying to have a child before we get too old." I was getting light-headed, so I had to stop talking long enough to suck in some air and compose myself. "Daddy, we would like to do it on Saturday if you can squeeze us in. And not at the church. We want to exchange vows in your living room, like me and Maggie did."

Mama and Daddy looked at each other and smiled before she wobbled up off the couch and came up to me with her arms outstretched. She hugged me and patted my back. "Bless your heart, son. Getting a new daughter-in-law would be such a blessing. Especially a fine Christian woman like Jessie. And another grandchild would be icing on the cake." Mama sighed and gave me a pensive look. "I can understand y'all wanting to start a family while y'all still young enough to enjoy them. Me and your daddy are at the age when most people already have great-grandchildren."

"Sure enough. And conceiving kids is hard at any age, so time ain't on you and Jessie's side." Daddy got up and grabbed my hand and shook it so hard I thought it would fall off. "I'd be glad to join y'all together next Saturday. Three o'clock sounds like a good time, so don't be late."

"Y'all going to send out invitations?" Mama wanted to know.

"Uh-uh. We just want some of our family members and a few friends from church present. Mama, if you don't mind, could you throw together a few things: a cake, some snacks, and juice?"

"I'd be glad to, baby." Mama paused and scrunched up her face. "Jessie's folks is kind of worldly, so we'd better pick up a few bottles of champagne, I guess."

"No! If they want to drink spirits, they'll have to do it someplace else. There's plenty of colored saloons operating in this part of town that they can go to after the ceremony," I said as fast as I could to make my lips and tongue move.

Daddy gave me a curious look. "You had champagne at your birthday get-together a few weeks ago. You drunk a whole glass yourself and you looked like you enjoyed it," he pointed out.

"I did, but I woke up with a humdinger of a hangover the next morning. That's why I don't want none at my wedding." I exhaled and nodded at Mama, then at Daddy. "I'm sorry for dropping such a big bombshell on y'all so suddenly. But now I need to skedaddle back home and sit down with Jessie so we can start organizing our plans. You two have a blessed rest of the evening."

Chapter 39
Jessie

I COULDN'T WAIT TO GET TO WORK ON MONDAY SO I COULD SHARE my good news with my coworkers. Especially Conway. He was still trying to get me to go have a drink with him. Knowing I had a "boyfriend" didn't make no difference to him, but maybe me having a husband would.

I usually got in before Quinette and Glennola, but today Quinette beat me. I found her in the room next to the lobby, where she had been ordered to bathe a unconscious woman who was so frail, she couldn't do nothing for herself no more.

"Good morning, Jessie. Happy birthday."

"Don't remind me," I groaned.

Quinette rolled her eyes and whimpered. "I know just how you feel. Mine is coming up in two months. And please don't remind me."

"I won't," I snickered. "Why are you here so early?"

"They couldn't get in touch with you, and Glennola ain't got no telephone, so they called me to come in early today. One of the men in the room at the end of the hall passed during the night. I had to clean him and his room up. Right after I finished doing that, they sent me in here." Quinette turned back to the old woman in the bed and gazed at her for a few moments. "Something tells me one of us will be prepping this one for the undertaker any minute now."

Quinette opened her mouth to speak again, but the biggest, most mean-spirited of the white nurses stormed into the room before she could get another word out. She marched right up and stopped smack-dab in front of me with her face so close to mine, I could smell her foul breath.

"Gal, didn't I tell you to go in the bathroom and scrub the inside of that commode last week? Do you want to keep this job?" she barked.

"Yes, ma'am," I mumbled. My stomach was churning with fear. When I left my job, I wanted to leave on my own, not because I got fired.

"Get it done today before you leave!" This woman never talked to one of the colored workers without wagging her gnarly finger in their face.

"Yes, ma'am," I said again. The nurse glared at me with her thin lips pressed so close together, it looked like they'd disappeared. She didn't say nothing else before she spun around and stomped back out of the room.

"That heifer," Quinette hissed. "Why didn't you tell her that you did clean that damn thing last week?"

"What's the use? It's easier to go with the flow than argue with these people. Sometimes I think there ain't no devils in hell because they are all here. But they ain't all white. There's just as many colored ones," I remarked. Blondeen's face flashed through my mind.

"Ain't it the truth. When I get a chance, I'm going to fill up a cup with water out that same commode and put it in that water pitcher them peckerwoods drink out in the break room." We snickered. "Like I was saying, I don't think this old lady is going to make it through the day." She gently patted the woman's shoulder.

"She's always been so nice to us. I sure will miss her. I'm so glad most of the white folks I've known are real nice." I sighed and smoothed down the sides of my stiff uniform.

"I'll testify to that. The lady I used to do laundry for before I came here treated me better than she treated her own daughters. It's a shame that a few white folks decided to make life miserable for colored folks just because the Jim Crow laws says they can." Quinette shook her head.

"Oh, well. Reverend Wiggins says that God saw fit to put us here, so we have to make the best of it. Hubert tells me the same thing all the time. Is there anything you want me to do before I go get busy? Do you want me to help you turn this old lady over?"

"No, I did that before you got here. But you can take a look-see at that nice blind man across the hall. He got up a little while ago and wandered into the kitchen and fell. It's a good thing Conway walked up in the nick of time to pick him up and take him back to his room."

"Before I do that, I wanted to let you know, I'm fixing to get married," I gushed with my chest puffed out.

Quinette looked at me with her mouth hanging open. "To who?"

I rolled my eyes and gave her the most exasperated look I could come up with. "Hubert."

She gasped. "Reverend Wiggins's son? When did y'all get this far, and so soon after his wife's passing?"

"I wish folks would stop harping on the fact that his wife ain't been gone that long. He is the one who decided he didn't want to wait no year or longer, like some folks seem to think he should. It's his life so he can do whatever he wants. Shoot."

Quinette pulled the covers up to her patient's neck and motioned me to follow her out of the room. "I'll go check on the blind man with you. Tell me about you and Hubert before we get too busy."

We started walking down the hall. Two nurses nodded at us as they passed by, but they didn't speak. Most of the white workers was nice and friendly, but they rarely spent time talking to us unless it was about work.

"Me and Hubert have been close friends for so long, I guess things was bound to turn out the way they did, now that we are both single again. He wants to try and have a baby as soon as possible."

Quinette stopped in her tracks. "Don't take this the wrong

way, but don't you think y'all a bit long in the tooth to be talking about making a baby?"

Before I could answer Quinette's rude question, Conway shuffled out of the blind man's room with a bucket of water and a mop. "What y'all crowing about this time?" he asked with a smirk on his face.

"Jessie and Hubert. They fixing to tie the knot," Quinette answered.

Conway couldn't look more indifferent if he tried. "I declare, I don't know if I should congratulate you or pray for you. Middle-aged marriages usually don't last."

I was in too good of a mood to let him know how annoying I thought he was. "How would you know that?" I asked. "You ain't middle-aged and you ain't never been married."

"I ain't got to eat a piece of spoiled meat to know it ain't good for me." He snorted and continued in an even more annoying tone. "My mama, two of my aunties, and a heap of other older women I know got married late in life. None of their husbands stuck around too long."

"I ain't worried about a man walking out on me before we even get married," I said firmly.

When Glennola approached, she joined the conversation. I was glad they didn't spend too much time talking about me and Hubert. But I was also glad that they—even Conway—wished me well and wasn't upset about not being invited to the wedding.

The day went by so fast, I lost track of time and decided to give the commode another scrubbing before I left. I spent more time on it than I usually did and didn't realize it was time to go home until some of the folks who worked the next shift showed up.

Glennola and Quinette had already left by the time I walked out the door. The bus I usually took was pulling away and I would have to wait another hour for the next one. When Conway drove down the road in his noisy old Chrysler and seen me sitting on the bus stop bench, he stopped and rolled down his window.

"You want a ride?"

"No, I can wait for the next bus."

"The last bus that leave from this location don't go to the colored neighborhood. You'd have to get off downtown and walk the rest of the way, and that's a long walk. It ain't safe for no colored woman to be roaming around by herself, day or night these days. It's just a matter of time before that crazy man snatches and kill another one of y'all."

A chill crawled up my spine. I was just as concerned about that killer as everybody else, so I knew it was in my best interest to take Conway up on his offer. I opened the passenger door and got in.

"I'll give you some gas money on payday."

He shook his head. "Don't worry about that. I been wanting to get you alone for a long time."

I sighed and gave him a dirty look. "Conway, I'm fixing to get married, remember?"

"I don't care. I still want you to know that if you ever want to try something new, just let me know. I promise, you won't regret it. I bet I can make you feel a whole lot better than that geezer undertaker you fixing to marry. Shoot. Ain't you squeamish about getting tied down to a man who is that close to dead folks all the time? There ain't no telling what kind of odd things he do to them dead women behind closed doors. I heard about a undertaker in Huntsville that got caught having his way with a dead woman."

I shuddered at the thought of something that gruesome. "Hush up. That was just a rumor started by one of the workers the undertaker had fired. If there was something odd about Hubert, I would have figured it out by now. He's almost as perfect as a man can be."

I didn't know if Conway believed what I'd just said, but I sure did. I was convinced that once I helped Hubert get over his performance problem for real, he would be perfect again. Just like Maggie used to tell me he was.

Chapter 40
Hubert

I PLANNED TO BE AS GOOD A HUSBAND TO JESSIE AS I HAD BEEN TO Maggie. I would let her do whatever she wanted, so long as it wasn't something that would embarrass me or the church. I was even going to try and limit the number of lies I told her.

For some reason, it seemed like the closer I got to Jessie, the closer I wanted to get to Leroy. It was a challenge having to balance the two relationships. More so than with Maggie because I hadn't needed to lie to her about my boyfriends. Now I had to stay alert at all times and that helped keep me focused.

I wanted to keep Leroy in the loop about everything that was going on with me and Jessie. This new development was a load I couldn't carry too long by myself. The minute I got home from work on Monday, I dialed his number. I didn't even greet him or ask how he was doing before I said real quick, "I need to see you as soon as possible."

"I'm attending my niece's engagement party tomorrow in Mobile. Her folks is having a get-together afterward, so I'm sure I'll spend most of the day with them. I should be home by eight p.m. Can you come then?"

"I can't wait that long. I need to talk to you tonight, if possible. I'd like to leave as soon as we get off the phone. I won't stay long because I have to be back home in time to celebrate Jessie's birthday."

"Can you come after that?"

"I guess I could. But I might be a nervous wreck by then."
Leroy's silence made me nervous. What he said next made me
even more nervous, and he said it in the most serious tone I'd
ever heard him use.

"Hubert, I hope you ain't going to bring me some bad news—
like you done met somebody else and want to end things. I'm
getting too old to keep having to look for somebody new and—"

"Hush up! I can't believe you would even think that that's
what I need to see you about! I want to spend the rest of my life
with you. There is something else going on. I'm feeling real conflicted about it."

"You sound mighty distressed, and I would love to make you
feel better. But I don't think you should be driving all this way by
yourself tonight. Why don't I come to Lexington? You can give
me a call after you and Jesse finish celebrating and I can leave as
soon as we get off the phone."

His offer shook me up so bad, I almost dropped the telephone. "Good God, no! I don't ever want you to come over here
to see me."

"Hubert, as long as we don't let nobody see us, we ain't got
nothing to worry about. Besides, if somebody sees us together,
you can tell them I'm your out-of-town cousin, like I tell people
over here about you."

"Everybody who knows me knows all of my kinfolks. Even the
ones that don't live in Lexington," I explained. "Do you really
think I sound too bad to be driving?"

"Yes, I do. If something was to happen to you, I would feel so
guilty I'd never forgive myself. Besides, we had a pretty bad
storm over here today. I don't think it's over, because I heard
some thunder and seen some lightning just before you called. It
ain't smart to drive in bad weather if you don't have to. Why
don't you calm down and let's discuss this again tomorrow when
I get home from the party, or Wednesday, okay?"

"All right."

Leroy was right. I was in no shape to be driving too far by myself. My hands was shaking after I hung up the telephone. I was

fine by the time Jessie came over to celebrate her birthday. Mama and Daddy showed up a few minutes after she did with the cake Mama had made and presents for Jessie. I was so distracted I could barely keep up with the conversation. It turned out to be a nice evening, anyway. But I still was anxious to talk to Leroy.

I was feeling much better by Wednesday evening when Mama and Daddy dropped in, before I had time to dial Leroy's number. They stayed until it was almost their bedtime. I was tired and didn't want to call Leroy so late at night.

I called him right after I got out of bed Thursday morning, but he didn't answer his phone. I called him again a hour later as I was about to leave for work and he still didn't answer. Now I was not just frantic about my situation with Jessie, I was concerned about Leroy. I couldn't use the telephone at the mill, so I came home on my lunch break and called him at his shop. If he hadn't answered, I would have gone to Hartville after I got off work to see what was going on with him.

The second I heard his voice, I blurted out, "Where you been? I was worried to death. I been calling and calling."

"My house phone was out of order," he explained. "I called you from my shop phone around eight thirty this morning. You didn't answer and I couldn't call you at work. The telephone man didn't come until this afternoon."

"Oh. Praise God it was something that tame. I was getting real worried. Can I come over when I get off work today?"

Leroy offered to come to Lexington again, but I insisted on driving to Hartville.

"All right. But be careful. You still don't sound too steady to me," he said.

I didn't go home first to change out of my work clothes. I got to Hartville in record time. "You sounded awful on the phone. What's going on?" he asked as I stumbled into his living room and plonked down on the couch. He sat down next to me with his arm around my shoulder.

He didn't say a word as I told him about Jessie being pregnant and that I was going to marry her this coming Saturday. He drew in a long, deep breath and patted my hand.

"Damn. That's a heavy price to pay because you had too much to drink. You do what you got to do. I'm with you all the way."

"I want you to know that my business with Jessie ain't going to change nothing between me and you," I assured him.

He gave me a pensive look for a few seconds and then he smiled. "I'm sorry you got all worked up over this, but I never thought what you had going on with Jessie would interfere with our relationship."

"I'll never let that happen. But the more I think about getting married again and having a baby on the way, the more I realize it's a pretty big responsibility. And, I'll admit, it's a little scary too. I didn't think this would be something I'd be going through at my age."

"You and Jessie getting drunk and having unintentional sex ain't nothing to be too upset about. It ain't like you was some stranger that clobbered her over the head and dragged her into the bushes and had his way with her. But I will say this, she should not have encouraged you to drink more than you was used to."

"I know and I should be mad at her about that, but I can't blame her. She didn't hold no gun to my head."

"I think it's a good thing for you to get married again. Having a wife is the best way to hide the truth. That was the only reason I married my wife."

I drew in my breath. "You didn't care nothing about her?"

"Oh, I cared about her. Probably the same way you cared about Maggie. The difference was, I desperately wanted children, so I had to play the role to the hilt." Leroy gave me a sheepish grin as he went on. "She's a gorgeous, traditionally built woman. Sex with her was a unique experience and there was plenty of times when I actually enjoyed it."

"Do you think you'll ever get married again?"

"Not a chance. I don't want to get involved with a woman again, because I don't think it's necessary in my case. I know several other divorced and widowed men my age and nobody thinks there's something wrong with them because they ain't got no wife or girlfriend. Besides, I'd rather spend *all* of my time with the man of my choice. I admire you for being able to have a relationship with me and Jessie and not get wore out."

"I just hope I never get wore out," I replied, sighing. "Well, I'm glad to hear you got something out of having sex with a woman—other than kids. I guess that's something I'll never know. I just wish I hadn't been so drunk when I made love to Jessie, so I could determine if I could enjoy having sex with a woman."

"It ain't never too late. I'm concerned about how long she'll put up with you if you never touch her. I mean, holding her off for a few months or even a few years with that concocted story about your manhood being on pause will eventually die out. Her being a woman, she might decide to get a divorce and marry somebody else. Or she might stay with you and just get a boyfriend to take care of her physical needs. From what you done told me about Jessie, she's as normal as a woman can be. And I don't think there is a normal woman in the world in her early forties who could go the rest of her life without sex," Leroy said.

"You got a point there. Oh, well. If she leaves me because I won't make love to her, at least for all my troubles, I'll have a child."

I felt so much better. I wasn't in the mood to have sex, but when Leroy started massaging my knee, I couldn't get to his bedroom fast enough.

Chapter 41
Jessie

W<small>E HAD A TORNADO THE DAY BEFORE THE WEDDING. WE WAS</small> lucky this time because it wasn't nearly as destructive as some of the ones we usually had. It blew some branches off the walnut tree in my backyard and flattened the shed where I kept odds and ends that I should have got rid of a long time ago. It also shattered the window in my bedroom. I didn't care about any of that because I had already packed up most of my stuff that I was taking with me to Hubert's house after our wedding reception.

But the storm had interrupted electricity on some streets, including my future in-laws. Reverend Wiggins called me Saturday morning. As soon as I heard his voice, I got nervous. My first thought was that he had decided not to marry me and Hubert and we'd have to find another preacher. There was three other colored preachers in Lexington, but I had no idea if one would be available to marry us at such short notice. I breathed a sigh of relief when Reverend Wiggins told me the reason he was calling.

"The electricity just came back on over here. Them chicken wings Mother was going to fry for the reception spoiled overnight. So we won't enjoy the same kind of feast we usually enjoy at a wedding reception."

"Oh, I don't care what we eat. And I hope our guests don't. I done already cleaned out my icebox and gave the meat I had left to Yolinda, so I can't fix nothing to bring myself."

"I'm sure we'll make do with whatever Mother can throw together. I just wanted to let you know."

"Thanks. Well, I guess I should get up and pack up the rest of my stuff."

Reverend Wiggins stayed silent for a few moments. "Jessie, do you really love my boy?"

I had to catch my breath because his question caught me off guard. "I *love* Hubert from the bottom of my heart." I made sure I put a lot of emphasis on the word "love." I added for even more emphasis: "I ain't never *loved* a man the way I *love* him."

"What about your first husband?"

"I loved Orville, but in a different kind of way."

"I didn't know there was more than one way to love a person."

"Well, I loved Orville because he was good to me in the beginning, and he was so pitiful with his bad heart, I felt sorry for him. I love Hubert because we both love the Lord, he respects me—which was something Orville never did—and he is dependable, caring, thoughtful, and treats me like a queen. I guess he learned all that from you . . ."

"Uh-huh. We raised him according to the Bible." Reverend Wiggins cleared his throat. "And if you don't mind answering my next question, I'd like to know when you realized you loved him?"

I was caught off guard again. The first thought that popped into my head was that he was fishing for information to see if I'd had feelings for Hubert before Maggie died. "Well, I only realized it about a month ago."

"And why was that? Did something in particular happen between y'all for you to come to that conclusion?"

"No, it didn't. The thing is, me and Hubert are both single now. One evening during supper, we got on the subject of how hard it is for people like us who'd been married for so long to be single again. I told him I couldn't wait to find another husband. He told me that he wanted to get married again too. All we had to do was find the right person. Well, it didn't take long for us to figure out the 'right person' we was looking for was already in the picture: us. I fell in love with Hubert that night. It

took him a few more days to realize he felt the same way about
me. You ain't got to worry, we ain't doing this on a lark. God
brought us together and you been telling us for years that we
should never question God."

"I see. Well, I stand by my words. Bless your soul and welcome
to the family."

We'd only invited a dozen folks to see us get married in the
Wigginses' living room. I wore the pink dress Hubert liked so
much. He had bought a new blue suit and looked so dapper in
it, I couldn't take my eyes off him. I couldn't believe that this
man was finally going to belong to me, legally and in God's eyes.
It didn't bother me one bit that I'd had to use deceit to land
him. I wasn't the one who had come up with the saying "All's
fair in love and war." But I totally believed in it.

Mama was the only one in my family who came to see me get
married. I was pleased that she wore one of the bulky yellow
dresses she wore to church, and not one of the outlandish, snug-
fitting outfits she wore when she hosted a get-together at her
house, or when she was going to a juke joint.

"Sister Inez, I am so glad you was able to join us at such short
notice," Hubert told her as she waddled throughout the living
room, fanning her nut-brown moon face with her hand, and
wheezing up a storm. Mama had asthma and a few other problems with her health, but she never let that stop her from having
a good time.

She stopped fanning and let out her breath. "Son, I wouldn't
miss this event for nothing in the world. Jessie married a frog
the first time. This time, she's marrying Prince Charming."
Mama laughed and then she turned to me, looked me up and
down, and said in a stern tone, "Jessie, you know your Bible, so
you know that even if he does something out of character and
upsets you, it's your cross to bear. You going to stay with him, no
matter what. If you ever do leave him, I'm going to make sure
you take him with you."

I seen Hubert from the corner of my eye fidgeting and rolling his eyes. "Mama, that's the last thing you should be saying before our wedding," I scolded.

She waved her hand in my face. "Humph! I mean every word I just said." She glanced around and sniffed. "Something smells good up in here. I hope y'all got enough food so I can take a plate home. What y'all got to drink? I sure could use a buzz."

"There ain't going to be no alcohol served, Sister Inez. I'm sorry," Hubert said.

Mama's face froze. "A wedding without spirits?"

"This is a very special occasion for me and Jessie. We want everybody to have a clear mind today."

"Oh, well. I'm sure it'll be a real nice affair anyway."

I was glad Mama didn't say nothing else inappropriate. She glided across the floor and stopped in front of Hubert's mama. Sister Wiggins had on a dress that was almost the same style as the one I had on, except hers was green. She and Mama immediately started talking about dress patterns and hair appointments.

I was disappointed Minnie had not been able to come so I could visit with Earl for a little while. She and her husband had to attend another wedding at the same time as mine. It was her goddaughter's, so she couldn't miss it. Hubert had offered to pick Earl up and take him back home after our reception. But when I asked Earl over the phone if he wanted to come, he said he'd rather go to the wedding Minnie was going to.

My other siblings had previous plans and they scolded me about planning a wedding at the spur of the moment. "Why don't y'all hold off a little while?" my big brother, Karl, had asked. "If y'all so much in love, y'all can do it next week or next month."

"We don't want to put it off," I shot back.

"Why come? You scared Hubert might change his mind?"

"No, smarty-pants. I know he'd never do that." That was one thing I was sure of.

Right after Reverend Wiggins pronounced us man and wife, and Hubert kissed me—on the mouth for the first time—we mingled for an hour with our guests. I enjoyed the snacks my new mother-in-law had prepared. A hour later, after a fifteen-minute-long prayer led by Reverend Wiggins, me and Hubert left.

I never expected Hubert to make a miraculous recovery so that he'd be able to make love to me on our wedding night. But I hadn't expected to spend such an important night playing checkers! That was just what we did until almost midnight.

"Maggie hated checkers," Hubert said after he'd won three games in a row. "And she'd rather get a whupping than play dominoes with me."

"Well, I like checkers and dominoes, so you ain't never got to worry about me not wanting to play with you." I hated both games from the bottom of my heart. I couldn't think of anything more boring. But I was going to say whatever I thought Hubert wanted to hear from me for the rest of my life.

He was already in the bed by the time I came out of the bathroom in the see-through pink nightgown that I'd bought especially for my wedding night. He yawned as I approached the bed.

"Jessie, you going to freeze to death in that skimpy thing. Ain't you got no wool or cotton nighties?"

"I didn't unpack them yet," I explained as I got in the bed.

"Then I'm going to get one of them quilts out of the closet that Maggie made. I don't want you to catch your death of cold on your wedding night."

Hubert tumbled out of bed and trotted to the closet. He came back with one of the thickest quilts I'd ever seen in my life and laid it on top of the sheets, a blanket, and a bedspread already on the bed. I immediately started sweating. I didn't care what I had to put up with now because I had completed my mission.

Chapter 42
Hubert

Me and Jessie had been married a month and things was working out just fine. She'd sold all of the furniture from her old house and we'd put the money in the bank. I told her to use as much as she needed to turn Claude's old room into a nursery and purchase some things for the baby.

Business was going well at my funeral home, but I didn't want to get slaphappy and start buying things we didn't need. Undertaking was a fickle business. I never knew when I'd get a body and there had been a few times last year when I'd had to wait for over a month. Miraculously, I'd been averaging at least two a month since last summer. The payments for them five murdered women in less than a year, not to mention that teenage girl that drowned and a heap of old folks, had really kept me and Tyrone and Floyd busy, and our wallets full. I was even happier now. I was convinced that I'd be as content with Jessie as I'd been with Maggie.

My relationship with Leroy was so strong now, I was also convinced that I would never have to look for love again. His birthday was coming up this week, on Thursday, May 9, and his kids was going to spend a few hours with him that evening. I would go over after work on Friday and me and him would celebrate it then. But I had another good reason to go make the trip to Hartville again and I'd already told Jessie about it. I wanted to visit one of my used-to-be high-school teachers over there because he was on his deathbed. His family had contacted as many of his favorite former students as possible to come pay their last respects. I was one of the first ones they'd called. I figured I could pay my respects Saturday morning, and spend Friday night and part of Saturday and Sunday with Leroy.

Before Jessie could even ask to go with me, I had a story already made up to tell her why she couldn't. "Tyrone and Floyd need a break, so I told them to take the Saturday off. I need for you to be at the funeral home to cover the phone from nine in the morning until five in the evening," I told her as I packed a few things.

Jessie gulped before she spoke with her voice trembling. "That place gives me the heebie-jeebies. When I used to go there with Maggie, I'd usually wait for her outside. Now you want me to be up in that scary place by myself? I would drop dead in my tracks if I seen a ghost."

"*Pffftt.* So long as I been running the place, I ain't never seen nary ghost."

"There's a first time for everything," Jessie pointed out. "And, other than the cemetery and the nursing home, there ain't no other place where spirits hang out more. Can I have Yolinda, or somebody else, stay there with me? I don't like going to the funeral home, even when I go there with you."

I tried to make light of the situation by chuckling. "I don't care if you take Yolinda or somebody else with you. If they don't want to go or can't stay with you the whole time, there's a Bible on the shelf behind the embalming tables. Anytime you feel spooked, take a hold of it, read a few Psalms, and then keep it nearby until you leave."

I left my house Friday evening a few minutes after six p.m. and met up with Leroy at his shop. He was cutting the hair of one of his regular customers that I had seen in passing a couple of times, but never spoke to. After I wished Leroy a belated birthday, he introduced me as his cousin from Toxey who had come to town to go fishing with him.

After we went up to his apartment, I was amazed to see balloons, birthday cards, and presents from his kids and other family members all over the place. He proudly showed me the new fishing reel his sons had chipped in to buy for him.

"I sure do miss my boy," I said with a sniff. "We didn't go fishing or nothing like that, but we spent a lot of time together picking blackberries and maintaining things around the house."

Leroy gave me a sympathetic look and a quick hug. "Well, if you have a boy this time, you can do all of them things again."

We dropped down on the couch at the same time. He unbuttoned his shirt and gave me a quick peck on the lips. "Honey, after you visit your used-to-be teacher tomorrow, we'll have a nice quiet supper and cake."

"You want to go to a movie or something tonight?"

"You ain't too tired after that long drive?"

"Leroy, I'm never too tired to do something with you. But let's stay in tonight." After we made love, we cuddled in bed and listened to the radio.

Whenever we wanted to go out together in public, I'd meet Leroy at wherever we was going and make out like we'd bumped into each other by accident. A few times he had suggested that we go to the Half Moon Diner, where I'd seen him kissing on that man New Year's Eve. The only reason I didn't go there with him was because I didn't want to run into Ralph Cook, the juke joint owner who had "warned" me about Leroy. The last thing I wanted to do was add fuel to that flame.

Ralph struck me as the kind of jackass who liked to run his mouth. If he was bold enough to tell me—a man he hardly knew—what he thought about Leroy, there was no telling what he'd tell the folks he knew really well. I would rather spend time with Leroy alone in his place anyway.

When we got up Saturday morning, I called up my old teacher's wife to let her know I was on my way. She told me not to bother and went on to tell me between sobs that her husband had took a turn for the worse and passed during the night. I went to visit her anyway to offer my condolences and to ask if I could help with the arrangements. This family always spent a lot of money on flowers and expensive caskets when their loved ones died so I would have made a heap of money. I was disappointed when I learned that the funeral was going to be in Slidell, Louisiana, where the family was from.

Me and Leroy spent the rest of the day lounging. Even though I enjoyed his company, knowing that I hadn't been able to say good-bye to my former teacher had put a damper on my spirit. That was the only reason I went back to Lexington early Sunday afternoon.

Jessie had already started cooking supper when I got home. It saddened her when I told her my old teacher had died before I got to see him.

"That's why it's important not to put nothing off," she said. "I'm so glad we got married when we did."

I was surprised when Jessie told me that nobody had called the funeral home yesterday to request my services. I knew several folks who was on their death beds. Some families didn't wait until one of their loved ones passed to call me. Sometimes if the person was close enough to the end, a family member got in touch with me a few days before their departure to start making final arrangements. I was glad Jessie hadn't seen no ghosts at the funeral home, not that I thought she would. She had stopped on her way home and bought a plump chicken from a man down the street who raised them in his backyard. She and Maggie used to do business with him at least once a week. They got the chickens real cheap because they had to tote them home still alive in a crocus sack. Then they had to wring their necks and pluck them. I used to help Maggie with that nasty chore, but Jessie had already done the deed by herself today.

"You look tired. I want you to sit back and relax while I finish cooking supper. I got everything under control." She took my hand and led me to the couch, gently pushed me down, and pulled off my shoes. "After I check on the chicken, I'll come back and give you a foot massage."

"Thank you, sugar," I muttered. I was pleased as punch that

God had blessed me with two earth angels. Between her and Maggie, I couldn't decide which one was the best.

We sat down to enjoy the fried chicken supper, along with some yams, turnip greens, and hot-water corn bread. Jessie swallowed the clump of greens she'd been chewing and gazed at me with her eyes narrowed.

"What's the matter?" I asked with my heart pounding. By living a double life, I had to deal with paranoia on a regular basis.

"Tyrone came by the funeral home yesterday before I left. I had the strangest conversation with him," she told me with a puzzled expression on her face.

"What was so strange about it?"

"When he asked if anybody had died and I told him no, he looked disappointed. And then he said he hoped business wasn't about to go back into a slump, like it had last year."

I raised my eyebrows. "We had a lot of business last year."

"I know. But earlier in the year, Maggie complained about how slow things had been before Orville and a bunch of other folks died in the next few weeks."

"Tyrone is worried that the Fuller Brothers is taking too much business away from us. Him and Floyd got families to support, and lady friends on the side that they like to spoil. Naturally, they'd be concerned about me having to cut back on our hours of operation."

"But don't you pay them for every day they work, whether y'all get any bodies or not?"

"I do, but only part of what I give them when we got more business."

"Well, I just hope they don't jump ship and go work for the Fuller Brothers or move to a bigger city and get jobs with one of them bigger funeral homes."

"Let's change the subject. I'm still grieving my old teacher's passing. You want to go out for a drive or to a movie?"

"Not really. I'd rather stay home and play checkers and listen to the radio. Besides, my stomach is feeling kind of queasy."

"I see. Well, that's to be expected when you expecting."

"Expecting what?"

I reared my head back and looked at her like she was crazy. "You fixing to have a baby." I had to scratch my head and wonder why she'd asked me such a odd question.

"Oh yeah! I don't know what comes over me sometimes. This pregnancy got me so frazzled, I don't know if I'm coming or going. Just like when I was pregnant with Earl."

"Well, a woman's body goes through a lot of changes when she's expecting. Mama told me that when she was carrying me, she would leave the house and not be able to find her way back home." We laughed. "By the way, I noticed you ain't had morning sickness yet. Maggie suffered with it almost every morning her first three months. You ain't puked nary time."

"Yes, I did!" she said quick. "It happened a few times last week after you had left for work. And twice today."

"Oh. I was just wondering. And another thing, your belly is still as flat as it always was. Maggie didn't start showing for a while, but almost every other pregnant woman I know started gaining weight in other places right away."

Jessie laughed and waved her hand. "When I start looking like a Guernsey cow, don't say nothing. In the meantime, I don't want to buy no maternity clothes until I actually need them."

Chapter 43
Jessie

HUBERT DECIDED TO GO VISIT HIS PARENTS WHEN WE FINISHED eating supper this evening. "You want to go with me?" he asked as he picked his teeth with a straw he'd plucked from my whisk broom.

"No, I'm going to make some tea and relax. I got a slight stomachache," I said, which was a fib. I just didn't feel like answering any of his parents' nosy questions. I ended up wishing I had gone with him. His mama didn't waste no time calling me when he got there.

"Sugar, Hubert just told us you think you're pregnant," she said in a low tone. "Ain't it kind of soon for you to know that?" Now she sounded suspicious.

"Um, I'm pretty sure I am. I been throwing up. My back, feet, and other body parts is aching. And my stomach feels queasy. I was only a month along with Earl when I started having them same symptoms."

"You was young then. Your body done went through a heap of changes since then so them symptoms could mean something different this time."

"Uh-uh! I know my body. I knew I was pregnant with Earl right away and I *know* I'm pregnant now," I insisted.

"I declare, I can't tell you how happy I am to hear you say *that*! I just hope you're right. And you better be careful. We can't allow you to get too sick and jeopardize the baby's health. Is your doctor giving you anything for them symptoms?" she asked.

"Huh? Oh! I ain't been to see no doctor yet."

Mother Wiggins gasped so loud, it sounded like she was standing right next to me. "What? How come?"

"I'm going to go to the clinic one day next week and get something for my stomach," I lied.

"All right, then, sugar. If you don't feel well enough by tomorrow, I'm going to come over there and tend to you myself. I make a mean pot of fish-head soup."

I did not want to have my overbearing mother-in-law breathing down my neck. But I was more concerned about the comment Hubert had made about my flat stomach. I thought about strapping a pillow around my waist in a week or so, but that thought didn't stay on my mind long. Some of the folks I knew was the type to do a lot of unnecessary bear hugging when I ran into them. It wouldn't take long for somebody to notice how fluffy my stomach felt. And I wouldn't put it past one of them nosy busybodies to lift up my blouse before I had time to stop them. I couldn't imagine the look on somebody's face after seeing a pillow tied around my belly.

When Hubert got back home a hour later, we went to bed. He snored like a moose every night, so it took me a while to get to sleep, especially if I had a lot on my mind. I sure had a lot on my mind tonight. It didn't look like Hubert was going to pleasure me no time soon. I'd gone without some for so many months, it was finally beginning to get to me. The last thing I wanted to do was get involved with another man, especially while I was "pregnant."

My condition didn't stop Conway from flirting with me. "I'm still trying to get close to you," he teased on Monday while me and him was eating our baloney sandwiches on our lunch break.

I laughed. "If I didn't bite your hook before I got married and pregnant, what makes you think I'd bite it now?"

"I'm just playing with you, *Mrs. Wiggins.* A lot of women would love to be in your shoes."

I swallowed a plug of baloney and gave him a confused look. "What's that supposed to mean?"

"Girl, you know how many other women wanted to snatch up Hubert? My old lady don't know I know it, but she had her eye on him before you took him out of circulation."

"Whoever your old lady is, you need to concentrate on her so she won't be getting no ideas about my husband. I know a lot of the colored women in this town. What's her name?"

"Oh, it ain't important. I doubt if you know her. She ain't the type that a unworldly lady like you would associate with."

I hunched my shoulders. "I was just asking. I don't really want to know nothing about her anyway. You told me right after I met you that she was a battle-ax, and that's enough for me."

Conway snickered and gave me a knowing look. "Yup, she is that. I ain't no angel myself, though. But I'm slick enough to do whatever I want and not let her catch me. My woman is a beautiful, smart, juicy-butt woman who can cook up a storm. She is also a liar, dishonest, gets jealous at the drop of a hat, and can't hold a job. You want to meet her so you can see what I'm talking about? Maybe you'd show me a little more sympathy."

"I just told you, I don't want to know nothing about that woman, let alone meet her. I got enough problems."

"Anyway, her name is Blond—"

I cut Conway off before he could spit out her full name. *"Blondeen Walker?"* I had heard months ago from a couple of people that Blondeen had a new boyfriend living with her. Them women knew me and her didn't get along so they didn't talk about her much around me. If they had mentioned the name of her new boyfriend, I had blocked it out. Blondeen fooled around with so many men, I couldn't keep the names straight anyway.

He nodded.

"Lord, have mercy! I already know her. She's probably the most mean-spirited woman I know. We used to work the night shift together here until she got fired for stealing money from a patient. She's had a beef with me ever since then because I'd refused to lie—and risk getting fired myself—and say she'd been with me when that money got stole."

Conway's eyes got big. "It was you that got her fired?"

"She didn't tell you it was me?"

"Not by name. She just whooped and hollered about a snooty black bitch causing her to get fired."

"She got herself fired."

"Well, she still blames you. If I was you, I'd stay out of her way because she ain't nobody to mess with."

"Humph! You think I don't know that. But I'll tell you now, if she ever tries to do harm to me, she better do it right. Because in the end, one of us will be dead."

Conway laughed and waved his hand. "I know her better than you. She's a mad dog, but I swear her bark is worse than her bite. Blondeen might threaten or actually coldcock you, but she wouldn't do nothing real violent because she can't stand the sight of blood. She puked and fainted when we witnessed a dog get run over by a bus."

"I don't want to find out if she would do anything violent to me. I hope you never mention my name to her. I'd hate for her to get ugly with you because of me."

"*Pffftt!* You ain't got to worry about me bringing up your name in front of her. When she goes on a rant about somebody, she stays on it for hours and it causes me a lot of stress."

I went back to work and didn't give Blondeen another thought. I had decided that I wasn't going to waste any more of my time and energy on her.

When I got home, Hubert was in the kitchen on the phone. From the sour expression on his face, I could tell that he wasn't having a pleasant conversation. "All right. I'll go get the hearse and get there as fast as I can." He hung up and gave me a weary look. "Remember that elderly woman down the street who used to bake tea cakes for Claude when he was a little boy? She had a stroke last night and passed. That was her husband I was talking to."

"Oh, I'm sorry to hear that. You going to collect the body now?"

"Uh-huh. Her family is too skittish to be in the house with a dead body for too long." Hubert swallowed hard and looked me up and down. First he felt my forehead. "You look flushed."

"I think that baloney I ate for lunch was too old." When he reached out to touch my belly, I yelped and stumbled backward. "Don't do that!"

Hubert's mouth dropped open so wide and low it looked like a soup ladle. "My goodness. I know pregnant women get a little crazy, but that's my baby too. If you act this territorial already, there ain't no telling how you'll act when he or she gets here."

I forced myself to laugh. "It's just that, uh, my stomach feels a little tender right now. Every time I touch it, it feels like it's going to turn upside down. I'm going to go lay down for a few minutes."

"Well, you do that and don't worry about nothing. I'll cook them greens you picked up from the market yesterday when I get back. Oh! Before I forget, Mama told me to tell you she's going to come pick you up this coming Saturday and take you shopping to pick out a few things for the baby. I declare, she is so giddy about becoming a grandparent again. Daddy is too. I can't believe that my misbehavior turned into such a blessing. Having another child is a dream come true." Hubert looked like he was going to attempt to hug me, but I moved away in time.

"I'd better go on and lay down for a while before I fall down," I insisted.

I went to the bathroom first and stared at myself in the mirror for a few seconds. "Girl, I do believe you fixing to have a miscarriage any day now," I whispered.

Chapter 44
Hubert

I'D ALREADY PREPARED THE ELDERLY LADY WHO HAD DIED ON Monday, two days ago. The family was anxious to get her buried so the funeral was going to take place today at ten a.m. I was glad that they wanted to have the service early in the day so I could attend it and be on my way before noon to go visit Leroy for a couple of hours. I had told Jessie not to expect me home before six p.m. She didn't like funerals, so I didn't have to worry about her taking off work to go to this one.

I liked having some free time to myself during the week. That way, I got to spend more time with Leroy. When I got to his barbershop a few minutes before one p.m., I looked through the window before I entered. I stopped in my tracks. There was a young man I didn't recognize cutting a customer's hair. I panicked at first. My first thought was that something bad had happened to Leroy. I ran around to the back of the building and took the stairs, two at a time, up to his apartment. He had gave me a key, but the door was unlocked, so I opened it and went in.

"Leroy, you home?" I called out. He didn't answer. "Leroy! Leroy! Uhhhhhhh, Leroy!"

A split second later, he shuffled into the living room from the kitchen. I was surprised to see that he was already in his long underwear and bathrobe.

"Baby, are you sick?"

"I'm fine, sugar," he chuckled as he waved his hand.

"Who is that downstairs cutting hair?" I asked as I followed him to the couch.

"Him? He worked for the man who used to own the shop. He contacted me recently and told me he was available to fill in for me when and if I ever needed backup. I had a slew of phone calls to make and a little housework that I wanted to get out of the way before you got here."

"Oh." I bit my bottom lip and looked at Leroy from the corner of my eye. "Is he . . ."

"One of us?" Leroy shook his head. "At least not that I know of. But you don't have to worry about him. I already told him that my 'cousin,' meaning you, stops by from time to time." Leroy looked me up and down. I still had on one of the three black suits I only wore to funerals and weddings. "You came straight from that woman's funeral?"

"Yup. I didn't want to waste no time. I'd like to be back home around the time my wife gets off work. She's been having a few problems with her pregnancy, but she keeps telling me it ain't nothing serious."

"That's good. I know how bad you want that baby. Hey, you want to go out for a little while? There is a sale on chicken gizzards at that meat market on Pike Street. Then we could catch the tail end of that flower show on the same street."

"No, I think we should continue to have most of our get-togethers at your place. The less people see us together in public, the less likely they'll get the wrong idea."

Leroy gave me a curious look. "Why would you think that? Other than you and my used-to-be lovers, don't nobody know my personal business. I been careful all my life. Besides, we don't look or act like sissies, so nobody would have a reason to think otherwise when they see us in public."

I exhaled hard before I asked the next question. "How well do you know a man named Ralph Cook?"

Leroy gave me a confused look and shrugged. "Hmmm. Ralph . . . Cook." He scratched the side of his head and raised his eyebrows. "Oh yeah! He operates a place in Toxey where he pushes cheap homemade liquor, and even cheaper women. I've been there a few times and conversated with him. I don't know him that well, though. Why?"

"Well, before I found out about you, I ran into him at the Half Moon Diner over on Beacon Avenue. We got to talking and he warned me about places to avoid if I didn't want to be pestered by sissies. Your shop was one of them places." I paused and watched as Leroy's eyes got bigger. He didn't say nothing at first, so I went on. "He was surprised when I told him how you'd been cutting my hair for years. He knows about you."

Leroy's face looked like it had turned to stone. When he started talking again, his lips was quivering. "That blabbermouth fool! Yeah, he knows about me—and I know about him. A few weeks after I got home from the military, me and my boyfriend at the time went to his place for a few drinks. While I was talking to some young ladies who had pounced on me, I seen Ralph's hands feeling up and down my man's neck. I thought he was just being friendly because he was drunk, but when I seen them smooching, I knew the score." I had never seen Leroy angry before and it was so disturbing, I hoped that this would be the last time.

"What did you do?"

He shrugged. "What could I do? I was young and still learning the ropes, so I didn't know half as much as I know now about the proper protocol for people like us. I pretended like I didn't notice. Anyway, I found out the next day, from the same ex-boyfriend, that Ralph swung both ways. Why else would he allow sissies to hang out at his place? Most of the other moonshiners back then and bar owners didn't allow us to socialize in their places."

I gave Leroy a thoughtful look. I was happy to see that he didn't look so angry now. "He sounds like a hypocritical troublemaker. If I ever see him again, I'm going to run in the opposite direction."

Leroy suddenly looked so weary, I wanted to change the subject. But he stayed on it. "Hubert, you know we live a dangerous lifestyle. We can't switch it off and on. All we can do is act as normal as possible and keep hiding everything any way we can. I don't know if Ralph was curious about it at one time, or what. Maybe he tried it and didn't like it and decided to only see women. And, let me tell you, he went overboard in that area. Last time I heard, he had seven babies by five different women. I'm glad he made that comment about me to you and not one of my other customers. I need all the business I can get in these hard times."

"I know just what you mean. That's why I don't think we should spend too much time in public. You never know who you'll run into. If Ralph seen me out in public with you, he'd wonder how come I didn't heed his warning. And just like he ran his mouth to me about you, he'd run it to somebody else."

"I guess you're right. Well, whenever we really do need a change of scenery, we can spend a little time in that motel where we first got together," Leroy said with a nostalgic look on his face. "That place will always be more special to me now."

I was still ready to change the subject, but I knew I had to ride it out to the end. "That suits me fine. Or we could drive over to a place in another county, where we don't know nobody. Folks there will think we are just two men friends out enjoying the day." I squeezed Leroy's hand and looked into his eyes. His smile made me feel warm all over. "That's much better," I said as I squeezed his hand harder.

He leaned over and gave me a long kiss. "Hubert, let's concentrate on today. I don't know when I'll see you again."

"If Jessie is feeling well enough to be left alone, I'll try and come back again tomorrow."

It turned out to be a very enjoyable afternoon.

When I got home at six thirty and found Jessie sitting up in bed with a damp washcloth on her forehead, I was shocked. I ran up to her as fast as I could.

"Jessie, what's wrong, sugar?"

She looked fine, but sounded like she was at death's door. "H-Hubert, I done lost our baby," she sobbed.

Chapter 45
Jessie

"**N**O!" Hubert boomed as he eased down on the bed and started rubbing the side of my face. I hated seeing him so upset. But I would have been more concerned if he hadn't been. "You sure about that?"

"Y-yeah, I-I'm sure," I stammered, nodding toward a few splotches of blood on the floor by his feet that led all the way into the bathroom. I had used some blood from the chicken I had cut up to fry for supper.

He looked down and sucked in some air so fast, he hiccupped. "I better get you to the clinic—"

I cut him off right away. "You don't have to do that."

"Why not?"

"Because I'm fine. Honest to God, I am. It happened early this morning and I feel a lot better already." Another lie blew up in my head like a balloon so fast, I thought my head was going to bust open. "Uh, one of the nurses at the home checked me out."

"A nurse?"

"Uh-huh. She's one of the nicest people there." I had to stop talking so I could organize my words so everything I said made sense. "Anyway, she drove me home and looked me over real good. She even gave me a pill and stayed a couple of hours to make sure I was all right."

Hubert started breathing through his mouth as his eyes roamed all over my face. "I declare, Jessie, this house has been in my family for over forty years and no white person has ever set foot inside."

"You can't say that now. You got a problem with a white woman coming here?"

"Goodness gracious, no! I'm just surprised she was willing to go all out for a colored woman. I been knowing my boss at the mill for over twenty years and I been to his house before, but he ain't never set foot in mine." Hubert let his breath out and began to look more relaxed. "Remind me to give that nurse a call to thank her. If she's agreeable, we'll have her join us for supper as soon as you feel up to cooking again."

"I will. But she's in the process of moving to Texas in a few days, so I don't know if she'll be able to take time from her packing to come have supper with us."

"Bless her heart. When you see her, let her know how much I appreciate her helping you out." Hubert stared at me with his eyes squinted. "Well, what happened? Did you lift something heavy after me and Mama and Daddy and everybody else told you to avoid too much physical activity?"

I shook my head. "I was getting ready to mop the hallway when I started feeling real crampy. My supervisor seen me doubling over and heard me moaning, so she told me to go sit down for a while. But she changed her mind in a flash and made me come home. I made it into the house in the nick of time. I felt something wet and warm between my legs and ran to the bathroom and plonked down on the commode. Next thing I know, a pain I wouldn't wish on Satan shot through my stomach and something slid out of me and splashed into the commode. I was with my sister Minnie when she had her miscarriage, so I knew what was happening to me."

"What did you do with the baby?"

"I flushed the commode. What was I supposed to do?"

"I . . . I wish you had scooped that poor child out so we could have a proper burial."

"'Burial'? What in the world are you talking about?"

"When my mechanic's wife miscarried, they had me pick up

the baby and take care of the final arrangements. It was a boy and they even named it."

"She was way further along than me because mine hadn't even formed into no baby boy or girl yet. It was just a big clump of blood and stuff."

"Well, in that case, you did the right thing, I guess. I can't believe we ain't going to have no baby." Hubert's voice was raspy and he looked so weak, I got scared that he'd end up in the bed too.

"Not this time," I said in a strong tone of voice.

He gave me a puzzled look. I had no idea what was going through his mind. But if he was wondering how come I suddenly sounded so strong, I had to squash that. I squirmed and moaned with a grimace on my face.

"Jessie, are you all right?"

"Uh-huh. It's just that when I move a certain way, a sharp pain goes all through me."

"Then don't move a certain way."

"I won't. Um, I been thinking. We are still young enough to make another baby. And, as soon as you get back to normal, we can start trying."

He nodded, but the deadpan expression on his face confused me. "It could take a while. I'm forty-three years old and ain't made but one baby."

"Two."

"Huh?"

"You made one with Maggie and one with me. You can't overlook Claude just because he's dead."

"You're right. Anyway, I ain't made but two babies, so my jism must not be that strong. The older I get, the weaker it's going to get, so it ain't likely we'll ever make another baby."

"But God's the one in charge so we'll have to live with whatever happens. In the meantime, let's put this behind us and move on with our lives. I ain't told nobody else about the miscarriage, but we need to let your mama and daddy know soon."

"I don't want to tell them over the phone. So, before I go to bed, I'll take a ride over there to let them know."

"Hubert, I'm sorry I disappointed you. I know how important the baby was to you."

"Don't worry about it. These things happen."

"I . . . I feel like less than a woman now." I was pleased that I was able to conjure up such a wimpy tone of voice and act so woeful. From the tortured look on Hubert's face, it was very effective.

"You ain't no less of a woman because of what happened than I am less of a man because of my situation."

"If you want to divorce me and marry somebody else—"

Hubert couldn't have looked more stunned if I had pulled a knife on him. "What's wrong with you? You're my wife. There ain't no way in the world I'd want to leave you for another woman. I married you for life and I'm going to stay with you until one of us is dead." He abruptly stopped talking and gazed at me with his eyes blinking hard. "Now, if you want to get rid of me because I ain't the man I should be—"

I couldn't cut him off fast enough. "I ain't going to leave you for nobody." I exhaled and forced myself to smile. "I'm pleased to hear that you feel the way you do. I'm going to rest a little longer, and when I get up, I'll clean up the bloody mess I left on the floor."

"I'll take care of that." Hubert stood up. "You get some more rest and don't worry about nothing. We'll be all right."

Chapter 46
Hubert

*I*DIDN'T GO STRAIGHT TO MY PARENTS' PLACE WHEN I LEFT MY HOUSE. I went to the cemetery first. Maggie and Claude had been buried side by side, I'd made sure of that. I squatted down between their graves and a great big tear oozed from the corner of my eye. I wiped it away with the back of my hand and had to cough to clear my throat before I could talk. "Maggie, I miss you so much! I thought I was going to have another complete family, but I was wrong. I hope you ain't mad at me for getting drunk and taking advantage of a God-fearing woman like Jessie. You knew her better than me, so you know how saintly she is. She ain't your replacement, though. If anything, she is a extension of you. I couldn't have asked for a better second wife."

I swallowed hard and turned to Claude's grave. "Son, you know by now that I wasn't your birth daddy and I hope you don't hold that against me. Me and your mama only did what we did because we didn't have no other choice. Having a child was so important, we didn't care how we got one. You two angels rest in peace and sleep well until I see y'all again. I hope that the spirit of the child me and Jessie just lost is already up there with y'all."

Since Jessie was my family now, I felt obligated to include her in my declaration. "Jessie will also spend eternity with us. I don't know which one of us will get to heaven first, so please be patient."

It took a lot of effort for me to wobble up off the ground. My feet felt so heavy, it was a struggle to keep them moving long enough for me to make it back to my car and get back in it. I was so overwrought, all I could do was sit there and boo-hoo for the next five minutes. When I decided I had cried enough, I sopped the tears off my face with my handkerchief and headed to my parents' house.

Mama had a distressed look on her face when I dragged my feet into the living room. I didn't waste no time telling her and Daddy the last thing I knew they wanted to hear. "Jessie lost the baby today."

Mama wailed and stumbled backward. When she reached the couch, she dropped down on it so hard, I heard a whooshing noise. "Lord, help us!" she boomed.

Daddy stood a few feet from me with his hands on his hips. He hadn't looked so beside hisself since Maggie and Claude died. "Is Jessie all right? Did you take her to the clinic?" he asked as he choked on a sob.

I took a deep breath and stumbled over to the couch and sat down next to Mama. She and Daddy was staring at me so hard, I got goose bumps. "Y'all calm down," I said as gently as I could. "We don't know what happened, but she's fine now. It started this morning while she was at work. One of the white nurses drove her home. She made sure Jessie was all right before she left."

"I'm sure that poor Jessie is prostrate with grief," Daddy said. "And we had such big plans for that baby." For such a big, strong man, he sounded as weak and small as a baby. I felt bad for me and Jessie, but I felt even worse for my parents.

"I guess it wasn't meant to be," Mama said in a gentle tone as she fanned her face with her hand. "We need to thank the Lord, Jessie's all right."

"She's a healthy woman and still got a few childbearing years left. We might still get lucky," Daddy said as he winked at me.

"Sure enough," I agreed. "I'm going to go on back home to be with her." I stood up and stretched my arms. "I don't like to leave her alone for too long."

"You want us to come with you?" Mama asked.

"No, I don't think she's up to seeing nobody just yet. She's feeling so guilty about what happened, I want her to have some time to get over things before she has company. I'm sure she'll be happy to see y'all in a day or so."

Daddy moved closer and clapped me on the back. "Go on back to your wife, son. We ain't but a phone call away if y'all need us to come have a prayer session. In the meantime, me and Mother will be praying nonstop."

When I got back to my house, Jessie was in the kitchen sweeping the floor. I was surprised to see her up and about. "Jessie! What's the matter with you?" I yelled as I ran up to her. "You need to take it easy for a few days. You want to fall out and hit your head on something and get brain damage next? Then you won't be good for nothing." I reached out to take her hand, but she backed away.

"Hubert, I feel fine. I done got enough rest. I been sitting on my rump so much today, it's numb. The nurse told me it was okay for me to move around, so long as I feel up to it."

"Put that broom down!" I ordered. "I'll sweep the floor before I go to bed." I reached out for her hand again. This time, she didn't move away. She dropped the broom and I led her to the living room. I sat down first and pulled her into my lap. "Let's just sit here for a few minutes."

"You want my rump to get numb some more?"

"No, I don't. When you feel that coming on, get up." I forced myself to laugh. Tears pooled in her eyes when I told her how Mama and Daddy had reacted when I told them about her losing the baby. "I'm sure Mama will be over here first thing tomorrow morning."

"Why? I'm going to work tomorrow."

"Please stay home at least one day. You know Mama will want to come look in on you and bring you some fish-head soup or something. She's hurting, Jessie. Can you imagine how she and Daddy must be feeling, knowing that they may never have another grandchild?"

"All right. I'll stay home. I just hope she don't come over here and make too much of a fuss over me. And I hate to miss out on a whole day's pay tomorrow, not to mention part of today."

"Honey, we are in pretty good shape with our finances. You can even shop for all new furniture."

"I can't do that right now. I don't know if I ever will," she said with a sniffle. "No matter what we do, we ain't never getting rid of this living-room couch."

"But it's old and lumpy and two of the legs is wobbly."

Jessie drew in a sharp breath and glared at me. "It's also where Maggie and Claude took their last breaths. We need to keep something in our lives connected to them."

My face was burning. I was ashamed of myself for not being more sentimental. "I hadn't thought about that. Maggie would be so pleased to see how well you stepped into her shoes. I'm so glad God brought me and you together."

Before I could say anything else, somebody knocked on the front door. It was a couple of our neighbors. They'd heard about Jessie losing the baby from Mama and decided to offer her some comfort. They looked so concerned, I didn't have the heart to turn them away.

For the next two hours, more neighbors streamed in and out like ants. Jessie seemed to love all the attention, but I think she was just being nice. One thing I could say was that she didn't look nothing like a woman who had lost a baby this morning. She was right resilient. The way she was laughing and prancing back and forth to the kitchen to get cider and snacks for our neighbors, you would have thought she was hosting a party. One thing I had to pat myself on the back for was the fact that I had a knack for picking strong women for wives.

It was almost midnight when the last person left our house. When me and Jessie went to bed, the last thing she said before she went to sleep was "Hubert, you are such a good man for me, I don't care if we never consummate our marriage. Even though it means we won't never have a chance at another child." She paused and gave me a meaningful look. "I know people would think I'm crazy for staying with a man who can't do what nature

intended. But I want you to know, I'm still very happy being married to you."

I didn't know what to say, especially with the big lump that had suddenly swole up in my throat. "Jessie, I'm glad you feel that way, but let's just take things slow and see what happens. So long as we are both happy with each other, nothing else matters."

She didn't say nothing else. She just smiled and pulled the covers up to her neck.

I was still feeling down in the dumps about losing my baby, especially since I knew there was no chance that I would get Jessie pregnant again. But I knew in my heart that me and her could still have a long, happy marriage anyway.

Chapter 47

Jessie

*I*T HAS BEEN A WEEK SINCE MY "MISCARRIAGE" AND EVERYTHING seemed to be moving right along, in the right direction. Except for one thing: me telling Hubert that I didn't care if we ever consummated our marriage. My feelings had changed about that. It was like something suddenly jumped up and shook some sense into my head. There was no way I would be able to go another thirty or forty years without sex.

I didn't think I had enough nerve to find another man to pleasure me, but I didn't know how much longer I could go on with the way things were. I tried not to think about sex, but no matter what I was doing, it always slipped back into my mind. Especially at work when I was around Conway. He always left the two or three top buttons of his shirts undone and his sleeves rolled up, so it was impossible not to see the top of his firm chest and muscled arms. If all that wasn't enough to make a woman (especially one going through a dry spell, like me) notice him even more, his pants looked like they was a size too small, so you could see his firm thighs and a few other items in the same vicinity.

"I'm going to swing by the county fair on my way home tomorrow evening. Quinette and Glennola want to go with me, and they said you might want to go with us," he told me Thursday evening as we was finishing up for the day. I'd just helped him clean up a mess on the floor, where a impatient patient had threw his bedpan after he got tired of waiting for one of us to come remove it.

"Thanks for asking. But I can't go with y'all this time," I replied.

Every year in May, our county sponsored a ten-day fair to help folks celebrate Memorial Day, which was the last day of the event. Colored people could only attend from six in the evening until it closed at eleven p.m. Minnie had brought Earl for a visit last Saturday and they had spent the evening at the fair with me, Yolinda, and my in-laws. Hubert had to go to Hartville that day to buy some more embalming fluid and stayed in a motel, like he usually did. He promised that he would go to the fair with me before it ended.

"Don't be a wet blanket, Jessie. You sure you don't want to go? We only planning to stay a hour or two."

"I'm going to go with my husband. Hubert loves going to the fair as much as I do."

"If you change your mind about going with us, let me know. You ain't got to worry about missing the last bus from the fair to get home. I'll take you all the way to your front door."

I shook my head and went on about my business. When I turned around, he was still standing in the same spot with a woe-begone expression on his face. I didn't know what was happening to me, but it seemed like the more I looked at Conway, the better he looked . . .

When I got home from work, Hubert met me at the door with a wide smile on his face. "Good news!" he gushed as he ushered me to the couch.

He sat down and pulled me into his lap, something he rarely did, but he seemed to enjoy doing it when he did. I didn't know if having me that close to him was for his benefit or mine. I wondered if he would keep doing it if he knew how much it excited me.

"What's the good news?" I asked as I dropped my purse onto the coffee table.

"I'm fixing to save us a heap of money!" he said with a grin.

I hunched my shoulders. "Oh? How are you going to do that?"

"I'm going to meet with the man in Meridian, Mississippi, that I purchase some of my caskets from. I been doing business with him from day one. He done finally got tired of competing with the white folks, so he's going to throw in the towel and retire. He needs to get rid of all his inventory first, though, and since I been such a loyal and regular customer all these years, I get dibs on everything before it gets picked over."

"That's wonderful!" I squealed. "There's a hat shop over there that me and Maggie used to shop at. I wouldn't mind going with you."

"Well, I wouldn't mind taking you with me, but I can't." Hubert sniffed and tickled my chin. "Please don't poke your bottom lip out. I hate it when you pout."

I poked my bottom lip out anyway. "I ain't pouting," I protested. "But I am disappointed. You never let me go out of town with you."

"I took you to that discount pork meat market, around a month ago, in Tuscaloosa."

"You took your mama and daddy with us. I'd like to go spend a night or two with you in one of them motels you stay at when you have to go to Hartville, or some other place."

"Jessie, I have to meet with the casket man tomorrow evening, so I'll have to leave work early. You don't want to miss work again so soon after the time you took off when you had the miscarriage, right?"

"That's right. It took me a while to get caught up on my chores and my supervisor rode my back the whole time, even making me work through my breaks."

"I'm going to stay at a motel because I don't want to try to make that long drive back home on a Friday night. I'm going to get up on Saturday and go look at some new car tires at a place that sells them real cheap."

"Do you think you'll be back in time for us to go to the fair before it closes?"

"I'll be back either Saturday night or no later than Sunday morning. I know I'll be tired, but we can go to the fair on Monday."

"Oh, Hubert," I said with a heavy sigh. "That's Memorial Day, so there will be so many folks there, we'd have a miserable time plowing through them crowds. And the fair closes on that day."

"Well, I guess I won't be able to go with you this year."

I shook my head. "I'll go with Yolinda again or some of the folks I work with. The lady that sells them blackberry pies will be there Saturday, and I'd like to visit that cloth booth to check out some of that fabric for a quilt me and your mama plan to make."

When I got to work on Friday, I went up to Conway fifteen minutes into my shift while he was mopping the hallway floor. "You still going to the fair after work today?" I asked. I didn't give him time to answer. "My husband won't be able to go with me this year."

Conway's face lit up like a lightning bug. "Sure, you can go with me. I'd like the company. Glennola took today off because some of her kinfolks from Branson showed up unannounced last night to visit her for the holiday. Quinette told me she's going to wait and go on Sunday with her family, so it'll be just you and me. I hope that won't be a problem for you, because I don't want to go by myself."

"Oh. Uh, what about Blondeen?" I asked.

"What about Blondeen?"

"If you really want somebody to go with you, why don't you take her instead of me?"

"*Pffftt!*" Conway waved his hand. "She don't want to go until Memorial Day so we can be there to see who all wins blue ribbons. Her friends Wilma and Sukey will be participating in the pie-baking contests this year."

"If you are going that day, why do you want to go today too?"

"Because today is the last day they'll be doing hog butchering and I want to get me a few pounds of that fresh pork butt. Do you want to go with me today or not?"

I was so conflicted, my head started swimming. I'd never been alone in a car with a man who made me tingle as much as Conway did. I needed to know for my own peace of mind if I was strong enough to stay as faithful to Hubert as he was to me.

"All right, then. I'd hate to wait another whole year before I can go again."

Me and Conway left work together at five o'clock. Ten minutes after he pulled onto the road that led to the fairgrounds, it started raining. That meant most of the exhibits would have to be shut down. "Dagnabbit! You can just drive me home, then," I told him.

"Come on, Jessie. Since we already together and had planned on spending some time at the fair, let's not waste it."

I swallowed hard and stared at the side of his face. "What else is there for us to do?"

He glanced at me and winked. "I wouldn't mind just taking a drive and gazing at the scenery along the way. Alabama is such a scenic state. Even in bad weather."

"What's wrong with you, Conway? There ain't nothing but cotton and sugarcane fields along the way in this part of the county. We both been looking at that kind of scenery our whole lives."

"I ain't tired of looking at it yet." He snickered. "I declare, Jessie, I wish you would loosen up. It took me long enough to get you alone in my car and I'd like to enjoy your company. You cute little thing, you."

His last sentence made me feel special and weak. "I'd rather look at something more uplifting than some fields," I said in a meek tone. From the smug expression on his face, I had a feeling he knew he was wearing down my resistance.

"Well, when I'm feeling down, I like to go out by Carson Lake and sit and clear my head. The last time I went, I met a real nice fisherman. He had a bucket full of catfish and he gave me a couple."

"I ain't been out that way since they started finding the bodies of them murdered colored women," I said with a shudder.

"Oh, we ain't going to be nowhere near that spot. That killer only dumps them women way off at the end of the lake in the thickets."

"All right, then. But I can't stay long." I was weaker than I thought, because I gave in quicker than I wanted to.

It had stopped raining by the time we got to the lake. Conway parked his car near some picnic tables. He reared back and stared at me like he couldn't figure out what to do with me, now that we was finally alone. I didn't wait for him to figure it out. I wrapped my arms around his neck and kissed him so hard and long, he started laughing when I turned him loose.

"I waited long enough for that," he said.

"Me too," I admitted.

I was surprised when all that backed-up passion I'd been holding in for almost a year oozed out of me. We scrambled out of the car and got in the backseat. I couldn't slide my bloomers off fast enough.

I experienced more pleasure in fifteen minutes than I had in years.

On the way home, we didn't discuss what we'd just done. Our conversation was all about work, church, and a few other mundane things. But when Conway stopped in front of my house, he asked, "When can I see you again?"

"What do you mean?" I asked dumbly.

"I hope this wasn't a onetime thing. Especially after it took me so long to get you to come around. And the way you was yipping and yapping and flipping and flopping, I know you had a good time."

My face burned. "I did, but maybe it ain't such a good idea if we do it again. If Blondeen was to find out, she would have a fit."

"You let me worry about her. You worry about your husband."

"Oh, I ain't got to worry about him. I can do whatever I want."

"What's that supposed to mean?"

"Nothing," I mumbled.

I didn't like the fact that I'd ignored my wedding vows, but I didn't feel the least bit guilty. As far as I was concerned, they was empty vows anyway. With the way things was going between me and Hubert, what else was I supposed to do?

Chapter 48
Hubert

*L*EROY CALLED ME AT HOME FRIDAY MORNING BEFORE I LEFT FOR work to tell me that his boys had decided not to come visit him this weekend, like he had expected. They wanted to go on a two-day fishing trip with a group from their church and then spend the holiday at a picnic. Leroy would have the whole weekend and Monday to hisself. He invited me to come over and spend as much of it with him as possible when I finished up my business on Saturday in Mississippi and I told him I would. Before I got back on the road to return to Alabama, I used the casket-selling man's telephone to call Leroy to let him know I was on my way.

I got to Leroy's place that afternoon a few minutes before four. I was surprised and pleased as punch to see that he had already prepared one of my favorite meals: barbecued chicken, dumplings, turnip greens, hot-water corn bread, and lemonade.

"You ain't going to stop until I'm so spoiled, you'll have to wean me like a baby," I teased as we sat down across from each other at the kitchen table.

He blinked and gazed at me for several moments before he licked his lips and spoke again. I had already started gnawing on a chicken leg. "That'll be fun. I'm going to do whatever it takes to keep you happy."

I stopped chewing and gave him a puzzled look. "I'm already

as happy as I can be. There ain't nothing else you need to do for me. I just hope that you are as happy as I am."

"I am, but I want us to get even more serious."

I laughed. "How much 'more serious' can we get?"

"I don't get to see you enough and I'd like to. I think about you all the time when you ain't here."

I gave him a woeful look. "Sugar, I'd come every day of the week if I could. But I got a wife. She's perfect for a man like me, but she's the kind of woman who needs a lot of attention. If I spend too much time away from her, she'll get suspicious, sooner or later, and start thinking I'm messing around with somebody."

Leroy's eyebrows shot up and he threw his head back and laughed long and loud. "If what you doing with me ain't 'messing around with somebody,' I don't know what is."

"I know that, and my wife said she'd never leave me, no matter what. But my mama didn't raise no fool, so I ain't going to count on her feeling that way forever. She's only human. Folks change all the time, especially women. I got too much to lose if she leaves me. First of all, every one of them other women who tried to snag me would be all over me again."

Leroy was beginning to look exasperated. "Come on now, Hubert. Can't you just tell them other women you ain't interested and to leave you alone? You wouldn't believe how many I had to beat off with a stick before I got married, and when my wife took off."

"Yeah, I could do just that. But I don't like to get on folks' bad side. Remember that Blondeen woman I told you about? Well, since I made it clear to her that I didn't want to be bothered with her no more, she's been pretty hostile to me and Jessie ever since."

"Avoid her. If she gets too hostile and bats your head with a frying pan, call the law on her."

"Yeah, right! As lax as the police is about colored folks committing crimes against each other, I doubt if they'll even bother to come to my house for something like a scorned woman beating me with a frying pan. It's easier for me to ignore Blondeen and them other women, so long as I got Jessie. But she ain't stupid. She knows that if I was interested in other women before her, I'm sure she knows I could get interested in them again."

"Hubert, I know how important it is for you to keep your wife. I been encouraging you to do that since we met, and I will continue to do so. But so long as Jessie ain't got no proof that you stepping out on her, you ain't got to worry about losing her. Nobody is going to find out about us," Leroy insisted.

"What if one of your used-to-be boyfriends start running his mouth to the wrong person? It would be just a matter of time before people like that bigmouthed Ralph Cook hears about you spending time with me outside of the barbershop."

"The same thing could happen to you," Leroy pointed out. "Somebody from your past might suddenly feel the need to come clean. About ten years ago, I had a casual acquaintance who'd had a bad breakup with his boyfriend. The boyfriend got so upset with him, he ran all over town blabbing about the relationship they'd been having for years. My friend's family and almost everybody else stopped speaking to him. You would have thought he had leprosy the way folks started acting when he went out in public. The cotton mill he'd worked at for thirteen years even let him go."

"I know things like that can happen. I pray about it all the time. What else happened to your friend?"

"Somebody turned him in to the police. He got wind of it before they caught up with him and moved out of his place and started living in his car. Things eventually got to be too stressful and he drove his car into Mobile Bay one night. The used-to-be boyfriend who had caused all the trouble was so guilt-ridden, he lost his mind and had to be locked up in the nuthouse."

I sighed and speared another piece of meat with my fork. "Honey, you better eat before everything gets cold," I advised.

"I will." Then Leroy gave me a sorrowful look. "I wish I hadn't brought up this subject. I get the vapors every time I think about it." He took a long pull from his glass of lemonade and let out a mighty belch. After excusing hisself and wiping his lips with his napkin, he went on. "I hate to bring up the next subject, but it's been on my mind lately." He sucked in some air and went on. "How long do you think your wife is going to put up with you not touching her? I bet she's climbing the walls from frustration."

"I don't think she's frustrated at all. When I told her about my so-called condition, she took it in stride."

"You don't think she'll start looking for affection somewhere else?"

I hunched my shoulders. "Well, anything is possible. I don't know what she'd do if the right man approached her. She is a good-looking woman, so that ain't so far-fetched. A heap of men gaze at her when we go out in public. I wouldn't be surprised if she got her needs fulfilled by another man."

"How would you deal with that if she did and you found out?"

"Well, so long as she don't flaunt it and make me feel and look like a fool, I'd turn a blind eye."

Chapter 49
Jessie

I COULDN'T FIGURE OUT WHAT HAD GOT INTO ME, OTHER THAN Conway. I'd only been with three other men before I married Orville. None of them—including Orville—had ever satisfied me as good as Conway.

Since the first time I got loose with him in the backseat of his car out by the lake a month ago, I'd been with him several more times. Each time was better than the last. I was sorry I hadn't gave in to Conway sooner. So that I wouldn't feel bad about what I was doing, I reminded myself that this was only because Hubert still wasn't able to take care of business the way he was supposed to. But I had to give him credit for being up front and telling me he couldn't perform in the first place. I had married him anyway and now I had to live with that. In the meantime, I planned to continue my frolics with Conway as often as I could until we got tired of one another, somebody caught us, or until Hubert was able to do his job.

Hubert told me the Monday before the Fourth of July that he was going to Hartville again on Friday right after work and wouldn't come home until Sunday. This time, it was to price new hymn books for his daddy's church. Since I'd started fooling around with Conway, it didn't bother me as much when Hubert left me alone for a few days.

When I got to work on Tuesday, I told Conway that I'd be

alone the whole weekend. If he could get away from Blondeen, we could spend as much time together as possible.

"I'd like to go somewhere other than the backseat of your car or that seedy old motel you took me to last week," I told him.

"Don't worry, sugar pie. I know how to treat a queen when I got a few extra bucks. I know just where to take you," he told me with a wall-to-wall smile on his face.

"Don't tell me where you taking me until we get there. I like surprises," I replied. "Can we go right after work today?"

"I don't see why not." Hubert had told me this morning that he'd be working a few hours overtime at the mill this evening because his boss had just returned from a two-week vacation yesterday and there was a lot of catching up to do.

Conway took me to a shabby house near the woods owned by a moonshiner. This man rented his spare bedroom to people who wanted to spend time with somebody other than whoever they was married to or involved with. He charged a quarter for every fifteen minutes. Conway paid him a dollar in advance so we could have a whole hour to enjoy ourselves.

I would have enjoyed being with Conway more if the accommodations had been better. The room was lit by a kerosene lamp sitting on top of a lopsided crate. There was a roll-away bed backed up against the wall with a naked mattress. The closet had a dingy horse blanket instead of a door. The only saving grace was stacks of clean sheets, a bowl of soapy water, and washcloths on top of a cardboard box next to the lamp. We covered the mattress with two fresh sheets, one on top of the other.

Despite my behavior, I thought too much of myself to ever sink low enough to return to this place again. I made the best of it, though, and couldn't get back in my clothes fast enough when we scrambled off that bed after we'd used up our hour. "Don't you never bring me to this hellhole again," I advised Conway as I wagged my finger in his face.

He chuckled and grabbed my finger and kissed the tip of it. "Whatever you say, Mama."

"And don't be calling me that! I ain't that old." Me and Conway never discussed the fact that I was more than ten years older than him. If our age difference didn't bother him, I wasn't going to let it bother me. But I didn't want to be reminded of it, especially by him.

He reared back on his legs and raised his hands in the air. "All right, I won't call you that no more, baby doll."

On our way out of the house, I spotted a woman I knew from church. She was on her way in, with her arm wrapped around the shoulder of the husband of another woman I knew. I didn't know if she seen me, because she was giving all her attention to the man she was with.

"Can you believe that hoochie-coochie jezebel is messing around with her best friend's husband?" Conway commented as we drove off.

"You got some nerve," I said with a snicker. "You got a woman, and I got a husband. We ain't got no room to talk about nobody else."

He glanced at me with a embarrassed look on his face. "You got a point there, Jessie. One thing is for sure, I ain't going to tell nobody I seen them out here, and I hope you don't."

"*Pffftt!* Do you think I'm crazy? There ain't no telling what Blondeen would do to me if the news got to her that you was in the same place with me."

"What about your husband? How would he feel if he found out his wife was fooling around with another man at a moonshiner's house? And since we on the subject, I thought you was so happy with him. You sure made me work harder than I ever worked to get some poontang."

"I am happy with my husband!" I snapped as I punched the side of Conway's arm. "What makes you think I ain't? When his first wife died, he became the most eligible colored man in Lexington. Blondeen even tried to get her hooks in him."

"I know." Conway sniffed and glanced at me. "She was real sweet to me at first and went out of her way to please me. That's why I moved in with her. But when she started accusing me of fooling around with other women, telling me what to do, where to go, and how to spend my money I knew I'd made a mistake. I'm going to be moving out of her house as soon as I can find a cheap room to rent. Then me and you can get together at my place. Or, since your husband has to go out of town so often, maybe we could spend some time at that nice house you live in."

My jaw dropped. "You must be out of your mind if you think I'm going to bring a strange man into my husband's bed. I would never be able to forgive myself."

"Humph! Well, he must not be doing his job in that same bed if you always so eager to get loose with me."

"What do you mean by that?"

"You tell me. I enjoy you being all over me when we sneak off somewhere, but I ain't no dummy. There has to be a reason why you act the way you do with me."

"I could say the same thing about you. If you was so 'happy' with Blondeen, how come you mess around with me and flirt with the other colored women at work?"

"I got a damn good reason. Blondeen is like a dead fish under the sheets. She wasn't so bad when we first got together. I guess she was trying to impress me, so she tried harder to please me. But she don't do that no more. Now she just lays there and hollers while I do all the work. That's why I have to go looking for quality attention from other women. And, baby, let me tell you, I really enjoy what you do for me." Conway kept his eyes on the road as he reached over and massaged my thigh. "I can't wait to see you again."

"We should slow down for a while," I suggested. "We don't want to get carried away too soon."

"'Slow down,' my ass. If anything, I'd like to be with you more often. I know about a motel over in Mobile that rents rooms by the hour too. For years, it's been the stomping ground for some of the ladies that provide service to a lot of the military men passing through."

"How would you know about a place like that? You been there with one of them ladies?"

"What's wrong with you? I ain't never had to pay a woman for nothing. I know a bunch of the men who go to that motel, though."

"Oh. Maybe we'll go there the next time my husband goes out of town. I'd also like to be with you even more often, but we can't press our luck."

"Aw, hush up! We ain't got nothing to worry about except getting caught. So long as we continue to be careful, that ain't going to happen."

I didn't care what Conway said, I was still worried about getting caught. I hadn't even thought about me getting pregnant by him, so I didn't waste no time thinking about that. One reason that wasn't a concern was because I hadn't conceived since Earl was born, more than twenty years ago. I didn't even know if I was still able to get pregnant. Before Orville's health went downhill, he used to pile on top of me several times a week, and not once did I ever get pregnant again.

The day after me and Conway's visit to the moonshiner's house, Quinette ran up to me while I was scrubbing the floor in a room where a patient had puked. There was a grimace on her face. "Girl, my monthly just snuck up on me a week early and I ain't got nary pad. You got some?"

"Yeah, I never leave home without a few in my purse and my sanitary belt."

Quinette followed me to the closet where we kept our personal items. My purse was hanging on a hook right next to hers. "My monthly is so regular, you could set a clock by it." I chuckled as I gave her one of the pads and the sanitary belt out of my purse. She thanked me and darted off to the restroom.

Before I closed my purse and put it back on the hook, a thought suddenly crossed my mind that made me freeze: My monthly was two and a half weeks late.

Chapter 50
Hubert

LIFE WAS AS GOOD AS IT COULD BE FOR ME. I FELT SO BLESSED, I went around humming and grinning like a man who didn't have a care in the world.

"Baby, I'm so glad you are back to your old self," Mama told me the evening before the Fourth of July. I had gone to the house to fix a leak in the kitchen sink, which Daddy had been putting off for weeks.

Me and Jessie had declined my parents' invitation to spend the holiday with them because they'd invited a crowd of folks. Jessie hadn't been feeling well again lately, so she decided she wanted us to spend the holiday alone at our house.

"That's because I am as happy as I can be," I almost sang. "If I didn't know no better, I'd swear Maggie was up there in heaven encouraging the Lord to make sure I'm as happy with Jessie as I was with her."

"That sounds like something sweet Maggie would do," Mama agreed. "She was such a helpful person. Now I can understand why God took her when He did. She's a asset to anybody she comes in contact with. She was the salt of the earth, when she was on earth."

I was glad I left when I did. I knew that if we talked too much about my blessed Maggie, we'd be in tears, and I was not in the mood for that today.

* * *

Jessie was still feeling under the weather when we woke up Thursday morning. I told her to stay in bed and I'd get our holiday meal going. Leroy had gave me the recipe to make the sauce for the ribs I planned to cook. It was one he had created hisself and was very scrumptious. I slathered some on just about everything I ate when I visited him, including eggs.

Just as I was getting out of bed, the telephone rang. I skittered to the kitchen to answer it. It was Tyrone calling from the funeral home. Even on holidays, I liked to have him or Floyd there in case somebody called. This time, it was Tyrone's turn.

"Did somebody call?" I asked.

"Not yet. I was calling you about another issue."

"Please don't tell me you done spilled the embalming fluid again, with your clumsy self!" I blasted. "I'll have to go back to Hartville to replace it—"

Tyrone cut me off. "It ain't nothing like that. I'm calling to let you know that while I was in the back room just now, somebody slipped a envelope under the front door."

"Oh? Who is it from?"

"Whoever left it didn't write their name on it. But it's addressed to you. You want me to open it?"

"Don't worry. I'll take care of it when I stop by on my way home from the mill tomorrow. It's probably a note from somebody in the family of a dearly departed soul who is having problems getting their insurance company to do their job. And they are too embarrassed to tell me in person that they'll be paying me late. We done got them kind of notes before," I stated with a chuckle. "I wonder why they didn't bring it to my house?"

"Um, maybe the reason is because there is something in it they don't want your wife to see."

Tyrone's comment made my heart skip a beat. Had somebody found out about me and Leroy? I wondered. I started talking so fast, I almost bit my tongue. "I'll be there as soon as I can." I hung up and turned around to see Jessie standing in the doorway, yawning and stretching her arms above her head. She was still in her nightgown.

"Who was that?" she asked as she sat down at the table.

"Tyrone. He said somebody dropped off a envelope addressed to me, so I need to tend to it straightaway."

"A envelope? Can't you pick it up later today or tomorrow?"

"You know how clumsy Tyrone is. He might spill embalming fluid on it and I won't be able to read it. Or he could misplace it."

"So? I still don't see why it can't wait. I thought we was going to have a nice quiet holiday together today. If I feel better in a little while, I'm going to go to that chicken-selling man's house and pick up a nice plump hen so we can have it to go with them ribs."

"Adding some chicken sounds good. But . . . uh . . . I have to go look into that envelope now. It could be some insurance paperwork that I need to turn in, say, by a certain date, and I might not have time to get from the mill to the funeral home to do it and get it in the mail on time. I ain't going to be gone that long, so we can still enjoy the holiday." I sprinted out of the kitchen, back to the bedroom to get dressed.

I was out the door ten minutes later and made it to my funeral home in less than five minutes. When I rushed through the front door, Tyrone was sweeping the floor in the room where we held the wakes.

"Where is that envelope at?" I asked.

There was a confused look on his dusky, bug-eyed face. "I put it in my pocket so I wouldn't misplace it. I just hope there ain't nothing in it that'll make you fret." He reached into the back pocket of his dingy overalls and took out a white envelope and handed it to me. His eyes got even bigger when he noticed my hand was shaking. "You sure you don't want me to open it and read it to you? You don't look too stable."

I gave Tyrone a dismissive wave. "Thanks, but I'm fine. I'll see you tomorrow."

"Ain't you going to open it now?" he asked.

I had already started walking back toward the door. "I'll open it when I get home. Jessie wasn't feeling good when she woke up this morning and I don't want to leave her alone no longer than I have to." I forced myself to smile and then I thought I should say something that would distract Tyrone so he wouldn't ask no more questions about the mysterious envelope. "You can go home at noon and spend the rest of the holiday with your family."

His face lit up like a lightbulb. "For real? What if somebody was to call here?"

"Well, let's not worry about that this time. If somebody can't reach nobody here or me at home, they can keep calling until they do. We been doing a pretty good job of being available all these years, so we can afford to play hooky once in a while." I spun around and dashed out the door. I didn't stop until I got in my car. I glanced back and seen Tyrone peeping out the window. So, instead of opening the envelope, I laid it on the passenger seat, started the motor, and drove off.

I drove three blocks down the street, before I turned the corner and parked at the curb. When I ripped opened the envelope and unfolded the sheet of paper that was inside, my mouth dropped open. There was a hand-printed message with words in big capital letters: *WHEN YOU AND THAT HIGH-AND-MIGHTY SOW YOU MARRIED FALL OFF THEM HIGH HORSES Y'ALL BEEN RIDING ON TOO LONG, I HOPE EVERY BONE GETS BROKE!*

"What the hell . . ." This note didn't make no sense to me. I was relieved that it didn't have nothing to do with me and Leroy. But who would leave me such a nasty message?

I knew some folks was jealous of me and had been for years. Rumors used to get back to me and Maggie that somebody had said we was uppity, or that we thought we was better than everybody else. We always laughed about it and wondered who it was that resented us, since we treated everybody we knew so well. I was never too concerned about that petty foolishness because I wasn't about to stop being who I was, to please other folks this late in the game. I hadn't heard any of them rumors in years, so I was surprised to know that there was somebody I knew who decided now to try and get under my skin.

One thing I had learned was that sometimes it didn't matter how nice you treated people, they could still get jealous. We didn't have no new friends, so it had to be somebody we knew. If they had to make their feelings known in a unsigned letter, they wasn't worth me and Jessie's time. I read the note again. It didn't sound threatening enough for me to be concerned. But I didn't want to dismiss it completely until I found out who was behind it, or until they sent another one. I didn't want to show it to Jessie, but I didn't think it would be a good idea to hide something like this from her. Especially if the culprit delivered one directly to her and mentioned the first one. She wouldn't like the fact that I'd hid something that included a reference to her.

Jessie was in the kitchen when I got home. I went up to her with a smile forming on my lips. "Is everything all right? What was in that envelope?" she asked.

"Oh, it wasn't what I thought it was. Somebody is playing a prank on us." I showed her the note and she read it out loud.

"Somebody is trying to be funny!" she hollered with her jaw twitching.

"I figured that out already. I guess they ain't got nothing better to do with their time. Have you disrespected anybody lately?"

"Not that I know of."

"Then let's not worry about this envelope."

"I know what to do about this one," she snarled as she snatched the envelope out of my hand. She ripped it and the note in two and dropped the pieces into the trash can next to the stove. Which was exactly what I would have done if she hadn't beat me to it.

I picked up the phone and called up Tyrone. "If some more envelopes come, don't open them. Call me and put them in a safe place until I can get there. Make sure you let Floyd know what I said."

"Okay, boss. I hope the one you picked up wasn't nothing serious."

"It wasn't. Some knucklehead with too much time on their hands was just trying to be funny."

Chapter 51

Jessie

*I*T WAS TWENTY-FOUR HOURS SINCE I FIRST SUSPECTED I WAS PREGnant with Conway's baby. My monthly still hadn't come and I had now started feeling achy and sick to my stomach. I was convinced I was pregnant.

There was no way I could claim Hubert was the daddy this time. Even if I could drug him again and say he took advantage of me a second time, I wouldn't believe a story that outlandish myself. The only choices I had was to claim a strange man had raped me or tell him the truth.

I had to tell him something soon, but I didn't want to ruin the holiday for him, so I decided to wait until the evening. First I'd offer to read a few of his favorite Bible Scriptures to him to get him in a spiritual mood.

Hubert did most of the holiday cooking, and a few minutes before three p.m., we sat down at the kitchen table to dive into the ribs and chicken he'd barbecued and all the biscuits, potato salad, and coleslaw I had prepared.

"I ain't never had barbecue sauce this good," I commented after I tasted the ribs. "Did you use one of your mama's recipes?"

"Uh-uh. I got it from a cook I met at one of the restaurants I eat at when I go to Mobile."

It took every bit of strength I had to act normal, but inside I was falling apart. After we finished our meal, Hubert went to sit on the couch while I washed the dishes. My stomach was churning the whole time. When I shuffled into the living room and sat down next to him, I took his hand in mine.

"Jessie, are you all right? I noticed you looked a little preoccupied while we was eating supper, and even more so now."

"I . . . um . . . I need to tell you something," I started. Before I could stop myself, I broke down. "I didn't mean to do it! Honest to God, I didn't!" I was crying and shaking so hard, I couldn't think straight.

Hubert wheezed. Even through my tears, I could see how frightened and concerned he was. "Do what? Jessie, what in the world is going on?" His put his hands on my shoulders and shook me so hard, my teeth click-clacked.

"I'm fixing to have a baby!" I finally managed to say. I was so distraught, I started confessing out of order. I should have mentioned the part about the stranger raping me first.

"Say what?" Hubert yelled. He sprung up off the couch and stood in front of me with his hands on his hips. *"By who?"*

Ideas was bombarding my brain like bullets. I stopped crying, but I was so confused, I ended up telling him a different story than the one I'd concocted about being raped. I managed to get my whole confession out between sobs.

"While you was in Hartville a while back, I went to Yolinda's house. There was this flashy musician there who started leering at me the minute I got in the door. Well . . ."

"He took advantage of you? How much alcohol did you have to drink?"

I shook my head. "I didn't drink nothing."

"Then how did this happen?"

That question threw me for a loop, so I suddenly decided to shift some of the blame on Hubert. I knew he wouldn't like it, but I didn't know what else to say.

"You . . . you don't want to touch me, and I was beginning to feel old and ugly. That musician kept going on and on about how good I looked. Before I knew it, I was so giddy and weak, it . . . it just happened. With you having that issue with your, uh, natural ability, I guess nature took over my mind and body and I couldn't resist the temptation."

Hubert sat back down and put his arm around my shoulder. "I'm sorry you feel the way you do. But I couldn't keep the truth from you about something so important in a marriage. I may not be half the man I used to be in the bedroom, but I'm whole in so many other areas."

"I know and I still don't care that you can't perform. In my heart, I truly believe that God will cure you someday." I cleared my throat and reared back on the couch. "I can go stay with one of my cousins in Mississippi, or even my uncle in Michigan, until I have the baby. You can tell everybody I'm out of town taking care of a sick relative. I'll leave the baby with them and we can go on like nothing happened. I swear to God, I won't ever let something like this happen again."

Hubert shook his head. "I don't want you to go nowhere. I'll forgive you for breaking your vows."

"But if I have this baby, what will we tell everybody?"

"We'll tell them that the Lord gave us another chance to be parents. What did this man look like?"

"He wasn't as handsome as you, but he was about your age and size and he had the same skin tone as you. His eyebrows wasn't as thick as yours, but he had the same full lips."

"Hmmm. So, if the child came out looking like him, nobody would think I wasn't the daddy, right?"

I nodded. "Uh-huh. You ain't mad at me?"

"I ain't mad, but I'm surprised and disappointed. I never expected nothing like this to happen to such God-fearing folks like us."

"I'm so sorry! If you want a divorce, you can have it. And I won't even ask for nothing. I'll go on to live with one of my out-of-state relatives."

Hubert rolled his neck so hard, I was surprised his head didn't spin off it. "Divorce? Lord, have mercy! I don't want no divorce. That would kill my mama. And I sure don't want you to move to another state and live with none of your kinfolks. Forgiving you is the Christian thing to do."

"I'm so ashamed, but I'm glad you still want to stay with me. But things change over time. How do I know you won't backslide and end up hating the child and me in the long run?"

"Jessie, as long as you been knowing me, have you ever heard me say I hated anybody?"

"No, but everybody likes you."

"At least one person don't—the one that dropped off that note don't," he reminded.

"Well, almost everybody."

"Listen, I'm glad you told me this now. We can't keep it to ourselves much longer. We should let our families know before we start broadcasting all over town."

"I just feel so bad about deceiving good Christian folks, like your mama and daddy. I'd rather cut off my tongue than lie to them." That lie left a bitter taste in my mouth.

"Honey, don't you worry about that. I done lied to my folks a heap of times and I don't feel the least bit guilty about it. Sometimes folks have to tell fibs to keep the peace, even good Christians like us."

I was so relieved to hear him say that. But I thought it was still in my best interest to continue to play the role of a pitiful woman who'd temporarily lost her way. "Hubert, I should have known you'd be understanding. This has been such a tribulation for me. I don't know how I managed to go this long without confessing to you and not go crazy. I'm glad I got this off my chest tonight, because it was becoming too heavy a burden for me to carry too much longer."

"I'm glad you did too. I'd hate for a dainty little woman like you to carry such a load on your shoulders by yourself. Let's pray."

Hearing him say that made me feel even more relieved. We went in the bedroom and got down on our knees by the side of the bed and prayed for fifteen minutes straight. When we finished, I wobbled up and felt so light-headed, I stumbled. My stomach started churning and I felt something warm and familiar sliding down my thighs. I made it to the bathroom in time to step out of my bloomers and plop down on the commode. I was shocked to see all the blood that had gushed out of me and left a trail on the floor.

"Hubert, I just had another miscarriage!" I screamed.

He didn't waste no time coming to me. He ushered me to the car and drove like a bat out of hell to the clinic. Within minutes after we stormed the emergency room, a doctor took me into a exam room and examined me right away. What he had to say was so shocking, I was glad I was already at the clinic, because my heart started beating so fast, I thought I was about to have a heart attack.

"You didn't have a miscarriage, Mrs. Wiggins. You weren't pregnant."

"Then why was my period so late if I wasn't fixing to have a baby?" I hollered.

"What you experienced was only a premenopausal symptom," the doctor said in a gentle tone.

"Menopause?" I yelled. "That's for real old ladies! I ain't but forty-two!"

The doctor gave me a pitiful look. "Some women start the process while they're still in their thirties or early forties, like you. Their monthly becomes irregular for a few months, then it might go back to what seems like normal for another few months, and it could stop for up to a year before the actual menopause kicks in. I see this all the time."

You could have knocked me over with a feather. I had made a fool of myself by telling Hubert I'd been with another man. If I had waited *less than twenty minutes longer* to come clean, I wouldn't have had to tell him nothing.

"What do I do now?" I asked in a meek voice.

"Go home and take care of yourself. It's the best thing you can do now." The doctor had me get dressed before he summoned Hubert into the room and told him everything he'd told me.

Hubert looked like he wanted to rise up and fly out the window. He started shaking his head and shifting his weight from one foot to the other and gawked at the doctor like he had suddenly grew horns. "Say what?!"

The doctor repeated what he'd just said and then he left the room.

Hubert looked so beaten down now, I felt even worse. "I'm sorry, Hubert. I've disappointed you again. I know how bad you want a child."

"Jessie, don't beat yourself up over what I want. All I really want is for us both to be happy and healthy, baby or no baby."

"I'm so glad we didn't tell nobody I was pregnant again," I said with a sigh of relief.

"I feel the same way. Losing one grandchild before its birth caused my mama and daddy a lot of pain. I doubt if they'd survive hearing about losing another one."

"Let's go home. This was quite a holiday. I think I'll take off work tomorrow so I can lay in bed and clear my head."

"I'll take the day off too," Hubert said.

"I don't want you to do that. I think I need a little time alone to think about everything."

"No, I'm taking tomorrow off too. I won't hang around the house, so you can have all the privacy you need. I'll take a drive to Hartville and have a nice long lunch before I come back home."

"I think that's a good idea. That long drive should do you a world of good."

Chapter 52
Hubert

I DIDN'T KNOW WHAT TO MAKE OF JESSIE'S CONFESSION. I WAS SORRY she had been weak enough to let what she did happen, but I was glad she'd been woman enough to own up to her sins.

I waited until I was sure she was asleep before I eased out of bed and tiptoed to the kitchen to call Leroy.

"I'm taking off work tomorrow. Can I come over?" I whispered into the telephone. "I'd like to come as early as possible. Before noon, if you don't mind." I figured I'd spend the first few hours in the morning with Jessie, so I could comfort her as much as I could.

"Sure. But I have several appointments on my calendar, so you'll have to hang out at the apartment by yourself."

"I don't mind doing that at all. I just need to get out of this house for a few hours."

"Did something happen?"

I didn't see no reason to tell Leroy that Jessie had been unfaithful to me. I would have told him if it turned out she really was pregnant by another man, though. "No, I'm just missing you."

"Okay. I'll see you tomorrow, then."

When I went back to the bedroom, Jessie was still sleeping like a baby. I felt so bad for this sweet woman. Life had not been kind to her. I cared enough about her to make sure I did all I could to let her enjoy some happiness. She was doing so much for me, I felt it was the least I could do.

* * *

I went to bed, and by the time I woke up, I felt different about needing to take a long drive to clear my head. Jessie looked so woebegone over breakfast, I didn't have the heart to leave her alone to deal with the feelings of guilt I suspected she was feeling about her affair. I had to call up Leroy as soon as I could to let him know I wasn't coming.

"What time are you going to go for a drive and where are you going?" Jessie asked in a raspy tone.

"Oh, I changed my mind. I think I should stay home with you in case you need something."

"You ain't got to worry about me. Other than some mild cramps, I feel fine. I can't wait to get back to work on Monday, so I won't have time to think about what I done to you."

"What do you mean?"

Jessie gasped. "Hubert, I cheated on you. How will you ever be able to respect and trust me again?"

"Don't make a mountain out of a molehill. Because you was brave enough to come clean, I'll always respect and trust you. You could have lied and claimed you got raped, or so drunk you didn't know what you was doing. But you didn't. The bottom line is, you made a bad choice, like every other human being. I done made some bad choices in my life, but I'm still a good man. So you are still a good woman in my eyes. The more I get to know you, the more I realize how much more you are like Maggie than I originally thought you was. And everybody knows she was perfect."

"She was a Christian to the bone. She didn't cheat on you or hurt another soul in any way. I don't have the gall to put myself on the level of a woman as saintly as Maggie was."

"Well, I got enough gall for both of us."

"Hubert, you sure know what to say to make a woman feel better. No wonder Maggie used to brag about you all the time . . ."

"She did?"

Jessie nodded and gave me a knowing smile. "Yup. She talked to me about *everything*."

"Everything?"

She nodded again. "I don't want to embarrass you, but she told me how well you satisfied her in the bedroom. That's one of the reasons I am convinced that you will eventually be able to perform again. And when you do, I hope I'll be able to keep up with you, because you'll need a lot of loving to make up for lost time. I know you never cheated on Maggie, and I know you'd never cheat on me, even if I had to take a break and turn you down a few times, once you get back on track. What I done wasn't just a bad choice, it was a sin and a shame of the worst kind. I swear to God, if I have to wait another whole year for you to get well, I won't never cheat on you again."

"Jessie, the less we talk about what you did with that man, the sooner we can put it behind us. If we continue to pray as hard and often as we been doing, everything will be back to where it was before you went to Yolinda's party. If you feel up to it later today, you want to take a drive over to Toxey and get some of that homemade ice cream from that parlor we went to a few weeks ago? Or if you don't want to go that far, we can take a drive over to the Seafood House and get something to eat and some of that ice-cold tea."

"I can't eat or drink nothing cold when I'm on my monthly. It'll make my cramps worse." Jessie sucked on her teeth and glanced at the door. "I'm going to go to that little jackleg store around the corner to get some ginger tea for my cramps."

"You ain't got to walk nowhere. I'll drive you. Besides, the man who runs that place is a ex-con. There is all kinds of shady people in and out his house."

"I don't want you to drive me. I need to get some exercise and fresh air. And you ain't got to worry about that ex-con. Me and him got baptized on the same day and he's always treated me like family. He wouldn't let none of his friends do or say nothing disrespectful to me."

"I'll walk with you, then. Lord knows, I could use more exercise myself." I pinched the roll of flab that had collected around my waistline in the last few months.

Jessie shook her head. "I'd rather go by myself in case I decide to go someplace else before I come home. I got a itching to pay that chicken man a visit and get a hen to cook for supper to-morrow. We've had pig tails for supper so many times in the last month, I'm surprised we ain't grew tails ourselves." We laughed.

I was so pleased to see that she wasn't too upset about being premenopausal, and I hoped she wasn't just putting up a front for my benefit. I would do all I could to show her that I hadn't lost no respect for her.

I waited about five minutes after Jessie left before I called up Leroy and told him I had changed my mind about coming to see him. He was disappointed, but didn't make a big deal out of it. After I ended the call to him, I checked in with Tyrone and Floyd to make sure everything was in order at the funeral home. I didn't think it was a good idea to call my parents' house; I didn't want to hear a bunch of nosy questions as to why me and Jessie took off work today.

While she was gone, I had time to reflect on everything we'd been through since we started our relationship. I still thought she was a good investment in my well-being, and I was convinced that she felt the same way about me. I had a feeling she wasn't telling me the whole story about that musician at Yolinda's, but I wasn't about to harp on it. I hoped she never brought it up again.

I wondered what she would think if she knew how many times I'd lied to her so I could be with somebody else. And a man, at that! Just the thought of her finding out the truth about me sent shivers up and down my spine. I moved all of them thoughts to the back of my mind because that was where they belonged.

When Jessie returned fifteen minutes later, she stormed into the house with a wild-eyed look on her face.

"Hubert, somebody just tried to mow me down with a car!"

Chapter 53

Jessie

"WHAT THE HELL HAPPENED?" HUBERT BOOMED.

My legs was so weak, I would have fell to the floor if he hadn't wrapped his arms around me and held me in place. He helped me to the couch and I laid down, wheezing like a old woman.

"Did you see who it was? You get hurt?" he asked, looking me over as he rubbed the side of my arm.

It took me a few seconds to catch my breath. I shook my head. "I jumped out of the way in the nick of time. It was a dark blue car, but I couldn't see who was driving."

"Do you know anybody with a car that color?"

"No, I don't."

"Praise the Lord, you didn't get hit. It's just a shame folks drive so bad these days, they cause accidents left and right."

"You think it was just a accident?"

"Who would be so mad at you that they would want to run you over?" A thoughtful look crossed Hubert's face and then he looked at me with his eyes narrowed. "What about the man who took advantage of you at Yolinda's house? He's probably married and now he's scared that you might blab to his wife, so he tried to shut you up."

"Um . . . I don't know. It could have been him."

I was saying what I thought was appropriate, but other thoughts was swirling around in my head. I couldn't overlook the fact that there was so much bad blood between me and Blondeen. She'd had it in for me for so long, it didn't make sense for her to wait until now to finally come after me. But if she'd recently found out about me and Conway, she had a new reason to hate me even more. Causing trouble between me and Hubert was right up her alley and that's why I was convinced that she was the one who had left that envelope at the funeral home.

One thing was for sure, I wasn't going to do nothing with Conway again, and I was so glad I hadn't told him I thought I was carrying his baby.

When I got to work on Monday, I went out of my way to avoid him. But just before lunch, when I went to get my purse from the closet, he followed me in and shut the door. Before I could get away from him, he wrapped his arms around me and kissed me long and hard.

"You stop that!" I hissed, and then I slapped his face.

He reared back, covered the spot where I'd hit him, and looked at me in slack-jawed amazement. "That hurt! What's wrong with you, woman? We kiss all the time," he whined.

"We won't be kissing no more! And we better get out of this closet before somebody catches us."

"Aw, shuck it! It's going to be awkward for us to make love and not kiss," he griped.

I glared at him and wagged my finger in his face. "You ain't got to worry about that, because we ain't going to be making love no more neither."

"Why not? You done found somebody else, huh?" he barked with a grimace on his face.

"Conway, I got a husband and you got a woman. Let's focus on them from now on."

"Huh? What's done come over you? You was fine the last time I seen you."

"We can't mess around no more. You need to get over me and move on."

He did a neck roll and huffed out a sharp laugh. "'Get over' you? Ow! That statement is so ridiculous, it hurts more than that slap on my face. There ain't nothing for me to 'get over,' so don't flatter yourself!" He snorted and folded his arms. "I ain't about to beg and plead with you to stay with me, with your goofy self. Besides, I done had much better tail than yours!"

"The same goes for your tail," I told him with my teeth clenched. And then I brushed past him as fast as I could. I opened the door and sprinted out with my cleaning bucket in one hand and a mop in the other.

It was a good thing I left the closet when I did. When I made it to the hallway, Quinette and Glennola was walking toward me. My feet was moving so fast and hard, it was a wonder I didn't bore a hole in the floor. "Slow down, girl! The place ain't on fire," Glennola said with a snicker.

"I just remembered I need to go into the restroom and clean the commode again and mop the floor," I said.

They stood there with puzzled expressions on their faces as I took off running.

I managed to avoid Conway the rest of the day. He didn't come in Tuesday, Wednesday, or Thursday.

On Friday, Quinette got on the same bus to work that I was on. She asked the woman in a maid's uniform who was in the seat next to me to move to one across the aisle so she could sit with me.

"How come you got on this bus and not the one you usually take?" I asked.

"I needed to come in early to do some of the work Conway left behind," she said with a growl. "That lazy sucker."

"He ain't been to work in three days. Is he sick?"

"Jessie, you ain't heard?"

"Heard what?"

"He called in yesterday and told his supervisor to mail him his last paycheck."

I gasped. "What? Who would quit a steady job when so many folks is still scrambling to find work?"

"Well, he found work. He's going to go chauffeur for one of them peckerwood lawyers that live on the hill."

"Oh? Well, good for him. I had no idea he was even looking for another job."

"I ain't going to miss him," Quinette said.

"I ain't neither."

Quinette narrowed her eyes, shook her head, and cackled with laughter. "Girl, you can end that act. I know you and Conway had a thing going. My cousin seen you and him together at the house of that moonshiner who rents his spare room to couples up to no good."

I was so embarrassed, I could feel the blood drain from my face. "Oh, Lord. I was a fool for letting him take me to that place!"

"I knew even before then. I got suspicious when I started noticing how you and him looked at each other. And then I seen y'all kissing behind the peach tree behind the home."

Now my stomach was turning too. "I hope you ain't mentioned it to nobody."

"*Pffftt!* So long as somebody ain't doing nothing that hurts me, I mind my own business. I ain't got no reason to tattle on you and Conway. Blondeen is the only one you need to be worried about."

"Well, I have a feeling she got wind of it too. You wouldn't believe the dirty looks I get from her out in public." I saw no reason to mention the nasty note I was convinced she had delivered to the funeral home.

"She still blames you for losing her job. But you won't have to worry about her for a while nohow."

"Oh? How come?"

"She gave up her new housekeeping job and got on a bus yesterday to go stay with her mama's sister in Austin, Texas. Her auntie's dying of cancer and needs somebody to help her kids take care of her. Her husband died a few months ago and she needs all the help she can get. From what I heard, she got about six months to live."

"Is that how long Blondeen is going to stay there?"

Quinette nodded. "Longer if necessary. It all depends on how long her auntie lives."

"What about Blondeen's house and all them bills she got?"

"Her mama and the rest of her folks will chip in and help Conway pay the rent and utilities until she gets back and finds another job."

"I'm sorry about her auntie," I said, and I meant it. But I was pleased to hear that I wouldn't have to worry about her for a while.

Chapter 54
Jessie

*I*T HAD BEEN THREE AND A HALF MONTHS SINCE SOMEBODY HAD dropped off that envelope at the funeral home. Hubert hadn't received another one, so I felt comfortable enough to put that mysterious incident out of my mind. He must have felt the same way, because he hadn't brought it up no more.

I hadn't seen Conway since he left his job at the nursing home. I missed making love with him, but even if he tried to get me back, and Blondeen was still out of town, I didn't want nothing else to do with him.

The days was flying by so fast, I couldn't believe October was almost over. Last year, on the night before Halloween, somebody snuck up on my front porch and stole the jack-o'-lantern that Earl had carved for me. When I took him out to collect candy the next evening, at almost every house we went to, the people made a fuss about him being too old to still be trick-or-treating. And they all knew he was slow.

Despite his mental state, my son was smart enough to know that there was something wrong with him. I'd never forget that time two years ago when he asked me, "Mama, will I ever be as good as other boys?"

That question brought a lump to my throat. "Baby, you are already as good as other boys. No, you're even better. Life is much easier on you. If something was to happen to me, you got a lot of kinfolks who will step in and look after you. You won't never have to work, struggle to pay bills, and support a family; and best of all, you won't never know how bad racism is. So you'll never know the kind of pain most colored people experience."

"Oh, okay. What's racism?"

"It's some crazy rules that a few mean white people threw together that keeps colored people under their thumbs. Their lives is so miserable, it's the only way they can make themselves feel superior to us—but they ain't. Racism hurts a lot of colored people when they experience it."

"I'm glad I ain't never going to experience it."

I was happy that Minnie had decided to let Earl and his cousins just have a party at her house this year and not go out to knock on folks' doors. With that killer still on the loose, most of the folks I knew had said that they wouldn't be opening their doors for the kids on Halloween night anyway, and I couldn't blame them. Hubert still wanted to pass out candy, but I talked him out of it.

Yolinda was having a Halloween party tonight and had invited almost everybody on our block, and a bunch of folks from other neighborhoods. Despite the fact that she was in the church and thought of herself as a respectable woman, she associated with some shady people. I seen some of the local moonshiners visit her house several times a month to play poker with one of the nephews who lived with her. I never stuck my nose in Yolinda's business about the company she kept, because it never interfered with the relationship I had with her. But I got annoyed when she bragged about the money she saved by buying spirits from the local moonshiners. I expected to see at least one of them at the party. Me and Hubert only planned to stay a little while, or until the party got too rowdy for us.

"And we ain't wearing no costumes," I'd told Yolinda this morning before I left for work.

"That's fine with me if y'all want to stick out like sore thumbs," she teased. "I just want y'all to have a good time."

And we did. Yolinda liked to go all out with her parties. She had several jack-o'-lanterns with evil-looking smiles all over her living room, and a scarecrow slumped on the couch. She had recently bought a phonograph and some old records by Bessie Smith and a singer I'd just found out about named Billie Holiday. When the phonograph wasn't going, a man who played the piano at Reverend Wiggins's church was strumming the blues on his guitar, so there was a lot of dancing. I seen several folks I hadn't seen in weeks.

Just as I was beginning to enjoy myself a little more, a woman wearing a black scarf tied around the bottom half of her face, like a bandit, approached me.

"Hey, Jessie. Long time no see."

I couldn't tell right off who she was, but I recognized her voice right away: Wilma McGinnis, Blondeen's friend-girl.

"I ain't seen you in so long, I thought you had flew the coop." I managed to give her a smile, but I wasn't glad to see her.

"Something like that. I finally left that ignoramus I married. Me and the kids moved in with my brother last Tuesday. I would have come to your house to visit you when I visited Yolinda, but Hubert makes me nervous."

"I don't know why that is. He ain't nothing like your friend-girl Blondeen. He don't bite," I said, trying not to sound too sarcastic.

"Blondeen got a mean streak, but she's a good friend to me. Did you hear the latest news about her?"

My heart started racing. I was hoping she was going to tell me that Blondeen had decided to stay in Texas for good. "What about her?"

"The auntie she was taking care of died last week and Blondeen's back in town. Girl, you wouldn't believe the mess Conway left for her."

Now my heart felt like it had stopped beating. "I'm scared to ask what he did?"

"For one thing, he'd been fooling around with some old gal. Blondeen got wind of it before she left to go to Texas, but she didn't have time to get all the information she needed so she could get in his face. And take care of whoever the wench was that he was seeing. The problem was, Conway fooled around with more than one woman. He even tried to hit on me. I never told Blondeen about it, though. Knowing the way her mind works, I know she would have put the blame on me." Wilma was talking so fast; she had to stop and catch her breath.

"Anyway, he was supposed to pay her rent and other bills with the money her kinfolks scraped up and gave him. He stopped paying everything a couple of months ago. When she got back to Lexington last week, the lights had been cut off and the landlord showed up the very next day and told her she had to move because her rent was behind. She was fit to be tied."

"That's a shame. I didn't know Conway was that irresponsible. I heard he got a new job driving for some fancy lawyer."

"And he moved into that rooming house on Morgan Street. The word is, he spent Blondeen's rent money on one of them women he been creeping around with. When she catches up with him, his life ain't going to be worth a plugged nickel."

I was glad Hubert approached before Wilma could go on.

"Hey, Hubert. How's business?" she greeted.

"It couldn't be better, praise the Lord," he replied with a proud look on his face.

Wilma shuddered and shook her head. "I don't want you to take this the wrong way, but shivers crawl up my spine every time I pass by your funeral home." She turned to me and shuddered again. "It don't bother you to know that your husband touches dead bodies?"

"I don't see why it should," I said.

"Wilma, you shouldn't feel that way, because you're going to end up at a funeral home someday. Maybe sooner than you want to," Hubert pointed out. He must have spooked her, because she abruptly excused herself and whirled around so fast to leave, she almost fell.

"Thanks for rescuing me. She was beginning to get on my nerves," I told Hubert. "I'm ready to go whenever you are."

I didn't mention that Wilma had told me Blondeen was back in town. I didn't see any reason to. If she knew that I had been fooling around with Conway, she had to know that I wasn't seeing him no more. And by now, she should have been over being mad at me for losing her job. I hoped that me and her could at least be on speaking terms again someday. Until then, I planned to avoid her whenever I could.

Chapter 55
Hubert

M E AND JESSIE DIDN'T GET NO PAID VACATION OR SICK LEAVE AT our jobs. But we decided to take off a few days in early November anyway. We had enough money saved up so we could afford to treat ourselves to a little vacation and take time off work without pay.

"You want to drive over to Miami?" I asked.

Jessie shook her head. "We can do that next year. I want to go to Hartville and meet some of the people you visit when you go over there."

I held my breath. "You do?"

"You know I do. I been wanting to do that for a long time and I ain't going to stop pestering you until you take me," she said with a hint of a pout.

We was laying in bed and had just finished saying our prayers.

"Okay, we'll go, then." I had put her off so many times, I was ready to take her to Hartville and get it over with. The only "friend" I could introduce her to was the man I bought the embalming fluid from. Him and Leroy was the only two people I met up with over there on a regular basis. If I introduced her to the folks I'd only interacted with once or twice since me and her got together, my stories wouldn't match theirs.

We headed to Hartville Wednesday morning at nine a.m. My embalming fluid supply was pretty good, but I decided to buy some more anyway.

The man I usually dealt with was in Mississippi visiting his grandchildren and would be gone a week. I played checkers with him every now and then, so he could have fit the bill of a friend. His elderly, slow-moving mother was filling in for him. She took two bathroom breaks in the first ten minutes after we arrived and answered the telephone three times. After Jessie had stood around for half a hour, stamping her feet and twiddling her thumbs, she got impatient and decided to go wait in the car.

I rejoined her a hour later. I loaded the embalming fluid in the backseat and got in the driver's seat. "It's high time!" she hollered. "I was fixing to come back in there to make sure you hadn't fell out or something. Let's get the heck up out of here. If I'd known this was going to be such a boring trip, I would have stayed home."

I laughed; she didn't. "Well, sugar, you wanted to come and meet some of the folks I deal with," I reminded.

"What about them other folks you spend time with over here?"

"I tried to get in touch with another man I been knowing for years, but his wife said he was working on a fishing boat in Mobile for the next month. Another guy I've known for years moved to Memphis last week."

"Good! Something tells me they are boring too. Let's get something to eat and check into that motel you always stay at."

We picked up some baloney, a loaf of bread, and a few bottles of Dr Pepper and headed to the motel. The minute Jessie laid eyes on it, she was horrified. A empty lot that was littered with trash was on one side. There was a deserted gas station on the other side, with every window broke out and even more trash out front than there was in the empty lot.

"I wouldn't let my dog stay in a dump like this," Jessie griped.

"It ain't no palace, but it's one of the few motels that'll rent to colored folks. The other two I know of look even worse."

"Hubert, don't get mad, but you need to take me home right now."

I was so overjoyed to hear her say that! "Do you mean to tell me that after all the fuss you made about coming over here, now you don't want to stay?"

"No! And you ain't got to worry about me asking to come over here with you no more. The next time we take time off from work, we'll go to a real vacation place, like Miami or Yazoo City, Mississippi."

"All right, sugar." I turned the car around and headed to the highway.

We spent the rest of our "vacation" at home, playing checkers and dominoes.

I was glad I'd visited Leroy twice the week before the anniversary of Maggie's and Claude's deaths. But despite how good he made me feel, when November 17 rolled around, I was so down in the dumps, I stayed in bed all day. I was glad it fell on a Sunday this year, so I didn't have to miss more work. I had thought about going to church because Daddy was going to include a few words about Maggie and Claude in his morning sermon. But I couldn't bring myself to be there. I only got up when I had to use the bathroom.

Jessie offered to serve me my meals in bed, but I didn't have no appetite.

"You have to eat something, Hubert. Laying in the bed ain't going to do you no good," she scolded. I was curled up in a fetal position as she hovered over me with her arms folded across her chest. "You want a pill?"

I looked up at her like she was crazy. "What good would a pill do me?"

"It might make you feel better. It's bad enough you won't eat, but you need to at least drink some water. Do you think Maggie would want you to get sick?"

"I ain't sick. I just got a case of the vapors."

"If that ain't sick, I don't know what is. If anybody should know that it's me. I had the vapors when Orville died and when Maggie and Claude died. They was even worse when I lost our baby."

I took a deep breath, winced, and finally sat up. But I didn't make no attempt to get out of bed. "Jessie, don't pay me no mind. I'm sorry for acting like such a baby. I ain't ready to eat nothing yet, but I'll take a pill and drink some water."

I washed down a pain pill with two glasses of water. I felt better about twenty minutes later, but I still didn't get out of bed.

By Monday morning, I felt good enough to go to work.

Jessie had a different idea, though. "You still look like death warmed over. Why don't you stay home today? I'll call in sick and we can go get some flowers for Maggie and Claude."

"We just put flowers on their graves last week," I said.

"I'm sure they are wilted by now."

"I don't want to go back to that cemetery again so soon. I think the best thing for me to do is get over Maggie and Claude, once and for all."

Jessie gasped and looked at me like I had a forked tongue. "Have you lost your mind? Get over them? Folks don't 'get over' people who meant so much to them. I don't know how you can say such a thing."

I didn't know how I could say such a thing neither. Maybe I had lost my mind. "You know what I mean. I declare, I need to stop whining about losing them. Maybe I need to pray a little harder."

"I feel the same way. Don't forget, I'm hurting just as much as you. I done lost a heap of loved ones," Jessie reminded.

"I know. And I hate to be acting like I ain't never lost nobody before. I'm sorry for being so gloomy."

"You don't have to be sorry. We got too much going now, let's focus on all the good in our lives."

"All right." Somehow I managed to smile. And I even got up and helped fix breakfast.

I offered to give Jessie a ride to work, but she insisted on taking the bus. It wasn't easy, but I got through the day without going to pieces. By quitting time, I felt much better.

Jessie usually got home from work before me. But today I beat her. I couldn't understand why she was running late. She hadn't mentioned working late or making no stops. When another half hour went by and she still hadn't come home, I decided to start cooking supper.

Just as I was about to put the pig snouts in a pan of boiling water, the telephone rang. It was Daddy. His voice erupted like a volcano.

"Somebody just tried to kill Jessie!"

The words hit me so hard, my head felt like somebody had batted it with a hammer. I gripped the phone harder and held it closer to my ear. I could barely form words, and when I did, it took a lot of effort to push them out of my mouth. My voice came out so meek and weak, it didn't sound nothing like me.

"Somebody tried to kill Jessie? Who? When?"

"I don't know who. But it happened about a hour ago," Daddy panted. It sounded like he'd been running. I knew that wasn't the case, because just walking was a real challenge for him nowadays.

"And you just now calling me?"

"We didn't know nothing until a few minutes ago. When Jessie got off the bus and started walking down Heggy Street, she said, somebody come at her from behind and clobbered her on the back of her head. She said it felt like they was using a baseball bat."

"My God! Is she all right?"

"She's fine, but there is a knot on the back of her noggin. Some teenagers found her laying unconscious on the ground in front of that deserted feedstore around the corner. If they hadn't come along when they did, the devil that jumped her might have come back and finished the job. Since the incident happened so close to us, them kids brought her over here."

"I'm on my way!" I hollered. Before I could hang up the phone, Jessie came on the line.

"Hubert, I don't feel good," she told me in the weakest, most heart-wrenching tone I ever heard her use.

"Just hold on, sugar! I'm fixing to leave the house to come get you! Did you see who done it?"

"No. B-but I got a feeling it's connected to whoever tried to run me over with that blue car."

"I don't know what this world is coming to. I can't for the life of me figure out who would want to hurt *you*."

"The only people I can think of is them women you used to take out before I took you out of the running."

"If I ever find out who it is that done this—and tried to run you over—I'll teach them a lesson they won't never forget! I'm going to hang up now. I'll be there as fast as I can. Tell Daddy to load up his hunting rifle and keep the doors locked in case somebody followed you."

The knot on the back of Jessie's head was about the size of a small turnip root. Mama had put some salve and a bandage on it. When I got her home, I put a fresh bandage on it and had her stretch out on the couch. No matter how much she claimed she was doing fine, I could see the fear in her eyes.

"Hubert, what if it was the same man who's going around killing women?"

I occupied the seat facing the couch. I was so fidgety, I couldn't sit in the same position for more than a few moments at a time. I crossed and uncrossed my legs so many times, I was surprised they didn't lock up on me. I scratched the top of my head and gave Jessie a skeptical look.

"I don't think it's that killer. The way them other women died, he knows what he's doing. He wouldn't try to run you over and miss. He wouldn't come at you with a baseball bat and leave, unless he was sure you was dead. If I ever find out who tried to kill you, the Fuller Brothers won't need to waste one of their caskets on them. By the time I get through, whatever's left of their vile body would fit in a Mason jar."

Jessie stared at me with a stunned look on her face. "My goodness, Hubert. I ain't never heard you talk like this. Would you really kill for me?"

"I sure would. I ain't going to let nobody get away with trying to hurt my wife."

"But I don't want you to go to prison."

I gave Jessie a thoughtful look. "Well, maybe I won't kill them, but I'll make them wish they was dead."

"I think we should call the police and let them know what happened to me. I know they ain't going to do much, but at least they'd have a report on file in case . . . um . . . in case something else happens."

"Uh-uh. Forget about calling the police, Jessie. Them peckerwoods won't do nothing but scribble something on a notepad and tell us they'll look into it."

"You're right, I guess. But I really do think that it's Blondeen or one of the jealous women that don't like me. The footsteps I heard running up behind me this evening sounded too heavy to belong to a woman, though. Whoever the heifer is, she's using some man to do her dirty work."

"Maybe I should buy a cheap car for you to get around town in. That way, you won't have to rely on the bus no more. You can drive yourself to and from work, door-to-door."

"Don't do that. That's a big expense. You just spent a pretty penny on that Singer sewing machine you bought me last month. I'll just have to be more careful." Jessie grimaced as she gently touched the back of her head where she'd been hit. "I'll start taking the later bus from work. It'll let me off closer to home, so I'll have only half a block to walk."

Chapter 56
Hubert

THE REST OF THAT WEEK WAS PRETTY QUIET. ME AND JESSIE ATE Thanksgiving supper with my parents. After we left their house, we swung by her mama's.

The minute we entered the barnlike house with mismatched furniture in every room, my mother-in-law told me for the umpteenth time, "Sugar, I'm so proud of you and how happy you done made my baby girl. It's a shame y'all ain't been able to make another baby. I ain't going to die until y'all do."

"I declare, Sister Inez, if that's the case, you going to live a very long time." I laughed, but she didn't. She just scrunched up her nose and gave me the fisheye.

"Humph! I just hope y'all still able to procreate," she said with a worried look on her face.

"Oh, I'm sure we can. But we ain't spring chickens no more, so it might take us longer."

"I was older than you and Jessie when I birthed her," she pointed out.

"Well, if it's God's will, He'll bless us with a baby. But it'll be in His time."

After I'd mingled with some of the other guests for a few minutes, I stopped a few feet behind Jessie and her look-a-like divorced sister, Annie Ruth. They was talking about a scarf Annie Ruth had borrowed from Jessie and hadn't returned. Then they abruptly started talking about me.

"Pssst. There's something I been itching to know." Annie Ruth got closer to Jessie and asked in a low tone, "Is Hubert as good as Maggie used to brag about all the time?"

This woman was too nosy for her own good! I couldn't wait to hear Jessie's answer to her rude question. "He's everything I ever wanted in a man," she replied in a shy tone.

"Everything?" Annie Ruth sounded surprised.

"Everything," Jessie repeated.

"Humph. Since when did *one* man have everything a woman wanted? That fool I divorced didn't have half the things I thought he had before we got married. I'm seeing two men right now, and I still ain't getting all I think I deserve."

"Well, I ain't lying."

Annie Ruth still sounded surprised. "I declare. If Hubert is all that, you ought to treat him like every day is Christmas and he's the best present you ever received."

"I do. And he treats me the same way."

I slunk back toward the opposite side of the room before Annie Ruth or Jessie said something I didn't want to hear.

I was beaming like a lighthouse to hear from Jessie's own mouth that she thought of me as her best Christmas present. She couldn't have said nothing more complimentary about me. I puffed out my chest so far, it was a wonder the buttons didn't pop off my shirt. I held her in such high regard, I could have said the same thing about her. Now I was looking forward to this year's Christmas more than ever.

I was so glad when December arrived. We immediately hung a wreath on the outside of our front door and bought some Christmas cards that we would send out closer to the holiday.

We did most of our Christmas shopping the second Saturday in the month. On the way back home, we stopped at a popular little restaurant near my daddy's church to eat supper. The Rib Shack had been around since I was a little boy. The food and service was good, and the prices was low. The only thing I didn't like about this place was that they passed out yellow plastic bibs for the customers to wear to keep the sauce from dripping onto their clothes. It hadn't bothered me when I was a kid, but I was too old now to be sitting around in public wearing a bib, looking like a baby.

"I don't know why you won't wear one of these bibs. You get barbecue sauce on your shirt every time we eat here," Jessie scolded before she started gnawing on a rib. "It takes a lot of bleach and I have to use the washboard to get your shirts clean."

"I don't need no bib," I protested. As careful as I was, I still got big splotches of sauce on the front of my shirt as soon as I started eating. "I don't like having nothing tied around my neck."

Jessie gave me a sympathetic look. "When you put it like that, I understand why. I bet there ain't a colored man or boy in this state, or any other state for that matter, who likes having something tied around their neck. My brother stopped wearing these bibs ten years ago when the Ku Klux Klan hanged one of his friends."

"That's pretty extreme, but since you brought it to my attention, I'll think about a noose every time I see a bib from now on."

Jessie glanced around the room at about a dozen other male customers present. "I guess most of the men in here feel the same way you do. I only see one wearing a bib." Her next comment made me squirm. "Maybe they think a bib on a grown man makes him look like a sissy."

"Oh? Do you think that?" I winced because knots was tightening up in my stomach.

Jessie shook her head. "I never looked at bibs that way." She reached across the table and patted my hand. "You could wear one every day and you'd still be a real man, so I ain't got nothing to worry about." Her eyes suddenly got big. "Why do you look so surprised to hear me say that?"

"Um . . . nothing. It's just such a high compliment, it caught me off guard. Thank you, sugar. Uh, we better hurry up and get going if we want to get to that Christmas tree place before they close."

I paid the check and was waiting for the waitress to bring my change when two women sashayed through the door. I didn't recognize the short, dark-skinned one in front, but behind her was Blondeen. She spotted us right away and looked directly at me with a hateful expression on her face. Jessie's breath caught in her throat. She heaved and covered her mouth like she was fixing to puke. I was so glad she didn't. With Blondeen's big mouth, that embarrassing news would be all over town before the end of the day.

"Oh, Lord," I hissed. "That's the last woman I want to see."

"I feel the same way," Jessie agreed with her teeth clenched.

"Let's haul ass."

"What about your change?"

"I don't want it that bad." We bolted out of that place so fast, you would have thought somebody was chasing us.

The Christmas tree lot was only a block away and there was only two other customers, so choosing a tree didn't us take long.

When we got home, we spent the next hour decorating it.

"Boy, do I miss the good old days," Jessie muttered. "Christmas was so much more fun back then."

I looked at her with my eyebrows raised. "You don't think it's fun now?"

"Oh, it's still fun. But it was more fun when we was kids," she said with a wistful look on her face. "Me and my sisters and our brother got up at the crack of dawn every Christmas morning. Our folks didn't have much money, but there was always a pile of presents under the tree for each one of us."

"Yup. Them was the good old days. Every year, me and Daddy went out to the woods and chopped down the biggest, nicest tree we could find so we wouldn't have to spend money on one. I had stopped believing in Santa Claus when I was eight. But I didn't tell my folks that because I wasn't ready to start getting boring things like clothes instead of toys." We laughed.

"I believed in Santa Claus up until I was twelve. I was so disappointed when I found out he wasn't real. I'd been suspicious all my life, though. But me and my siblings never questioned why a great big, fat, bearded white man in a red suit would come to colored folks' houses to drop off presents when the law said we couldn't even eat at the same places he ate at." We laughed again.

After we put on our sleeping clothes, I brought the big boxy radio from the bedroom and set it on the living-room coffee table and we got comfortable on the couch. We listened to a few Christmas gospel programs until the reception got so bad we couldn't enjoy them no more. It was just as well. I was ready to turn in for the night, and from the tired look in Jessie's eyes, I had a feeling she was too.

"Baby, I'm tired. I'm going to turn in for the night." I stretched my arms way up above my head and yawned.

"I'm tired too. But I'm going to take a bath before I turn in."

I was dead to the world when Jessie got in the bed. The next thing I knew, the lamp on the nightstand by my side of the bed came on and woke me up. Jessie had a lamp on her side, so I couldn't understand why she was turning mine on. Before I could say anything, I rubbed my eyes and looked up.

"What in the world—" I couldn't finish my sentence.

What I seen made me freeze: Blondeen was standing at the foot of our bed with a wild-eyed look on her face, and a gun in her hand.

Chapter 57

Jessie

"GOOD EVENING, LOVEBIRDS," BLONDEEN SNARLED. HER TEETH was clenched together so tight, I wondered how them words was able to squeeze out. She was glaring at us with enough hatred in her evil eyes for ten people. "Good news! I'm going to bring a mess of flowers to y'all's funerals." She threw her head back and guffawed like a hyena. "Twice as many as I brought to Maggie's and Claude's home-going. Hubert, something tells me that them Fuller Brothers undertakers will be tickled to death to handle your funeral—after all the business you stole from them over the years."

"Woman, what the hell are you doing in my house?!" Hubert roared. He tumbled out of bed with his arms flailing. He didn't even look scared, but I could have seen how mad he was through a blindfold. I was just as mad. Blondeen had been tormenting me long enough. She crossed one line too many tonight and I wasn't going to put up with her antics no longer. The only problem was, she was the one with the gun.

Blondeen suddenly exploded like a hand grenade. "Y'all don't look so high and mighty now! You get out of that bed too, you cheesy-ass black bitch!" The hand she had the gun in was shaking. I was scared it might go off accidentally before she decided what she was really going to do with it. I couldn't bring myself to believe she was actually going to kill us. If she only planned on scaring us, she'd done that. But I wasn't that dumb. Nobody breaks into somebody's house with a gun just to scare them.

I was too petrified to move, so I just laid there, stiff as a plank. I couldn't even feel my lips moving, but words shot out of my mouth like rocks. "Blondeen, do you want to go to prison?"

"'Prison'?" She laughed long and loud again. "We'll see about that."

"We sure will! I'm going to call the police right now!" Hubert screamed and attempted to leave the room. But Blondeen blocked his way.

"Don't you move, *Romeo*!"

"What do you plan on doing, Blondeen?" he asked.

"If you ain't figured that out, you dumber than I thought. And deaf too. Didn't you just hear me say I was going to bring flowers to y'all's funerals? Did you think I was going to let you get away with leading me on the way you did?" She looked so burning mad, it was a wonder smoke wasn't coming out of her mouth. "I'm going to settle everything, once and for all, tonight!" she threatened as she wagged the gun.

Hubert gulped. "Settle what? We ain't done nothing to you!"

I couldn't tell which one of us was trembling the hardest, him or me. He started sweating and shifting his weight from one foot to the other.

"Blondeen, I don't know what you are really up to, but I know you ain't crazy enough to shoot that gun."

"You fixing to find out just how crazy I am!"

"Then don't be a fool! You are too smart and got too much going for you to throw away your life over a little misunderstanding." Hubert sounded like he was grasping at straws. "If me or Jessie done or said something to offend you, we apologize." He whirled around to face me. "Right, Jessie?"

I nodded so hard, my neck ached. Hubert even attempted to smile, but it looked more like a sneer.

"'Apologize'? You two *Beelzebubs*? Humph. That don't even sound sincere to a sow's ear, let alone mine. I'm surprised you even know that word!" she screamed.

Hubert held up his hand and said in a firm tone, "I advise you to get up out of here and don't never come back. Me and Jessie won't tell nobody about this, and we'll forget it ever happened."

She was still blocking his way, so I didn't know why he didn't haul off and knock that gun out of her hand and then grab hold of her.

Blondeen must have thought he was fixing to do that because she cussed under her breath and stumbled back a few feet. With her heavy makeup smeared and the wild-eyed look on her face, she looked right beastly. She shook her head so hard, her wig-hat shifted, and the bangs almost covered her eyes.

"And if I don't leave?" she asked as she adjusted her hair, which now looked like a wet mop because of all the sweat pouring out of her.

"You are going to be real sorry when the police get here! I'll see to it!" Hubert blasted.

Blondeen laughed again. For something to be so serious, her funny bone sure was working overtime. "By the time the police get here, if they do, I'll have done my business and be back home in my own bed, snoozing like a possum. But you ain't going to call nobody! The only person you need to be thinking about calling is God to let Him know y'all on the way to meet Him!" She swallowed hard and then glared at me with such a evil look on her face, my blood ran cold. "Correction. Make that call to Satan, because hell is where I'm sending y'all!"

"Blondeen, be reasonable. Let's sit down, have a cup of coffee, and talk this over like reasonable folks. Please," I whimpered. I never thought I'd see the day I would grovel so hard. "I'm begging you not to do something that would hurt so many people, including yourself. I don't care how mad you think you are. If you kill us, you will regret it for the rest of your life. I . . . I . . . am so sorry for hurting you."

For a split second, she looked so sad, I almost felt sorry for her. But the next thing I knew that evil look was back on her face. Then she said the last thing I expected her to say: "Hubert, I would have made you a good wife. I'm still young, I could give you three times as many babies as that old fossil laying there like a deadweight."

The look on Hubert's face was so incredulous, it looked like he had put on another man's face. "I don't know what made you think I'd marry you," he said with his hands on his hips, looking at her like she was crazy. "I liked you and enjoyed spending time with you, but you was never more than a casual friend to me."

"Blondeen, you got a man. If you ain't happy with him, a young and pretty woman like you can get somebody else," I threw in.

"I got a man? Humph! I know you ain't talking about that low-down funky black dog Conway! Ain't you heard? He ain't my man no more!"

"Get another one," I suggested.

"For what? One's just as bad as the next!" she barked. And then without warning, she confessed to something I'd been right about all along. "That fool I paid to run your ass over using my cousin's car, and beat the dog shit out of you with that baseball bat, couldn't do nothing right. He was the one supposed to come over here tonight and wrap up this business. But I decided not to take no more chances with that incompetent idiot."

My heart was beating like a drum and I braced myself to hear her tell Hubert she heard that I'd been fooling around with Conway. Even though it was true, I didn't want him to know it. Despite all the lies I'd told him, I didn't want him to know I was sleazy enough to mess around with a man who was in a committed relationship with another woman. He was too good of a man to live with such deceit.

Before Blondeen could let the cat out of the bag, Hubert lunged at her and grabbed the hand she had the gun in and they started tussling.

"Y'all stop that!" I hollered. I was finally able to move my legs and get out of the bed. I grabbed the lamp off my nightstand. Just as I was about to trot over and clobber Blondeen upside her head, the gun went off. It was a little bitty gun, but the shot sounded like thunder. I dropped the lamp.

Hubert yelped so loud, I thought he was the one the bullet had hit. He froze, I froze, and Blondeen hit the floor.

I couldn't tell who screamed the loudest, me or Hubert. I couldn't even feel my feet on the floor as I ran over to him. I snatched the gun out of his hand and tossed it onto the bed. He was in such a daze, he just stood there and rubbed his head and gawked at Blondeen's body.

"Jessie, we need to get her to the clinic straightaway!" He squatted down and gently slapped the side of her face. Her eyes was wide open, but she didn't blink, budge, or make a sound. She had on a white blouse, so the red stain forming on her bosom really stood out. Hubert let out a loud groan before he wobbled back up off the floor.

"Is she all right?" I asked.

He shook his head. "She's as dead as a doornail."

"No! That can't be. That little bitty gun looks like a child's toy. It would have to get off more than one shot to kill somebody. Check her again!" I yelled.

In a calm tone, Hubert looked me in the eyes and told me, "Jessie, I been a undertaker half of my life. With my eyes closed, I can tell if a person is dead."

I sucked in a deep breath and stumbled to the bed and plonked down so hard, my tailbone ached.

"Hubert, what have *we* got ourselves into?" I wheezed.

Chapter 58
Jessie

"Go get the Bible so we can recite a few lines and pray for Blondeen's soul," Hubert told me.

"Pray for her? Hubert, the woman came here to kill us! If anybody needs to be prayed for, it's me and you."

"You got a good point, I guess." He heaved out a loud breath and looked around the room. "We need to get something to sop up that blood off the floor."

I had to trot to keep up with him as he rushed toward the kitchen. I thought he was going to get a dishcloth or some old newspapers for us to clean up the bedroom floor. Instead, he picked up the telephone.

"I'll call the police."

I snatched the telephone out of his hand. "Don't you know that killing a woman in your house that you used to date will cause a major scandal? Who is going to believe you didn't shoot Blondeen on purpose? You and a lot of folks know she had a ax to grind with me," I reminded as I shook the phone in his face.

"She broke in here with a gun. I was just protecting us," he protested.

"It don't matter. Both of our reputations would be ruined for the rest of our lives—not to mention the damage this would do to your mama and daddy."

"A woman is dead, Jessie. What are we supposed to do?"

I gave Hubert the most desperate look I could. "Think about it. Don't nobody but me and you know what happened here tonight." I was talking as calm as I could so I wouldn't look as hysterical as I felt inside. "I don't want to go to prison, and I know you don't. If they ever turned us loose, we'd be so old, our lives wouldn't be worth living no more."

His eyes darted from side to side and he started breathing through his mouth. "Blondeen's kinfolks will report her missing and somebody might track her to us. What if she told Sukey and Wilma or whoever she got that gun from what she was going to do tonight? And she probably told the man she paid to try to kill you. And if she didn't tell nobody, one of our neighbors might have seen her come in here. If we come clean now, maybe the law won't be so hard on us."

"Hubert, it don't matter when we 'come clean,' because the law would still put us in prison and throw away the key." A idea popped into my head so suddenly, it made my head spin. "I got it!"

"You got what?"

"We can haul her to them woods by Carson Lake and dump her in some bushes, like that maniac did with them five women he done away with. That way, everybody will think he killed Blondeen too."

Hubert scratched his head and gave me a pensive look. "You might have something there, Jessie. I hadn't thought of nothing like that, and it just might get us out of this jam. Do you really think folks will pin this on that killer?"

"Why wouldn't they? Look, we can't stand here and keep yakking." I gave him the sternest look I could come up with. "The longer we do, the more blood we'll have to clean up off the floor. If we don't do nothing tonight, by morning her body will be so stiff, it'll be harder to move her. Now let's get dressed so we can put her in the car and get this over with."

"Lord, help us," Hubert moaned, wringing his hands as he gazed at Blondeen's body.

"We'll deal with the Lord later. Now let's get this done!"

* * *

After we put our clothes on, Hubert drove his car to the back of our house and put a thick blanket on the backseat to keep Blondeen's blood from dripping on it. The neighbors who lived behind us wasn't as nosy as the ones in the front. Most of them was so old and decrepit, they'd sleep through the eye of a hurricane, so we didn't have to worry about them peeping out their windows in the middle of the night.

When Hubert returned, I was taking off Blondeen's clothes. "Why are you doing that?!" he yelled. He sprinted across the floor and dropped down next to me. "Ain't we done enough to this woman? We ain't got to take away her dignity too."

"This ain't got nothing to do with taking her dignity," I snapped as I removed her brassiere and dropped it onto the pile of her other clothes. "Every single one of them other murdered women was naked when they was found. If we don't stick to the way the real killer operates, it might raise doubt in somebody's mind," I explained. "We can burn up her stuff tomorrow. The gun included." I shook my head as I removed her wig-hat last. "It's a shame to get rid of all this gorgeous fake hair."

"Put that back on her head. Her real hair looks like a black sheep's butt and it'll look even worse after she's been laying in the elements for we don't know how long. Let's let her have *some* dignity."

I put the wig-hat back on Blondeen's head. Hubert grabbed her arms and I took hold of her legs and we lifted her up. I couldn't believe such a small woman felt so heavy. We almost dropped her twice before we made it to the car.

We didn't say nothing during the ten-minute ride to the lake. When we parked where the trees and bushes was the thickest, a great big owl perched on the hood of the car and started hooting so loud, we both got scared.

"One of them creatures showing up is a bad omen! Especially one bold enough to get this close to us," I said with my lips quivering.

Hubert didn't say nothing as he got out of the car and grabbed a stick. Before he could hit the owl, it flew away. He motioned for me to get out of the car.

"Jessie, come on and let's get this done."

After we placed Blondeen's body in a clump of bushes, where somebody had dumped some old car parts, we sprinted back to the car. The owl was back on the hood! Hubert picked up the same stick and chased it away again. A split second later, he bent over and threw up on the ground. His hands was shaking so hard, I had to drive us back home.

"Jessie, I wish none of this had happened," he whimpered as we inched along the dirt road.

"It wasn't our fault," I reminded. "That woman brought this on herself. Now all we have to do is wait for somebody to find her."

We didn't have to wait long.

The very next day, Yolinda stormed into our house and ran straight to the kitchen, where me and Hubert was eating breakfast.

"Y'all ain't going to believe it!" She had to stop to catch her breath. "Blondeen is dead!"

Hubert gulped and his face froze.

"Who killed her?" I blurted out.

It was a stupid thing to say, and Hubert let me know that by kicking my foot under the table.

Yolinda looked at me with her eyes narrowed. "I only said she was dead. She could have had a heart attack or got bit by a snake. How did you know somebody *killed* her?"

Chapter 59
Jessie

Yolinda's question caught me by surprise. But I was able to think fast and come up with a good reply: "She was mean to so many folks, I assumed somebody decided to finally stop her."

"You took the words right out of my mouth. I thought the same thing when my niece told me this morning. That wasn't the case, though. A man out hunting for possums this morning stumbled up on her body out by the lake. Near the same place they found them other murdered women. But I bet it was Conway who killed her. Wilma told me he had threatened to blow her brains out when she confronted him again about squandering her rent money and not paying her bills while she was in Texas! How could he do something like that?"

"I guess he thought he could get away with it," Hubert suggested.

"I guess he did." Yolinda shook her head and sucked on her teeth. "I declare, this is a hell of a thing to happen with Christmas right around the corner. And it ruined today for me. I had planned to get up and go do some more of my shopping. Now all I want to do is go back home and read my Bible."

When Yolinda left a few minutes later, I asked Hubert, "What do we do now?"

"There ain't nothing for us to do now but wait and see what happens next," he told me in a tired tone. "I guess I need to get in touch with Tyrone and Floyd so we can pick up Blondeen's body."

Just like Yolinda, several other neighbors told us that they suspected Conway had killed her. That idea got squashed when it was made known that he'd been laid up at the clinic since Thursday night with head wounds he'd got during a juke joint brawl. On top of that, a heap of people said they had talked to Blondeen Friday morning. Since Conway couldn't have killed her, everybody assumed she had been killed by the same man who had killed them other colored women.

Every time somebody knocked on our front door, or when the telephone rang, we almost jumped out of our skin.

"Jessie, we need to get a grip. We can't be acting this nervous at the funeral tomorrow," Hubert told me on Monday night.

Five minutes later, Yolinda barged into the house without knocking. Me and Hubert was sitting on the couch, feeling as distraught and helpless as everybody else.

"Would y'all believe that a policeman just showed up at Blondeen's mama's house this evening—and she had called them Sunday morning? All he did was ask four or five questions and scribble a few notes! The whole time, he was smoking a pipe while everybody in the house was writhing in grief!" Yolinda shrieked before she plopped down in the chair facing us.

"They ain't going to do much more than that. They claim to still be 'investigating' all of them other murders and ain't made no progress yet," Hubert pointed out.

"I'm so glad I don't live by myself," Yolinda said with a heavy sigh as she crossed her legs and started fanning her face. "And I ain't about to be out gallivanting up and down the street unless somebody is with me."

"Blondeen hardly ever went anywhere by herself. Almost every time I seen her, Wilma and Sukey was tagging along. I wonder how that killer got to her?" I said.

"Maybe he caught her when she was by herself, like all of

them other women," Yolinda suggested. "She had moved back in with her mama, but she liked to go out by herself every now and then. Blondeen's mama said she didn't know that Blondeen had left the house that night until she got up before daybreak to use the bathroom and seen her bed hadn't been slept in. So we know the killer didn't break in the house and snatch her. He caught her out walking."

Hubert was fidgeting in his seat, so I knew he was still just as anxious as I was for this to die down.

"That sounds like what happened. He'd probably been watching her for a while. I'm sure Conway is relieved that they can't pin this murder on him," he said.

Just hearing Conway's name made my chest and face tighten up. As subtle as I tried to look, Yolinda noticed something was amiss right away.

"Jessie, you sure seem upset about what happened to Blondeen. I can tell from your puffy eyes that you been crying as much as the rest of us. I guess you done got over all the misery she caused you, huh?"

"Yolinda, I ain't one to hold grudges. She had lightened up on me, so her messing with me in public wasn't no big deal to me no more," I replied.

"Poor Blondeen. She was a spitfire, but she didn't deserve to die the way she did," Hubert said, stretching his arms high above his head. "I'm sure her family will be pleased with the funeral I done organized."

A curious look crossed Yolinda's face and she started talking in a low tone. "Y'all want to hear something strange? I been thinking about it ever since that last woman got killed before Blondeen."

My chest was feeling so tight now, I was surprised it hadn't squeezed the life out of my heart, which was beating so hard, I could barely sit still. "What, Yolinda?" I asked.

"Every single one of the murdered women's families had Hubert handle the funeral arrangements, not the Fuller Brothers," she answered.

Me and Hubert looked at one another and hunched our shoulders.

"So?" he said. "Maybe they all like my work better, and I don't charge as much as them Fuller Brothers."

"And each one of them women was connected to Hubert in some way. They either belonged to, or had visited, his daddy's church," I pointed out.

"Not only that, but they'd also all been to my mama's house numerous times for her to do their hair," Hubert added with a snort. "What's your point, Yolinda?"

"Oh, I ain't got no point. Now it makes sense that all of them families came to you to handle everything. Plus, I do have to admit you make corpses look much better in death than they looked in life. They even still look alive. The Fuller Brothers do such a shabby job of sprucing up dead folks, you would think they was going to spend eternity at a Halloween party. I'm glad you made them let your mama do Maggie's makeup and hair. She looked like the angel she was." Yolinda's tone suddenly dropped so low, we could barely hear her. "I just hope that killer bypasses me. Everybody around here knows I spend hours at a time alone during the day with the kids either at school or running the street and everybody else working. That hound dog my nephew bought to protect the house plays possum more than a possum. I declare, I hope they catch the slimy murdering devil that's causing so much grief."

"When they do catch him, I hope they put him away for life," Hubert said with a nod.

"*Pffftt*. He ain't going to get off that easy. The state will kill him for sure, if the kinfolks of them dead women don't get their hands on him first," Yolinda insisted.

I was glad she left a minute later. This subject had wore me down to a frazzle. The only person I felt comfortable discussing it with was Hubert.

"Do you think they'll ever catch the man who killed all of them other women?" I asked.

"Sure, they will," he said with confidence. And then he dipped his head and gave me a puzzled look. "Why are you still looking and acting so distressed? There ain't nothing for us to worry about. We covered our tracks."

"I know we did, but I was wondering . . ." I paused for a bit and sniffed. "When they catch that man, what if he admits he did kill all of them women except Blondeen?"

"They'll know he was lying. Who in their right mind would take the word of a admitted killer?"

Chapter 60
Hubert

I HADN'T SEEN LEROY SINCE LAST THURSDAY WHEN I LEFT WORK EARLY and went to spend a couple of hours with him. I had told him I'd talk to him soon, and because I hadn't, when I finally called him last night while Jessie was taking a bath, he was frantic.

"Baby, you told me you'd call me in a couple of days. That was *four* days ago. I thought you had forgot about me," he whined. "How come I ain't heard from you until now?"

As much as he loved me, I didn't know how he'd feel about being involved with a killer. I wasn't crazy enough to tell him the truth, even though he probably wouldn't have never told no-body. But I didn't want to burden him with such a heavy secret.

The only thing I could do was rattle off a bald-faced lie. It would be the first one I ever told him, and I hoped it would be the last.

"Um, my wife's been very sick. I was worried about her, so I had to give her all my attention."

"Oh. I hope it's nothing too serious."

"Um . . . just some female issues. She's fine now."

"When will I see you again?"

"Well, I got a important funeral coming up tomorrow. The lady was a member of my daddy's church, so her kinfolks want me to handle all the arrangements. I'm going to be busy tomor-row. I'll pay you a visit after we get her buried."

"Okay. I'm sorry about that poor woman. Was she a close friend of yours?"

I wasn't sure how to answer his question, so I said the first thing that came to my mind. "Yes, but we wasn't as close as we used to be." When Leroy didn't say nothing right away, I decided to offer up a little more explanation. "When Maggie died, this lady consoled me a lot and brought all kinds of home-cooked meals to me. I even took her out a few times—as well as a few of the other women who consoled me and fed me during that trying time."

"Bless her soul. How did she die? Was she sick?"

The second lie I told Leroy rolled off my tongue so quick and easy, I was worried that I'd be telling him even more in the future. I would try my best not to, though.

"She got murdered by the same man we believe killed five other colored women since last year."

"My God! I remember reading a little piece in our newspaper a few months ago about them killings. It was up to three then. Do the police have any suspects?"

"Not that I know of. They are still 'investigating' the first murder. It's unlikely that they'll ever investigate the others much."

"When and if that maniac starts killing white women, them crackers will work around the clock seven days a week until they catch him. I'll pray for your friend's family."

"Thank you, sweetie."

I felt better when I got off the phone, but I was still a wreck. I had so many wild thoughts dancing around in my throbbing head, I was afraid that a nervous breakdown was the next thing I'd have to deal with. The more I thought about everything that had happened, the more my head throbbed. I just couldn't believe that Blondeen felt that killing me and Jessie would make her feel better. What was the world coming to? I wondered. Just thinking about her upcoming funeral was too much for me. When I went to bed, I tossed and turned half the night before I was able to fall asleep.

*　　*　　*

There was at least a thousand other places I would have chose to be at instead of Blondeen's funeral Tuesday morning. On top of listening to so many terrified folks moan and groan about Blondeen being murdered, we had to sit through another one of Daddy's long-winded, foot-stomping testimonies about all the evil in the world. He said pretty much the same thing he'd said when them other women got killed: "Satan done plucked another one of God's flowers out of the garden of life."

Blondeen had always called herself a Christian, but never spent much time in church, even though my daddy had baptized her when she was a teenager. Like at every funeral I ever sat through, a bunch of folks went up to the pulpit and talked about how "good" the dearly departed was. No matter how big a devil they had been.

"I watched Blondeen grow up," Yolinda sobbed. "She was a good girl. Whoever the devil was that took her away from her family and friends, he will surely pay for his crime!"

The whole congregation yelled, "Amen!"

Sukey went up to speak next. But she was so distraught, she couldn't get no words out, so a usher escorted her back to her seat. Then Wilma went up and went on and on about what a good friend Blondeen had been to her.

Conway showed up with white bandages covering his head like a stocking cap. He didn't say nothing to nobody, and the way he was crying, you would have thought somebody was whupping him. I wasn't surprised when he slunk out of the church halfway through the service.

The families of the other women who had been murdered was howling like coyotes. Two hefty women fainted and had to be carried out by the pallbearers. The man who had killed the other women, or somebody from his family, could have been sitting on the same pew with me and Jessie, crying up a storm hisself! Just thinking about that sent a chill all through me.

There wasn't a dry eye in sight. Me and Jessie was two of the ones sobbing the loudest.

* * *

After the service ended, everybody gathered in the dining area and folks started eating like pigs at a hog trough. I managed to eat half a plate of greens, a chicken leg, and a piece of corn bread. Jessie only nibbled on a biscuit and a chicken wing.

A few minutes after I finished eating, Blondeen's mama, Vellamae, came and gave me a bear hug. Even with a head full of gray hair, lines going every which way on her face, and seventy-five extra pounds, she looked so much like Blondeen.

"Hubert, before my baby married them other two fools, she used to sit around talking about how she wanted to marry a man like you. I kept telling her you was too old for her, but she didn't care about that. I know you liked her and took her out a few times last year, and I'm so sorry things didn't work out between y'all."

"I guess the good Lord didn't mean for me and Blondeen to be together," I said.

"And we can't question the Lord's actions," Sister Vellamae said, then sniffled and hugged me again. "Your mama and daddy done a good job raising you. I can't thank you enough for not charging the family for the funeral expenses. Me and my kids had to chip in every penny we could afford to pay for my brother's recent funeral in Birmingham and my sister's in Texas. And that low-down funky black dog Conway didn't pay her insurance while she was out of town, so they canceled it."

"That's a shame. Well, the Lord done blessed me in so many wonderful ways, I'm duty-bound to give back to the community in any way I can," I told her.

Sister Vellamae looked at me with so much awe, I cringed. I wondered what she'd say and do if she knew I was the one who had took her child's life. "I would have been proud to call you my son-in-law." She glanced at Jessie and said something that shocked me. "Jessie, I never got to know you and your family that well, but I ain't heard nothing but good about you. It would have been nice if you and Blondeen got to know one another and become close friends. You being older and so pious, you could have took her under your wing and given her some guidance that would have made her life much better. Maybe you could have introduced her to one of Hubert's friends and she could have at least had one more husband before she went to be with God."

Them words really got to Jessie. She took a gulp of air and stumbled. She wiped more tears from her eyes with the handkerchief that was already soaked clean through. "Um . . . I wish the same thing," she said with a sniffle. "This was a wonderful service. Blondeen looked beautiful."

"Sister Vellamae, we'll be praying for you," I added. "Your baby girl will never feel pain again."

"Humph! She won't, but what about the next one that killer get his hands on? Whoever he is, he must have Satan's protection. People been paying good money to every hoodoo in town to bring that black devil down and it ain't working."

"Well, I don't condone the use of hoodoo. The Bible warns us about any form of witchcraft because it's just part of Satan's plan to deceive us. I advise you to let go and let God do His job," I said firmly.

"When they catch the man who killed my baby, they better hide him good. Otherwise, his family will be arranging his funeral!"

I nodded and hugged Sister Vellamae so tight, I could feel her heart beating against my bosom. "I'm glad to see you're coping a little better now. My wife is not feeling well, so we'll be leaving soon." I excused myself and ushered Jessie toward the door.

We didn't say nothing during the ride home.

As soon as we got in the house, Jessie busted out crying again. I pulled her into my arms and led her to the couch, where we flopped down. "Hubert, I don't know how much longer I can hold on. I'm about to lose my mind over what we done! It's beginning to sink in deeper and deeper each day."

"Look, we didn't do nothing that anybody in the same predicament wouldn't have done! Blondeen started this mess!" I exclaimed. My outburst made Jessie flinch, so I softened my tone. "Trust me. So long as we trust in Jesus too, we'll be fine."

She sniffled and blinked at me. "Do you think . . . for the rest of our lives, we'll be able to keep to ourselves what happened?"

I gave Jessie a weary look. "I know how to keep a secret."

"I know how to keep one too," she mumbled without hesitation, which I couldn't ignore.

"Well, if you got a deep, dark secret, that's your business. As long as it ain't got nothing to do with me, I don't care. Keep it to yourself. But this one about Blondeen affects us both. So, if you ever decide to tell somebody, keep in mind that you'll be ruining both our lives and maybe even sending us to the state penitentiary."

Jessie shook her head. "You ain't got to worry about me saying nothing. If you got any secrets that don't concern me, keep them to yourself too. I just want us to continue being a happily married couple."

"And we will be," I vowed.

I didn't care how many more secrets I had to hide or lies I had to tell to avoid a scandal, stay out of prison, and keep folks from knowing the truth about me. And, as remorseful as I was about accidentally killing Blondeen, I would kill again if I had to.

"I been thinking"—Jessie paused and gave me a hopeful look—"when you get over your problem, and if we ain't too old, maybe we can try to have another baby."

"Maybe. Now let's go to bed and get some rest." I sighed.

When we got in the bed, I kissed her on the lips for the first time since our wedding day. I didn't feel nothing this time neither. She moaned and shook like she was having a mild spasm, so I know it did something for her.

"That was nice, Hubert. I needed that. There ain't nothing more soothing than affection, no matter how limited it is . . ."

"I feel the same way."

I pulled her into my arms and kept her there until she went to sleep.

Amen.

AUTHOR'S NOTE

In the first book in The Wiggins Series, entitled *Mrs. Wiggins*, the title character, Maggie, tells her side of this story in graphic detail. In the third and final book in the series, the killer of the five women in *Empty Vows* will be revealed in a twist so shocking, even *I* didn't see it coming!

EMPTY VOWS

Mary Monroe

ABOUT THIS GUIDE

The suggested questions that follow are included to enhance your group's reading of this book.

DISCUSSION QUESTIONS

1. Do you think Jessie would have gone after Hubert if her sister hadn't put the idea in her head?

2. After losing his wife, son, and being dumped by his long-term gay lover at the same time, Hubert became extremely lonely and distraught. He was also very vulnerable. Do you think Jessie should have given him more time to grieve before she started scheming to land him only a few weeks after the funeral?

3. Were you happy for Jessie when Hubert decided she was the best woman to replace his first wife?

4. Were you surprised when Hubert told Jessie he hadn't been able to perform in the bedroom since his wife died?

5. Were you surprised when she told him that didn't matter to her?

6. Jessie believed Hubert had become impotent, but she was determined to help restore his manhood and she didn't care how she did it. Did you think she went too far when she decided to set a trap for him?

7. Just being Hubert's "friend" was not enough for Jessie. She wanted to replace his first wife, especially in the bedroom. When she decided to drug him and make him think he'd raped her while he was drunk, he believed her. Do you know anyone who pulled a similar trick on someone they "loved"?

8. A month after the "rape," Jessie told Hubert she was pregnant with his child. Did you think he would propose to her as fast as he did?

9. Hubert was happy being married to Jessie for more than one reason. One was because she was a good prop to help him hide his relationship with Leroy, his new boyfriend. Hubert's first wife knew all along that he was gay and was happy to help him hide it. Do you think that if Jessie had found out, she would have stayed with him?

10. When Jessie had a "miscarriage," Hubert was devastated because he wanted a child so badly. Did you get angry with her for duping him?

11. Hubert continued to claim that he was still unable to be intimate with Jessie, so she had an affair with a coworker. Did you blame her for turning to another man?

12. Blondeen Walker was angry because Hubert had chosen Jessie over her. When she broke into his house in a jealous rage to kill him and Jessie, did you think she'd be the one who would end up dead?

13. Hubert and Jessie made it look like the same man who had killed five other black women was responsible for Blondeen's death. That's what everybody assumed, so Hubert and Jessie thought they'd gotten away with murder. People rarely get away with such a heinous crime. It usually affects them in ways they never imagined. Do you think Hubert and Jessie will be able to go on as if nothing ever happened?